THE A

Born in Liverp
educated in M
National Servic
journalism and spent ten years in Fleet Street
before becoming the *Sunday Times* correspondent in Turkey and Greece. Two years working
for a French news agency was followed by a
move to Australia, where he was variously chief
leader writer for *The Australian*, a writer and
presenter in film and television, and head of the
Fraser Government's media unit. In 1971 he
published *The Dreamtime Society*, a politico-
economic survey of Australia. THE ANDROS
PASSAGE is his first novel. John Hallows now
lives in Sydney, where he writes, and sails his
26-foot yacht.

Also by John Hallows

THE DREAMTIME SOCIETY (non-fiction)

JOHN HALLOWS

THE ANDROS PASSAGE

FONTANA/Collins

First published in Great Britain by
Fontana Paperbacks 1989

Copyright © John Hallows 1989

Printed and bound in Great Britain by
William Collins Sons & Co. Ltd, Glasgow

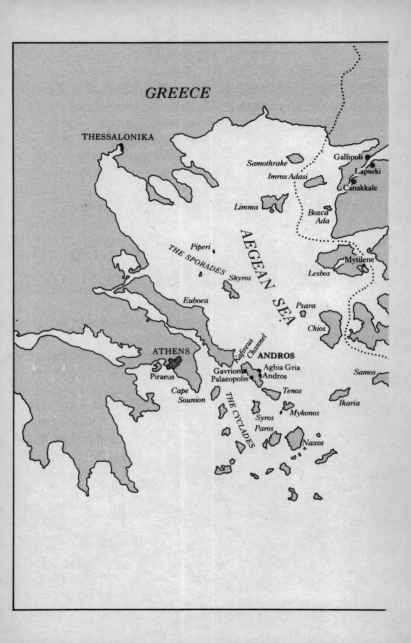

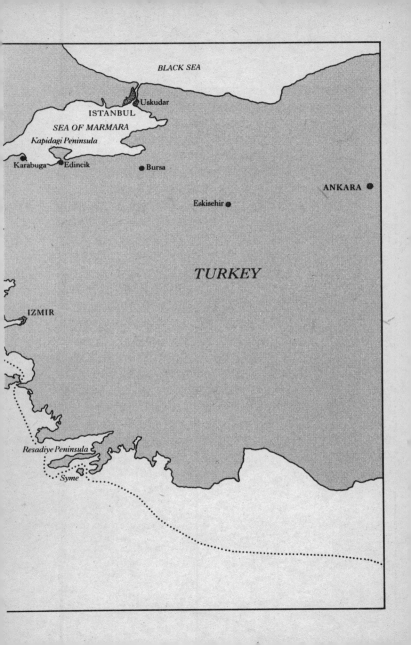

CHAPTER 1

The Caique

If I had known what was going to happen I would never have steered my boat within a sea mile of the white yacht ahead. But when I first saw it, with a near gale blasting across the Aegean sea and the fierce sun striking diamonds off my wet, heeling deck, there was no reason for suspicion. The yacht was just a dancing speck on the horizon, as threatening as a girl in a bridal dress at a church porch in the corner of your eye. I had no reason to think of that distant flash in the dark sea as anything other than an occasional mark to steer by: I was too busy trying to hold my big ketch on course, and persuading myself I had enough of a sailor's stomach to take the yacht through the storm.

Andromeda soared and crashed in the spume like a horse in a nightmare steeplechase, heaving at a huge angle over the wave peaks and then pitching with a jolt into the troughs. She was a forty-four-foot ketch, built in Taiwan to an American design along the sea-kindly lines of the East Coast tradition, but these waters were not the Grand Banks the New England fishermen understood. The Aegean is a shallow sea. Parts of it around the Cyclades are less than 100 fathoms deep, and for that reason the big *meltemi* winds that blow from the north for most of the summer kick up a savage wave pattern which makes sailing something close to misery. I was clutching the wheel, wedged into place in the cockpit, braced against the jarring thumps as we pitched, and almost losing my grasp whenever the boat heaved irresistibly upwards to a crest. As *Andromeda* soared on the bigger waves, I felt the same sense of numbed shock in the face of implacable physical force that I remembered from when I was a freshman running-back, hitting a top college defensive line for the first time.

It was the unexpectedness of the whole situation that struck me, before the nausea crept up. The wind-scoured Greek sky was a brilliant blue; the sun so strong the light was white. On shore the litter of island tourists would be sunning themselves peacefully behind barriers of wicker windscreens and Ambre Solaire sun-oil. Down here at sea level it was warm enough for me to be comfortable in just a windcheater and a pair of jeans, but I was sailing through a near gale as vicious as the Atlantic winter. The boat was carrying two reefs in the main and the mizzen was bare, but even so she was thrashing across the steep seas on a steady 25-degree heel. The needle of the automatic log was fixed at ten and a quarter knots. And then, after a couple of hours, I began to feel seasick.

There was not a lot I could do about that. In the first place, I was single-handed. That had seemed sensible enough when I was planning the voyage on a two-week stop-over in Turkey beforehand: *Andromeda* was easy to handle, and in the summer Aegean the wind direction is so steady there would be no need to change sail. All I had to do was steam across to Greece like an express train. The idea had been to wait for strong winds and do it in a day: that was, in fact, the whole point of the voyage. Technically, this is simple enough in the summer *meltemi* season. You know the North wind is going to be sweeping down from Turkey five days of the week.

In the second place, I had *Andromeda* on a reach, with the Force Seven blast just aft of the beam, which is the most comfortable point of sailing for any boat. I was in the open Aegean, nine hours out from Izmir and heading sou'-west on a line between the islands of Skyros and Chios: if I turned and ran for shelter in the lee of Chios to the east I'd have to gybe, swinging the mains'l boom across the deck with the force of the wind behind it. This is not the safest manoeuvre for a single-handed sailor in a near gale. And if I got through that exercise I would be almost on a dead run, which is no simple thing to handle in *Andromeda*, either.

But the overwhelming argument was the importance of making the passage in a single day. I had something to prove, and perhaps a new career to find in proving it. The first step revolved around crossing from Izmir in Turkey to Euboea in Greece in some seventeen hours of sailing, after weighing anchor at two a.m.: if I gave up and headed for Chios the effort would be wasted. I had brought *Andromeda* across the Indian Ocean to the Mediterranean from Hong Kong with the sole aim of making this voyage, to prove that the nineteenth-century English poet Lord Byron had been a pirate before he won literary fame and fortune. If I weakened today, just because I was out of practice in bad-weather sailing, the entire summer's plan would be lost: I wasn't just trying to reach Athens, I was trying to steer my life out of the doldrums of news-agency reporting into a new dimension as an independent TV producer. And I'd hocked fifteen years' agency severance pay and two cashed-up life insurances to buy my Taiwan ketch and take that chance.

I was using *Andromeda* to duplicate the voyage to Greece that Byron made aboard the Royal Navy frigate *Salsette* in 1811. The poet had been on his way home from Turkey that October; *Salsette* caught a strong *meltemi* on the beam and whisked him through the Cyclades in a few hours. According to every reference book in the British Museum, that was supposed to be the only time Byron saw the Aegean. I knew it wasn't. I'd spent eighteen months based in Athens covering the Middle East for the agency, and in that time I took a good look at the poet's story. When I discovered the truth I realised it was too good to file for the news service. By sailing the same route in the same time I was going to prove that *Salsette*'s wild dash through the Archipelago could not have given Byron the vast and detailed knowledge of the islands he kept writing about for the next ten years. *Salsette* never even saw some of his favourite places – like Naxos, the island to which Byron always told people he would return, and buy a house.

Byron was curiously silent about his real experience in the Aegean. I believed I knew the reason why. Once I disproved the *Salsette* explanation for his Aegean expertise, I knew where to find what amounted to written proof that Byron left the frigate at the last island she passed en route for Athens, and returned secretly to the Cyclades. There the nineteenth century's bestselling poet fell in with Greek pirates, and joined a band based on the island of Paros.

If I duplicated *Salsette*'s trip myself and proved the point, I had the basis for a first-class TV film about the poet's romantic villainy. It could make me a custom-tailored reputation in a fresh field. And for an out-of-work news agency reporter betting his life's capital on the result, the idea of giving up on that chance, or even delaying it, was a prospect far worse than a Force Seven summer gale in the Aegean.

I'd been in the agency business for a decade and a half: fifteen years as an anonymous observer at other people's wars and revolutions, a kind of scorekeeper without even the power to throw an official's yellow flag on the play. I'd had enough of being shot at and not carrying a gun; of recording events as a set of corporate initials on the tag-line of agency news stories. I was sick of keeping the score: I wanted at least to interpret the play, to produce something original myself.

So I really had only one choice. Which was to try to keep my stomach, avoid keeling over into a retching helpless heap on the rail, and sail *Andromeda* on course.

There is a way to hold nausea back when you are steering. It's the old seaman's trick of fixing your eyes on something outside the boat. You don't want to watch the compass bobbing in the binnacle just for'ard of the wheel, so you steer by any object you can find on the horizon. Mostly a sailor uses a cloud, or a distant point of land. But there are no clouds to speak of in the Aegean, and there were no islands in sight. Instead, I started judging my course by that one particular flash of white, dancing on the horizon ahead of me, and tried not to look at the intervening maze of white wave crests and dashing spray.

That is why for nearly two hours I watched the white yacht, heaving in the distance like a lantern held by a staggering man, without taking any real notice of her. Of course, I knew the glittering speck there in the distance was a ship, but I had no reason to consider

13

her further. She was just another leading mark: I fixed her with a vague eye, and kept her about one point off *Andromeda*'s port bow.

And in time, I drew up to her.

It was a curious accident, really. If I had not been sick, I would not have gone near the white *caique* – far less gone aboard her. The whole thing started just because I was out of the habit of sailing in big seas: if I had done just a little more cruising in the time I was waiting to set off across the Aegean from Izmir, instead of vainly plotting to screw the Hon Rosemary Bulltine of the British Embassy, Ankara, or if the voyage across the Indian Ocean had not been so calm, the whole thing would never happened. But then, Nina would be dead, and other people would still be alive I prefer not to be. On the whole, perhaps I don't altogether regret I let myself slide in Izmir.

I was thinking of quite different things as I came into clear sight of the strange boat. I was wondering, during the bouts of nausea, why I had not looked around for new crew when the two Australians who helped bring my ketch to the Mediterranean had paid off in Izmir to go ocean-racing in Sardinia. In darker moments I wondered, too, why I'd persuaded myself it was necessary to sail across the Aegean to prove the Byron theory anyway, since I could do it almost as well with the charts and *Salsette*'s log. It should still be in the Royal Navy's archives.

But after two weeks at Izmir the trip had become an obsession, a sort of personal hostage to fortune – make the voyage alone and *deserve* the new breaks – and in the end I'd even let go my promised moment with the tall and lovely Bulltine in my fever to sail. That

14

shows the force of obsession. Just to look at Rosemary, striding around a room discussing politics with the light of a bright Ankara morning shining through her dress, was to contemplate a delightful suspicion – that behind the cool self-possession the British aristocracy cultivate so well lay, in Bulltine, the white-hot abandon to which the British aristocracy is also no kind of stranger.

But when she finally wired from her post at the British Embassy that she was coming down to Izmir, the itch to be off on Byron's track had become too strong. It was the night before I was due to leave, and I coldly wired back to tell her to stay at her Third Secretary's desk.

How I regretted that now. There's something about the first onset of seasickness which is peculiarly unsettling: doubts rise simultaneously with the sensation of being out of synch with the swirling world. When *Andromeda* heaved worst I found myself questioning almost my whole career, wondering at the late age of thirty-seven if I shouldn't have been a flyer like my British father after all. It would have kept me out of small boats. My old man had been quietly expecting me to follow him into the Royal Air Force, when in the nick of time he was posted to a job in the British Embassy in Washington, and I was sent to a local high school and on to college. That left me with an accent that never knew which way it was going to pronounce a word before I said it, and different ambitions to my father's. I'd come to college football too late ever to develop a quarterback's arm, but at seventeen I was six foot three inches, and I could run the hundred in even time: for a couple of years I saw myself as a pro running back. The Cleveland Browns were the hot team at the time. Sanity arrived by graduation day – I'd broken a few ribs by then – but the American education my father imagined would be so useful in a NATO officers' mess left me with a wider view of the world than seemed likely to be satisfied by the peacetime professional Air Force. Journalism is a logical step when a liberal schooling has left you with no foundation for a constructive future, and your father has given you a name which sits nicely in a newspaper by-line. My pa, who liked the rhythm of his own title, Group-Captain Lancaster, christened me with my mother's maiden name, Harrison. 'Harrison Lancaster, Saigon,' has the spurious ring of authority the media appreciates. Which is one major reason I found my way into the International News Agency, to survive Vietnam, Iran, Afghanistan and every other extraordinary risk of the next period of modern history. Until the 80s recession and the economy cuts.

You don't survive wars without developing the habit of covering for contingencies. Even my best friends would say that courage comes somewhat lower on my list of priorities than a careful assessment of personal risks. The college football coach expressed this more forcefully. That doesn't bother me. When I say I can live with it, I put the emphasis on 'live': I had a lot of braver colleagues in Vietnam, and a lot of them got left there. What I was kicking myself for now was the stupidity of getting caught out at the end of this long career of objective calculation by an assessment that was idiotically wrong. I'd successfully kept my ass down in two wars and an Islamic Revolution, not to count several problems in South America. I'd prepared *Andromeda* for every eventuality of storm and pirate attack on the risky voyage through the Malacca Straits and the Andamans: as witness the .30 cal machine gun under the quarter berth, in addition to my two sea anchors, half a mile of cable and two sizes of storm jib. A .30 cal is a useful piece of equipment for a yacht in Asian waters: I really had tried to think of everything.

And after all this, to come adrift (possibly literally) out of simple over-confidence! To have assumed that my seamanship would take me across the Aegean single-handed in a day-long storm, without even considering the possible protests of the inner-ear canals. I mean, I should have thought of that. Sea-sickness bothered even Admiral Nimitz, every time he went to sea.

I was miserable, and low – and apprehensive, too – when my gloomy, watering eye finally focused properly on the white *caique*, now just a couple of miles away on my port bow.

I was surprised, then, to have caught up with her so quickly. I would have made five miles on her in two hours. It crossed my mind that whoever was aboard must be a rank amateur: probably one of those wealthy West Germans who hire bare-boat charters out of Piraeus and then spend two weeks waiting for calm weather to motor round the Aegean. She was rolling into the wind in a curiously purposeless way.

I wondered what the hell they were doing, and got the glasses out of the cockpit locker to take a closer look. Stupid, I thought. She should have been footing better: she was one of the *varkalas* type of coaster they still build on Samos, with a clipper bow and a nice sheer halfway back to her transom stern. She'd obviously been converted to a yacht and rigged as a gaff schooner. Big: about fifty feet overall, I judged, with a wide beam in the local style. An easy sort of boat for heavy weather, and she was running under reefed main and jib with her foremast bare between them, which is a comfortable rig for a two-master sailing on a reach in a blow.

On the other hand, I realised suddenly, she wasn't *on* a reach. Two hours before she must have been on the same course as *Andromeda*, with the *meltemi* just aft of the beam. But now she was on the wind if anything, her bow headed into the near gale and the seas at about 40 degrees. In which case she would have sailed better with a reefed for'sail instead of her main. Even so, it was strange that she could make no better headway.

Then I noticed that her jib was backed.

Was she hove to? If so, she wasn't doing it very effectively. When a boat is hove to she is parked in a position where the pressure of the wind on her sails offsets an opposite pressure on the rudder, so the boat sits more or less at a standstill with her head to weather. The trick is to back your jib so the wind pushes the boat's head down to leeward, and at the same time lash the helm down the other way so that the rudder tries to turn the boat in the opposite direction, up into the wind. The balance between the two holds the boat reasonably stationary. It's not a move you see much these days. Few yachtsmen even know how to go about it, which is why I was watching the *caique*'s performance with a superior smile, at first: if they thought they'd hove to, they'd got the steering part quite wrong. The way the boat was slewing round to the waves it seemed her helm had been left unlashed.

And even as I watched, the *caique* lurched so heavily she came right round under the wind, her bows bearing away and her stern crashing up into the advancing wave. For a second or two she hung stern-first to the weather. Then as the succeeding wave lifted her up into the full force of the wind she came further round, and the main boom jerked across her deck in a standing gybe. The impetus brought the bows back into the wind: she leapt forward as the jib filled again. But even as the jib drew, the bows paid off once more. She continued slowly turning, until the jib was backed in the original position.

Not even a fool could be doing that. Whoever was aboard must be sicker than I was. But I couldn't see anyone in the cockpit: if someone was steering he must be huddled down below the coaming. And by the look of what the boat was doing he was either ill or injured.

My first thought was, Christ, I'm in no shape to render life-saving assistance at sea. The sensible thing would be to play the marine Pharisee and pass by quietly on the other side. I clutched at the hope there was no one left aboard.

Freud was quite wrong in the belief that sex is the underlying human motivation. In my view it's cupidity. I might just have tried to get a line aboard that *caique* to save a human life, albeit with fear and massive reluctance. I wouldn't have done it for a fuck, even if you had told me the entire sophomore year at Vassar were lying naked in the cabin stroking themselves in anticipation. But when the hope flashed through my mind that the *caique* could have been abandoned my stomach began to surge at the possibility of gain: the hope of salvage money.

It's curious how the prospect of action immediately alters the physical state. The moment my mind formulated the word 'salvage' it swept aside all sensations of nausea. I had need of that money. *Andromeda* had cost me my entire severance pay from International and the bulk of my other capital. By the time I'd shipped her to Hong Kong and fitted her out for extended cruising I had very little left. There was no more than $4,500 waiting to my credit at the American Express in Athens. A *caique* yacht conversion had to be worth ten times that: a quick salvage agreement could save hunting around for loan money to make the Byron film. At least it would stake me to a worthwhile assault on the European television stations; at best, even pay for the cameraman and sound recordist I needed to tape the programme.

Certainly I calculate the risks, but when the prize is worth it I can gamble, too. If the *caique* was abandoned, I knew I was going to try to get aboard. *Andromeda* was driving hard, still heeled steeply although the wind was falling now to around Force Six. I calculated we would be level with the disabled yacht in about twelve minutes. I had to work out in that time how a single-handed sailor could safely get over to another boat in a high sea.

Now let me just say that crossing between boats single-handed is something you have to think carefully about in mid-ocean, even if there's a mirror-flat calm. The iron rule for someone alone in a boat is not to leave it without ensuring absolutely that he can get back: if the boat starts to drift unexpectedly you're likely to find out very quickly what the airline navigators mean by the point of no return.

To achieve the trick in a sailboat when there is any sort of wind up depends essentially on getting the boat hove-to. Some boats with short fin keels won't do this at all: they just spin aimlessly round in drunken circles. But *Andromeda* was a long-keel design, and she could heave to very steadily.

Once I'd gotten her into that position, the trick would be to use the inflatable life-raft, and let myself hand-over-hand downwind to the *caique* on the longest line I could get together, maintaining contact with the ketch all the time. I'd have to heave to as close as possible on the weather side of the crippled schooner, and hope the two craft remained together for a few minutes. I knew from experiments – the kind the other crew obviously hadn't made with the *caique* – that when *Andromeda* was hove-to she would for'reach slowly across the wind and down to leeward at about one and a half knots. If I assumed the *caique* stayed in one spot, which of course she wouldn't, that gave me at best five minutes before *Andromeda* drifted 200 yards away, which would be near the limit of any cable I could put together. In that time I would have to get the *caique* into the same stable hove-to attitude as my own boat. Even then she would be unlikely to drift at the same rate as *Andromeda*, but at least we'd be moving in the same direction and I would have a little more time to get a cable between the two.

The real risk was that the *caique* could broach across the wind as I tried to get down to her – even as I kept the glasses on her she went round and gybed again – which would be likely to take her out of the limits of my lifeline. The *caique*'s helm was probably running free. The first thing I would have to do – if I got aboard – would be to jam the wheel to balance that backed jib.

Andromeda was well fitted out. Despite low Asian prices the gear had cost me a small fortune. Most of my main anchor rode was chain, which wasn't going to help, but after I had lashed the wheel to hold us on course for the crippled yacht I rummaged in the peak for the second bower's rope cable, and brought it aft to the cockpit. I had seventy-five fathoms of that, and another fifty from the sea anchor. When I joined them in a double sheet bend this gave me 250 yards of strong towing

21

cable. I coiled it as neatly as I could on the stern deck and in the cockpit, arranging it to run out through the stern mooring chocks from a secure hitch on the portside headsail winch. Then I had a moment of inspiration and took the fifty fathoms of light line off the sea lead and bent that onto the anchor cable. Now I had 350 yards of line to leave between myself and *Andromeda*: perhaps seven minutes of time aboard the *caique*.

This part of the theory was sound enough, but I saw the drawback as soon as I'd attached the lead line to the thicker cable. I had a cold flash of fear for a second, kneeling there on the wet heeled deck with one arm clasped round a liferail stanchion to hold me aboard. I started to feel sick again immediately: I hadn't been thinking as clearly as I assumed. The anchor cable was going to be too heavy for the inflatable to tow. The weight of it would swamp the life-raft the moment any quantity of cable got into the water. I needed the anchor cables' strength to keep the two boats together, but to succeed I would have to get aboard the caique before the 100 yards of lead line ran out: once I had to depend on the heavier rope I would be at risk. If I was still in the raft when the bower cable paid out, I was gone.

Andromeda bucketed through the chop while I thought it out a second time. There *was* a way through: I had spare halyards and spare sheetlines, and thick but floatable warps meant to be streamed out from the stern in heavy seas. Together there were more than fifty yards of halyard, twenty yards of sheets, and all of fifty fathoms of storm warp. All up it would make for 170 yards of alternative line – nearly four minutes of time on the last calculation.

I dragged it all out of the various lockers, and bent all the ends together, with the thick warp at the inboard end made fast to the headsail winch. Now I had two long lengths of cable – the light, floatable stuff to use as the dinghy's lifeline to the main winch, and the heavy towing cable fixed to the stern bitts. To connect the two I took the outer end of leadline which was attached to the anchor cable, and bent it to the outboard end of the thick storm warp. With the last length of light lifeline paralleling the light first length on the towing system, I could float the life-raft out to the *caique* on the manageable line of halyards and storm warp, and still pull myself back safely to the ketch if I missed her. But if I got aboard the derelict on the end of the floating lines I would eventually bring in the leadline connecting me to the heavy anchor cables. By pulling that in, I would establish a tow.

I thought it through again when I was finished. It still seemed logical. By this time we were just about half a mile from the *caique*. I was sure now that there was no one on deck.

Boarding the *caique* was no longer merely an interesting idea. The doomful moment had arrived when the next move would take me over the top. Once you begin any dangerous enterprise your actions tend to follow in an automatic sequence: the mind switches off, probably to preserve its balance, and the momentum of that first commitment carries you through the course you have started. It's only the opening shot which requires courage. For the rest of the battle you are running a pre-set pattern like a well-trained football player. I'd discovered that, choking on my own fear in Vietnam: just make yourself take the first step, and the rest will follow.

I brought *Andromeda* into the wind to ease the pressure on the main, and then lowered the wild canvas and began to reef it down to the third and last set of reefing cringles. In that sort of sea just moving about a boat is an ordeal. The lurching of the boat turns your own weight against you: you are light when you expect to be heavy, and then at the next moment leaden-limbed with the momentum of the roll. But there was a spare slab-reefing line in a cockpit locker, luckily, and in a few minutes I had it set. I could heave to without the skimpy triangle of canvas that now remained, but I calculated *Andromeda* would be steadier with it, and I could manoeuvre better. I brought her back on course and crept up on the weather side of the wallowing *caique*. The schooner started to go around again: I could see a lashing on her wheel when we got closer, but it seemed to be just loose enough to let the rudder play a little, so that the occasional bigger sea could turn her bows across.

I hailed her as she turned. There was no response. The deck was empty. I pulled on some light spray gear and a big life-jacket. Now I was going to have to go.

The *caique* turned slowly through a great circle to leeward, and when her bows came back into the wind she was astern of me and further off. If that happened while I was in the life-raft I would have to haul myself back inboard from the end of my line and bring *Andromeda* back into position for another shot. On the other hand if I could heave to close enough, my lee might protect the *caique* from the larger waves, so that she would point steadily for a minute or two. But I would have to take *Andromeda* right round her now to come up close enough to begin. I needed to gybe the main to circle to leeward of the yacht. I was glad now that I had left it set: the manoeuvre would have been cumbersome under the jib alone.

The turn was difficult enough as it was, with one hand on the jib sheet and the other nudging the wheel round, but *Andromeda* slid across perfectly, the main boom coming up short with a contained crash on the secured mainsheet. It was a quieter motion now, as we came under the *caique* in an arc about 600 yards across. I eased the jib sheet a good two feet and then brought her up comfortably back onto the wind. We were on port tack, coming gently up onto the *caique*'s beam. I brought *Andromeda* down a little and then slipped up past the *caique*'s counter. She was no more than eight feet away.

Now I had to move very fast. I spun the wheel to port and brought *Andromeda* back on the starboard tack: the momentum carried us up onto the *caique*'s starboard beam and we almost turned into her as the backed jib took hold of the wind. I thrashed the wheel back to starboard. The rudder bit. The wind noise in my ears died instantly, as *Andromeda* quietly steeled herself and hove to.

I lashed the wheel into position quickly and then dragged the life-raft canister to the stern rail. We'd come into place only about fifteen feet from the *caique*, but in a minute or two's drift she would be out of our lee and the boats would begin to separate. I tied the life-raft painter to a stanchion, pulled the ripcord and flung the canister over the side. There was a huge rush of compressed air and in five seconds the four-man raft was bobbing ready in the sea. With the end of the coiled halyard line tied round my waist I clambered over the heaving rail, and pulled in the raft. Then as she rose for an instant towards

25

Andromeda's stern, I half jumped, half stepped, out onto the rubber floor.

By now I had twenty-five or thirty feet of water to cross to the *caique*'s pitching bow. But as the raft slipped further away from *Andromeda*'s stern it began to leap into violent motion: I spread my legs to try to wedge myself against the sides but the raft seemed to jerk all ways at once in the seas, going sideways on the advancing face of a wave and then rushing forwards as soon as it passed. I was gripping the side lifeline with my left hand as I reached with the other for the paddle, bobbing in the sea on the end of its safety line from the raft floor. I needed two hands to use the paddle with real effect. But for the moment I couldn't bring myself to release the raft lifeline.

I made a couple of ineffectual stabs at the sea. They hardly seemed to have an effect on the raft's direction. There was no choice but to force myself to use both hands: I couldn't risk drifting down on the *caique*'s lee bow for fear she would round again and sweep me away from *Andromeda* in the turn. Frantically I dug the paddle in. The raft answered slowly: as the next wave peak lifted it I managed to push us to the left towards the weather side.

The *caique*'s bow heaved up on the wave above me and I came to the next problem with an awful inevitability. The big sheer on the old, high-bowed design gave her a good six feet of freeboard at her prow. I couldn't pull myself up to that height from the raft. It would be like a swimmer trying to heave himself onto a boat from the water: anything over three feet is impossible without a ladder. As the raft hit the *caique*'s side I had to throw myself forward and fend the inflatable down along the hull to the lower sections amidships, praying the plastic was not suddenly going to rip on a sharp projection. There were ominous rubbery squelching noises as we rubbed down towards her stern. Then, relief – a life-rail stanchion loomed up on the rail within reach of my right hand. I hitched the raft's painter to it quickly, and heaved myself aboard.

The motion on the *caique* was different again. She was wallowing, with a kind of stupid aimlessness, as the wheel at the stern moved to and fro on its loose lashing. I tied the light halyard line from my waist to the schooner's foremast, linking her tenuously to *Andromeda*, and stumbled aft to secure the wheel. The *caique* seemed to steady slightly. I judged she would at least keep her bow to weather, now.

Andromeda was for'reaching. She'd moved thirty yards ahead, with wild water starting to open up between us. I went for'ard again and began to pull in my lifeline. The linked halyards came in slowly. It was a minute or more before the join with the parallel sea-lead line appeared at the rail, with the heavy cables that represented safety behind it aboard *Andromeda*.

I untied the knot and brought the lead line back to a headsail winch in the cockpit to get a purchase. After a minute or so winding, the floating line went suddenly heavy as the anchor cable on *Andromeda* slipped into the water and submerged. I cranked the winch endlessly, muscles straining. Then, slowly, the big anchor cable came inboard.

The jubilation and the relief was almost like being suddenly drunk. I hadn't realised how frightened I must have been. But the worst was over: I'd got a towline aboard, and as soon as I had brought in the join between the two anchor warps, to remove the risk of the knot parting in the heavy weather, I could make my bower line fast and feel safe.

When I made the big warp secure through the mooring bitts at the bow I slumped for a moment by the foremast, starting to shake a little. But I'd got it done. I'd made the first part of the salvage.

The question now was whether there was any damage to the old schooner. She had been rolling helpless in the storm for several hours: there would be water below. There was also the mystery of what might have happened to the crew. I got to my feet and went hand over hand down the cabin coaming to the cockpit again.

This time I saw immediately something that seemed to explain the missing crew. Just aft of the cabin hatch, on the lee side, were three dark patches running indistinctly across the wet decking. It dawned on me after a split-second what they were. Where the last wave had come across the deck it had washed some of the stain away, and as this ran down the grooved planks it was light red. The dark patches were blood. One of them was very large, with a great tongue at the edge suggesting some spouting artery. When I looked there were faint traces of blood on the side life-rail, too. Whoever was bleeding had gone over the side.

I glanced for'ard to the anchor cable. It was holding comfortably enough. If anything the weight between the two boats was improving their joint ability to keep head-to-weather. It seemed safe enough to take a look below at the cabin.

There wasn't much headroom on the shallow-draught *caique*, and I could not see clearly for a moment or two after the bright sunlight outside. About a foot of water washed round my ankles where I hunched just inside the hatchway, letting my pupils dilate to the gloom. After a moment I could see that the cabin was packed with some kind of cargo. Every berth and most of the floor space was taken up with rough crates and large square shapes covered with sacking, soaked with the overflow from the bilge. There was a smell of damp and old cloth, like the remains of a flooded junk shop.

Christ, I thought, drugs. I'd hit on an abandoned smuggler.

The nearest crate was jammed into a settee berth just for'ard of the navigator's table on the right of the hatchway. I swung over to it by the grabrails on the cabin head, clutching them against the *caique*'s jolting motion, and pulled back the sacking top. Inside were large packets wrapped in grubby tissue paper. I pulled a couple apart with my free hand: one contained an old brass Turkish coffee mill and the other a set of copper coffee pans. Perhaps it *was* a junk shop.

The rest of the packets in that crate seemed to be similar. The next contained a selection of small rugs and the square pieces of carpetry the peasants on the Anatolian coast use as shoulder bags. None of this made sense: in the middle of the storm-blasted Aegean, the derelict's cabin held the remnants of some floating tourist souvenir stall.

Like a damp and discomforted chimpanzee I moved hand over hand along the grab rails, through the ankle-deep water towards the forepeak section. A louvred door swung in the entrance to the for'ard passageway, with a hanging locker on one side and presumably the yacht's heads on the other. I pushed through a further pair of louvres into the for'ard cabin. Then I stopped short in the hatchway, staring at the derelict's final surprise.

On the portside berth lay a woman, very nearly naked, with her shirt ripped back off her shoulders and her hands tied up above her head to the ornate bunk rail with a length of cord. The rest of her clothing had gone. There was blood on her legs. Vomit stained the mattress round her. I thought for a moment she was dead or at least battered unconscious. But she flinched when I touched her and her eyes opened slowly in confused fear.

I wiped some of the mess from her face, saying something highly ethnic and suitable like 'Jesus fucking Christ', and she just groaned for a while as I untied her hands.

'Oh God,' she said in an American voice, 'who the hell are you?'

'I just came aboard,' I told her. 'I thought the boat was abandoned. What the devil happened to you?'

'Turks,' she said. She brought her hands down from the berth head rail and cradled them to her breasts, moaning quietly. 'Turks.'

One hand began to scrabble on the bunk for a scrap of grubby blanket that was lying crumpled between the mattress and the inside of the hull. The boat pitched into a wave trough with a heavier crash than before and her eyes came wide again. 'Where are they?' she said.

'There's no one else on board,' I told her. 'Whoever the Turks were, they've left. From the look of the blood on deck, they went violently.'

'Bastards,' she said, and for a moment her eyelids dropped again and she looked as if she would pass out. Then she began to pull herself up, weakly. 'Christ, I'm so sick. I've got to clean myself up. For God's sake find me some clothes.'

I helped her aft, holding her firm against the lurching motion, into the head. She half fell into the cramped compartment, the door swinging behind her, and I watched her splashing water on herself for a moment. There was nothing in the cabin she could wear apart from an old spray jacket in the hanging locker. I passed it in to her. The water was slopping around the cabin floor and I wanted to get back to *Andromeda* as quickly as I could.

'I've got this hulk in tow at the moment,' I told her. 'We need to get over to my ketch as soon as you feel able. It'll be a rough trip in a life-raft. Can you make it?'

She stopped scrubbing her thighs for a second or two. 'Just get me off,' she said. 'Just get me away.'

'Put the spray jacket on and come back to the cockpit,' I said. 'But don't go beyond the coaming. I've got to get the sails down before we leave.'

I fought back through the chaos in the cabin trying to work out the way to tow the *caique*. Obviously the jib needed to come down because it would just make the tow harder, but there was more water in the cabin than I'd hoped. I would have to leave the main up, reefed, to try to steady her in the sea. I took a quick look at the bilge pump and gave it up. It was a smart-looking electrically operated model: a couple of attempts to switch it on confirmed that the yacht's batteries were beyond resurrection.

The jib was no problem. When I crawled to the foot of the foremast I found the halyards worked on an old-fashioned block system, in place of a winch: all

I had to do was slash through the line and the halyard went screaming through the masthead sheaves, with the peak of the jib blasting out to leeward. I unshackled the bottom edge from the sheets and the bow and the whole sail took off into the Aegean. But without the steadying pressure of the sail the *caique* began throwing her head about like a neurotic horse, and reefing the main became quite another matter. The heavy gaff spar was banging violently now and when I started to lower it the canvas suddenly ripped through near the mast. In a second the tear flashed outwards to the leach and the mainsail tore free, cracking out across the liferails after the vanished jib. I cut it loose and let it go. There was no option now but to lower the gaff and let the *caique* take its chance. I had no time to hunt up a storm trysail.

The girl was up in the cockpit now, holding on like death to the hatchway rails, pale-faced and frightened.

I clawed back down the cabin-top towards her, shouting through the wind to try to ease her tension: 'That's one quick way to reduce sail!'

The joke vanished like the canvas on the wind. Her eyes were wide: 'I'm not going in that life-raft in this sea.'

'It got me here.'

'I'm not doing it. I'll stay.'

I looked across to *Andromeda*. She was nearly forty yards upwind now. 'You have to come,' I said. 'I don't know if the schooner can stay afloat. We've got several hours ahead of us.'

'Oh, Jesus,' she said.

The trip back to the ketch was no attraction to me either, now. I went back to the bilge pump and cut out the thick neoprene hose line from the mechanical parts. It would protect the anchor rode from chafing in the *caique*'s bow chocks. With the slashed hosepipe on my left wrist I took hold of the girl and steadied her up over the cockpit coaming.

'You have to,' I told her.

We inched for'ard along the cabintop rail to where the life-raft jumped and tumbled back at the *caique*'s side. When I'd fixed the hose onto the tow-cable at the chock, and the girl was ready, I retrieved the lifeline from the foremast and climbed down into the life-raft. I was clutching at the bigger boat's toe-rail, trying to steady the raft against the schooner each time it rose to within reach of the deck. Three times the raft rose and each time the girl hesitated.

I bellowed at her: 'If you trust me I can get you over to the ketch. But if you're on the *caique* and she starts to sink I can't save you.'

Her face set firmer. Then she jumped, a little too early as the raft rose towards her, and she cannoned into me on the wet rubber. There was the punch of her knee in my stomach and her cold wet belly on my face. Her breath was coming in quick sobs. 'Hold tight to the lifelines and wedge yourself in,' I told her, 'I've got to pull us back to the ketch along the line.'

I unhitched the dinghy painter and got up to a kneeling position, hauling on the halyard around my waist. Then with a great sideways slither we swept out from the schooner's side across the white water. I hauled in on the floating line and slowly pulled the raft's head towards *Andromeda*.

The raft pitchforked upwards on the first wave. With the line taut to the ketch she was held hard against the rush of water and we were submerged waist deep in the breaking peak. But the raft wasn't going to flip: she was designed to survive broken water and though we were full to the gunwhales, once the peak was past I was able to pull the raft rapidly down the back of the wave. It was terrifying – but I thought we were going to make it.

The steep wave pattern threw us and thumped us up and down like riders on a nightmare hobbyhorse, in white water up to our chests but still with the bulging bulwarks of the inflatable holding us up in the swirling foam. We could only breathe in the skittering downhill rushes towards the distant ketch – then shut our eyes and faces in the crash of the next rising wave. But in those downhill jerks I was slowly hauling the raft towards *Andromeda*. My arms felt like breaking. When the raft dived into an oncoming wave I had to clutch the protesting halyard like a man making love to a nervous water python. But gradually the raft was edging towards the stern of the ketch.

The last twenty yards were the slowest.

And then, at last, when my strength was almost gone, we reached *Andromeda*. I made fast to the bucking stern and pushed the girl, freezing and shaking uncontrollably now, onto the safety of the deck.

She pulled herself over on hands and knees into the cockpit. As soon as I could haul the life-raft back onto the deck I joined her, and helped her down into the main cabin. She half fell onto the settee in front of the navigator's table. Once I'd collected myself I tossed her a woollen sweater out of the spare clothes net hung over my own berth opposite. After an exhausted minute, she started to pull it on, very slowly, like the half-dead victim of a bomb blast.

When I got my breath back I found a can of bouillon in the galley cupboard, heated it up and handed her a mug. She held it in both hands and sipped.

The question that was in my mind now seemed to have an obvious answer, but indelicacy comes naturally to ex-reporters and I asked her, all the same. 'Did they rape you?'

She looked up at me, sick and weary. 'Yes and no,' she said. 'I mean, yes – but not in the usual way. You know the Turks have a taste for boys.'

CHAPTER 2

Heel and Tow

The girl was as comfortable as she could be, under a light blanket on a main cabin berth. *Andromeda* could look after herself in the hove-to position for a while, and while the girl finished the soup I warmed us up a can of stew on the galley stove. The ketch was pitching, but not rolling around in the waves like the *caique*, and the girl seemed to feel better with the steadier motion. I wedged myself in the hatchway and considered the position as she slowly spooned up the stew.

I was glad, briefly, that she had not actually been raped in the normal sense. This was not going to be much solace to her for the moment. When I looked at her face, ravaged like someone just taking in the sight of a horrific highway smash half an hour before, I decided immediately to leave this comfort till later: she was in no state to appreciate that it might be better to be forcibly sodomised by two rampaging Turks than risk impregnation. There was little I could do for her now apart from offering what physical comfort the boat could provide. In this high sea that was not too much, but even so it seemed to be helping. She finished her stew and gave a sort of half smile. Then she settled back on the berth and closed her eyes.

The immediate question was what to do with the

boats. I had the radio, of course, but I was not going to ask for help if I could avoid it: a tug would cut my share of salvage. I had to try to tow the *caique* to shelter, and I took a look at the chart on the navigator's table by the hatch to work it out. The nearest island now was Andros, but when I started to reckon our position I realised that if I made for the main harbour, in the eastern half of the mountainous island, we would be on a dead run almost due south. That was going to be risky in this weather with the *caique* in tow: she would continually be over-taking *Andromeda* down the leeward slopes of the swell, a threat to the towing warp if nothing else. There was another point to consider, too. On the voyage out from Hong Kong I had read Denham's sailing guide to the Aegean from cover to cover, and I knew the modern port on Andros was open to a northerly gale. It would be better to take the *caique* on a broad reach for the Kafireus Channel, the Andros Passage round the western tip of the island. A reach would be an easier point of sailing for the tow in any case, and once through the channel I could swing back south-east for the older, sheltered port of Gavrion round the corner. That way the tow would be safer while we were in the open sea, and the anchorage surer when we arrived. The girl was asleep: I shut the hatchway on her, and moved into the cockpit to bring *Andromeda* onto course under main and jib. Then I switched on the diesel and brought it up to half power, to keep a steady tension on the towing cable.

Once *Andromeda*'s starboard quarter was turned to the gale her motion was not too bad, though the wind wasn't going to ease much more until hours after sun-set. With a little experiment I found a way to handle the tow. The wave pattern was producing major peaks about sixty yards apart. Our course slanted across it. When I adjusted the slack on the cable to hold the *caique* at just about the same point of the pattern as the ketch, the pull of the diesel kept the cable taut as we both rose up the windward side of the waves. Then once the ketch passed the peak I could head her off the slant and straight down the wave for a moment, so that the extra speed of the ketch's descent took in the slack as the *caique* astern began to plunge down her own slope. It meant I couldn't relax and use the self-steering gear, but I began to hope the towing cable would at least stay in one piece until we got into the lee of Andros. My expectations of salvage increased.

After about an hour the girl opened the cabin hatchway on the starboard side of the stern cockpit and stood for a moment, pale and bare-legged under my sweater, blankly looking out.

'Have you got any antiseptic?' she asked, faintly. 'I'm feeling a bit better. I thought I'd wash up.'

'There's a shower for'ard of the main cabin on the left,' I said. 'It's a bit rough now to use it, but you can wash and there's a bottle of antiseptic and tubes of Savlon cream in the cupboard.'

She would not look at me, but I could feel she was straining herself to find a defence against what had happened. She tried to be tough; but the attempt proved brittle.

'You reckon you could get syphilis in the asshole?' she said.

'Certainly. But it's easily curable. Look at it this way: at least you won't need an abortion.'

She looked at me now. 'I suppose you think that makes it better,' she said. And she drew in her breath and as the boat lurched again down a wave I waited for the first tears. They were close, but she would not let them begin. 'I'm going to wash,' she said. The set of her face as she looked at me was halfway between fury and anguish; then she bent back through the hatchway into the cabin.

The sea was like a regiment of charging white bonnets: the ketch was slipping over and down the waves easily enough, but I had to concentrate at the wheel. I was glad for the first time that the Taiwan builders had installed a smooth-rimmed destroyer wheel instead of the spoke-handle traditional variety I'd sentimentally ordered. My hands were moving constantly, almost as if I was driving a tricky car on a serpentine circuit, and projecting spokes would have obstructed control and jarred unwary fingers. I reckoned we were twenty-five miles from the tip of Andros, with another fifteen to sail through the Strait before we came under a lee. It was going to be a hard-working afternoon: and I noticed as I glanced regularly at the *caique* astern that she was making heavier weather of the tow, as if she had taken in more water from the constant rolling.

The island of Andros, ahead, and Euboea to starboard were well in sight when the girl reappeared on deck, a couple of hours later. She was bringing me a mug of soup, with another in her hand for herself. She seemed to have slept again: she was clean, and calmer, and she had found a pair of my shorts to wear under the sweater.

'I'm sorry I snapped. But, you know. . .'

'That's OK. I'll find you something better to wear once I can leave the wheel.'

'Where are we headed?'

'Andros. That's the island you can see on the port bow.'

Andromeda's cockpit was shaped like a wrong-way-round letter 'L', with the upward leg formed by a starboard passageway that leads past the rear cabin to connect the wheel position with the main cabin hatch, for'ard. She came through, gingerly, handing me the soup mug, and found herself a place on the lee side out of the spray.

'It beats the place I thought I was going.'

'Where was that?'

'The bottom of the Mediterranean.'

'Jesus,' I said. 'How did it all happen?'

To my astonishment she laughed, just for a second.

'Do you think we ought to be introduced?' she said. 'I'm Nina Millen. I'm an archaeologist, from Columbia, and I'd like to tell you I don't make a habit of going around being raped by Turkish smugglers.'

'Harrison Lancaster,' I said. 'Journalist, until a little while ago, and now impoverished yachtsman and historical researcher. I kind of assumed the *caique* was a smuggler.'

'Sure is,' she said. 'I'd guess there's around a hundred thousand dollars of illegal antiquities aboard that yacht.'

It didn't surprise me greatly. There's been a trade in archaeological smuggling across the Mediterranean virtually since the end of the Second War, and it has survived every attempt by governments in the area to stamp it out. Every kind of antique relic, from Neolithic arrow heads to amphorae dredged up from ancient Greek shipwrecks and figurines stolen from Near East archaeological digs, run the smuggling route westwards to the art markets in

40

European capitals. On the other hand the contents of the *caique* had not seemed exceptional.

'It looked a lot like junk to me,' I said.

'Believe me,' said the girl, clutching her soup against the heave of the ketch at the top of the next wave. 'Archaeology is my business. And they killed to keep it quiet.'

'What happened?'

She hunched herself up where the aft cabin and the cockpit made a corner, and stared at the soup in her hand.

'I've been on a dig up on the shores of the Black Sea near Samsun for eighteen months,' she said. 'It's a land dig, but I want to make underwater archaeology my speciality – I'm a qualified scuba diver.

'A Turkish guy on the expedition called Manoli' – her face screwed up for several seconds, and she bit her lip – 'Manoli was interested too. There's been a theory round for years that Jason's Golden Fleece – Jason and the Argonauts, you know? – was actually a cargo of gold ingots in the shape of a hide, from Colchis in the Black Sea. They've found copper ingots cast that way in Bronze Age wrecks all along the coast of Turkey, but no one's found the golden ingots yet.

'The trouble is it's difficult to dive in the Black Sea. There's plenty of wrecks there from the first 2,000 years BC, but most places you've got problems with Turkish military security. So we thought we'd use our three weeks vacation to scout for likely wreck sites on the Aegean coast. That's where most of the ingot cargoes have turned up so far.

'We hired a car and took a slow look down the whole Aegean coast south from Canakkale. We just

41

stayed nights in village inns, with sleeping bags, and cruised around looking at the headlands and bays, anywhere a Bronze Age galley might have been caught on a lee shore and wrecked.

'One morning early in the second week we were looking at a really deserted piece of coast east of the Gulf of Syme. Manoli was wading in the water examining a little headland at the end of a long bay, and I decided to climb over to look at the next one.

'When I got the top I saw the *caique* moored in the shallows, and a group of men loading a dinghy with bales and cases. I mean, one glance and I was turning to go: obviously it was something illegal and rape is a national sport in that country, anyway.

'Then another man came out of the bushes behind me, doing up the buttons on his slacks. He must have been the lookout, but he'd been busy taking a leak and missed me.

'He just grabbed me, and I screamed and struggled.

'After a minute Manoli came running up the little hill, and the guy just dropped me, turned, and stabbed him. Just like that. No questions. He just jabbed him twice, and Manoli fell down. He didn't make a sound. I think he was dead immediately.

'The Turk grabbed me again – I was simply standing there, too shocked to move. And he took me down to the beach. They tied me up and put me aboard the *caique*.'

'Jesus,' I said. 'But I suppose it's a prison sentence, even for smuggling old junk. And they'd kill for a quarter, out there in the backblocks.'

'It's not junk,' said the girl. 'They left me tied up in the cabin for a while and I saw what they were loading.

There's one piece that would be worth at least $50,000 in Paris even on the black market. It's a big head of Apollo, early Hellenistic period I'd guess. They were struggling into the cabin with it and the carpet wrapping got torn away.

'When they realised I'd seen that, they tied some cloth over my eyes. I couldn't see a lot more after that, but who knows what else they'd got?'

'Fifty thousand dollars, though.'

'Easily. OK, a lot of the stuff the archaeological smugglers move out is nickel and dime material. They'll take anything they can find on a dig – up at Samsun we even lost pieces of kitchen pottery that was nothing more than historic household trash, really. But really valuable material gets stolen, too. The Apollo's Head was a good piece, but it wouldn't be the biggest item the smuggling trade's shifted in its time. Last year a French expedition lost a statue they were almost certain was the famous Aphrodite of Cnidos by Praxiteles, the Greek sculptor from the fourth century BC. That would have been worth millions.'

'On the black market?'

'Sure. You don't know what that kind of thing is worth if you're not in the business. The Cnidos Aphrodite was one of the wonders of the classic world, but it hasn't been seen since the third century AD. All we've got is a second century copy in the Vatican. The French people found a statue that looked very like the Vatican version during a dig on the Resadiye peninsula near the ancient site of Cnidos. They had it locked up at the diggings for two days, and somebody broke in and stole it the third night. It'll be in Paris or Rome by now, and the Apollo's Head was about to take the same trip.'

43

'Big stuff, eh? I'd assumed it would be drugs, when I first got on board.'

'Maybe that, too. But it's big, all right. It's an international gang. After they put the blindfold on me the leaders came aboard. I couldn't see much through the cloth, just people's shapes, but they were a couple of tall guys, and they talked in English. Come to think of it they sounded like Englishmen. One of them hit his head on the cabin roof and swore like an Englishman. You know, "Bloody 'ell, mate," the way they do, "this boat's built for dwarves." '

'Yes, I know. I was English myself, originally.'

'I thought you were. There's still traces in your voice. I'll never forget the accent now. Right after that he spoke in Turkish to the crew, and the other guy just drawled "Tell them to take the girl with them and drop her over the side before they get to Marseille." '

'Nice.'

'The Turks had other ideas first.'

I didn't want to make this conversation too difficult for her. She was only narrowly holding on to her control. I watched the waves ahead and considered. But while I thought about it all she made the decision herself.

'There were only two of them crewing the boat. Once the others had gone and they were under way, they decided to have a little fun with me on the voyage to France. I had two hours of them, one after the other.'

She was quiet, swilling the remains of the soup around the bottom of her mug.

'How did they start to fight?'

'The younger one wanted to keep me alive, at least until they got closer to Marseille. He wasn't too bad, in between times. At least he loosened the ropes and

44

brought me something to drink. But the older guy seemed to be in control and he was getting nervous. He wanted to drop me over the side as soon as he'd finished the second time. They argued about that.

'Then the young one had a second go at me, and when he'd finished the old fellow wanted to do something else.'

She broke off, staring emptily at the tossing horizon. Then she looked at me out of the corner of her eyes for a second and drained the last of her soup, quickly.

'What he had in mind was a very nasty game with the boat hook. The young one told him I'd be no good after that and they started to push and shove each other. In a flash they had knives out. One way or another they'd been arguing over me for an hour and it suddenly snapped. You know what Turks are like. Or maybe you don't.'

'I've got an idea.'

'Anyway, one chased the other out of the cabin and they were shouting and screaming for a while. Then there was silence. The boat began to roll around like something in a washing machine, and I guess I must have passed out.'

'I wonder how long you'd been there by the time I came aboard?'

'Hours. It was night-time when most of this was going on, you know. It would have been dark when the two hoods went over the side.'

'And I didn't pick you up until late afternoon.'

'No wonder I needed the soup. When do you suppose we'll get to land?'

It was nearly dark already. The sun would set just after six, and we were not making quite the speed I had expected. The 3,000-foot peaks of Andros were high on the port bow now, and perhaps just around sunset we would lay the headland and turn sou'sou'west into the channel. That still left another three hours before we would find a lee.

'Maybe not till midnight,' I said. 'We've got twelve miles of open channel to sail before we get into sheltered water on the other side of the island. And the port's another ten miles on after that.'

'Maybe I should go find something to eat for us,' she said.

'That's good thinking,' I told her. 'I can't leave the wheel in this weather while we've got the tow. There's a few cans of stuff, bread and *feta* cheese in the galley, and some Turkish beer in the icebox.'

She took my empty mug and went down to rummage in the cabin. I watched the high mountains of Andros for a while, as they grew tall above the pitching bow. We were close to the north-west point of the island now, and soon we would enter the race through Kafireus Channel. I kept to the same course as the headland began to slip with slowly increasing speed from the port bow to the beam: I wanted to take *Andromeda* out in the centre of the channel, where the current would be faster and less complex, before I changed course to pass through.

Nina came back to the cockpit with a plate of cheese, Turkish butter, and long bread rolls that had kept reasonably fresh, wrapped in plastic in the icebox. In the other hand she had a litre bottle of the yeasty Turkish beer that is supposed to be lager, but tastes just a little flatter than normal, like an old-fashioned draught beer drawn from the wood in a tavern. Beer is a good thing to drink at sea in bad weather – on Norwegian whalers they used it as a remedy for seasickness – and the meal gave both of us a small touch of fresh life.

For the first time – nausea virtually gone, the dramas of ship and rescue overcome – I had a chance to look for a while at my ravaged passenger. It registered, almost with surprise, that she had the kind of face which inevitably, with terrible ease, conquers my heart. Oh God, I thought, almost unwillingly, one of mine. High cheekbones, sweeping out in a sort of sensuous Russian steppeland below Slavic eyes which had that straight-edged lower lid that suggests slow, interior contemplation. A wide mouth, longish, straight black hair. Slim hands that were steadier, now, as she ate and her horrors receded. A woman for a long affair: this thought was not quite welcome, because it involved me where I did not wish to be threatened, in emotional contemplation of what had happened to her.

'I don't think you're right about the drugs,' Nina said suddenly. 'If those two kooks had been stopped by a coastguard patrol or something they would have been arrested the moment somebody saw what was in the cabin – I mean the Apollo's Head, not me. Why would you risk putting drugs aboard a boat which was that vulnerable?'

'Because once the antiques were found the patrol probably wouldn't look much further. At any rate for a while. The crew would be expendable as far as the organisers of the voyage were concerned: they could stay in a jail on charges of smuggling antique junk, while somebody from the gang went back aboard the *caique* to recover the drugs. The antiques would be a cover.'

'They're too valuable for that,' she said.

'Are you sure?'

'That head of Apollo is a good piece,' she said. 'There's not too much stuff around from the second century BC, which is where I'd put it from the brief glance I got. I told you, it's worth fifty thousand in Paris, easy. Plus they're bound to have had a lot of smaller things, figurines or whatever, in the other cases.

'I guarantee you, there's maybe $100,000 worth of antiques on that *caique*. Who needs heroin?'

'Well, we won't know until we look in the bilges,' I said.

'That's true.' She took a brief glance up from her loaf and cheese at the coast of Andros, moving aft now along our rail, and said, 'That island seems to be moving off to stern. When do we go into the channel?'

'Any time now. We'll get a much quicker, smoother ride in the middle of the race.'

Actually I was surprised myself to find how much better the conditions were in the centre of the strait. The wind was still blasting from the north, and the current through the channel was from the north-east, but the strength of the stream seemed to be flattening out the waves here in the centre, and its force started to move us rapidly. We'd hardly been making five knots with the tow in the open sea: from the way the coast of Andros was beginning to move in the rapid gloom of the quick Aegean evening, I thought we were approaching seven at least.

'I tell you what,' I said, 'I can put her on course now.' The current had us firmly in its teeth and and it took only one turn of the wheel to settle *Andromeda* and the tow onto the south-western heading. 'The channel current is keeping down the wave pattern, here in the centre. Do you think you could take the wheel for a while so that I can go below to check the course?'

48

'I thought you'd never ask,' she said.

And she grinned suddenly, quite out of keeping with the image of a respectable young American girl who not long before had been forcibly buggered by the Turks, as she moved across to take *Andromeda*'s wheel from my hands.

'I like boats,' she said. 'And if I can steer for a while it'll help keep my dinner down. Concentrating on something outside the boat, you know?'

'Just keep us on that heading,' I said. 'We've got enough way on now to hold the towline taut.'

Andromeda's navigation table is on the right of the hatchway steps, a little cramped area between the starboard side settee berth of the main cabin and the rear bulkhead that separates the main accommodation from the aft cabin. I found the Cyclades chart and the sailing instructions for Andros and considered the possibilities. I knew already that with the current behind us we were going to clear the Kafireus Channel faster than I'd thought, but now another consideration came up. The half-litre of beer had hit me like a sledge hammer at the end of this strenuous day in life-rafts and boat rescues. And I didn't like what I read about the entrance to Gavrion, if I was not going to arrive there in razor-sharp condition.

I pulled myself back into the cockpit and told her the good and bad news: 'The way the boat is going we'll get into the lee of Andros in a bit over an hour. If I go for the port I had in mind we've got two hours' sail after that.

'I don't know about you, but I'm just about to fall over with fatigue. And the sailing instructions say the Vovi shoal at the entrance to Gavrion is difficult in the dark.

'What do you say I find a sheltered bay round the point at the end of the strait and we cast anchor for the night?'

She nodded her head, taking her eyes off the course for a moment. 'Why don't you,' she said. 'I don't think I can stay awake much longer.'

'You can have the aft cabin,' I said. 'I wouldn't recommend it in a seaway but you'll be comfortable there at anchor.'

'Harry,' said Nina, 'don't worry about the proprieties. I've had just about enough for one day and if it's all the same to you I'd rather you didn't try to fuck me. But if you did, I think I might be just too tired to notice.'

I let her steer for most of the hour we spent in the southerly race of the channel. The rapid Aegean evening faded into dark like a theatre's house lights soon after she took the wheel, but with a half moon and the star-littered sky we could see the coastline of Andros clear to port, the mountains silver with the night light. The current was stronger now, but here in the middle of the channel we were clear of the eddies and confusing swirls that a channel race produces closer to headlands and bays. Nina steered competently, adjusting *Andromeda* direct to the course with clear, unhurried movements of the wheel, never losing way from the boat's progress: the current and the diesel together were enough to keep the towline tight. The *caique* was lower in the water but rolling less as the current flattened the wave tops. I thought we were doing as well as we could.

Just before seven-fifteen we came level with the north-western tip of the island, where the channel broadens out and the Andros coastline begins to veer first to the south, and then sou'sou'east.

'I'll take the wheel now,' I told her. 'There's a big bay about a mile and a bit further down, with shelter from the *meltemi*. I'll bring her in on slow ahead and anchor. But stay on deck for the moment: I'll need you to help when I take the jib off.'

As the channel widened the current eased, and I brought the two boats a little to port, creeping down the slant of the coast. For half a mile or so beyond the point the land still bears south-west, but once we came under the lee of the mountain just inland the *meltemi* fell away to an occasional sudden whisper, and there was nothing of the storm but a following stern chop from the channel. In the newly-quiet air I caught a faint scent of the mountain herbs, blowing off the land.

Nina said quietly: 'God, I feel better already.'

'Those are big mountains up there. This side of the island should be quiet apart from a few sudden gusts.'

I spoke too soon. Almost the moment I saw the dark, telltale front racing towards us across the silvered water, a squall sweeping down from the mountain slopes abeam struck *Andromeda*. The sail on the main boom gybed savagely across the boat and the jib backed with a loud crack. I cursed as I put us into the wind: fatigue had dulled my caution, and I should have brought the sails to the other tack the moment I began approaching the coast.

Even as I was swearing and *Andromeda* heeled to the gust, Nina swung herself up to the port heads'l winch and loosened off the cracking jib. I was looking to jam the wheel and secure the starboard sheet, but she shouted 'OK, I've got it,' and moved down to pass the line around the other winch and wind it home.

The incident was over as quickly as the gust. 'It's nice to have another sailor aboard,' I said. Nina grinned,

51

tiredly. 'If you take the wheel again,' I told her, 'I'll get the headsail down.'

I was confident enough of Nina's steering to stay at the mainmast when the jib was handed, and con the ketch around the next headland into the big bay that takes a double bite out of the coast, just before Andros starts to slope away south-west. I called to Nina to bring the diesel control back to quarter speed: with the heavy *caique* behind we crept slowly into the dark shore. About fifty yards off Nina cut the diesel and let go the main sheet. *Andromeda* lost way and I released the main anchor chain. Even in the starlight I could see the anchor and the chain falling for some ten feet through the still sea. The chain clanked on for a few seconds and slowed to an irregular, occasional rattle. The anchor bit in about twenty feet of water. We were safe in a harbour, of sorts.

Nina watched for a minute while I winched in the towline to hold the *caique* close to *Andromeda*'s quarter. When I shone the deck torch on the warp it showed fairly desperate signs of chafing near the *caique*'s bow, from the strains of the long tow. I told Nina wearily I would have go aboard to fix it before we could settle for the night.

Now the need for action was removed she seemed almost at the point of collapse. Her face fell forward and she yawned heavily, her eyes closed. She said slowly: 'I might just see if your shower is working – since the boat's stopped leaping around like a buckjumper.'

'Not only is the shower working,' I told her, 'the diesel's been running all afternoon, and you'll even get hot water.'

'My God. That's more civilised than the average Turkish hotel. It'll be my first hot shower in six weeks.'

'I thought you'd realised,' I said, 'you're on a better class of ship.'

It took a few minutes to adjust the towing warp so that the chafed section was inboard of the anchor bitts. The tow would hold now through the night and the morning's short trip to Gavrion. I had a quick look below in the *caique* to check how much water she'd taken in during the afternoon. There was more than when last I'd seen it, lapping about a foot high on the cases in the cabin, but the boat seemed in no immediate danger. It would wait until morning. When I got back below on *Andromeda* there was a cloud of steam from the shower in the for'ard passageway. Nina, naked and dripping wet, was opening one of the lockers in the bulkhead. I froze on the cabin steps, starting to apologize.

She looked round and grinned. 'Don't worry about it,' she said. 'You saw most of this on the *caique* anyway.

'Have you got a spare towel, though?'

I found her one from a different locker, noticing — as I had not before — what very pleasant breasts she had, when one tilted nipple carried a large droplet of water above my arm and let it fall to my skin as I passed the towel. I raised my eyes to her face quickly and Nina smiled, tiredly, turning back towards the steam. This quick flash of desire, so unexpected after the desperate day, felt strange and almost unwelcome. It submerged immediately in the knowledge that only a little while before the object of my sudden lust had been suffering a sexual abuse which must surely have left her chilled to any further approach. But I felt that Nina had detected it, and further, that she was unsurprised.

She shut the door of the shower behind her and I was left in a confusing welter of emotions. There is something about a tit that possesses a disturbing and inexplicable power to derange the logical course of events. I mean, for reasons I do not entirely understand I would rather look at a girl's breasts than other areas of that fascinatingly different arrangement of flesh: and I say this having seen my share of interesting tricks with cigarettes and Coke bottles in Bangkok and all points east. Yet why, one might ask? I mean, a tit is a tit, and once you've examined it carefully and fondled it and sucked it and maybe whacked it with your dick a couple of times *nothing much more happens*: there's no great event at the end and you're not going to go off or anything with the overwhelming delight of it all. Indeed, I've always found that in a topless bar in the East even wall-to-wall breasts seem perfectly normal after thirty seconds or so, and one carries on with regular conversation. So what is so specially unsettling about a breast? I do not know. But it happens. And I thought about Nina's, newly seen and first appreciated, and while I considered them it also occurred to me to find her some fresh clothes to wear. I looked her out a shirt from my locker, and hung it on the shower door, calling out to her that the sweater she'd worn against the *Meltemi* until now would be too hot in the cabin.

Even as I spoke, I knew that even without imagining I was thinking about it, I had picked the thinnest Hong Kong cotton in the pile. Her nipples would show through.

Now, this was a terrible situation. To start having randy thoughts about someone to whom I had believed I felt only protective threatened the erosion of the proper course of events. It kept going through my mind that she had been horribly raped less than eighteen hours before: I felt I needed to try to salvage the reputation for decency of the entire human race, not just for the sake of this abused girl but for me, for my own peace of mind. Yet the philosopher's curse resides just below the belt, where the bald-headed inhabitant remains stubbornly independent of all finer feeling in the upper regions. Just as when one is totally exhausted at the end of a desperate day, thinking apparently of nothing but sleep, one's dick rises with a loud cry to arms, quite out of the exhausted mind's control and insisting with a painful throb on satisfaction of the primal urge; so now, when I should have been considering only the girl's care and comfort, I started to fancy her.

I tried to think about food instead. I found I was very hungry: we'd had nothing to eat all day but the mug of stew and the scraps of bread and cheese that afternoon. What I really wanted was a steak, but the lusty Australians had eaten all the meat I'd packed in the freezer in Hong Kong, and there had been little good steak to replenish it with in Turkey: all I had been able to pick up at Izmir was some fresh lamb. But the alternative was fish, and we'd had enough of the sea for one day. I went into the galley and got the lamb out the refrigerator to start preparing a kebab.

Nina came aft from the shower and looked round the galley bulkhead, buttoning the shirt, just as I finished slicing the meat. I noticed, of course, that I could see her nipples through the cloth. She had smallish breasts, but her nipples were big and darker than the normal virginal pink. As somebody remarked to me in Greenwich Village once, I do like a tit that makes a *statement*.

55

'My God, are you going to cook?' she said. 'I don't know if I can stay awake that long.'

'If you look in the drinks cabinet over the chart table you could find us some wine. There's a good Turkish red in there. This won't take five minutes. It's just a lamb kebab.'

'Now he wants to feast,' she said in a small exhausted voice. 'Kebabs. You going to light a charcoal barbecue or something?'

'I'm going to cook them the Greek island way, sear them in the frying pan with a little olive oil. You could make a salad.'

'I could make my bed,' she said. She made half a movement across to the drinks locker and then turned back. 'You know, I just don't understand myself,' she said. 'After everything that's happened in the last twenty-four hours I should be making a great production. I feel I ought to be flying home to mother, or screaming, or suiciding. I should be doing something exceptional. I certainly ought to be seeing a doctor right away for the biggest shot of penicillin in captivity.

'Instead of that, for some reason I'm just . . . carrying on. It's like being caught in a rut. You want to live, so you get in a life-raft, you get on board another boat, and then you just go on yachting, for Chrissakes. As if we were on an ordinary vacation sailing trip around the Greek islands!

'And now we're discussing cooking and you want me to make the salad. . .'

She sat down heavily at the chart table, and started to cry, suddenly and completely.

'Nobody can help what happened,' I said. 'But you have to eat.'

'Yeah, let's have a dinky dinner,' she said, 'it's quite good cheeky little Turkish red, I suppose.'

I put my arms round her, pulling her weeping face into my chest. 'It's over,' I said. 'It's not still there in some little room you can open the door and look at.'

'It's in my head, still.' The voice was muffled against me. But she stood up and went on very quietly.

'Give me the fucking knife. I'll make the salad. We're still living. I guess having two rampaging Turks up your asshole is just a kind of everyday misfortune in this part of the world.

'Do you know,' she said, sniffing over the tomatoes as I went back to the frying pan, 'I knew a girl in New York who got raped eleven times. Once is carelessness and twice is stupidity, but eleven times! It got so she was having more rapes than normal screws.'

'I know it seems unlikely now, but you'll live through it.'

'Yeah, sure,' she said. 'Oh shit, let's open the cheeky Turkish red.'

We ate the meal at the dinette table in the cabin, almost in silence. She drank two glasses of wine and picked at the meat without great interest. I tried to talk about the boat, explaining I didn't like dinette arrangements anyway and would have preferred the old-fashioned centre table with settees and pilot berths on each side. But with *Andromeda*'s twelve-foot beam that had seemed impossible to arrange. The words flowed on: I was trying to keep her mind occupied by chattering about the boat's peculiar lay-out, which is the result of the designer combining the stern cockpit steering position that's comfortable at sea with the separate after-cabin arrangement that gives the owner a little privacy from the main accommodation. So you get in a way the worst of both worlds, I told her: three berths in the aft cabin, then in the main section the galley and the navigator's table facing each other across the hatchway, the starboard settee berth and the portside dinette across from that, the shower and lockers beyond the bulkhead and finally three berths in the for'ard cabin, which is uncomfortable in a seaway. The end result is three usable berths when we're at sea, one in the main accommodation and two in the after cabin, where I converted the impracticable starboard double berth into a single backed with a row of lockers, and shelves for my books.

Nina observed that the dinette was a table, and she supposed that was enough.

When she had finished eating she looked across the cabin at the settee berth and added: 'And that, Harry my lad, is a bunk. Forgive me, I'm going to use it.

'Don't be long putting out the lights.'

She moved across to the berth and collapsed onto the blanket I'd put there for her in the afternoon. She was almost asleep already. I settled the pillow at her head and arranged the covering over her. I stood there looking at her, wondering whether to kiss her softly. Her eyes opened and she smiled sleepily, seeing me caught undecided in the approach.

The smile became, for just a second, the wide grin I had noticed before. She swept the back of her hand gently and very swiftly across my groin – which despite the fatigue waxed instantly at the touch.

'No fun and games tonight,' she said softly. 'Maybe I'll thank you properly when we get to shore.

'I can be a lot of fun when I haven't just had an assfull of Turks.'

I did not doubt this, at that moment, for a second. But she was already asleep. I took myself off to the aft cabin and fell onto the single bunk under the skylight. I didn't even think to open it before I fell into a thick, undreaming slumber.

CHAPTER 3

—❦—

Gavrion

The Greek islands lie embalmed in their special scent, unlike the flavour of any other part of the world. Mediterranean passenger liners cross from the Ionian Sea into the Aegean on a night-time track three or four miles off Cape Matapan, at the southern tip of the Peloponnese. If you are standing on the deck at midnight you know the precise moment when you pass from an Italian to an Aegean world: the flavoured tang of wild oregano and thyme carries for all that distance in the warm dark, borne by the night wind off the great mountainsides that lie hidden in the horizonless velvet away to port.

I love Greece. The familiar herb-filled scents welcomed me back the moment I stepped onto *Andromeda*'s deck a little after dawn the next morning. Nina was still asleep: I had washed in the after cabin's miniature heads to keep from waking her, and then crept on deck to see what I could do about the water in the *caique*'s bilges. But there seemed to be no hurry when I got into the fresh Greek air and looked at the bare grey mountains, imperturbable with time, towering 3,000 feet above the anchorage in the little bay and clearing before my eyes in the growing light.

The day was on its way to a brilliant morning, the white sunlight beginning to clear the peaks to the east and slant across the hillsides just ahead of me. During the night the wind had fallen away to nothing, as quite often happens the day after an Aegean storm. Far below us Egypt lay cooled from the night, ceasing for a time to suck her neighbours' air. The sea in the bay was mirror flat and not a breath fell off the mountains to disturb it. There might still be a breeze on the north coast, but here on the sheltered side we would have a calm sail to Gavrion later that morning. I sat on the aft cabin's coach-house roof and lit a Turkish cigarette: I was as calm as the day, back in Greece among the oregano scent from the hillsides, where life has posed no really new problems since the Trojan Wars.

There was, it was true, the question of the water in the *caique*. I considered it from a Delphic distance: I could hardly get it out with *Andromeda*'s bilge pump, since I did not possess a hose long enough to link the two boats. On the other hand it seemed to my now-relaxed spirit that even two Turkish seamen as incompetent or as murderously distracted as the *caique*'s crew proved to be would hardly have set out on a voyage to Marseille without some system of pumping the bilges; which implied there had to be some method of doing so other than the so obviously long-dead electric system.

Five minutes' search on board the *caique* proved that there was: an older hand-pump in a cockpit lazarette that had escaped me in the frantic minutes on the derelict the day before. I worked with it for half an hour and reduced the water in the cabin to a level just above the floorboards. For a moment or two in the cabin I considered whether to shift the more valuable cargo items to the ketch. The old *caique* was certainly a risk. She looked to be some seventy years old, judging from the old-fashioned lines of her steep sheer, the little stepped poop at her stern, and her wide beam. Though she had recently been repainted the timbers must be suspect, and yesterday's tow would have severely strained her seams.

Then I looked at the largest package in the cabin, a bundle about six foot high and three across, tied up in a massive layer of old carpet. There was a rip along one side and when I lifted the flap I could see the grey surface of weathered marble, carved into the lines of a man's ear and upper cheekbone. The Apollo's Head. I tore away a little more of the cloth: the side of the face came dustily into view, serene and perfect.

I could feel my heart pounding. The Apollo was a discovery, a beauty: as I pulled away more of the rotting carpet I believed I knew a little of what Schliemann must have felt when he unveiled Agamemnon's golden mask. But the head was hugely heavy: I had pulled away a two-foot length of carpet and only bared the lower side of the face. I guessed the head would weigh 400-500 lbs. Moving it would have to wait until we got to Gavrion. Doubtful though the *caique*'s seams might be, she would survive an hour's tow in a flat calm.

I went back to the ketch and made Nina a tray of Turkish coffee, bread, butter and honey – the *vouteri-meli* Greek island breakfast. By this time it was seven o'clock and she was in the shower again. This morning the water was almost cold, because the diesel of course had not been running through the night, but she splashed in there for a long while, scrubbing away at her savage memories. I made a mental note to refill the fresh water tanks as soon as we got to Gavrion.

Nina came out of the shower, towelling her hair, when the coffee was on the table.

'I slept,' she said. 'I don't know how, but I slept like the dead, right through until a few minutes ago. Jesus.'

'Have your coffee.'

'Yeah,' she said. 'What's the plan this morning?'

'When we've finished breakfast we'll motor down the coast to Gavrion. There'll be a police post there. We can report in. Maybe there's a doctor – if not, there'll be one in Andros town. It's only a ninety-minute drive through the mountains.'

'Then what?'

'Hours of interviewing policemen, I should think. But at least you're safe.'

She nodded, without great enthusiasm.

Nina sat in the cockpit, wearing the shirt and shorts and a baseball cap one of the Australians had left in a locker, while I winched up the anchor, and set course under the diesel for Gavrion.

Once outside the bay, you would hardly have believed we had sailed in at the end of a storm the night before. There was a touch of swell, perhaps; but the water was an unbroken blue. Here on the sheltered south-west coast of the island there was no other trace of yesterday's gale, no foaming collar of surf at the throats of the steep rock cliffs along our track. The ketch rolled a little as the diesel thumped the two boats down the coast. After an hour or so we rounded the cape which protects Gavrion's bay, and Mt Kovari, the island's main peak, opened up on the port bow. I threaded the ketch through the ring of islets which guard the bay to seaward, and headed up towards the port as soon as we had cleared the

63

Vovi shoals between the islands and the harbour. I let go the anchor in three fathoms of water off the village itself, deciding to leave the quay and the jetty to the car ferries which run most days from Piraeus, or Rafina on the mainland.

The stillness seemed sudden when the diesel cut off. *Andromeda* and the *caique* lay calm at the anchor. We could hear little morning noises from the village, going about its own leisurely affairs 300 yards away.

'I'll get the dinghy overside,' I said, 'and take us ashore.'

Nina held one hand to her head briefly.

'All the talking,' she said. 'Oh God.'

'The sooner we start doing it, the sooner it's done.'

'Yes,' she said, but we were both wrong.

The Greek police sergeant at Gavrion sat in a high-ceilinged, whitewashed office, and wore, from the moment of our urgent, unbuttoned entry, a mask of utter puzzlement.

He had idly watched from his office window as two largish foreigners rowed across the mirrored harbour and awkwardly climbed from their tiny dinghy. *Andromeda*'s tender was barely ten feet long. The sergeant watched merely to pass the time for a few minutes: he assumed the harbourmaster would look after papers and other formalities. Indeed, the fat port official insisted on doing just that, before I could get away from his office on the quay. But when the police sergeant saw the female member of this strange pair breaking off from the quay and headed directly for the police office he began to anticipate some strange and unwelcome intrusion on his peaceful morning routine.

By the time I arrived in his office he had resisted this well enough for several minutes, being unable to speak anything but Greek and quite proof to Nina's efforts to explain. Then I swept in with the village's resident Greek-American, one of those retired ex-immigrants who return to die on their native islands, boasting of their tobacco store in Chicago and complaining about the hometown donkeys shitting on the streets. The Greek-American was about to have his big moment after years as the scorn of local youth: he was already voluble with excitement when he entered the sergeant's office a pace ahead of me.

Johnny the Greek was at a crescendo instantly, de-claiming at top speed like a Schmeisser machine gun. The sergeant's brow knotted with incredulous dismay. Rape. Piracy. Murder. Robbery. Unnameable offences upon this delicious *Amerikani*. The big man has salvaged the murderers' *caique*.

The sergeant's eyes tightened almost to slits with the horror of it all. Not merely the horror of the story: with what if anything was the more immediate horror of hearing it told in his quiet office, of all police stations in Greece available for the exercise. You don't get to be sergeant of a Greek island village out of any record of enthusiasm or notable excellence. You look forward to a life concerned with the orderly completion of forms, the control of dogs which insist on barking during the Government-ordered siesta season, and the punctual arrival of mid-morning refreshments from the café across the road. There is no crime to speak of, bar an occasional petty theft when the wilder elements from Athens are in town for the summer holidays. And now to have to cope with what looked like amazing international brigandage.

The sergeant's eyes closed altogether. There were no precedents in his experience. He would telephone Andros.

The sergeant started slowly on the telephone, but in a minute he, too, was shouting down the instrument at racing speed. Greek is that kind of language: most of the words are long and they emphasise the last syllable, so that even asking for a cup of coffee sounds like a declaration of war.

'The sergeant speaks to his captain,' said Johnny the Greek-American, satisfied as if this triumphal conclusion was his own creation.

'Is he calling him "Sir"?' asked Nina tiredly.

'Huh?'

'Forget it.'

The conversation took ten minutes. When it was over the little sergeant appeared visibly exhausted. He said something to Johnny.

'The captain drives over from Andros immediately.'

Immediately, in the Greek bureaucracy, can mean anything. I have just enough Greek to insist that the lady needed a doctor right away. *'Y ginaika thelai to yiatro, tora. Katalavenete? Prepei.'*

The sergeant's jaw went forward in a grimace. The captain was already on his way. The doctor does not come to Gavrion today. The lady must wait to see the captain, and perhaps go back with him to Andros to the doctor.

I began to rise at this, but Johnny the Greek-American halted the argument.

'You won't find the doctor anyway, till maybe five o'clock,' he said. 'This island only got one doctor: God knows where he is this time of day, out seeing the peasants maybe. You get him later for sure.'

The sergeant spread his hands: there was nothing else to be done. The captain would arrive in an hour, probably.

'Maybe you folks go get something to eat,' said Johnny. 'I show you the restaurant. Then the captain'll come, you talk to him, he take the lady to see the doctor. OK?'

Nina looked at me and bit her lip. 'You can't beat the system,' she said. We filed slowly out of the sergeant's office in the trail of Johnny.

We had very little left to say, now. The Greek-American took me to the village branch of the agricultural bank to change some money, and then showed us to a sidewalk table at a little restaurant on the quay. Fortunately he now had something else to do and did not stay to eat. Deflated as we both were, I found I had an appetite and Nina ate keenly too, in silence, when the waiter brought fried whitebait, bread, tomatoes and a litre of *retsina*.

There was nothing to do for the moment but wait. I bought a second can of *retsina*, and we sliced through a large melon.

'Why were you sailing alone to Greece anyway?' said Nina. 'Seems kind of a waste.'

There was plenty of time to tell her. 'I was on the track of a nineteenth-century mystery,' I said.

'You know the poet Byron was the last century's best-seller? He spent half his life writing about the Greek Cyclades. Several times he told friends he planned to retire to a castle on Naxos and live what he called the life of a Pasha.

'The funny thing is, according to the record he only ever saw the islands once. That was from the deck of a British frigate bringing him back from Turkey to Piraeus.

On that voyage he can't have seen Naxos at all. The frigate came across the Aegean in a strong *meltemi* on July 18, 1810, and went through the northern islands in a few hours. Byron apparently was going mad on the poop deck, exclaiming about the scenery and refusing to go below for meals. Once they were out of the islands he wouldn't even stay aboard for Piraeus, but insisted on being put ashore at Euboea with his servant Fletcher, allegedly to go on overland to Athens a few days later.

'Now, the frigate's track took her through the Sporades islands, past Chios and Psara. But the only Cycladean island Byron can possibly have seen, from the deck of a sailing ship on a direct run, was the one we're on right now – Andros.

'Yet when he wrote later about the Cyclades in poems like *The Corsair* he put in exact geographical descriptions and references to what you saw on particular points on Paros that he could hardly have known about unless he had been there. Plus he spoke about living on Naxos, a place he had officially never been, as if he knew what it was like.

'So my theory is that after the *Salsette* landed Byron on Euboea he didn't go direct to Athens after all, but hired a *caique* and sailed back to the islands for a while.'

She was interested, but not unduly impressed. 'Byron's life has been pretty well written. No one suspected this before?'

'Not in this century. But he wrote very few letters back to England after he returned to Athens. His travelling companion Hobhouse stayed aboard the *Salsette* to go back to England when Byron and Fletcher went ashore on Euboea. But in 1825, after Byron died in the Greek War of Independence, one of his fellow-volunteers wrote a book anonymously claiming that Byron sailed as a pirate in the Aegean and fathered a Greek child, on that first trip out there in 1810.

'So I believe he *was* a pirate. But the key to the mystery is the *Salsette*'s voyage across the Aegean. I was retracing it when I found you, to show the frigate was never within sight of Naxos. The idea was maybe to get a TV programme together later this year.'

History is like playing detective with a bunch of safely-dead criminals, and once the fascination of the game gets you it never lets go. The archaeologist in Nina was beginning to take an interest now, despite herself.

'How did the anonymous guy know all this? It happened seventeen years before his book was published.'

'Off-duty conversations with Byron during the War of Independence, I suppose. But in any case he didn't have the story quite right. He placed Byron's island sojourn upon Mytilene, in the Sporades, although the pirate base Byron described in *The Corsair* was on Paros. And that description was exact, incidentally: we know the principal pirate lair in the Aegean was in the precise place, the bay of Naousa on Paros, where Byron says it was. Another British traveller was there a year later – the uncle of the scientist Charles Darwin. Strangely enough he'd travelled across to Turkey with Byron on the outward voyage.'

'It's still going to be difficult to prove,' said Nina.

'Not necessarily. Byron himself was always hinting at some secret scandal during his second year in Greece.'

And the discussion occupied us for another hour, before the police captain from Andros joined us at the table. Word of Nina's ordeal and the captured *caique* had spread through the village during the sleepy

69

lunchtime. When the spick-and-span captain appeared, his mirrored sunglasses attempting to add a touch of formidability to his tubby and very average form, silent onlookers gathered at the restaurant fringes to watch Johnny the Greek-American demonstrate his translation skills. The captain heard my story out and then surveyed the growing crowd. He preferred to dispense with the Greek-American's assistance when he spoke to us, although he found it useful when we replied.

'I need to see the *caique*,' he said, after a little thought. 'Then I will take the lady to Andros, to the doctor.'

'And then?'

'You must both stay on the island, for a while.'

Nina made a small face. 'Why don't you come back here?' I suggested to her. 'I'm not keen to leave the boat for long – I can book rooms at the hotel.'

In the back of my mind, of course, was the thought that before long one room might be sufficient.

'I suppose so,' said Nina.

'Then I'll meet you either at the hotel or here, for dinner. In the meantime, you'd better take some of the money with you in case you need something. Pay me back later.'

I separated a couple of thousand drachma from the new wad of notes, and the sergeant escorted Nina back to the police office. The police captain led me to the quay, leaving the Greek-American behind, disconsolate at his loss of a place in the scheme of things. It was beneath the captain's dignity to be rowed across the harbour in a ten-foot dinghy. My little tender was towed behind as the captain stood in the stern of a small fishing boat with its commandeered skipper, motoring the five hundred yards to the two moored yachts.

70

He clambered aboard the *caique* awkwardly, took one brief glance around the deck, and as I followed went straight below to rummage through the navigation position for her papers. I noticed water was showing once again above the *caique*'s floorboards.

I lifted the carpet flap around the packaged Apollo and showed him the other crates of smuggled goods. 'These are the antiquities the girl saw brought aboard.'

He glanced at them. 'They are Turkish,' he said. This appeared to dispose of that point, for the moment.

In a locker behind the navigation table the captain now discovered all sorts of papers. He looked at them, compressing his mouth, for a little while.

'The papers are Turkish,' he said.

'Turkish yacht, I suppose.'

He looked at me sideways. Without shifting his glance or changing his expression he pointed up at a beam across the cabin top. I followed his hand and saw two Greek letters and a number carved into the wood. The captain had seen more than I had managed to observe.

'Maybe now,' he said.

'Well, I don't know. The whole thing is a puzzle. But what about the antiquities?'

The captain gave the *caique*'s shabby cargo another perfunctory glance, and then sniffed at the water damping the soles of his highly polished black shoes. He stepped back into the dry on the bottom rung of the companionway, looking away from me and around the cabin. There was one of those long, ruminating silences which policemen normally use as a disguise for unresolved thoughts.

The captain threw out his chin suddenly and shrugged his shoulders a little, which in Greece

71

is a mime for a man of the world expressing informed doubt.

'These things were stolen in Turkey,' he said. 'Everything happened in Turkey.' He shrugged again. 'Maybe you win the boat.' He turned and clambered back up the stairs to the waiting fishing boat, to chug off across the harbour again. They had left my dinghy tied up to *Andromeda*, moored alongside.

It would be several hours before Nina returned to Gavrion. The quarter inch of water showing on the *caique*'s floorboards was beginning to worry me a little. Her seams had probably opened more than I suspected in the wild tow the day before. It was time, I thought, to take off at least the more valuable pieces of cargo. I went across to *Andromeda* to look out my bigger billy-tackle. I'd shipped it to handle work on the diesel and battery installations: it ought to lift 500lbs, if I put a purchase on the *caique*'s main boom.

I was sweating in the afternoon heat even before the tackle was fixed on the spar. When I went below in the *caique* I found further problems: the Turks had stowed the Apollo's Head as close to the hatchway as possible – it was too heavy to move further into the cabin – but it was not directly on a line of access. I cleared a way as much as possible, moving two crates of the smaller antiquities onto the chart table. But the big sculpture would still have to be lifted through a kind of dogleg towards the hatchway.

At least it made a problem in elementary mechanics to while away the afternoon. After thirty minutes I had a marvellous cat's cradle of lines fixed between the *caique*'s boom and the statue to steady and guide the heavy stone, once I could pull it to the cockpit. A lever lifted the carpeted head sufficiently to pass a carrying harness underneath, and then with the lever and the lines I managed to heave it into the centre of the cabin on a clear path to the hatchway. I fixed a small block on the cabin's for'ard bulkhead and passed another line through it from the statue harness back out to the deck, so that as I lifted it on the big six-block billy tackle the for'ard line held it from crashing into the steps.

Out on deck under the boom, I heaved on the billy with both hands and held the statue steady through the for'ard line, lashed round my hips. The great, carpet-covered mass rose inch by inch as several feet of rope came hand over hand from the billy tackle. Finally I had the thing hoisted to deck level inside the cabin: now I secured the billy, and gingerly let the mass swing forward into the cockpit with the line round my hips.

So far so good. I lowered the stone and went across to *Andromeda*, tied up alongside, with the billy haul and the line from the *caique*'s boom. The other ropes were finished with: all I had to do now was haul the statue up to above gunwhale level, and swing the boom across to *Andromeda*.

It took several minutes to raise the weight above the height of the *caique*'s cockpit coaming. The tackle groaned; my hands began to chafe with the effort of pulling down yards and yards of haul from the billy. Finally I seemed to have brought it high enough. I began to swing the boom slowly over to *Andromeda*.

Something happened very quickly now that I had not bargained for. As the statue swung away from the *caique*'s midships centre of gravity, the massive weight made the boat heel, first just a little and then with an increasing rush of momentum. I had a line to pull the boom across, but I hadn't thought to fix a restraining line on the other side: the statue crashed through the arc uncontrollably, crunching the biggest headsail block on the schooner's gunwhale, sweeping over to the ketch, and ending up like a lethal pendulum swinging above *Andromeda*'s cockpit.

Jesus, that was a narrow shave. Thank God it came over at the point it did, or I would have lost a winch or two as well. I lowered the statue very carefully to the cockpit floor just behind the wheel.

I saw, then, the other damage I had done. Through the torn carpet where I had ripped the covering to inspect the statue, was a massive scar of bright new stone, where the Apollo's ear had been.

Christ, I thought, I've smashed the Head. You take in facts instantaneously in this kind of disaster: I saw in this same second that some of the ear was lying in fragments around the damaged winch on the *caique*. The rest of it, of course, was in the water.

I felt as if I'd taken the arms off the Venus de Milo. What do you tell yourself when you've wrecked a 2,400-year-old masterpiece?

You tell yourself, all of a sudden, many bitter things indeed.

Until you look closer and recognise that there is something very odd about the new white marble where the ear used to be. That it isn't marble at all. That it looked remarkably like some kind of epoxy compound, tricked up with stone dust to make a surface like weathered marble. And filled with lead somewhere, presumably, to give it the weight.

The Apollo was a fake.

I went back aboard the *caique* and looked more closely at the rest of the cargo. Most of it also looked like trash, to me. I shifted one box of small figurines and artefacts across to *Andromeda*, and in order to get the bulky obstruction out of the way, hauled the Apollo up again on the billy tackle and stowed it in the stern lazarette locker under the spinnaker and spare main bags. The Head lay low down and fairly well wedged on a line amidships between the figurine crate and some engine spares: *Andromeda* would carry the weight well enough.

All this was very puzzling. Not that the Head, and presumably much of the rest of the cargo, was a fraud: there is a thriving little industry in Anatolia creating fake antiquities. But why would anyone take such risks to smuggle fakes? On the other hand, had the Turks known they were carrying imitations? They might themselves have been tricked.

I took the most sensible action possible in baffling situations of this sort. I had a long drink of beer out of the fridge, and went to bed for the rest of the afternoon.

It was just after six, and the middle of the swift Greek twilight, when I woke. I had a rapid shower – there still seemed to be a reasonable amount of water in the tanks despite Nina's indulgences – and rowed across to Gavrion to book rooms in the hotel and stroll down to the restaurant on the quay.

Nina was quite late. I had several *ouzos* and two plates of barbecued octopus, which smells like martyred early Christians over the charcoal, but tastes as sweet as a summer dawn at sea on the plate. Finally, well after eight when Gavrion's villagers were in full summer-frocked procession along the quay for the evening promenade, a taxi from the main town rumbled to a halt at the edge of the restaurant tables and she appeared. She looked clean, she was smiling, and she was wearing a new, high-necked embroidered dress that appeared to have come straight out of the tissue paper at a tourist store in Andros.

'The doctor's bill wasn't going to worry Blue Cross,' she said. 'I had plenty left over so I bought this to give me a new outlook on life.

'Looking to my front instead of my rear, if you see what I mean. I hope you don't mind.'

'Not a bit,' I said. 'You look delightful.'

And of course she did. The dress was dark blue, with red and light gold embroidery across the front. It set off her charcoal hair and the face which despite its slight tan still suggested a light, delicate quality about the cheeks. The skirt came just below her knees, flattering her slim hips and smooth legs.

'I don't exactly feel it,' she said, hooking the last piece of octopus with one of the toothpicks provided in place of forks, and borrowing a sip of my *ouzo*. 'I feel just about as pleasant as anybody does with an assful of penicillin. One way and another that particular portion of my anatomy has taken just about as much as it wants, over the last couple of days.'

'You look good, though.'

'Well, you're sweet,' she said. She grinned suddenly, like an old confederate. 'But don't just feed me with compliments. Buy this piece of slightly damaged goods the best damn dinner a tumbledown waterside restaurant can provide on this island. I'm just starved, Harry.'

I ordered a litre of *retsina*, a *megalosalata* with tomatoes, peppers and *feta* cheese swimming about in olive oil, and a double dish of *keftedes*, meatballs spiced with oregano and cheese and fried in olive oil. As soon as the salad arrived Nina began mopping up the oil with her bread.

'The police seemed to have started taking all this seriously, suddenly,' she said. 'The captain from Andros drove back with me. Apparently a top guy from Athens is coming over by helicopter tonight to talk to us.'

'I don't have too much energy left for more talks with the fuzz right now. I just plan a quiet dinner and a retreat to the hotel. I got us rooms, by the way.'

'Well, I don't think it was anything I said, so don't blame me when the top brass walks in. The captain seemed more interested in the *caique*, if anything. That, and whether I'd ever seen you before.'

'It must look like an odd story to them, when you come to consider it.'

'That boat has them freaked, for some reason. The captain was going to take the Athens bigwig to see it as soon as he touched down.'

The rest of the meal had arrived by now, and for a while we ate it seriously without thought of talking. For both of us it had been a long time since lunch.

It was simply for that reason that I did not mention my discovery about the Apollo's Head that afternoon.

Certainly, it was not that either of us felt uncommunicative. But Nina was starved, and I had been waiting for her a long time. For myself, a sense of deep peace first created by the *ouzo* had taken over. I looked at Nina and thought of long days ahead waiting for nature to take its course and lay mine for her bedroom. In this state of calm, there was no urgency either to hurry in that direction, or to break any immediate news.

We had called for a plate of grapes and Nina was using bread as blotting paper for the last of the olive oil when I finally said: 'I think the police are interested in the *caique* because there *are* drugs aboard, after all.'

And I was just about to mention the fake of the Apollo's Head when a trim figure in the grey-green uniform of the Greek police appeared in the corner of my eye, at the edge of the restaurant table. His shoulder lapels bore a captain's insignia, but this was plainly a superior officer to the island commandant from Andros. For one thing he was younger, neater, and surer of his presence: for another he was not wearing the mirrored sunglasses with which most Greek policemen reinforce the authority of their uniform. This captain wore a different kind, gold-framed and lightly tinted in brown.

'Forgive me interrupting your dinner,' he said in perfectly accented English. 'I am Captain Theodoropoulos, from Athens.'

'Sit down, Captain,' I said. It helps to be polite to the men who are really running things. I offered him a glass of *retsina*.

He took a chair, but declined the wine.

'I have seen the *caique*,' he said. 'Did you know she was Greek?' He looked at me carefully.

'The captain from Andros seemed to think so,' I said.

'Yes, she is,' said Theodoropoulos.

'Well, the smuggled antiquities are from Turkey,' said Nina.

'I'm not greatly interested in them,' said the captain. 'I am concerned with a stolen Greek *caique* yacht. When you have finished your meal, I would like to ask you to accompany me by helicopter to Athens.'

'Oh, Christ,' I told him, 'we're hardly interested in a night flight to Athens right now. We've both had a rough couple of days, Captain: we want to finish eating and get showers and a full night's sleep at the hotel here.'

'I am sorry,' said Captain Theodoropoulos, 'I didn't mean to suggest that the trip was entirely voluntary.

'Not to put too fine a point on it, I'm *taking* you to Athens. If you want to argue the question, I'm taking you under arrest.'

CHAPTER 4

The Problem for Thais

I never liked helicopter travel even before Vietnam. The noise and the vibration constantly remind you of the technology's tendency to flutter fatally to the ground like an incendiary dragonfly. The police helicopter was a small French model which made as many concessions to comfort as a baby Citroën car, and though the seats were crammed together the noise prevented any communication with Nina, sitting in the row in front. She managed to do no more than knot her brows in puzzlement at me a couple of times, as the machine swept nose-down in the dark across the straits to the mainland, before the policeman sitting beside her told her to look to the front with an admonishing finger. We had not been alone since the Athens police captain had appeared at our table in the restaurant.

There was a chance to think, though. Once the helicopter was in the air the racket of the engine and the heightened tension that kind of travel produces began to sweep my mind clear of the dulling effects of dinner, the wine and the *ouzo*. It had been a meal which would normally produce an overwhelming desire for slumber with no thought even of making love – assuming Nina would have been willing – but adrenalin overcomes lethargy when an immediate air flight underlines the visible threat of an unfriendly police captain.

Captain Theodoropoulos sat up for'ard alongside the pilot. Nina was in the second row with one policeman: I was crushed in the back seats with a third, a dark-jowled cop who was well below six foot but whose shoulders, unhappily for our comfort in that confined space, had no need of the padding in his uniform jacket. I had some forty minutes' flight for silent thought.

I have been picked up by the police quite a lot in the course of fifteen years' reporting news around the world. The first reaction to this kind of situation, with me, is surface acquiescence. Yes, of course I will come to the police station with you, officer. There's no point in arguing, he's going to take me anyway, and the man who has nothing to hide will establish this fact at the charge desk. He will also have time to think it all out, on the way.

What comes almost immediately after is sheer atavistic anger. Fuck 'em. I'm certainly not going to help: the men who arrested me are my antagonists, and never mind the justice of their cause, they threaten mine and I develop that kind of Nordic berserk unreasoning fury my father used to call the 'red mists'. This happens in silence, but whatever condition I was in when they picked me up, it produces very rapidly a state of fierce, intense calculation devoted to the destruction of the threat.

Once the helicopter jolted me out of the wine fumes into this mode, I was immediately grateful I had not chosen to mention either to Nina or to Theodoropoulos that I had moved the Apollo's Head across to *Andromeda*. I needed to keep counsel about that some time longer. When Captain Theodoropoulos started poking around in the yacht's lockers he would discover among other things the .30 cal machine gun, which would take some explaining.

Further, whatever had caused Theodoropoulos' suspicions and whatever they actually were, I was not all of a sudden entirely sure about Nina. I had only her word that she was what she said, and in newspapers you learn not to believe anyone's story until you can cross-check it. There could easily be more to the *caique*'s voyage than I knew: a much more solid link between the girl I found on the boat and the smuggled goods. It seemed to me now that the explanation had to be drugs, and that Captain Theodoropoulos knew something more about it than he had revealed.

I was going to need someone in Athens to bail me out before the .30 cal machine gun and the transferred Apollo's Head complicated the situation more than it need be. The police would probably allow me a phone call, expecting me to contact the US Embassy. In fact, I could do much better than that if an Englishman called Mike Bassington was still in Athens. I had met him when he was a radio reporter in Saigon. We had all known there, as the foreign journalists in Athens had understood later when his network transferred him to Greece, that he also had a function with British Intelligence.

The British, like the CIA, use journalism as a cover very frequently. But unlike the CIA, who tend to work through name journalists likely to pick up by-lines now and then because they make more working trips abroad, London prefers people who are little known: night-shift copy-editors on *Agence France-Presse* in Paris, and similar occupants of the media shadows. Bassington, big, heavy-hipped and amiable as an English sheepdog in a pipe-stained tweed jacket, was one of these. Of course it was a gamble that he was still in Athens. But he was more likely to be able to fix any problems which might hit me than a Third Secretary at the US Embassy.

The helicopter dipped over the lip of the Attic mountains and the bowl of midnight Athens opened up ahead, like a carpet of flickering matches far below. We crossed the city fringes at a height of around 500 feet, watching the passing canyons of yellow apartment buildings and the little knots of people at street stalls or dotted in the flare-lit gardens of open-air tavernas. The amber-lit Acropolis rose above the helicopter's port side, and the chattering machine let itself carefully down on the police helipad. The policeman crushed against my right shoulder led me ducking out under the slowing rotors: we waited for Theodoropoulos and the others, and then at a nod from the captain my guard took my arm, to march me briskly down the headquarters' corridors to a cell, bare but for a deal table and a scrawny bed.

I lay on the cot, loosened my belt and closed my eyes. But thoughts still raced through my mind and I could do no more than doze through the next hour or so. Then, as I had expected, the squat guard returned to retrieve me. He motioned me to follow him: Theodoropoulos was plainly faithful to the orthodox police belief that interrogations are best performed at night.

Theodoropoulos sat comfortably in the wide glow of a desklight, his uniform unbuttoned and his short collar loose, but still wearing the amber sunglasses. He nodded at the unshaven cop behind me. The man sank back into the shadows and I was allowed to sit at the chair in front of Theodoropoulos' desk.

'I'd like you to inform the American Embassy of my arrest,' I said.

'Of course,' said Theodoropoulos, 'in time.'

I see, I thought, then I am arrested. But for what, I could still not imagine.

Theodoropoulos arranged the pencils on his desk, and straightened a group of papers in front of him. I studied his office and waited for him. As far as I could make out beyond the light from the desk the room was more comfortable than most police accommodation I had seen. Theodoropoulos' chair was leather-covered and well-padded. Bookshelves on one wall held files and a thick collection of what I took to be law books. Behind him venetian blinds covered a wide window, and between the bookshelves and the blinds a second door stood partly ajar into a darkened side-office.

No ordinary captain, I thought.

'Would you like to explain to me,' said Theodoropoulos, 'what your movements were during the month of November last?'

'Certainly. Most of the time I was in Hong Kong preparing my ketch *Andromeda* for the voyage across to the Mediterranean.'

Theodoropoulos looked at me steadily. He had the detective's trick of fixing his gaze on the bridge of someone's nose, rather than the eyes: you can stare with total comfort at that little patch of innocent flesh for minutes at a time, whereas straight eye contact requires concentration if you are not going to blink, or make the involuntary movements that suggest the reassurance of communication.

'No,' he said. 'Your passport tells me that from November 8 you were in Europe.'

He had obviously picked it up from the hotel in Gavrion.

'For a week or so, yes,' I said. 'I was in London for ten or twelve days around then. I had to see some TV networks, and do a little library research at the British Museum.'

'A little longer than that. Your passport says you landed in London on November 8 and returned to Hong Kong on the 23rd.'

'Well, then.'

'Do you have a British passport as well?'

'No. Not with me. I've been an American citizen for seven years.'

'Precisely. But since you were born in Britain you were presumably travelling on a British passport before that, and British passports are valid for ten years. As the holder of a British passport you would be able to travel countries of the European Common Market at will – EEC countries normally don't even bother to stamp Common Market passports at the frontier.'

'So what? I haven't one with me, and I don't really know where it is.'

Captain Theodoropoulos smiled all of a sudden, very thinly.

'We have a problem, Mr Lancaster. The yacht you say you salvaged north of the island of Andros is a Greek yacht. Registered in Panama now, and owned by a Mr. Tafu Karanakarthorn' – he said the name with a little difficulty – 'of Bangkok. A wealthy Thai gentleman, apparently. However, the *caique* was built here, had a Greek crew, and until the night of November 15 last year was based at the Tourkolimano yacht harbour just outside Piraeus.

'That was the night she was stolen, Mr Lancaster. She was attacked by men from an unknown ship somewhere off the island of Samos, while returning from a cruise in the Dodecanese. The only people on board were her paid crew of two, both Greeks, and the owner's secretary. The crew had their throats cut and were dumped over the side. The secretary was injured in the attack, but jumped overboard, took the dinghy that was under tow, and escaped in the dark.

'He describes the leader of the gang as a tall European speaking in English, Mr Lancaster. He believed him to be British.'

I was totally stunned for several seconds. I could see now where Theodoropoulos was coming to, and ridiculous as it was, as easy as it would surely be to disprove it, the accusation was shattering. Then the words began to well up: 'Good Christ!' I practically shouted at him, 'there are plenty of tall Englishmen around.'

'But only one tall Englishman,' said Theodoropoulos, 'turned up on the self-same boat out in the Aegean eight months later. When the boat was apparently making a smuggling trip – and had certainly run into difficulties.

'It was very *fortuitous* that you happened to be just in that spot just at that time, Mr Lancaster.'

'For God's sake, why would I bring her into a Greek port?'

'What else could you do, Mr Lancaster? You had two large yachts to handle in a stiff Aegean gale, and you could hardly tow the second one all the way to Marseille, or wherever she was intended to go.

'The girl, of course, would make a very convenient cover. She had only seen the Turks who loaded the *caique* and crewed it: she never saw the European

86

leaders of the gang clearly, but merely heard their voices. She says they sounded like Englishmen, by the way, did you know that?

'If you brought the *caique* into an island port, you could expect the local police to be absorbed in the girl's story, and then perhaps you would be able to tranship onto your ketch whatever the *caique* was smuggling. Turkish antiquities, I understand.'

Oh Jesus, of course I *had*. And I had carefully kept that information to myself. I cursed that decision, silently. I'd assumed the drugs would be safely stowed away in the bilges, leaving the fake antiques to be used as cover if the smugglers were stopped by a patrol. It now occurred to me with awful force that the Apollo's Head could easily be stuffed bang full of heroin. Its weight hardly implied that it was hollow, though.

'When you get excited,' said Theodoropoulos, 'you sound to me to have more of an English accent than an American one.'

Then he raised his voice. 'What do you think, Miss Millen?' He looked at me, grinning again, and turned towards the darkened outer office.

Nina, pale, wearing a look of worried concern, came slowly into the light.

She said nothing for a moment, biting her lip. Then she said, hesitantly: 'It could be the same voice. I suppose.'

'The English voice you heard on the *caique*?'

She nodded.

'Harry,' she said, 'I don't know anything about you. . .'

'I think it is time for a small identification parade,' said Theodoropoulos. He looked across at my guard, in the shadows, and said something quickly in Greek. 'I'm told the witness is here, now.'

As they led me away I told Nina: 'If you get a chance tonight just do one thing for me – inform the Embassy.'

'Yes,' she said, miserably. I had the sinking feeling I was going to need both Bassington and the diplomats, now.

'That will be looked after,' said Theodoropoulos, unconcerned. 'Later.'

We hustled down bare corridors and finally into a large room, lit by three powerful unshaded globes, with the tiger stripes of a comprehensive height scale all along one wall. They let me sit on one of the two chairs on the other side for about thirty minutes until the rest of the ID parade arrived. Theodoropoulos had found difficulties rounding up anyone else over six foot. There were a couple of big Greeks, but they were built like wrestlers, as large men tend to be in the Mediterranean: their heads came up to my ear, but they must have outweighed me by 50lbs apiece. Theodoropoulos' men had brought in two German tourists, pulled off the streets of the Plaka by the look of them, who were tall but quite the opposite shape. One blow would have broken both of them in half. Theodoropoulos filled the rest of the line with jacketless policemen looking ill at ease in their shirtsleeves and quite unlike civilians. They were all dark-haired, as well: it was hardly the line-up of similar-looking men these tests are supposed to be.

All the same, I could not see how Theodoropoulos' witness could identify me, unless I had a double rampaging the Aegean as a boat-napper. College football and a raw-boned North British ancestry left me with a fairly distinguishable face: unless the man they were looking for also had a broken nose and a big jaw the witness could hardly make a mistake. My confidence was feeling better as I chose my place in the line-up between the Germans and one of the Greek wrestlers.

Then they brought the witness in, and my heart fell suddenly.

He was a Thai.

The problems a Westerner has in telling one Chinese face from another, unless he knows the man well, is exactly the reverse for Orientals. Europeans, in their eyes, are the indistinguishable possessors of identical monstrously large noses, unhealthy complexions, and cumbersome bodies. We all look the same to them, too.

The Thai took one long glance at the line-up. Then he walked unhesitatingly to the biggest man in the parade, and tapped me firmly on the shoulder.

They brought me a miniature cup of Greek coffee at six a.m. next morning, with half a loaf of yesterday's bread and honey, but no butter. I had managed four hours of fitful sleep. I gave myself a thorough wash in cold water at the basin in the corner of the cell, but I had no razor, of course. They had taken my belt. I sat there unshaven in a day-old shirt, crumpled cotton trousers, and dusty espadrilles feeling, and certainly looking, like a trapped criminal.

The circumstances were closing around my throat. The eye-witness to the theft and murders had picked me out: the witnesses to my real story were missing. The Australians who had crewed *Andromeda* to the Aegean had gone their own ways, God knew where after the race in Sardinia, and in any case they could only support me on recent events. The people who knew where I had been the previous November amounted to a half-dozen television executives in London, who could testify where I was in the early part of the month. But where had I been on the 15th?

I had planned to wind up my selling trip to Europe with a riotous few days in Paris with the former love of my life, but when she turned up at the London hotel the night before with a handbag full of grass and a readily-engineered row I recalled precisely why I let her go in the first place, and plans altered. There had been an empty hole where Marilyn used to be, caused by something a little stronger than ordinary hash, I suspected, and I had taken myself instead out to the wilds of Wales. By train – I hadn't even rented a car from a company to show the record. I had not met anyone I knew in Caernarvon and the Snowdon range – I believed an old friend kept an inn there but I didn't find him. The only record of my trip lay in a few hotel registers. I hardly remembered what they were all called anyway. The hotel register evidence would not only be thin, but difficult and time-consuming to establish from a police cell in Athens.

The position was assuming desperate proportions.

About an hour after the thimbleful of coffee, they took me down the corridors to Theodoropoulos' office again. The captain was spruce this morning. A clean-shaven police officer has an automatic advantage over the suspect who has spent a razorless night in the cells. His uniform jacket was fresh-pressed and neatly buttoned. His dark hair was meticulously brushed. He smiled at me sweetly through the amber-coloured glasses.

'I hope you were not too uncomfortable,' said Theodoropoulos. 'But then, you are used to the spartan conditions of small boats.'

'I would like the American Embassy and a lawyer as soon as possible,' I said.

'All in due course.' Theodoropoulos arranged the papers on his desk, still with a slight smile, confident that everything else was also in its place.

'I shall be charging you with complicity in the theft of the yacht, in the first instance,' he said. 'That is, that you and others knowingly stole the *caique* yacht *Despina*, property of Mr Tafu Karanakarthorn, somewhere off the coast of Samos on the night of November 15 last.

'I am aware, of course, that you had left the yacht by the time the two crewmen were thrown over the side, but you were there when they were first attacked – the Thai secretary is sure of it. So you will be asking yourself why I do not charge you also with complicity in the murders.'

'I wasn't there at all,' I said, 'and given a little time I will prove it. I was in Britain, in West Wales.'

Theodoropoulos smiled again, brilliantly. 'Perhaps you will,' he said. 'But at the moment I doubt it. Well then, I am not going to charge you with murder immediately because you may wish, as you Americans put it, to plea bargain. Do you begin to see what I mean?'

'No,' I said, 'I don't.'

Theodoropoulos stood up and paced slowly around his desk, first to the window, and then out into the room. 'We're really very intrigued by this case, Mr Lancaster.

'Consider some of the points in it. A group of men, we presume they were Turks, under leadership of a tall European speaking English, seize a large *caique* in Greek waters. Of all the yachts at Tourkolimano, this one happens to be owned by a Thai. This is curious in itself. There are plenty of foreign millionaires with yachts based in Greek waters, but we do not see many Thais.'

'I was regretting the coincidence myself. You realise they can't tell one big European from another, don't you?'

Theodoropoulos gave me a reproachful little smile, deprecating this feeble defence.

'It is also curious that a group of Turks come to Greece to steal a boat. Curious that they choose a Thai-owned yacht for the purpose. Even more curious that when the yacht next turns up, once more under the command of a tall European with an English accent, it is evidently taking part in a smuggling expedition – and the tall European happens to have spent much time in the Far East, most recently a few months ago in Hong Kong.

'I don't think we will find merely an assortment of second-grade Turkish statuettes aboard that vessel, Mr Lancaster.

'I think that when we start taking her apart, which I shall arrange to do as quickly as possible, we will find a large quantity of drugs. Perhaps raw Turkish opium: more likely, refined Thai heroin. But in either case, a large cargo of drugs on its way to Marseille.'

'I wouldn't be surprised either,' I said. 'It seems the likely explanation. But the girl says the antiquities are valuable.'

Theodoropoulos sat on the corner of his desk. 'I am not concerned with Turkish junk,' he said. 'I am not concerned with the Turkish end at all. What interests me in the first place is that two Greeks were killed –

though I begin to suspect they may have been no great loss – and in the second and major place that this strongly suggests a drug-smuggling operation has been running here, in Greece. In Greek waters, with a Thai-owned yacht operating from a Greek port.

'In short, I would like to know a great deal more about Mr Tafu Karanakarthorn. I suggest that you think over what you can tell me about him. If you begin to cooperate, it might well be that the more serious charge' – he tilted his chin up and shrugged his shoulders slowly, in the Greek suggestion of things to be considered – 'it might be that this could be made easier for you.'

Then he clapped his hands, as they do in Athenian restaurants to call the waiter, and the guard reappeared to take me back to my cell.

Back on the greasy cot, I cursed myself for asking Nina to ring the Embassy. I needed to contact Bassington now, not as a fixer and organiser of corruptible policeman, but as a character witness. He had known me in Saigon as a journalist and we had spent a lot of time sailing together at the recreation bases on the coast and on R & R in Hong Kong. There had been long hours of easy drifting over the limpid waters of the South China Sea and nothing to do in the misty calm but talk: we had grown close, he knew my background, and after I took up the Near East agency post in Beirut and discovered him again in Athens, I had also told him about my dream for the Byron film. He knew what I was in the Aegean to do: he would be able to convince Theodoropoulos.

If he could not, I now saw myself faced, at the least, with months in jail before I could prove the Welsh story. God knows what would happen to *Andromeda* in the meantime. Worse, the year would be gone, the chance of making the film delayed until the following summer, and my slender resources of capital exhausted. I had to get hold of Bassington. But they had taken my money into safe keeping along with my belt. There would be little chance of bribing a guard to get a message out. I had to pray that Nina got through to the Embassy, and then persuade the Embassy to find him – whenever the Embassy were able to get through to me.

There was nothing more I could do. I curled up on the cot, and started to catch up on my sleep.

When the guard woke me a couple of hours later and hauled me off through the labyrinth again to Theodoropoulos' office, the captain was no longer in a good humour. He stood stiffly in front of his desk with my belt, wallet and money clip in his right hand. A young American with a face so clean you could almost taste the aftershave sat in a chair on his left, wearing a Brooks Bros gaberdine suit that apparently did not feel the heat.

'You are being released into the custody of the American Embassy on 20,000 drachmas bail,' said Captain Theodoropoulos, grinding the words through a set jaw. 'Sign the paper for your possessions.'

Relief flooded through me. The young American stood, and took my hand. 'Munro,' he said, 'Third Secretary.' He did not smile.

'I'm very grateful for this,' I said to Munro and also to Theodoropoulos, over his shoulder.

'Don't thank me,' said the trim captain. 'You are temporarily freed purely through a political decision which is over my head.

'But you can rely on it we shall be talking again, very quickly. The police will of course retain your passport.'

I signed the paper and started to tell the policeman I would naturally help all I could, but that this would not be a lot, when Munro took me by the arm and moved me out of the door. Theodoropoulos stood silent and angry watching us go.

'Don't argue any more,' said the diplomat as we stepped into the corridor. 'This may be no more than a breathing space. Wait until we get in the car.'

The heat of a July Athens morning blasted me at the headquarters' door. The Third Secretary moved briskly to his small Opel saloon, parked in the shade of a clump of cypress at the edge of the small police parade ground. Even here, in a modern quarter of the city that was mostly five and six storey office blocks separated by low belts of conifers and dusty eucalypts ornamenting strips of well-weeded sand and gravel, the smell of summer Athens was immediate: harmonics of grilling meat and cooked peanuts, over the solid, pervasive bass of roasting coffee.

Munro opened the car doors and put on the air conditioning as soon as we were inside. Considering my day-old, slept-in clothes, he may have hoped this would make me a more tolerable passenger.

'First of all,' he said, 'the Ambassador requires your solemn undertaking not to try to leave the country.'

'They still got my passport.'

'Even so.'

'OK, you have it.'

He breathed out, it seemed with relief. 'We may not be able to keep you out of jail for long. But at least it's a chance for you to get some money, and start organising a defence. I presume there is a defence?'

'Why did you get me out of the cell, if you doubt it?'

'Nina Millen came to the Embassy in the early hours of this morning. She said you had been an American journalist. Some of the Embassy staff remember you – apparently you were based in this area for a while.'

He started the car and swung it out into the wide boulevard.

'Have you got any travellers' cheques or anything? We'll fix a lawyer for you, but it would be a help if you could pay him a small deposit.'

'I've got some money with American Express. But I don't know how I pick it up without a passport.'

'I'll tell them the Embassy vouches for you,' said Munro. 'They'll accept that. I'll take you straight away to their office in Constitution Square.'

'And while we're there,' I went on, 'I need to make some phone calls. I've got a defence all right – dammit, there's an alibi – but it's in Britain. I was there at the time the *caique* was stolen.'

For the first time, Munro looked relaxed. '*Right*,' he said, 'get working on that.'

'Not so easy. I'm going to need help. There's someone who should still be in Athens who could arrange that help for me, fast. I need to find Mike Bassington, do you know him? British radio man.'

'I don't know him,' said Munro. 'I've heard of him, I think.' His face was expressionless. I began to think that whatever he did at the Embassy, he was not part of American Intelligence.

I found the letter of credit in my wallet as Munro edged through the beeping midday traffic into the centre of Athens and Constitution Square. The American Express office was full of girl tourists in khaki shorts and corrals of rucksacks around the floor. It took a little time to present

96

the letter and draw $750 in drachma: the clerks didn't approve of the absence of passport documentation, and Munro had to lean on the manager with all the diplomatic authority he could find. Then I went to the phone booths to try to raise Bassington. Munro was getting tense: he'd had to leave his car in a side street 400 yards away. I suggested he wait for me outside in the parade ground of umbrellas and café tables, but he was unwilling to leave my shoulder. I gathered the responsibility for me was serious.

Bassington was a freelance and he worked from a little one-room office between Omonia and Constitution Squares, shared with another stringer. Between them, they scraped up the weekly wage for a girl whose principal duty seemed to be translating the daily papers and taking messages. Bassington was still in Athens, she told me to my intense relief. He was out to lunch, at the usual place in the Plaka.

'It's in Odos Diogenes, barely half a mile round the corner here,' I told Munro. 'I've got to eat soon anyway, and I guess you do too – let's eat there, and I can find Bassington.'

To my surprise – he seemed almost to think we should be handcuffed together – the crisp Third Secretary agreed to this.

There wasn't any point in taking his car, of course. He would not find anywhere to park where the old quarter's narrow streets start to climb the hill towards the Acropolis. We left it where it was, tilting drunkenly in a deep gutter outside a tiny Byzantine church that now wears the overcoat of a modern skyscraper built all round it like protective styrofoam packing, and walked through the sidestreets to Odos Diogenes – Diogenes

Street – where Bassington's favourite open-air taverna spreads its tables under large olive trees and in between the pedestals of broken temple columns.

We found Bassington at the back of the courtyard, seated happily alone with a large meal: octopus in red wine, a salad, a *moussaka* and a half-litre of the rose-coloured *retsina* called *kokkinelli*, which you normally only get in Athens. Bassington always liked his food. For some reason you do not think of him as a *fat* man: but he has the girth and the jowls of a man of pleasure. He exploded in a great bearish profusion when we came up to the table; the welcome was all hugs and slaps and exultation; he forced us to chairs either side of him and called for fresh glasses of iced water and another litre of *kokkinelli*; and yet I sensed he was not really surprised.

Because I have never known Bassington taken aback by events I've come to visualise him, in his absence, as invariably clad in secure old tweeds, firm, imperturbable, impossible to find flustered. He has all the solid certainty of some gleaming steam loco pulling the full complement of nineteenth-century Pullman coaches, and a dining car where immemorial traditions are maintained among the starched tablecloths and silver cutlery. Of course, this was a July heatwave day in Athens, 90 degrees in the shade everywhere except where the breeze sloughed through the shadowed courtyard of an open air taverna, and he was wearing an open-necked white shirt and light tan slacks. But when I saw he was not surprised, Bassington, as usual, gave me hope.

I told him I had been arrested.

'Yes,' said Bassington, 'you made two of the morning papers, you know. They didn't use your name, of course, but they had the guts of the story. Dramatic rescue, stolen *caique*, held for investigations and so forth. I was astonished when enquiries this morning revealed it was you. But I thought you might make contact when the initial problems were sorted out.'

'It's all an incredible mistake.'

'Yes, of course,' said Bassington. He went back to spearing his octopus, and at his invitation, I joined him.

Through a mouthful of octopus I told him: 'The alibi, unfortunately, is in West Wales.'

'Ah,' said Bassington. His great limpid brown eyes turned on Munro. 'Do you think you'll be able to secure it?'

'We haven't gotten to discussing that yet,' said Munro.

'No, I suppose not.' Bassington looked quickly from the side of his eye for a moment and found Munro interested in the octopus. He turned his eyes to me, without moving his head, and gave me a slow, very meaningful wink. I could not understand this, yet.

'Well, you will need to eat,' said Bassington. 'This is likely to be a very long day.' He winked at me once more. Then he raised his hand for the little scurrying waiter.

We ordered extra food. Munro was relaxed again now. We were in a much more understandable situation, having lunch, a civilised discussion.

Bassington said to me again: 'I thought you'd probably make contact.' It seemed to me there was a meaning intended in this repetition. He said: 'I'm always glad to be of help, you know.'

'It looks like I'm certainly going to need it,' I said.

'Oh yes,' said Bassington. He helped himself to some tomato and cucumber and then, as if on an afterthought, fished out a notebook from his shirt pocket and wrote a few lines on the last page. He replaced the notebook and looked thoughtfully at the olive trees.

I'd finished eating now. I felt a great deal better. I leant back in my chair; the smell of the warm trees, food from the tables around, the wine and the underlying roasting-coffee fragrance of Athens was giving me a very European kind of confidence. European, because it is the feeling you get there that your problems are no more than one more tiny error, fading to insignificance in a history which has forgotten so many previous thousands.

But Bassington caught my eye again. Very deliberately he flickered a pupil to the still-eating Third Secretary as if to exclude him, and then winked slowly once more.

He collected himself and said casually to Munro, 'Of course, one small difficulty does occur to me when I think of it.'

'What's that, Bassington?'

'Lancaster is not an American citizen. He is a British subject. I'm not sure that the American Embassy should be taking responsibility, are you?'

Munro dropped his fork in consternation. 'The hell you say.'

'Perhaps you really ought to pass him over to our people.'

'He's *British*!'

'Of course,' said Bassington. He looked at me slowly, just slightly narrowing one eye. 'Isn't that so?'

I had no notion what Bassington was doing. But up to now I seemed to have made every possible mistake by following my own reasoning. I said: 'Sure, I have a British passport.' Which was, in a sense, true.

'There you are,' said Bassington.

'Christ!' said Munro. 'We thought – you've apparently been working for an American news agency for years – oh, God. What are we going to do about that?'

Bassington let him think for several seconds.

'Well, if I were *you*,' he said, 'I rather think I'd let your Embassy know right away. I mean, it really ought to be our people who take responsibility to the police for Lancaster, don't you think?'

'I most certainly do,' said Munro. 'Do they have a phone here, do you know?'

'Yes,' said Bassington, 'inside the restaurant. Your people would be back from lunch by now. If you want to give them a call, I could probably take you and Harry up to our Embassy straight away.'

'Right,' said Munro, and he rose all in one action from the table and flashed in towards the interior of the taverna.

I could not for a moment follow what was going on. 'What the hell *is* this,' I whispered hoarsely to Bassington, 'I've lived in America since I was sixteen, I've had a passport for seven years. You know I have.'

'Yes,' said Bassington, 'so does the Embassy.' He was speaking with a new, low urgency. 'But it'll take about three minutes for Munro to find someone to confirm that. He must be a very junior officer.

'That gives you three minutes to get out of here.'

He took his notebook from his breast pocket and rapidly tore out the page he had written earlier. 'There's no time to give you a proper explanation. Just believe me, this situation is much more serious than you think. You've got about one real chance, which is to get out right now and make your way to the address on this paper.

'It's a safe house in Piraeus. You can trust them there. Wait for me to come, and I'll explain everything.

'But go now.'

I did not understand. But Bassington was about the one man in Athens I knew, and believed I could trust. It was the moment to decide: but in a large sense I was already committed to him. If he said he knew, I believed he did. And I could not do much worse than I already had.

I got up and ran through the back of the courtyard, out onto the street behind the restaurant where the alley turned into a file of mule steps climbing to the Acropolis. No one would expect an escapee to start running uphill.

I had taken the chance.

CHAPTER 5

The Black-eyed Blonde

The most likely way of getting down to Piraeus in anonymity was going to be to join the crowd on the Athens subway, which comes up to breathe halfway to the seaport and makes the whole journey in about twenty minutes. Going by subway I would leave little trace for detectives to pick up later: if I took a cab I might get there quicker, but the driver would be likely to remember me. The problem was that racing up the Plaka streets I could not work out how to get to the nearest station. From memory I thought it was on the other side of the Acropolis hill and if I was right, it was too far to run. Instead, I had to play percentages and head in the direction I was sure of, even though that meant a longer, riskier way round.

I ran about 200 yards up the hill to where the sidestreets turned into narrow stepped passages, and then cut off right for a few minutes until I could turn down the hill again towards the Agora quarter. The roadway widened now to some six yards across, terraced houses on the right and the open excavated area of the ancient marketplace to the left. But it still descended the last slopes of the hill in steps. I'd seen people drive little French Citroëns down muleways like that, but I felt safe from Munro in his Opel, even if he had managed to follow my general direction. And that seemed unlikely. I slowed to a rapid walk in order to be less noticeable, crossed the Agora at the bottom of the steps, and found a ramshackle cab cruising in a mainstreet just beyond. I had to force myself to check the fare to Omonia Square before I booked him, so everything would seem normal – the meters rarely work in Greek cabs and if I had not haggled over the fare first the cabbie would have found me suspiciously unusual. Five minutes later we were at Omonia, and I ran down the subway steps three at a time to buy a ticket for Piraeus.

I believed I had made it, now. I was standing in the corner of a crowded carriage rumbling through the tunnels southbound under the city barely twenty minutes after hurtling out the back of the taverna in Odos Diogenes. Piraeus was another twenty minutes away. Theodoropoulos, even if Munro got a message through to him immediately, would hardly have had the time to mount a city-wide manhunt even when I got off the train.

At Piraeus there was, in fact, one policeman on the platform under the big barrel roof, but he was paying no attention to the crowd and I slipped away down the stairs at the entrance without delay, and onto the wide waterfront area. I was free, here. My pulse had slowed, my breath was easy. For a second or two I had a mad desire to buy a steamship ticket and slip aboard one the tall-funnelled ancient ferry steamers that run to the out-of-the-way Aegean islands – they use more modern boats for the tourist destinations – but since I'd committed myself to Bassington's sudden plan it made sense

104

to stick to it. All I needed to do was to find his safe house.

A newspaper–tobacco kiosk on the quay sold me a packet of Papastratos cigarettes and a street map. I walked slowly off eastwards down the waterfront street, through the late lunchtime crowds around the peanut roasting stalls and the *souvlakia* grilled meat vendors, maintaining, as I hoped, the camouflage of an idle tourist. I looked grubby and unshaven, of course: but so do a lot of the European hippies who wander Greece in the summer. About a mile away from the station I found a sidewalk café table, and stopped to study the map and order a beer. Perhaps this wasn't strictly sensible, but after the run through the Plaka in 90-degree heat I had to have fluid.

The cold Fix beer and a couple of cigarettes began to restore me. It was getting towards mid-afternoon now and it was time to go: the crowd in the streets and on the café terraces was thinning for the siesta. Bassington's safe address looked to be about twelve minutes off through the back streets, and as I cut away from the waterfront there was hardly a soul about.

The address was a newish three-storey concrete house near the end of a narrow and otherwise ramshackle street. Each lifeless window on the ground floor was protected on the outside with bars; the ones above were shuttered tight against the sun. Rusting reinforcing rods jutted skywards from the fringes of the flat roof, where the hopeful builders had proposed adding another story later when the money arrived. Instead the decaying iron now supported a clothesline from which an immense collection of motley towels and sheets hung limp in the heat, giving the whitewashed blockhouse the air

105

of a seedy South American battleship on a local Independence Day. I knocked discreetly, and then much louder, on the peeling door. At last it was opened, still on the chain. Almost at my own height, an area of seamed, brown flesh surrounding one examining male eye appeared in the gap.

'Bassington,' I said, offering the paper. The section of face in the slit nodded without looking at the paper. The man unlatched the chain, out of sight, opened the door slightly, and motioned quickly with one hand to bring me inside.

He was tall, lean, in his late thirties, and totally expressionless. The eye that had been hidden from me at the door was dull, its lid permanently drooped from some old injury.

'The bar is closed,' he said. 'You rent a room, eh? Sleep. . . *hypnos*. . .*schlaffen*? Thousand drachmas.'

I gave him the money. There was nothing resembling a bar in sight, and I presumed this was the back door. He led me up two flights of stairs to a small room, bare apart from a double bed dressed with threadbare sheets and a handbasin with one cold water tap on the wall. There was silence throughout the house.

'The girls come later,' said the one-eyed man, moving slowly out through the door again, 'when the bar opens.'

Bassington, it dawned on me slowly, had sent me to the safe cathouse. It was probably as good as anywhere else.

It is only in Asia that the cheap brothels have air conditioning, and the room was stifling even after I opened the windows behind the slatted wooden shutters. A slight smell of sewage mixed with grilling meat drifted in with the tepid air from the street. Far away there was occasional traffic noise from the waterfront, but in this area there was nothing but the dusty quiet of a hot Greek afternoon.

I found some soap, but no towel, in the handbasin. I washed myself as well as I could and dried off on my shirt, hanging it on the inside of the shutters afterwards. There was nothing else to do now but smoke the Papastratos and wait for Bassington.

Lying on the bed, going over what had happened, it seemed barely credible that events had gotten so out of control. Twenty-four hours before I'd been in command of a well-found ship with all my papers in order, a modicum of money in the bank, and a scheme in mind that if it wasn't certain, was at least a respectable and even prestigious project. Now I was hiding in a Greek brothel with a murder charge over my head and the police hunting me all across Athens. I was without a passport and presumably bereft as well of the protection of the Embassy, since I'd been persuaded to deny my citizenship in what I began to feel was a flash of insanity. What I needed above all else was to get *Andromeda* out of Greece: I had the dull, growing certainty that a sane man would have waited, whatever time and interruption was required, to ensure that prime necessity. Yet I still trusted the solid Bassington.

After two cigarettes the heat took me over. I joined the rest of the neighbourhood, and drifted off to sleep. Things, I told myself, must surely get back to normal soon.

It was getting dusk outside when the one-eyed man woke me with a glass of iced water and a cup of Greek coffee. He brought a folded towel, too, evidently fresh off the washing line on the roof.

'You want shower, *douche*?' he asked me as I drowned my parching post-siesta thirst with the water. When I agreed he indicated the location of this unsuspected luxury with a nod of his sombre head in the direction of the hall. I thanked him and began to drink the coffee, lighting a cigarette. He went to the shutters and removed my dried shirt, holding it out to inspect the size.

'You give me pants, too,' he said. '*Kyrie* Bassington speak telephone. He say you want new clothes. I get.'

That seemed like an intelligent plan. The shops would be open again now, after the siesta.

'Three thousand drachmas,' said the one-eyed man. 'I have to get from shop. You no leave house, *Kyrie* Bassington says.'

'OK,' I said wearily. 'There seems to be a hell of a lot of time payment in this runaway business.' I gave him the money and my old pants. He looked at me briefly and went off down the hall. I got hold of the towel and went to find the shower.

It was cold water, of course, but amazingly welcome. After the first blasting shock of it I luxuriated in the wash like a football player after a tough game. It was almost as if my problems were sloughing away with the street dirt and the old sweat. All things were going to be manageable: come quickly now, Bassington, let's get this whole mess sorted out.

When I finally emerged from the shower cabinet, the one-eyed man had returned. He was waiting for me in my room with a whole pile of towels, bottles, scissors, an old-fashioned razor and a set of clothes still in their plastic wrappers from the supply store. I pulled the pants out of the pack and put them on: they were a kind of metallic-coloured French cotton, a little short in the leg, but wearable. The one-eyed man put his razor and the scissors on the ledge over the washbasin.

'Shave now, and change hair,' he announced. '*Kyrie* Bassington say new hair. Different.'

There was a kind of professional air to all this. The one-eyed man seemed to be different, too, as if he had now been reassured about the situation. He knew his job, as well: he tucked a towel skilfully round my neck as I sat on the edge of the bed, soaped my face with a shaving brush, and whisked away a day's stubble with his cut-throat razor. When he got to the top of the right side of my face I felt him slash away most of the sideburns in front of the ears. I wasn't very happy with that and made a gesture, but he continued to take them all off and followed suit in front of the other ear.

Then when my face was dried and he got out his scissors I understood why. My hair was still a long lank mess from the shower. He took hold of great handfuls and with a sequence of savage slashes cut off most of the crop I'd let accumulate through the last few weeks of cruising on the yacht. He scissored it back to something little longer than a crewcut, and then brought out a serrated razor to thin what remained into shape.

I was certainly going to look different. But after combing it into shape perfunctorily he indicated he was not finished with me, and got me to kneel by the washbasin. He began rubbing the contents of one of the bottles into my scalp, getting me to hold a towel to my face. Evidently I was to get some kind of dye, too.

I was quite passive about this. I'd sometimes wondered what I would look like with black hair instead of my normal light brown, anyway. The process seemed to be going on for ever. The first rinse was allowed to set for some minutes, followed by another stronger smelling solution from a different bottle and then washed off in the basin. I was made to sit after the final wash with my head swathed in a towel.

After twenty minutes the one-eyed man took off the towel and surveyed the result.

'Good,' he said.

He combed my newly-short strands into place and passed me a hand mirror.

'Good,' he said again, '*Deutsch*.'

I stared, aghast, into the glass. Things were nowhere near getting back to normal. An escapee from the Afrika Korps stared back. I had been turned into an ash-blond.

'Put on clothes now,' said the one-eyed man.

The other packets contained a dark blue cotton shirt and a light tan zip jacket. They were both my size, but the jacket was cut on a very European style, with stiffly square shoulders.

'Ah yes,' said the one-eyed man. '*Deutsch*, now.'

When I held the mirror away at arm's length I understood his point exactly. With my white blond hair and square jacket I looked ready now for a march to Nuremberg.

The one-eyed man gathered his towels and implements together. From below, a low wail of sound and a heavy rhythmic bass filtered up from the ground floor. Someone had put a *bouzouki* record on a player.

'The bar open downstairs, now,' said my barber. 'You be OK there. You wait in bar, not go outside. *Kyrie* Bassington come later tonight.'

I was nervous about showing myself, but Bassington's man was obviously the expert. Certainly I no longer looked much like the passport picture which by now would presumably have been issued to searching police. I followed the one-eyed man down the narrow stairs and through a door opening onto the back of the bar.

It was a long, dimly lit room with tables in secluded booths down one side and a row of stools at the bar on the other. The *bouzouki* music was delivering a tragic slow march from a small juke box by the window. Three bar girls sat facing the machine, shrugging an occasional shoulder to the rhythm without a great deal of interest: an older girl serving the bar broke away from their end and came up to take low instructions from the one-eyed man, while he put his implements away in a cupboard and went out. I asked for an *ouzo* and sat at the furthest bar stool from the window, where I could watch the door to the street.

The smallest of the three round the juke box turned to look back at the bar. Her eyes did not exactly settle on me, so much as widen: almost in the same instant she slipped off her stool and glided rapidly across, like a cat moving soundlessly to its prey, before the others noticed custom had arrived. Her face was alive with interest: I had the impression that in addition to normal business concerns, ash blonds were a wow in Piraeus.

In fact, we were almost the same colour. As she fixed my eyes with hers and moved the next bar stool closer to mine, I found myself wondering if our hair came out of the same bottle and the one-eyed man performed part-time services as *coiffeur* to the whole house. Her hair, fluffed into a bouffant helmet around a face that looked no more than nineteen, was almost as pale as mine now was. The effect of youthful freshness was

111

only marginally reduced by a large blue bruise showing through the powder below and around her left eye.

'*Deutsch*,' she said, smiling and swirling her wide skirt up over both our legs as she perched up on the stool.

'*Ja*.' I might as well accept the part.

She pointed to herself happily and said '*Nicht Deutsche*.' That seemed to dispose of any possibility of conversation, but the little blonde seemed quite undisturbed. She settled herself comfortably close to my shoulder.

'Do you want a drink?' I said, trying to assume a guttural accent in English.

She did not speak English either, but when I gestured with my glass she accepted joyously, calling to the girl behind the bar for what looked like a Greek vermouth. The small blonde sipped it decorously, and spread her skirt wider across my thighs. She held up the hem an inch or two and looked at me inquiringly. After a moment it dawned on me that this was an invitation to have a feel, but I was a little slow to take it up. Her hand moved to the low-cut neck of her dress, instead. She pulled it open to show me her breasts, looking into my eyes all the time. Even a slow-witted and distracted runaway could now recognise this as the Piraeus pick-up.

'Very nice,' I said. I did not want to do anything about this – not in my present circumstances – but some sort of explanation was necessary.

'I'm only here to listen to the music,' I said, forgetting the *Deutsch* accent in the consternation of the moment.

Small blonde shook her head, in concerned non-comprehension.

'*Y musiki*,' I said in Greek.

'Ah, *Y musiki*,' she said contentedly.

112

The juke box was playing a sad, slow song now, one of what the Athenians call the 'heavy' *bouzouki* variety that are not regarded as quite respectable because they have a strong Turkish influence and are supposed to have homosexual connotations. It was intoned by a male singer with an immensely deep bass voice and it appeared to be about the sea: the phrase '*Y thalassa*' rang monotonously through the refrain, as if the singer was mourning some great marine tragedy.

I liked the tune suddenly. It suited the mood the disasters of the last twenty-four hours had created. I thought I would ask small blonde the name of the song: my Greek is hardly conversational, but it seemed to be up to me to communicate something.

'*Ti enai to onoma tys musikis?*' I said, more or less correctly.

'*Y musiki,*' said the small blonde, very definitely. Of course, 'music' was called 'music'. Yes. I gave up. My Greek accent was worse than I thought.

By this stage I had decided to take advantage after all of the invitation to knead the girl's upper thigh. My hand was buried in the folds of her voluminous skirt, clutching a slim and attractively firm expanse of cool flesh. I bought the small blonde another vermouth and took a refill of *ouzo*. As my glass was poured, she leant forward suddenly and said something quickly in Greek to the girl behind the bar.

The girl listened and then asked me casually: 'You want to fuck the little blonde? She ask eight hundred drachmas for one hour. She got number one very good pussy.'

Well, by now the idea was developing attractions. I mean, if I was going to be a wanted criminal on the run from a potential murder charge, perhaps I should store up such moments. I knew the condemned man was supposed to have his choice of last breakfasts, but I doubted that even in Greece there was pussy available on Death Row. But I could not afford to miss Bassington.

'Tell her later on,' I said. 'I'm waiting to see someone. Can we maybe get something to eat, meantime?'

Small blonde was overjoyed when this thought was translated to her. I could see we had 'A Date', now. As we moved to one of the booths by the wall I was almost wearing as many of the wide flounces of her skirt as she was. She pulled open the neck again, and would not rest quiet until I reached inside and took hold of her left nipple. It was quite hard. She kissed me as I pulled it even stiffer. It seemed that holding her nipples promised me to her, somehow. She told me her name now, with signs: Christina.

The one-eyed man came back into the bar and offered to bring in food from a stall down the road. I ordered *souvlakia* and eggplant: I could not understand what my new love ordered, but the meal when it arrived included courgettes in batter and fried prawns. It was all surprisingly good. We opened a bottle of wine and I began, incredibly, to enjoy the situation, with my small bruised blonde feeding me prawns on a fork and nuzzling me in the intervals, while I picked at the skewered meat. We moved onto Greek brandies and coffee afterwards: she was going to want more than 800 drachma for this length of time, I reflected. But what else was I to do?

It was after ten before Bassington arrived. 'Sorry to be so late,' he said appearing suddenly large round the booth wall. 'I had to be sure none of Theodoropoulos' men were following me.'

114

He sat down comfortably, putting a large canvas grip under the table. 'They weren't, of course. It's not a particularly efficient police force, I'm afraid.'

I forgot Christina immediately: 'For Christ's sake, Bassington, tell me what's going on. . .'

'Yes,' he said, 'in a minute. We'd better just ask your young friend to wait a while at the bar, first. Just in case.'

The one-eyed man had appeared with a beer for Bassington.

They spoke rapidly and the situation was explained to the small blonde. She gave me an anxious look and drifted over to linger, desolately, on a bar stool at the end. Bassington called after her: 'Tell it's all right, there'll be time later.' Christina brightened when she was reassured, and Bassington turned back to me.

'Listen,' I said, 'things have gotten quite out of control. I'm on the run from the police, I must have amply confirmed Theodoropoulos' suspicions in doing so, I've left my yacht on Andros, and now for Christ's sake your one-eyed heavy here has given me a Fire Island hairdo. You've got to make some sense out of all this.'

'You look absolutely fine,' said Bassington. 'Perfect for your new papers.' He drew a dark document out of his inside jacket pocket and handed it across the table. It was a West German passport.

'Genuine, too,' he said. 'The Jerries want it back when this is all over, though.'

I flipped it open. 'There's a blank in place of the photograph of the holder.'

'Not for long,' Bassington said. 'I brought a Polaroid in the bag, here. That passport will get you out of Greece tomorrow morning.'

115

'I've got to get my boat back, Bassington. What the hell is happening?'

An abstracted, thoughtful look replaced the organising briskness in Bassington's expression. He drank a little of his beer, slowly.

'I suppose I have to tell you I'm still thinking that out,' he conceded.

'Terrific.'

'Well, it's clear – clear to me, anyway – that you've managed to stumble into something much bigger than either you or the Greeks understand. I realised that the moment I heard about the way you turned up on Andros.

'Now, it happens that my great and powerful friends elsewhere' – he gave me a quick glance to ensure I understood him – 'have for some time very much wanted to resolve this very problem. When I saw you walking into the Odos Diogenes I felt it was a golden opportunity. You could help us, and in return we could help you escape a rather unfortunate situation in which you would spend the next twelve months closely examining the wall of a Greek police cell.'

'Christ, I'm innocent. Would it take me that long to produce the truth?'

'Very likely,' said Bassington. 'The problem in a nutshell is that the Greeks aren't talking to anybody at the moment. They're not talking to the Turks because of the *impasse* over Cyprus. They're not talking to the British because of the Elgin Marbles and another row about NATO. They're being nice to your people, until further notice, because they want American support over Cyprus. That's why their Foreign Office told Theodoropoulos to let you out of jail. But since

Washington can't agree to side with them against the Turks that won't last more than a day or so. Which is why everyone knew you would be back in a cell again very quickly.

'Now, this all makes life very awkward for us all.

'It means among other things that when you turn up with a raped archaeologist and what we all presently assume is a boatload of smuggled drugs, the only thing that interests our Captain Theodoropoulos is the fact that it's a Greek boat – and you are suspected of stealing it.'

I lit the last of my Papastratos in desperation. I was beginning to see how this formerly-incredible trap had closed around me. Bassington went on:

'The fact that this is part of a much more serious thing in Turkey – I believe – doesn't interest the Greek police at all.

'Now, you say you've got an alibi in Britain, and I've no doubt we could dig it up. But they don't like us very much at the moment either, and it's not a sure thing.

'From your point of view, if you had not very sensibly taken my advice and scarpered from Mr Munro's arms at the restaurant, you'd be facing at best a year or so in jail waiting trial, and at worst, perhaps conviction and a long sentence. You've been identified by the only eye-witness, after all.

'I imagine even half a year in an Athens jail would be a serious handicap just now, wouldn't it?'

'Of course it would,' I said. 'But the only thing I own of value is a $130,000 ketch sitting in the harbour at Andros, Mike. I can't hightail it out of Greece and leave the only thing I've got behind.'

'You can't have everything,' he said.

117

'You're such a wonderful help. But what on earth do you expect me to do?'

'Tell your story in Turkey, and clear yourself,' said Bassington. 'That's where you'll find the evidence you want, because that's where the smuggling gang is operating. As far as you're concerned, the quicker the Turkish end is cleared up, the faster your Greek problem will be resolved, and the sooner you get your boat back. Once we get the proof even Theodoropoulos will have to accept it.

'And as for us, we need that gang smashed.

'You see, I'm fairly sure that somewhere underneath the pile of elderly statuettes on your *caique* will be a cache of drugs destined to finance the purchase of arms for European terrorists. We have believed for a long time that a major drug smuggling ring operating out of Turkey, using small boats in just this way, has been used to finance and arm the major European terrorist groups: the IRA, the Red Brigades, and the Bader-Meinhof clones in Germany.

'Unfortunately, because we've never had hard evidence until now, we've never managed to get the Turks to act. It's been the familiar problem of bureaucratic politics. Since we can't prove anything, their security arm just says it isn't happening and drugs aren't their problem. The narcotics branch says it isn't happening and terrorists aren't *their* problem. It's the old Ottoman torpor all round, old son.

'And since the Greeks aren't talking to the Turks, Istanbul won't take any notice of *your* find, either – until we produce you and say Look, this chap was there, he can prove to you that at least one shipment has gone over in just the way we said was happening.

'That's what will get them off their Ottoman backsides. And that's why I was able to get you a nice new genuine German passport, of course.

'Though they want it back afterwards, as I said.'

This was all becoming too complex and too damned big. 'After what?' I said.

'Well, what I propose, if you're agreeable, is that we slip you complete with nice new German passport – oh, some visas have already been put inside it, by the way – on the Turkish passenger liner which is leaving for Istanbul tomorrow afternoon. When you get there you will be met by one of my colleagues, who will take good care of you until I arrive in a few days to introduce you to an officer I'm fairly confident about in the Turkish security police.'

It seemed thin, to me. 'There's only one flaw,' I said. 'I only know what the girl told me. I never saw the Turks at all. How do I prove anything?'

'You saw the boat.'

'It's Greek.'

'You know where it came from.'

'Only in very general terms. And that's only hearsay.'

The lines of something like concern began to register on Bassington's rotund features. 'You did look at the cargo,' he said.

I believe I had seen this opportunity developing for several minutes.

– 'Ah, yes,' I said slowly.

'And as it happens, the major item in it is now aboard *Andromeda*. Most of the stuff looked like bazaar junk to me, but there was also what appears to be a large stone bust of the god Apollo. The girl thought it was valuable, so I shifted it onto my boat as soon as I could.

'But when I did, I discovered it's a fake.

'Perhaps that's the proof you need.'

Bassington stared at me for a second, his face suddenly lightening.

'*Shit, yes*!' he bellowed all at once like an army sergeant at drill instruction. There was a flurry of taffeta skirts back at the bar as the girls turned to look at him. His voice regained its confidential tone. 'Christ, it was a sudden hunch to snatch you out of the Embassy's protection, but it was a *good* one.'

Bassington took a long pull at his drink, and regarded me with avuncular satisfaction as he put it down.

'That's the oldest trick in the dope-smuggling book,' he said. 'Back in the 70s half the stuff from the Golden Triangle was coming out as faked antiques – Buddha heads, ceramics, you name it. In 71 two big earthenware Thai pots were shipped into Australia that had the Sydney trendies on Cloud Eleven for six months.

'It's six-to-four odds there's no dope in the bilge of that damned *caique* at all. The stuff'll be tricked up as part of the antiques cargo – it's the cover for moving it around until they break it down.'

'Well,' I said, 'the Apollo's Head is aboard *Andromeda*. And she is under arrest in Gavrion harbour.'

Bassington thought for a moment, pulling out his Peterson pipe and starting to stuff its bowl. 'The problem's not insuperable,' he said. 'If you agree to the scheme, I could get the ferry across to Andros tomorrow morning and pick her up for you myself. Is there plenty of diesel in the tanks, by the way? It'd help.'

'You expect just to sail her off without any questions?'

'Why not?' said Bassington. Clouds of thoughtful smoke began to rise above him. 'Theodoropoulos is only interested in the *caique* for the moment. He's having her brought over to Piraeus, did you know? Your ketch is just lying at anchor in Gavrion harbour without anyone taking any notice, you may be sure. You know how honest they are on Greek islands: nobody would dream of stealing the gear or anything, so we can rely on the fact she will not be guarded through the night.

'And if there are any questions it's quite simple. You registered her in Hong Kong, old boy. British ship. I shall have many official documents with me to say that I'm picking her up on behalf of her proper owners and delivering her elsewhere.'

'You're taking a helluva risk.'

'Not really.' Bassington had worked it all out, now. 'Once away from Gavrion harbour I'll turn due north and head up for the Athos peninsula before I swing east for the Dardanelles. No-one's going to be looking for your boat there, even when they miss her at Gavrion. And by the time that happens I should be 100 miles away, beyond Skyros: she does about eight knots under power, I'd say.'

It began to seem possible. I knew there was at least enough diesel left in *Andromeda*'s tanks for 700 miles. I told him this, wondering.

'It'll work, then,' said Bassington, 'if I do it tomorrow night. Wouldn't want to leave it much later.

'Very well. Michaelis here' — he gestured at the one-eyed man — 'will get you onto the *Samsun* tomorrow morning. You'll be in Istanbul next day.'

'How much is that going to cost me?' I asked. 'The German clothes and the new gay hairdo made a bit of a whole in my ready cash.'

'That sly fucker Michaelis,' said Bassington admiringly. 'I told him we'd pay for everything. I shall have to reimburse you. Anyway, you'll need some spare funds.'

He drew a thick envelope from his other jacket pocket. A rapid look inside revealed it contained US dollar bills.

'More than kind. How are you going to get me aboard the boat for Istanbul, though?'

'It's a little tricky,' Bassington said, 'but easier than getting you on a plane. They'll be watching all the airports and waterfronts, of course, with particular attention to ships and flights heading for Turkey, since that's where Theodoropoulos seems to have convinced himself you're criminally involved. There are various ways of getting you onto a liner, though: I'd say the easiest will be for Michaelis to bring you a ticket from Athens to Istanbul tomorrow morning, together with one of the boarding cards they give the transit passengers who want to get off and spend a day in Athens while the ship's in port.

'All you do then is mingle with the passengers coming back from the day trips, and get on board the *Samsun*. Once you're there go along to the purser's office with your ticket and present yourself as a new passenger joining the ship at Piraeus. Your new name – Horst Reinhardt, by the way – will be on the purser's list already, so you'll just be given a cabin and it'll be assumed you've already been through Greek immigration. Once out of Piraeus, you're under the Turkish flag.'

I believed in the whole plan, by now. Relief poured into me: I ordered another bottle of *Demestica* and a new packet of cigarettes.

'I'm immensely grateful, Mike,' I told him. 'You're going to a hell of a lot of bother for me – and you must be in trouble already, after this morning's exercise.'

122

'Not at all,' said Bassington. Smoke was pouring in heavy clouds from the Peterson's. He had his tobacco specially sent him from London, I remembered: the Greek pipe tobacco is amazingly acrid stuff.

'No. I mean, apart from helping out a chum, this is a rather important problem to us, you know. And you represent our first chance to demonstrate to the Turkish authorities that the problem really exists, and that it's on their territory.'

'This morning, though.'

'Ah,' said Bassington, 'Theodoropoulos could hardly say anything to me because after all I don't have any sort of official authority to apprehend people who just happen to leave restaurants in a rush. It hasn't struck him that I was in any way dishonest in suggesting you still had British nationality, because that's the trick he believes you've been using to travel easily around Europe anyway.'

'Munro will start problems with the American Embassy.'

'Munro is a young sucker,' Bassington said decisively. 'He was certainly more than peeved when he found you'd gone, but there are one or two people higher up in your Embassy who understood the point of it all and sympathise. They couldn't have kept you free more than a couple of days, you know.

'If I say it myself,' Bassington went on, leaning back in the booth and sucking his pipe contentedly, 'this morning's was one of the best spur-of-the-moment notions I've had for a very long time. You'll enjoy Istanbul with Tom Pollock, too. He's our man there, and one of yours as well, I shouldn't wonder.'

Christina, still sitting alone at the bar, had been wistfully watching her colleagues picking up a pair of

Norwegian sailors at the other end. From the corner of her eye she saw Bassington leaning back, the serious part of the conversation apparently over, and now she drifted across with inquiry in her eye. I made room for her on the booth bench and she settled back into her former position, with every evidence of overwhelming delight.

'It looks to me as if you'll be having one for the road,' said Bassington. 'Make sure to hold on tight to our money.'

I assured him I would, and he ordered more beer; telling the bartender at the same time, with a jovial avuncular air like a London clubman treating the flower girl, to bring a new vermouth for black-eyed Christina. She toasted him with a serious Greek '*Sygea sas*', taking on the formal manners of an established mistress in solemn reaction to his gesture.

Thinking it all over across the wine, I said: 'I suppose it *has* to be drugs: the girl claimed the antiques were valuable, but they looked like fakes to me. She may well have been fake, too.'

'Oh, Nina Millen is genuine,' Bassington puffed. 'We checked her out this afternoon. But it's got to be drugs or arms – you wouldn't mount that kind of operation just for antique statues. We'll find out for sure in Istanbul.'

Christina was beginning to get affectionate again. I could tell from the way she pushed my right hand down the neck of her dress.

'Before you get distracted,' said Bassington, 'I'd better take your snap for the passport.'

He reached under the table and fished for the Polaroid camera. While he was opening the bag, my small blonde managed to unzip my flies and started pulling my cock.

She was looking at me dreamily. Bassington brought the camera up and began focusing, oblivious to Christina's apparently innocent proximity to his subject across the table. But when she saw the lens she ducked.

Which is largely why the photograph on my temporary German passport displayed the happiest Harry Lancaster portrait any Immigration official has inspected anywhere in the world.

When he took it, she was under the tablecloth, with my dick in her mouth.

Bassington must have noticed some slight distraction, though. He said: 'I'll leave the passport with Michaelis, when I've fixed the stamp on the picture. Pollock will meet you in Istanbul.

'And I'll be off once the passport's done. It looks as if you'll be busy tonight.'

He smiled, angelically. I started to suggest to Christina that we move to my room. She agreed energetically the moment her head was back on deck and she understood what I was saying.

As we left, Bassington said: 'Only one thing, old son. Make sure she's got a prophylactic.

'Piraeus is the syphilis capital of Western Europe.'

This is not precisely the kind of news you want to hear as you drag yourself wearily to bed with a new small lover. Christina was beautiful. She washed herself carefully all over at the basin on the wall, demonstrating that this was to be a major affair of the night and not an incident of an hour. She was attentive and erotic. She made wonderful noises, thrust her tongue at me in a knowing way, rubbed my hands over her breasts and opened her legs at me with little darting, hiding motions of her hands designed to tease.

I couldn't raise a stout enough intent. All right, there is penicillin, but still – the thought Bassington had wickedly planted festered away all traces of manhood.

I felt like the fool one would expect in that situation, and all the worse because I could not imagine how to explain to the little Greek. But Christina had thought of her own explanation.

She thought I would like to make love to her like a boy: a popular variation in the eastern Mediterranean. She turned over, her cheeky little black-eyed face grinning at me over her shoulder, and indicated her buttocks.

The Greek phrase she used meant 'like a man', or similar: in modern Greek the word for man is 'Andros'.

Oh yes, I thought. Well, to hell with Nina Millen anyway. In some way the idea liberated my loins: all reservations vanished. So I went ahead. It seemed impossible to get in, at first, but Christina, passionately interested, produced some white cream from her handbag and suddenly the entry was made. Tight, but astonishingly deep.

Christina was squealing and moaning with what I first feared was pain. She was a very small girl, and I'm in proportion to my size. Then I realised the noise came from genuine pleasure. I too was becoming beside myself. For some crazed, inexplicable reason it is a wildly erotic sensation when your loins are thumping at a girl's slim buttocks instead of her belly. And it was, I suppose, the second time in three nights I traversed the Andros Passage.

CHAPTER 6

Ticket to Leave

You can't sleep late in Piraeus. The world's ship-building industries may be in the silent depths of depression everywhere else, but someone along the Piraeus waterfront starts banging boilerplate at six a.m. every day of the week. I woke to the racket of distant rivetting. Christina lay comatose, the bruising around her eye newly vivid in the morning light reflecting through the shutter slats. I gathered my clothes and took a cold water shower down the hall.

One-eyed Michaelis was making coffee in the bar. He nodded at me and poured a second cup unhurriedly. As I drank it he handed me my new German passport from under the bar counter. There was now an embossed stamp certifying the Polaroid picture of the white-blond, wild-eyed individual who stared back at me from the page: both the stamp and that impersonal photograph gave the authentic passport look.

'The steamship office opens at eight o'clock,' said Michaelis. 'I get you the ticket then. But you stay in the bar until we go to the ship this afternoon, OK?'

'What time does she sail?'

'Five.'

It was going to be a long, nerve-racking wait. Christina eventually surfaced, paper-pale, and was sent protesting to the baker's for fresh bread. When he had eaten Michaelis strolled off down the street to a steamship office. Half an hour later he came back with a new Turkish Maritime Lines ticket from Piraeus to Istanbul, and a buff card bearing two lines of printed Greek script and a large number. He slipped the card into my German passport and told me to put the ticket in the other pocket of the zip jacket.

'You go aboard just with the passport and the card, OK? Then on the ship, take the ticket to the purser's office.'

The morning passed very slowly. I played several games of backgammon with Michaelis, in silence punctuated by the occasional thunderous crash of my opponent bearing a man in grim triumph off the board. Between games we drank a slow beer.

The bar girl brought in a morning paper. Michaelis scanned it briefly and left it on the booth table when a delivery arrived outside. I picked it up, painfully trying to translate the headlines, when my eye suddenly fell on a smudgy version of my own picture on an inside page. I could not follow the Greek, but it was obviously the story of my escape. The picture had been taken from my genuine passport: it was a kind of reassurance that it looked as little like me now as the new one resembled the real me. Michaelis had not spotted the newspaper picture. It seemed to me that I was just another job, to him, and he neither knew nor wished to discover the reasons for my flight.

I wondered if it would make a difference if he found out I was wanted by the Greek police for a crime against a Greek. Better not risk it: I started to fold the paper up, to push it somewhere out of sight, when he came back to the booth. He had noticed the page I'd been looking at and took it from my hand.

He just looked at the photograph for a few seconds, and finally raised an eyebrow. Then he looked at me, back at the photograph, and raised his chin with a small sardonic smile. He gave me back the paper. All he said was the brief word *'Endaxi'* – meaning everything is under control, or as I took it in this case, they'll never spot you from that.

When the slow afternoon had ticked round to a little after three-thirty, and the shipyard noise and the street traffic had died away into the siesta period, Michaelis finally calculated the time had come to go. Christina, who had been sopping up some fish soup with bread and listening to the juke box, rose to give me an enthusiastic farewell, with admonitions translated by the bar girl to promise to find her again on my next trip to Piraeus.

Michaelis watched the embrace and then seemed struck with a sudden thought. He spoke to her rapidly. 'I'm telling her to come to see you off,' he told me. 'Three of us on the streets, no one will look too closely.'

At first there seemed to be no one about to notice us at all. The side routes we used to get to the main waterfront were quite empty. Even on the wide quay itself there were only occasional porters to be seen in the distance, and small knots of people at café tables attending to the aftermath of their leisurely lunches. Michaelis would not allow us to walk too quickly. We strolled across the roadway onto the waterside, out in the strong sun where no sensible policeman would be standing to survey the scant afternoon traffic, and turned left in the direction of the liner berths. Christina insisted on carrying the cheap compressed-cardboard suitcase

Michaelis had produced halfway through the morning, and filled with old newspaper and my newly washed clothes of the day before.

About a mile round the curve of the quay we came to the point where the Turkish liner, white and cool with the crescent on her scarlet-banded funnel, lay at the edge of a plain of concrete wharf that was criss-crossed with rail lines and the metal girders which made up the tracks for mobile cranes.

Michaelis halted us at a corner café table with a view of the wide quay. Nothing was moving at the liner's side: there was an occasional dark head at her rail, and there were two officials, a policeman and a Customs– Immigration officer, somnolent and small at the gangplank foot. But the Greek stevedores were having their siesta-time break, and the mobile crane stood motionless above a small platoon of cars waiting among the crates to be shipped into the liner's holds.

Michaelis motioned me to sit with my back to the ship. He ordered coffees and placed himself to command the quay while Christina automatically moved her chair to nuzzle my shoulder. I rubbed my cheek against her hair and drank the coffee, hearing intermittent traffic noise at my back.

What sounded like several cars and a couple of trucks had gone by when Michaelis said, 'The tourist bus is arriving.' There was a deep diesel noise and from the corner of my eye I saw a dark-windowed coach painted white and blue glide by towards the quay.

'You go now,' said Michaelis. 'We follow to get your case on board. I will be the porter to bring it on. Wait for me to bring the case before you take the ticket to the purser's office.'

I kissed Christina briefly, shook Michaelis' hand, and walked purposefully off the café terrace and across the road. I chose the direction which would keep the tourist coach between myself and the liner's gangplank. I reached the rear of the coach just as the last of its passengers were emerging to join the straggling line making its way across the mobile crane tracks: as I came round the coach I merged with the last group, my passport and boarding card ready in my inside pocket.

Then I saw Theodoropoulos at the gangplank, chatting to his officer.

In a reaction even without thought I halted and patted both jacket pockets as if I had just lost something, turned, and retreated under cover of the bus. Without looking back I started to retrace my steps to the café. Michaelis was halfway towards across the expanse of concrete, with a large tin porter's badge now pinned to his shirt and my cardboard suitcase in his hand. His expression did not change as we came towards each other.

Theodoropoulos must have driven up in one of the cars that passed us at the café as my back was turned. Of course: it was a Turkish ship, he believed I was part of a Turkish gang, and he would see the necessity to check himself not only the day's flights but the departure of a Turkish liner.

'One of the policemen at the gangplank knows me,' I told Michaelis.

'Ah,' he said, 'Theodoropoulos.'

'I was with him twice, for an hour at a time. He's going to recognise me.'

'Make it look like you left your wallet in the café,' said Michaelis, turning round to retrace his steps across the quay. I went with him, slapping each of my pockets in turn, without looking back at the gangplank.

Michaelis swore quietly. Then he put a restraining hand on my arm. 'Not too much,' he said, 'you don't want the police to come across to help.'

'What now?'

Michaelis thought, until we reached the safety of the shaded café terrace once more. We sat as we had before, Michaelis looking out at the liner.

'Maybe Theodoropoulos goes away,' he said. The waiter came up for fresh orders. We had no stomach for coffee, now. '*Tris ouzo*,' said Michaelis.

Thirty minutes ticked slowly by. Michaelis said suddenly: 'He's not going to go. We have to use a car to get you aboard the ship. We do this now, before the workmen come back.'

He spoke quickly to Christina, who nodded, kissed me goodbye yet again, and walked off down the quayside street towards the far side of the distant liner.

'You have to get in one of the cars waiting to be loaded,' said Michaelis. 'You hide, then they lift you aboard ship in the car. They tie the cars down on the afterdeck.

'You got a watch? Good. You must wait in car until after dark, seven o'clock. Then the ship will be out at sea and no one will be on deck. You get out of the car, go to the purser's office and give them your ticket. Say you been in the rear bar until then.

'I will take your case on board after you are in the car, leave it at the purser's office, and tell them you are on the ship someplace I don't know.

'This is OK. Not as good as walking aboard, but better than seeing Theodoropoulos.'

132

'Anything is better than that,' I said.

'Yeah.'

He watched Christina's slowly vanishing back for a while. Then at his signal we got to our feet, leaving the suitcase at the café table. We walked off slowly in the opposite direction to Christina, making a wide circle across the quay until we were approaching the stern of the liner just as the girl turned to walk towards it from the other side.

Christina was sauntering up to the big white ship along the edge of the quay, looking up at it in apparent admiration. By this time in the late afternoon the onshore breeze was whipping across the harbour. Her skirt kept blasting waist-high at her inattentive hands.

The policemen watched her approach with heightening interest.

Their backs were turned to us. Michaelis now walked quickly towards the cars parked by the mobile crane, watching the rear of the two policemen intently. He halted suddenly by a Renault with a Paris number plate. It had a couple of bedrolls and what looked like a small inflatable canoe pack in the back seat.

'You hide under that,' said Michaelis. He had a piece of wire in his right hand: within a half second the rear door was open, and locked again behind me.

I was cramped in the rear of the Renault even after pushing the front seats forward, but at least I seemed to be completely hidden from view under the bedrolls. But the car had been parked in the broiling sun all afternoon: it was oppressively, bakingly hot. Both rear windows could come down an inch or two without increasing the chance of detection and I stripped immediately to lie in my shorts under the baggage. Nevertheless I was streaming with sweat like a man in a sauna. I wasn't too sure how long I could take this solar-powered oven without collapsing, and it seemed a wry fate: I'd wanted to get onto a Turkish liner, not into a Turkish bath.

But Michaelis had timed the attempt almost to the minute. I was still settling into position on the car floor when the mobile crane clattered into action outside. There was the noise of voices, and chains being secured; a volley of shouts, and the racket of the crane again. The stevedores were back from the afternoon break to load the cars aboard the ship.

The Renault's turn came in time. As I lay there trying to keep still in my pool of sweat, a clanging at the front of the car told me the carrying cradle was being attached to the wheels. I waited for the same noise at the rear.

Instead there was the sound of a key in the front door. My heart almost stopped as it opened: I lay frozen under the baggage waiting for Theodoropoulos to tear the coverings off me. Instead I heard the grating noise of the handbrake being let off, and somebody grunted near the front wheel. The Renault shifted forward slowly along the uneven quay and there were other shouts from outside the car from the rear and at the front.

I understood suddenly: the method of loading was to lay the cradle on the ground in front of the car and roll it forward into position. The Renault moved a few feet and the hand brake was notched back into place. The car halted with a low shudder, and the front door banged shut. There was a noise of some sort of net coming into position higher on the car's sides, a volley of shouts from the quay, and I felt the vehicle rising and swinging high into space on its way across the liner's side.

We spun a little in the air but of course I could see nothing. After what seemed an endless interval and felt like some wild blind helicopter ride, the Renault came gently to rest. The front door was opened again; the car was pushed back and the unseen cradle removed; and then the crash of shackles began in earnest as she was fixed into place on the liner's deck.

The noises faded as the stevedore gang turned to the other autos in line for transportation. I was safe: all I had to do now was wait for dark. I think I even dozed for a while before I felt the ship's engines reverberating through the bottom of the car, almost below the threshold of hearing. I lay there rigid with suspense until I heard seamen's shouts from the stern, and the hollow sound of a bridge officer, like God on the tannoy, giving the order to let go mooring lines. We were about to depart. I lifted the edge of the bedding roll above my head to give a slit of view through the window: the water of Piraeus harbour was so flat you could feel no motion, but the shaft of sun blasting through the windows above me slowly swung round to a new angle. The liner was away.

By degrees, the oven heat of the car interior eased. We were steaming into a stiff sea breeze now, fresh air was drifting into my baked lungs through the small gaps I'd made at the top of each window, and the sunlight itself was deepening to a mellower yellow from the white glare of day. Evening fell quickly and at the end I was almost comfortable. At six-thirty, some two and a half hours after Michaelis crammed me into the Renault, it was dark enough to slip out.

I got into my clothes again and opened the rear door on the side closest to the stern. I crept on my knees: there appeared to be no one about. I moved round the car in a crouch, as if checking its lashings. Then I straightened up, gave it a last inspection with a look of relieved satisfaction, and walked rapidly forward through a sort of gate in the railed-off cargo section of the deck, to the tourist accommodation amidships.

Since I had not gone through Greek Immigration at the dockside, my passport lacked an exit visa, but the clerk in the purser's was unconcerned. That was a problem for the Greeks: he merely glanced through the German passport for it, and shrugged his shoulders. The ship would not turn back to port because of this. Neither did he see anything peculiar about my late appearance with the ticket. I'd found a washroom on the way to the office and sluiced off the worst effects of spending the afternoon in the oven. What annoyed the clerk was the fact that Michaelis' late booking of my passage had messed up his accommodation plans. Michaelis had bought a cheap Tourist C berth, and the Greek agents had added the name to the manifest without bothering to check the cabin plans: Tourist C was full at this time of year, and the clerk, making angry faces, finally had to give up and allot me a place on my own in a far more comfortable Tourist A cabin. He was expecting a tip for this service, but the other problem which caused great groaning was the nationality of my money. I had a reasonable amount in Greek drachma, and given the uncertainty about the future I wanted to change that rather than break into Bassington's US dollars.

Drachma was not much use to the purser, he pointed out, or to me either on a Turkish ship. With enormous reluctance he offered a ruinous rate of exchange. I accepted, and then tipped him a handsome part of my new Turkish lira. His face softened, just fractionally.

By the time the purser's business was finished, and I had spent half an hour splashing with joyous relief in the shower of my new palatial accommodation, the liner was turning north-east at Cape Sounion for the Andros Passage. Her wake ran sternwards like white lines drawn with a ruler on black glass: the night's only wind came from the ship's own passage. I went up to the foredeck, just behind the lookout stationed at the bow, and watched the dark lump of Andros coming up behind Kea to starboard. Every breath of night air confirmed freedom. I strolled back into the tourist class to find something to eat and a bottle of Turkish wine in the dining room: I slept afterwards without dreams.

The minarets of Istanbul came up through the haze off the Sea of Marmara early the next afternoon. The German passport met no problems at Immigration, though the Customs man who went through my suitcase seemed slightly surprised at its sparse contents. I looked briefly round the crowded hall in the shipping terminal, as a casual arrival might, but there was no one obviously seeking me. It was only when I carried the suitcase out onto the concourse where the taxis waited that a slim figure moved alongside, and a voice with a New York accent said:

'Don't show too much surprise. I'm Pollock – I've been expecting you.'

He was a wiry figure in a shirt and slacks, a couple of inches under six feet, with a close mop of cropped brown curls surrounding a face that seemed bright and youthful until you noticed the lines around the grey eyes. Pollock's words came rapidly, one tumbling into the other, so that anyone who hadn't spent time in New York would have trouble following him. As we shook hands he said: 'Don't talk too much now or in the cab. In this town you can't tell who's understanding English without showing it. I'll take you to my place.'

He took the suitcase and steered me to the taxi rank, climbing into the back of a battered thirty-year-old Buick behind a silent, grease-stained driver who jerked the vehicle into motion without reply to Pollock's mention of an address. The Buick ground its gears up the steep street leading up from the international quay into the new part of the city. As we crept into the traffic Pollock said: 'Bassington should leave tonight.'

'There's a problem? He was supposed to sail the same day I did.'

'Wanted to be sure you left OK. But leave that for now.'

His apartment was a spacious three-roomed affair at the top of a modern concrete block on the hills of Pera to the east of the main thoroughfare, the *Istiklal Caddesi*, up in the new part of town where the streets are wide and lined with trees in an attempt to imitate the better Parisian boulevards. A modern hotel and a curving row of office buildings made up the main-street neighbourhood and you would not have known you were in Turkey, if it wasn't for the scent of spiced food wafting up from the side alleys, and the faint sound of a *zaz* lute playing in 6/5 rhythm somewhere behind the modern buildings. An enterprising cook had set up a restaurant in a back garden of one of the imposing office towers, and Turkey had triumphed over the camouflage of international conformity.

Once aloft and through the door of Pollock's twentieth-floor living room, I was confronted by a spectacular view of the Bosphorus. The apartment looked south-west, and the french windows which opened onto a small balcony commanded everything but the new bridge, out of sight to its left. Tiny ferries crept across in the hazy distance to Uskadar and the Asian shore: below to the right the ferry wharf busied itself under the gaze of Galata Bridge and the minarets of the Sultan Ahmed Mosque.

'Greatest view in the world,' said Pollock, locking the door behind him. He was grinning: the mental defences I'd felt in the cab were gone. He crossed to the window to find some glasses from the cabinet standing at the side.

'Not bad for a boy from Queens, uh? You know something, if you leave the bathroom door open you got the view of the Bosphorus while you use the can. I sit there every morning, taking a crap and looking out at the world's finest harbour, and I think just this, you know, just this moment, makes all the effort worthwhile.'

'What are you doing here?'

'Import-export and travel consultancy. I'm involved in some tourist development here, and on the trade side I got a connection in Turkish wines to Europe: some of them are good quality, and they're cheap. Plus I export carpets and rugs, of course.'

'And antiquities?'

'No way. That's illegal.' He'd taken the remark perfectly straight.

'I'm sorry,' I said, 'that was a joke. I thought Bassington might have told you all about this mess.'

Pollock fetched a litre bottle of Turkish beer out of the fridge in the kitchen.

'No,' he said as he took off the cap, 'all I got was a short code message to pick up a German called Horst

139

Reinhardt, who I'd then discover to be an American called Lancaster, and look after him until Bassington brings a boat across. You can tell me the rest if you want – or not, if you prefer. I'm assuming you want a beer anyway, though.'

'Very certainly,' I said, and I told him the story, over the next couple of bottles.

At the end I said: 'I guess I won't feel really secure until Bassington gets over here with *Andromeda*.'

'Bassington doesn't take stupid chances,' said Pollock. 'If he said he'd do it he must think he can. Considering what police security is like on small Aegean islands I don't see why he can't.

'The telex he sent me under cover said he would be leaving tonight, which I take it means with the boat, but he made no arrangement about radio contact. So I presume he isn't figuring on needing help.'

'Do you reckon they were smuggling drugs on the *caique*, or arms?'

'Drugs, naturally. Can you think of anything else they got here that's small and highly valued?

'And I tell you one thing,' said Pollock, 'that sure isn't the Turkish whores. They're neither – wait till I show you some. Later, when Basso gets here.'

Until then, Pollock wanted me to stay in the apartment, at least during the day. 'I want to hear Bassington's view of things before we take a chance on you going out in the open,' he said. 'What I got from Bassington so far doesn't tell me enough to take any chances.'

He showed me the telex, sent the day before to the address in Pera: Pollock had a Philips telex machine in the second bedroom where he now dumped my suitcase. After the address code the message read in clear:

140

POLLOCK COMMAGENT PERA, SENDING CONSIGN-
MENT GERMAN GOODS BRANDED HORST REIN-
HARDT EXAMERICAN ORIGIN LANCASTER AND CO
STOP PLEASE COLLECT TURKISH MARITIME LINES
ARRIVING ISTANBUL THURSDAY AND HOLD FOR MY
ARRIVAL STOP PLANNING LEAVE BOATWISE TOMOR-
ROW NIGHT ONCE CONSIGNMENT SAFELY SHIPPED
EXPIRAEUS = REGARDS LUBBERLY

'That's his code signature,' said Pollock, 'and of
course the message would have been filed by some
legman at the public telex – it doesn't come from
Bassington's machine. The meaning's clear enough
once you understand the terms we use.

'If he'd seen any need to arrange radio contact in
the meantime he would have included two date-time
groups. The first would have told me what frequency
he'd be using, and the second the time he'd call, so I
could listen out here. I guess your boat has a two-way
short wave set?'

'Standard issue for long-distance sailing.'

'He'd have known that. So he didn't anticipate
problems. At the same time there's no hint in this
as to which terrorist group he thinks may have been
behind the drug-smuggling. If it's a terrorist group at
all. That's the theory-of-the-month with Bassington's
mob at the moment, but I'm not so sure.'

'Aren't you British Intelligence?' I asked him.

He broke into a big, bubbling laugh. 'Jesus, no.
You think the name is Benedict Arnold Pollock?
Official British Intelligence here is a guy at the
Consulate, and the Turks know *all* about him. That's

why Bassington got me to pick you up, I imagine – the other guy would have been spotted.'

'So you're one of ours?'

'I'm not CIA either, if that's what you're thinking. Look, for your purposes just assume I'm wheeling and dealing – but I'm basically on Bassington's side.' The laugh had gone. The steel returned to his glance, as he led the way out of the small bedroom. 'There's a few other people around than just the Brits and the CIA, you know.'

Mossad, I thought, but I wasn't going to take the interrogation further. Pollock brought another beer from the kitchen, and sat down at the picture window with the glasses between us.

'The trouble is,' said Pollock, 'it doesn't quite fit together.' He put his small feet up on the table beside the beer and studied me for a moment.

'You ever heard of Occam's Razor? It's Middle Ages philosophy all about monks counting angels on pin-heads, but Occam had a principle there that makes a lot of sense in this business.'

'I know about Occam,' I said. I must have shown amused surprise, because Pollock took this up.

'Oh, I got plenty of time in Istanbul to do some reading, you know. Anyway, the basis of what Occam was saying is that if an obvious explanation hits you in the mouth, you don't need to waste time looking around for something more complicated. Smuggling goes on all the time round here. Unless there's some real reason to think differently, Occam's Razor looks to me like saying don't worry about the terrorist angle. It's an unlikely explanation you don't need.'

'The big statue of Apollo was a clear fake.'

'That'd be par for the course with a couple of Turks dumb enough to try to run a hot cargo through Greek waters on a boat that was stolen there in the first place.

'But OK, maybe it's stuffed with drugs, maybe there are more aboard the *caique*, that part's likely enough. What worries me is that because according to the girl the trip was set up by Europeans, Bassington concludes it's part of the Turkish urban terrorist link to Europe.

'Now that exists, sure. The problem is that apart from one group, the terrorists here have never been *into* heavy drugs. We've got two mobs with Palestinian links and at least another two who are Muslim fundamentalist and pro-Iran, and the local gang, the Turkish Grey Wolves, who are half radical urban guerrillas and half gangster. They go in for bank robberies, assassinations, and extortion and it's kind of difficult to distinguish the political motive from the profit each time.

'Now the Palestinians don't have good connections here and except for a little hashish-pushing they don't count on the drug scene. I can't see them setting up something like this. The Jehad Holy War group and the other fundamentalists are slightly to the right of the Ayatollah as far as religious fanaticism goes, and it's kind of unlikely they'd get involved with the heroin trade.

'That leaves the Grey Wolves. OK, half of them are straight hoods so they'd be interested in a drugs profit, and they've got links to the terrorist network with the Red Brigades, the IRA and the German factions.

'But they don't need to use boats across the Aegean to move their material. They have solid Soviet backing and they push anything they want to take to Europe straight through Bulgaria. That's how Ali Aca got to Rome to shoot the Pope.'

143

I didn't want to accept Pollock's doubts. They called Bassington into question, and I needed to believe in his omnipotence at this point. He had my ketch. 'Bassington told me the British believe Turkish groups have been drug-smuggling across the Aegean for a long time,' I said.

'That might be what the British believe,' said Pollock. 'You know what *they*'re like. Once they convince themselves of something they think it's a divine ordinance. But as far as I'm concerned, there's dope going out by sea, sure, but so far it hasn't been terrorist-connected.

'Maybe Bassington's got something new, though. But until I find out, you stay tight in this apartment.'

'Why?'

'Because we don't know who the other side are. We don't know who to be afraid of.

'When in doubt, don't put out, that's my motto. I'll send for some food from the restaurant down the back lane. It's not half bad.'

The colours were starting to deepen down on Galata Bridge, and the shadow from the hills of the Old Town towering up on the other bank of the Golden Horn crept slowly towards the crowded quays. I switched my drink to a glass of *raki*, the Turkish equivalent of the Arab *arak* and Greek *ouzo*. Until Bassington arrived it seemed the only way to relax.

Pollock said: 'OK, there's always a first time. Maybe the Grey Wolves have turned to using boats for some reason. But in this business it's always disturbing when something fails to fit the known pattern.

'It makes you suspect there's something you don't know.'

For the next two days I prowled around Pollock's apartment. There was nothing to do but wait, and I've been trained for that: days of waiting outside police stations and army headquarters for news that never arrives tend to develop a certain fatalism.

After a while the whole point is to endure, to demonstrate a capacity to survive unperturbed in the face of certainty that irreplaceable time is being wasted. But of course to achieve this you must have abandoned hope: the journalist exists on the other side of despair, to paraphrase Sartre, because in these situations he is telling himself 'My profession is the business of waiting for valueless things, the sacrifice of boredom in exchange for the details of meaningless murders and ephemeral trivia, and therefore patience and fortitude is the measure of my worth.' If you actually think that something *is* going to happen – worse, if you desperately *want* it to happen – this Buddhist calm can hardly be maintained. The boat was all I had, after all.

Pollock was no fool, and none of this was lost on him. 'Kind of difficult just to hang around, isn't it,' he said. 'Try to remember that if Bassington was in any kind of trouble he'd have a way of letting us know. He would radio to his Athens base, get a message to us. No news is good news.' There was indeed, no news. The Turkish papers had picked up a couple of paragraphs about the original salvage of the *caique* and my subsequent arrest, but after that there was nothing.

Pollock distracted me, very successfully, with a gale of conversation while he was at home in the apartment. Even after a full recital of his autobiography I could not be certain how he fitted into the intelligence network or

145

who his masters really were. Perhaps he was, after all, the wheeler and dealer he claimed to be.

He'd started life with ambitions to be a baseball player, he told me. He wanted to join the Dodgers, which placed him now near his forties, because they were still in NY at the time. After a stint as a conscript in Germany with the Army, he'd finally made it through the minor leagues into the Dodgers' spring training camp. By this time he was a lean and wiry pitcher very proud of his fastball; he hadn't made himself popular in training camp with the manager, who wanted him to throw more curves, and also I suspected because Pollock in his early twenties would have been brash to the point of being painful. Pollock's baseball career came to a sudden end in the second week of spring training. When the Dodgers' star batter of the year came to the plate the manager told Pollock to pitch curves and sinkers, since that was the batter's weak point, and the aggressive struggler from the minor leagues elected to throw a fast pitch instead. The way life works out, Pollock lost his grip halfway through the pitch, and beanballed the team's star batter on his first trip to the plate. As the Dodgers' hope for the World Series was being carried to the ambulance the manager consigned Pollock back to the minor leagues: the boy from Queens caught the next boat back to Germany instead.

'That was the end of baseball for me,' Pollock said. 'I figured if they were going to take a minor mistake that much to heart there wasn't much point spending another three years in the boondocks getting back into position to make another one. So I hightailed off to Germany to sell computer programs, and cars, and anything else that sounded better with an American accent. I always picked up languages fairly easily, and I'd learned plenty

146

of German when I spent eighteen months promising to introduce every Fräulein in sight to Private Elvis Presley back on base.'

He did not seem to have returned to the States for long after that. 'I started selling travel, representing US airlines, and I got involved in German tourist developments in Spain for a while,' he said. 'Travel's a good business to be in. Airline tickets fall off the ceiling every time you sign your name.

'That's how I came to Turkey originally. The future of Turkish tourism is in packaged resort holidays, which is something the Turks have been telling themselves for twenty years without doing anything about it.

'Istanbul's just a straight-out garbage tip, and the whole problem is that when foreign tourists come to Turkey they always arrive here. As soon as they've smelled the shit and seen the Topkapi Museum, Aghia Sophia and Theodosius' city walls they're off home vowing never to return.

'Istanbul doesn't have much else, when you think about it. It's not a comfortable city. Because it's Muslim there's no sidewalk cafés, no leisurely Paris-style street life the way there is in Athens, and the populace spits at Westerners in the street because they're infidels. The air is so polluted from the brown coal they burn on the Bosphorus ferries you get worse bronchitis in the summer here than they do in northern Europe in the winter. It just hangs about in the air because Istanbul is built at the bottom of a bowl of hills. The city's got good food and good ruins, and that's just about enough to entertain a foreigner for half a week.

'If the Turks want to earn a real tourist dollar they've got to concentrate on resort packages in decent hotels down on the Turkish Riviera – the Aegean coast. That's got everything. Great swimming, great snorkelling, lovely relaxing warm climate, plenty of Greek ruins. The food's better than Greece and the wine is excellent. If only the Turks would stop insisting on their lunatic official exchange rate, when every tobacconist will give you double even for American Express cheques, the whole thing would be Paradise at bargain prices.

'But somebody's got to build the hotels first. That's where my Munich friends come in. They see the Turkish Riviera as the new Spain, as far as they're concerned. And Pollock puts the two together, you see.'

'With all that, how do you find the time to get involved in intelligence as well?'

Pollock always refused this question with a laugh. 'Don't you worry yourself about that.'

The life-story revealed itself in instalments across the *raki* in the afternoons, or over large meals ordered from the restaurant behind, great portions of *doner* kebab, dishes of sliced lamb baked with aubergines, or fish from the Bosphorus, with high plates of triangular *borek*, light pastry shells stuffed with egg, cheese, and herbs. I learned to look forward to these intervals when Pollock would whisk me away from concern over Bassington and the boat into his whirling reminiscences. But there were also long periods when he left to pursue his affairs around Istanbul. On the second night he was gone for several evening hours at a meeting of the foreign press club in the Park Hotel: apparently he also found it useful to do some occasional stringing for the *National Inquirer*. 'Turkey's full of bizarre stories,' he said. 'Mayor and village council eaten by wolves – that was absolutely genuine. You don't need to invent anything, even for the American Bela

Lugosi newspapers. And a foreign press pass gets you a free first-class ticket on the rail system, you know.'

At other times he went into seclusion with the telex machine, tapping in full pages of tightly written German for mysterious correspondents in Munich. On the second afternoon I woke from a siesta to find him at work in French, as I gathered dully when he began to shout 'Fucking Frog lunatics!' and asked me if I knew the difference between *immeublement* and *ameublement* which the telex had somehow managed to confuse. 'I took it the first way,' he said, 'and assumed they wanted the block as *immeublement*, to buy on a real estate basis. Now it looks like the fools just want to rent furnished accommodation.'

In all his free moments he was trying to lighten my strain, and I was grateful. By the third day in Pera I think he had even succeeded: all things, when you were with Pollock, began to seem possible and even likely. When he left to make business calls in late morning, I enjoyed some beer, the view of the Bosphorus, and what almost passed for peace of mind.

Pollock was perfectly correct: his apartment had the john with the finest view in the world. In fact I was in there that evening, with the door open, taking a shower and singing to the lights of the Bosphorus with Pollock joining in from the kitchen, when Bassington finally arrived.

He was salt-stained, and sweaty, and anxious to take my place in the shower. He stood there massive in the little bathroom, strewing his clothes into its corners as he stripped in the middle of his first sentence, as ebullient as a fifteen-year-old who just pulled off something no one expected in a junior ball game.

'Perfectly simple trip,' said Bassington. 'Thirty-seven hours, up on the leeward side of Skyros and across to the Dardanelles. Never saw a soul – Theodoropoulos may not even know I've gone, yet.

'She motors very nicely, your boat: she's moored off a fishing village called Karabuga, halfway down the Sea of Marmara. I thought it best not to bring her all the way to Istanbul, but the village copper accepted your Turkish arrival papers from Izmir, plus a handful of dollars, and was as good as gold.'

Bassington was totally naked now, and halfway into the shower, as I began towelling myself.

'But something entirely expected has happened,' he said. He stood there without closing the glass door, his hair and his left shoulder blasted by the water, unwilling for the moment to plunge in.

'The boat is safe, at least for the moment. But the rest of our plan may have been sunk.

'Literally.'

CHAPTER 7

Bassington on Andros

After careful thought, Bassington had decided there was little to gain by trying to get hold of the ketch at Andros straight away. He sat in front of Pollock's picture window now, wrapped in a towel with his hair dripping water from the shower, and explained his change of mind.

Certainly, if he could have got to the boat on the same day I escaped from Munro in the Plaka, the attempt would have been infinitely safer. But Andros was eight hours away by island ferry: and after arranging the business with the German passport at Piraeus he began to realise that even if he left by the first boat, things would have changed by the time he arrived. By then, Athens would be bound to have ordered a local police watch on the ketch, in case their escaped prisoner tried to reclaim it.

Consequently, Bassington decided he lost no real advantage by waiting another day, and by doing so he made certain that the Piraeus departure had gone to plan. Once he knew the *Samsun* had been safely boarded he could leave for Andros with the probability that his cover story about the British Embassy's interest in the ketch would at the very least distract the island policemen. But if he went immediately, and in the meantime the *Samsun* affair went wrong, there was a good chance Theodoropoulos could blow the plan in five minutes' interrogation aboard the Turkish liner. The result would be more than a little embarrassing for Bassington when he found the island police waiting for him.

As it was, the cover story was hardly perfect. Bassington called round at the British Embassy to liberate some letterhead, and typed himself some impressive credentials. Then he manufactured a formal instruction to 'Captain' Bassington to take possession of the ketch *Andromeda* now at Gavrion Harbour, pending further inquiries in Hong Kong. He even tapped out some telex copy on his machine, purporting to be a request from Hong Kong to detain the vessel in response to unspecified debt claims. He felt fairly sure that this would give him a fall-back position if the Gavrion police began asking questions, and in some circumstances might even get him aboard the yacht. But of course an Athens detective like Theodoropoulos would not be impressed for a minute, and once Bassington left Gavrion Harbour and headed north it would fool no one. A consular official from the Athens Embassy would hardly be likely to steer in the general direction of Thessalonika and Turkey to take a yacht into safe custody for Hong Kong creditors: he should be bringing her back in quite the opposite direction, to Piraeus.

Nevertheless, after the *Samsun* left, Bassington felt relatively secure. The cover story was now reasonable insurance, but he hardly expected to require it. The island police would be watching the ferries for a tall, younger American to whom a stout, balding Britisher bore no resemblance. Of course, they would be keep-

152

ing an eye on the ketch as well, but that represented
no problem since Bassington proposed to go aboard at
midnight, when the two-strong Gavrion police force was
unlikely to be manfully maintaining a twenty-four-hour
watch. Particularly since they would have met every
ferry since its owner went missing, and knew he was
not on the island.

Bassington calculated that the earliest Theodoropoulos
could arrange any sort of air search from Athens would
be around ten a.m. the next morning. By that time
Bassington expected to be somewhere north of Skyros,
providing he could get under way from Gavrion around
midnight. That would put him 150 miles in the opposite
direction from the likely search area. Theodoropoulos
would naturally send whatever pilots he could obtain
to the approaches to the Turkish coast south of Chios,
which represented the most direct escape route to a
Turkish port. A yacht with a good diesel could reasonably hope to make most of the trip there in that
time. Bassington might even have taken this direction himself, and tried to sail up the Turkish coast
to Izmir: but he happened to know that it was the
precise area where most units of the Greek navy were
concentrated on manoeuvres, making an arrest at sea
almost inevitable.

On the northerly route, though, Bassington anticipated no problems. Once past Skyros he would cross
the northern Aegean virtually in open sea all the way
to the Dardanelles. There would be little traffic on the
route, and the closest he would sail to Limnos, the biggest island in his track, would be fifteen miles – at which
point *Andromeda* would just be an unidentifiable dot on
the horizon. The plan was good, Bassington thought. In

view of the importance of getting the Apollo's Head evidence to Istanbul, it represented only a modest element of justifiable risk.

It was never Bassington's habit to worry about a situation once he had carefully assessed it. He slept calmly after one-eyed Michaelis phoned with the news of the *Samsun*'s safe departure, and next morning boarded the Andros ferry steamer at Piraeus, almost with the feeling that he was going on holiday. Nice to be away from the office, he told himself: he had dressed in a thin shirt and canvas drill slacks, like any anonymous middle-aged lone male tourist, and in the duffel bag were his sailing sweater, jeans, and deckshoes.

The ferry was not one of the modern motor ships which ply the routes to tourist destinations on the smarter islands. An unfashionably tall funnel betrayed her earlier career on a northern European run in the 1920s: the black smoke wisping out of it into the hazy Piraeus sun also revealed that little had been spent on engine overhauls since Greek owners bought her, on the post-war second-hand market, for service in the Aegean.

There was still half an hour to go before departure. Several elderly Greek ladies, all in black, already lay flat out on the benches in the deck-class section astern, moaning softly and clutching cut lemons, the folk-remedy against sea-sickness whose uselessness they consistently proved on every trip home. One reclined comatose on the deck-boards, a small heap of vomit chiefly composed of horribly digested tomato a few inches from her face, the tribute she had paid the perils of the sea even while the ship was still tied up to the quay. Bassington lit his pipe and strolled amongst the infirm, favouring them with the disencouragement of powerful tobacco fumes like a malevolent reverse-image of Florence Nightingale doing the rounds. *Mal-de-mer*, he believed strongly, was all in the mind.

He was travelling deck-class to maintain the pose as a normal tourist, one of the swarms of Europeans who wander the rocky outcrops of the Aegean each summer with serviceable desert boots and easily portable luggage. It was a further advantage that when you bought a deck class ticket no one bothered to check the passenger's name. But he had not concerned himself to bring food and drink for the voyage. He knew that once the ferry had cast off, the crew tolerated foreign tourists deserting the scenes of distress astern for the bar in the more expensive accommodation.

The old ferry began to roll almost as soon as she slipped through the entrance in the Piraeus seawall, and after Sounion she was pitching heavily in the open sea. The deck-class now was totally miserable. Occasional cold douches of spray slashed over the weather rail across the miserable heaps lying in the open. There was a fair wind up, Bassington judged: but not enough to be a problem after nightfall, when the *meltemi* would die away. He took himself into the bar, and began to drink Fix beer until it came time for lunch. He had an eight-hour trip ahead of him.

Because of the boat's exuberant motion the bar had few active clients. The attendant seemed glad to have someone to serve: the other four people were there not so much for a drink as for the comfort of the leather armchairs. Bassington had two beers and took himself for a walk on deck to check the weather. From the look of the sea the wind was still no more than Force Five to Six, he thought: it was just that the ancient steamer had been designed for the Irish Sea or the Baltic, and was now demonstrating the tendency of her shallow draught and flat bottom to roll around even in a millpond. The Andros plan, like the ferry, remained on course. Which was more than could be said for the ferry's passengers: as Bassington ploughed his way through the oily chicken and tomato stew which was served for lunch in the dining salon he counted only three other takers: an old bearded priest making a quiet meal with his huddled wife in one corner, and a businessman lunching with an Athens paper in the other.

There were still some hours to go. In the bar Bassington found himself an armchair whose occupant had retired to the solace of a bunk, and went to sleep.

The throaty ferry siren woke him sounding for the entry to Gavrion when there was still some ninety minutes of daylight left to the afternoon. The ship's motion was a little quieter now, under the lee of the island, and a few of the passengers were beginning to stagger about in preparation for the landing. Bassington moved sternwards to retrieve his duffel bag, and stood behind the knot of deck passengers gathering at the gangway.

The engine note dropped a tone or two and quietened as the ferry moved into the flat water of the harbour, and the ship slid softly towards her waiting place at the quay. While the ferry slowed and brought up to the quay, Bassington, standing back from the rail, casually studied the boats in the harbour. He spotted the ketch, moored now to a buoy well out from the shore. Bassington noted her black hull and traditional sheer aft from the bowsprit with satisfaction: seen on the horizon, her shape would almost pass for an old *caique*.

But when his eyes came back to the quay he felt a pang of cold shock in his stomach. Standing in front of the harbourmaster and the straggle of grey-shirted wharf hands was a familiar figure in uniform shirt and slacks. Theodoropoulos.

Bassington eased himself into the protection of an alley between two deckhouses. For a moment he could only think that something must have gone wrong on the *Samsun*. Yet when his brain ceased racing this began to seem unlikely: if Theodoropoulos had somehow discovered the scheme to steal the ketch, he would have been waiting out of sight in the village for Bassington to make the incriminating attempt to board, not standing on the quay to meet the ferry. After all, Bassington's trip to Andros in itself meant nothing, and unless he was caught in the act of stealing the ketch, he was proof from arrest.

Bassington considered what he should do. There was certainly no point in meeting Theodoropoulos: it might be better to stay aboard the ferry for the trip round the island to Andros town, and swear blind to the crew that he was just a stupid tourist who mistook his destination. On the other hand, Theodoropoulos' open presence on the quay was intriguing. Bassington wanted to find out what he was doing there: if he went on to Andros town that would mean a trip across the mountain back to Gavrion in any case. If he could find a way of avoiding the police captain, he should go ashore now.

Theodoropoulos stood waiting for the seamen trundling out the ferry's gangway. As Bassington watched him from the cover of the deckhouse, the policeman seemed to catch sight of someone on the ship. His right hand waved above his head in a half salute, half wave. Passengers began to crowd down the gangway: a pushing bunch of the ladies in black, miraculously restored to health by the sheltered harbour and the prospect of landing, three or four grubby single tourists, and then the complement of the first-class cabins. Two army officers, the bearded priest and his wife. And now, a dark-haired girl, carrying a very new-looking blue canvas bag in one hand. She was an American, Bassington decided: no European wore that style of wide Bermuda shorts, with the creases and cuffs immaculately pressed.

She walked straight towards Theodoropoulos, who pushed through the disembarking crowd to meet her. The assumption had to be that this was Nina Millen. But why? Theodoropoulos was smiling, Bassington saw. The police captain took the girl by one arm and led her to the side, talking rapidly. They were moving towards a car, waiting at the end of the wharf. Once Theodoropoulos' back was turned Bassington joined the last of the jostling passengers at the gangplank. It was safe to go ashore.

Bassington walked quickly down the quay and turned to the left, towards the main village, since he had seen the car drive off to the right, away from the waterfront. He switched his thoughts to the question of what Nina Millen was doing there. Could she have been summoned to identify bodies from the *caique*'s Turkish crew? Hardly: they would not have been washed up on this side of the island. Much more likely she was there to give an expert opinion on the *caique*'s cargo of antiquities. But the *caique* was presumably in Piraeus by now: Bassington could see no sign of her in the harbour as he walked into the village.

He turned off into a side street before he reached the wide concourse on the harbour's edge, and doubled back behind the hotel and the waterside restaurants to find a small café out of its line of view. The harbourside was starting to fill after the ferry's arrival with villagers, strolling around in the evening promenade.

Bassington sat down inside the café, ordered himself an *ouzo* and *mezzes*, and studied the other occupants. There were two old men in fisherman's peaked caps playing backgammon, and a third, bare-headed, watching them. As the matronly proprietress fixed the drink and the snacks behind her bar, Bassington heard the syncopated clatter of a helicopter starting up, away outside the village beyond the quay. It had to be the police helicopter, of course. But if Theodoropoulos had that with him, why had he brought the girl over by slow ferry? The helicopter noise increased. It rose, crossed the village at a deafeningly low altitude, and faded slowly to the west.

When the woman brought his drink Bassington spoke in a tourist's slow, imperfect Greek to ask her, with apparent innocence: 'Has Andros got an air service to the mainland now?'

It was the police, said the woman. They were investigating the sensational crime of last week. A Turkish *caique* smuggling arms, and drugs, and a cache of immense wealth was seized after its American skipper killed the mutinous crew for raping his mistress. The *caique* was worth millions.

The backgammon players smiled.

But the helicopter, Bassington asked. Were they still hunting the criminals?

Oh no, said the woman. It was the *caique* that was lost, now. The police hired a big fishing boat to tow her over to Piraeus yesterday. The *caique* filled with water in the rough seas and sank in the Kafireus channel.

Bassington asked if the police could salvage the boat.

Of course, said the café owner, they were working on it now, with the helicopter.

The police *thought* they could, broke in the man who was watching the backgammon game. He began to cackle, and the two players sniggered. The café owner bridled. Certainly they would, she said shrilly. The conversation burst into the machine-gun speed of a Greek debate. They were arguing for their own amusement now, not for the tourist. The café owner, one of nature's conservatives by virtue of her modest asset, attempted valiantly to defend the forces of law and order. The old fishermen had more up-to-date knowledge.

The police divers gave up this morning, said the kibitzer at the backgammon game, triumphantly. The water was too deep for them. They had to wait now for an American expert to arrive from Athens to tell them what to bring up, and how.

The café woman snorted and went back behind the bar. Bassington, pretending not to have followed the rapid-fire discussion, juggled the information in his head until he made it fit.

Since the girl had arrived on the ferry, which sailed from Piraeus before noon, she must have been summoned early in the morning before Theodoropoulos understood the full problems involved in salving the *caique*. The problem would not have appeared so urgent, then.

Of course, Theodoropoulos should have known better, Bassington reflected. He doubted if there was anywhere in the Kafireus Straits less than fifty fathoms deep, and the problem would be worse still in the centre, where the scouring flow of the entire southerly Aegean currents concentrated in a gap that was only seven miles across at its widest. The fact that the police team dived at all suggested the towing crew had tried to get the *caique* inshore when she started to sink. All the same, the bottom shelved deeply in the straits and she could be down in as much as 150 feet of water: too deep for a scuba diver to descend without time-consuming staging on the way back up again. Divers who could spend only five to ten minutes on the bottom could take months to strip the wreck, let alone get into the bilges where the drug cargo was presumably being carried. That might even require a proper salvage vessel equipped with slings.

Bassington could see now why Theodoropoulos had been waiting so anxiously for the girl, and then whisked her off in the helicopter to look at the wreck site. Providence had conveniently provided him with a properly qualified underwater archaeologist, already on her way to the island from rest and recuperation leave in Athens. The logical thing to do would be to put her in police diving gear and send her down to check which antiquities were actually worth saving. The scuba team could then save time by dumping the rest over the side, before lifting the floorboards into the bilges to search for the drugs.

Sitting there with his *ouzo* in the fading daylight, Bassington now saw one other conclusion very clearly. It was imperative to get *Andromeda* away from the island that night, before the girl went down on the wreck and found the Apollo's Head missing.

The sound of the returning helicopter chattered across the village, and died in the area from which it had set out, away to the east. The woman behind the bar switched on the café's complement of naked light globes hanging from the ceiling. Once the purple twilight outside began to fade into proper dark, Bassington paid and left, heading westwards to the village outskirts and onto a dirt road behind. When he had walked about a mile into the hills he halted, and exchanged his clothes for the dark blue sailing shirt and jeans in the duffel bag. Then he found a side track, and branched off across bare country towards the lower slopes of the mountain overlooking Gavrion Bay. Every few seconds the lighthouse at its foot, looking out on the western side of the bay's entrance, flashed its beam across the water and the surrounding hillside. Though no one was in sight, Bassington tried to keep under cover of rock field walls and occasional gullies. He was tracing a long half-circle to cut back to shore less than a mile across the bay from the village.

After twenty minutes or so he made his way down the hill towards the bay, and found himself a convenient hollow, high enough to be out of sight from the waterside track, but with a clear view of the village and the moorings, now less than 900 yards from him. He took a Zeiss monocular from the duffel bag and studied the waterfront and *Andromeda*. He satisfied himself there was no one on board the ketch: the cabin hatch seemed to be firmly shut, she carried no lights, and there was no dinghy at her side. He concluded the local police felt it sufficient to keep an eye on her from shore. And, in fact, there was what appeared to be a policeman, recognisable from his cap, sitting under the bright lights of one of the waterfront restaurants.

Across the water came the noise of the helicopter again. Bassington scanned the sky behind the village with the monocular until he found the machine's flashing navigation light. As he watched, it rose into the sky and came towards him. It passed over his head and directly out to sea. Bassington hoped fervently that Theodoropoulos was on his way back to Athens to resume charge of the manhunt. He returned to his study of the waterfront, and found that there was a line of small fishing boats drawn up on the sand where the seawall ended – between his own position and the ketch. He had no need to go into the village itself to find a way over to the yacht.

There was not much more for Bassington to do, now. He set the alarm on his watch for midnight, and cradled his head on the duffel bag to sleep.

When he woke, one or two lights in the village were still ablaze, burning in abandonment on the quay and in the main square, with a forlorn sort of electronic reproach. The villagers had left these anachronistic totems of modernity to themselves, and gone to their familiar beds. Bassington's monocular discovered the restaurants tight-shut, and the policeman apparently vanished.

But when he looked out to the bay he cursed, fiercely. A straggle of acetylene fishing boats threaded slowly across its still black water, one man crouched in each bow behind the twin lanterns summoning the fish, his assistant standing in the stern, monotonously propelling the oars. The line crept towards the shoreline directly under Bassington's position, and painfully wheeled about for another pass. Twenty minutes later, at the other side of the deep bay, they swung round again, and returned. Bassington swore to himself. There would be no chance of reaching *Andromeda* undetected while the fleet worked the bay. Never had he wished so fervently for a poor catch.

The acetylene fleet went about for an hour. Bassington had almost abandoned hope when the lead boat finally veered off to round the opposite headland, and the others followed to work the next bay.

Bassington got stiffly to his feet and struck off sharply for the beach. He had less time now than he would have wished: the acetylene fishermen would not work all night, he knew. He had to be away before they returned.

In a few minutes down the waterside track he came to the line of beach where the rest of the village's small fishing boats were hauled onto the sand. On the principle that normal actions rarely attract an onlooker's attention, Bassington walked without attempt at concealment straight to the nearest rowing boat, threw in his duffel bag, and pushed it into the water. He climbed over the stern and found the oars. Then, careful to stand amidships facing the bow to row Greek-style, pushing rather than pulling, he set off with his heart pounding, across the dark water to *Andromeda* at her buoy.

As the boat slid silently to the mooring he strained his ears. There was no sound from the village. Quietly Bassington tied the rowing boat to the buoy and scrambled aboard the ketch. He found the boat key still hidden in the cockpit locker as he had been told. He unlocked the cabin hatch and the diesel controls, but left the motor silent for the moment. He merely unlashed the steering, rummaged for the sailbag with the jib in the side locker, and went for'ard to the bow with the sail.

Bassington congratulated himself on double fortune here. *Andromeda*'s number one sail set was a traditional brown, fitting the design and the hull colour, and now offering the additional advantage of night-time camouflage. In addition the boat's police guardians had brought her up to the buoy rather than leaving her at anchor: Bassington was saved the potential problem of alarming the sleepers on shore by a sudden clatter of anchor chain.

He hoisted the jib and watched the sail take in the light night breeze from the shore. There was barely sufficient to fill the canvas — happily, not enough to make it crack. With his knife Bassington slashed the line to the buoy, and made his way back sternwards to take the wheel, and haul in the slack of the sheet.

Slowly and silently the jib bit into the offshore air current, half-filled with the pressure, and bore *Andromeda*'s bows away from the buoy. Bassington put down the helm, and as the ketch turned for the black open sea, let out the jib sheet to belly the sail across the bow rail. *Andromeda* picked up a ghost of white ripple at her throat, and headed in total silence out to sea.

When he was just a mile out from shore, Bassington picked up the distant acetylene fleet from the corner of his eye. They were headed east, away from Gavrion and the ketch. He brought the boat around onto the starboard tack, heading for the Kafireus Strait: and after twenty minutes, he switched on the diesel. The time was one-forty a.m. He was behind schedule, but he still believed he could make it.

Once Bassington had Cape Kakogremi and the 2,200 foot mountain behind it between himself and the village, he pushed the diesel up to full power and turned onto a north-western course. At this late hour he thought he could dispense with his earlier plan to cross quickly to the Euboea shore in order to minimise the chances of detection. When he had brought the Cape Fassa

165

lighthouse sufficiently onto starboard to be sure of clearing the intervening headland, he set *Andromeda* on a course almost due north, to have the effect of crossing the Straits on a long slant as the current pushed her towards Euboea, and give himself a clear run for Skyros.

The current was stronger than he had hoped. Bassington locked the steering wheel and went below to rummage for the hand-bearing compass. He found it in a locker by the navigation table and returned to the cockpit to take bearings from Fassa and the light on Manhili island. When he transferred them to the chart he cursed: the current was bringing *Andromeda*'s forward speed down to some four knots. At this rate he would hardly be out of the Kafireus Strait by dawn.

There wasn't a great deal he could do about that, and for the next half hour he occupied himself handing the jib. Local trading boats rarely used one, and in daylight it would seem unusual from shore. When it was down, he set the mizzen as a riding sail. By this stage he was still not far beyond Cape Nikolaos on the Andros shore. Bassington decided to gamble, and swung the ketch westwards for Euboea.

An hour later, in the shallower water of the western shore, he reckoned the current was easing. *Andromeda* was making five and then six knots according to her bearings from the Fassa light. Then the big light at Cape Kafireus hove into view, at the northern end of the channel. *Andromeda*'s speed was picking up almost with every ten minutes that passed. Bassington began to breathe a little easier. By five a.m. he was just north of the Kafireus light, into the open Aegean, and hitting up eight knots.

At ten o'clock that morning he was nine miles west of Skyros, and, he believed, in the clear.

There was time now to get into the stern lazarette locker and take a look at the Apollo's Head, hidden at the bottom there under the concealing engine parts and spare sails.

CHAPTER 8

Night Games

Bassington's hair had dried in the breeze from the open window, despite the humidity of the darkening afternoon. The Bosphorus in the distance was all copper and purple, and the evening's rapid fall was only a breath or two distant.

'From Skyros onwards it was all plain sailing,' Bassington said buoyantly. He carried his success like a sporting trophy.

'I stayed on a track slightly west of north until I passed Piperi – saw nothing but a couple of fishing boats – and then swung east round about three in the afternoon to leave Limnos to the south around nine that night. By dawn I was halfway up the Dardanelles.

'I thought there might be awkward official questions if I brought her right through to Istanbul. So I parked your boat at the fishing village, Harry. Karabuga's just this side of the Dardanelles – the boat's anchored in quiet water, north-east of the rock in the middle of the harbour there. The village policeman promised to look after her.'

'But what about the Apollo's Head?' I asked him. 'And why do you say the scheme is sunk, when everything seems to have worked?'

'Well, it hasn't,' said Bassington. He got up from the window and looked around to refill his beer glass.

'The bottle's empty,' said Pollock. 'There's just *raki* now, if you'd like some.'

'Marvellous,' Bassington said. As Pollock produced glasses, water, and the bottle, Bassington began to purse his lips thoughtfully.

'For one thing,' he said, watching the clear liquor turning milky with the water and ice, 'I'm almost sure we've been wrong about the Apollo's Head.

'If you were hoping it was a hollowed-out plaster cast filled with grade one heroin you're going to be disappointed. I reckon it's practically all solid stone – the weight alone should have told you that.

'Admittedly, I didn't examine it thoroughly. It was too heavy to shift out of the cockpit locker while we were at sea, and there was no time later. But I had a damned good look at the part I could reach, round the top where you knocked the ear off.

'There's certainly been a very large fibreglass repair job on that side of the head. But underneath the epoxy resin there's solid marble, Harry. I buggered one of your chisels finding that out.

'We can't be sure, of course, but I really think that on the whole the girl was right, old son. It's a genuine Hellenistic carving, with a lot of restoration. So we're back to Plan A as far as evidence goes.'

'Terrific,' said Pollock. 'Now we're right up the Bosphorus without a paddle.'

'Oh, come along,' Bassington said quietly.

'Come along my *ass*, Mike.' Pollock was spitting with exasperation now. 'Just think about it. This guy here is talked into jumping arrest in Athens, and you yourself hi-jack an arrested yacht in Greek waters, all on the strength of uncovering a terrorist plot you're going to lay before the grateful Turks. And what have you got? Fucking nothing! One hot yacht and a badly damaged, slightly renovated antique curio.'

Bassington looked back at him flintily. 'You say peculiar things at times.' The rebuke fell cold between them. 'Very well, that statue's not what we thought it was and the drugs are still in the bilges on the *caique*. The Greek police will find them eventually, and in the meantime we can show that the smuggling run was attempted.'

'If there *are* any drugs,' said Pollock. 'Not only are you minus any evidence at all of terrorist involvement, you don't even know for sure there were drugs on that boat. Has it occurred to you they may just have been small-time street hustlers smuggling pottery souvenirs and old carpet?'

'Hold on,' I said, 'I agree with Mike, here.' Perhaps it was my own need to reassure myself: but I thought I saw a train of logic that gave us at least some purchase on the situation.

'If we analyse what we know about all this it obviously wasn't a penny-ante operation. From what Theodoropoulos told me in Athens, we know the *caique* was stolen in Greece by a mob led by a European. Europeans also turned up heading the mob that loaded her with goods for a smuggling run. We can assume it's the same gang: the odds have to be pretty high against there being two separate groups, both led by Europeans operating out of Turkey, involved in the one affair.

'OK, why does this gang go to the trouble of stealing a Greek yacht? There are plenty of old *caiques* they could get hold of round the coast of Turkey.

'Again, one conclusion seems irresistible. They were going to a lot of trouble to prevent being identified with the boat if the eventual scam went wrong. If they'd bought a *caique* in Turkey it could be traced to them. If they stole one in Turkey there would be a search for it.

'But if they stole one in Greece, the way things are between the two countries just now, there'd be no questions.

'Right. If it was worth their while going to those lengths to get a boat the scam must have been pretty heavy – something that meant long terms in the local penitentiary if they got caught. Plus, there's always Theodoropoulos' point: the *caique* must have been the only damned yacht in the Mediterranean owned by a Thai. Maybe she was already part of a drugs operation. Due to pick a shipment up, maybe. Or perhaps it was already aboard.

'But one way or another, Bassington's on the right track. The odds are there's a big drugs deal somewhere at the bottom of this.'

Pollock had quietened while I was talking. Bassington looked steadily at his glass. After a moment, Pollock said:

'OK, the drugs I buy. The terrorist connection I still say is a long shot. And that's why we're *still* down the Bosphorus without a paddle.'

'For Christ's sake why?' said Bassington, 'how does this change anything? Whatever the statue is, it's evidence of the girl's story, and it's enough to take to Ilderim until the Greek police bring the drugs up off the *caique*.' He turned to me with an explanation. 'Colonel Ilderim is the military cop who heads the anti-terrorist operation in Istanbul.'

171

Pollock slowly unbuttoned his shirt. 'You haven't got nearly enough,' he said.

'Listen,' I said, 'whether the theory is right or wrong, there was still a murder here in Turkey when they snatched the girl aboard the boat.'

'How many murders you think they have in Turkey every year?' said Pollock. 'You think you're going to tell Ilderim, "Look, a guy got himself killed down on some beach we can't precisely identify on the Anatolian coast a couple of weeks ago, and we think you should start digging up 500 miles of shoreline to find him"? Ilderim says "Oh, yeah," and goes back to his sherbet, or whatever keeps him happy in the afternoons.

'And that's the whole point. Ilderim's a straight guy as far we know, but he's not going to be an easy man to influence. The moment he decides you haven't got the evidence of terrorist involvement, the file goes straight across to the regular narcotics squad in the *Polis Karagah*. And that's what we can't afford. From then on everything's out of control. At the very least, it's blown Basso's chances of getting to the terrorists, if they exist.'

Bassington stood up and began to pace around the room, swilling the *raki* in his glass. 'I think we've got to make a start with Ilderim,' he said.

'Listen,' said Pollock, 'we've heard your tale of woe. Let me just give you a different analysis for a minute.

'Never mind convincing Ilderim you have international terrorism at work here, you haven't talked *me* into it yet. You're assuming just because the girl said she heard people speaking English when she was hauled aboard the *caique*, and there was a European involved in the theft off Samos, you've got a line to Red Brigades and Bader-Meinhof.

'Let me tell you, Mike, you don't have to look for terrorism to find European crooks in Turkey. There are Europeans here all ready to smuggle dope, or whatever you fancy, who wouldn't know the IRA from Irgun Zvei Leumi.

'Not only do you have no indication this is a terrorist stunt, logic argues it's much more likely to be just an ordinary criminal caper. When did the terrorist groups last use a smuggling run *across the Aegean*?'

'The French pulled a cargo of arms ten miles off Marseille six months ago,' Bassington said defensively.

'Which was shipped from the Lebanon.'

'The Turkish Grey Wolves are reported to be heavily into the heroin traffic.'

'Which they move through Bulgaria. Who's used the Aegean route apart from straight hoods pushing dope without a thought of politics?'

Pollock sat down again, wearily. 'I tell you what this'll turn out to be,' he said. 'An ordinary drug run, just like any other.

'What all that says is don't bother Ilderim's ass with this shit until you're sure.'

'Why not?' I said.

'You're in Turkey, kiddo. It's not just a matter of going to the cops, it's going to the *right* cops. Ilderim is solely involved in chasing urban guerrillas. If he passes the file on to someone else in the regular force, we could really have security problems, I can tell you. And we don't necessarily even get any action.'

Bassington said in a flat little tone: 'You can't guarantee the police in the drugs section?'

'Nope,' said Pollock.

Bassington considered for a while.

'What you're really saying is, to be sure of getting Ilderim in gear, we need the girl here as well as the Apollo's Head.'

'The chances'd be a whole lot better if you had. She can identify the location where the goods were loaded, she saw the European hoods.'

'Very well, then. I'll make every effort to get her across, starting tomorrow.

'But in the meantime,' Bassington added very firmly, 'I'm sorry, but we're going to have to at least broach the question with Ilderim. We have to play every card we can. I've just stolen a yacht out of police custody and probably screwed up my Greek residence permit for all time, and I'm damn well going to get a result out of it.

'I'll get the first flight to Belgrade tomorrow morning – using *my* shiny West German passport – and thrash back to Athens to somehow persuade Miss Millen to return to Turkey. I'll point out that it was her Turkish colleague who was killed, perhaps – she owes it to him to do something about it.

'One way or the other, I'll get Nina Millen here.

'But I have to introduce Harry to Ilderim before I go. The odds are I may not be able to return to Istanbul for a bit. Theodoropoulos is likely to be peevishly suspicious, to say the least.'

Pollock shrugged his shoulders, seemingly prepared to concede the logic of this. But he told Bassington: 'Just do us all one favour.

'Don't give Ilderim the entire information first off – in case things don't work out, and the file lands up on someone else's desk. Don't tell him you got the statue. Just tell him we're going to have something for him, and he'll get the evidence later.'

174

Bassington thought about that for a time. Then he shook his head. 'We need to give him the statue to get him interested,' he said finally.

Pollock watched him, quietly, as he went to the telephone to book himself an air ticket. First Bassington had to get an answer at the other end, and then there was an agonising wait while they found an English-speaker. Pollock winked at me. Out of the side of his mouth he passed the comment: 'A good soldier leaves himself room to disengage if need be.'

When Bassington had finished on the telephone Pollock dashed off the last of his *raki*.

'Now I know what it's all about,' he said, 'I reckon we can afford to show our faces on the streets. Who's for a night out in the fleshpots?'

Bassington brightened. 'What an excellent notion,' he said. 'I can always sleep on the plane.'

Bassington got into a clean shirt and pants, all we needed on that close summer night, and the three of us piled into Pollock's battered Opel. Pollock headed down the hill to the Istiklal Caddesi. 'Dinner first,' he said, 'to provide blotting paper for later.'

He found a restaurant near Taksim Square, and ordered an immense meal of skewered meat, and salads, and *imam biyaldi*. The name means 'the priest fainted': it is a dish of whole eggplant stewed with tomato, herbs and oil, set on the plate like an *imam* in an old-fashioned black robe lying flat on his back. Pollock claimed it was the best possible foundation for a drinking tour on the town.

Outside the windows the crowd on the sidewalk parted suddenly. There was a distant crash of approaching feet, hitting a stone surface in unison.

175

'Take a look at this,' said Pollock.

Up the rise of the *Istiklal Caddesi* came a file of giants. They were six massive military policemen in white pipe-clayed webbing, huge boots and snowdrop helmets that gave them the appearance of standing seven foot tall, all crashing up the street in the Turkish wrestler's march which stamps the feet into the ground from a high knee lift as the opposite arm is bent and punched into the air. They stared blankly ahead like Anatolian automata: they were terrifying.

'Get in the way, and they'd just stomp you into the ground,' said Pollock approvingly. 'Let's hope none of us ever falls into the hands of the military police. They beat you up on principle even if you're just a witness.'

'What the hell are they?' said Bassington.

'It's the nightly guard for the red-light district going on duty,' Pollock told him. 'They've got the place specially fenced off from the rest of the city, and they control it. We ought to go take a look, it's quite a spectacle.

'And you want to believe, it's safe. . .'

He drove us up after dinner to the high paling wall which surrounds the red-light quarter, with its entrances guarded by the Anatolian giants.

'I'd heard of this,' said Bassington when we got inside, 'but I never expected anything quite so hellish.'

The brothels were set up in low buildings on each side of a couple of wide streets, closed to traffic and garishly lit with sodium vapour lamps on the street poles. Each one was fronted by a long plate-glass window, behind which fifteen or twenty largely overweight whores sat around reading novels in their underwear, or paraded the floor trying to attract the attention of the jostling men outside. Bassington said it was like a sideshow alley at some obscene World's Fair. 'There ought to be someone shouting "Roll up, roll up, fuck the freaks for a quarter".'

But nobody seemed there to buy. The crowd stood eight or nine deep, shoulder to shabby shoulder, stockstill, staring with hopeless lust at the quarantined flesh behind the glass. Just once, in the ten minutes we watched, a man broke away from the audience, fumbling in his hip pocket, and walked rapidly through the sidedoor entrance, moving with the half-crouching embarrassment of someone who can no longer contain himself.

'Fascinating, isn't it?' said Pollock. 'Can you imagine being prepared to pay actual money for one of those large ladies? They charge around a dollar, too.'

A Turk in the crowd in front heard and turned to us, grinning. He spoke to Pollock and jerked his head encouragingly towards the window. Pollock lifted his chin in the traditional East Mediterranean negative gesture – 'Yok,' as Turks say, meaning 'No, in spades' – and grinned back. The man returned to his concentrated appreciation.

Bassington walked on. At the end of the alleyway a military policeman stood impassively.

'He's the only one who's not turned on,' said Pollock.

'Not the only one,' Bassington said.

'Don't worry. I'll take us on to a couple of clubs where the entertainment is more presentable.'

Pollock winked at me again, as Bassington led the way through the fence gates to the Opel. I felt there was some message I was not quite receiving, as if all of a sudden I was sitting helpless in front of a two-way radio set, with the reception crystals producing inadvertent code instead of a voice.

'Sorry about that,' Pollock said as he started the car beyond the fence. 'They're the only legally tolerated whores in Istanbul. And as you might say, literally beyond the pale.

'Strictly low class, as you see. But there are much nicer girls around, in the better-heeled clubs where they can afford to pay police protection. Where you get a wealthier sort of clientele. We'll go look 'em up.'

He drove back towards Pera. In one of the modern streets behind the *Istiklal* he found a place passing as a disco, but with a curious imbalance of men to women at the tables. We drank *raki* while a girl did a belly dance and the customers shouted encouragement.

'They're telling her to get her top off,' said Pollock. 'Some nights she does, depending how she feels.'

'Bangkok this is not,' said Bassington, 'although I'm not complaining.'

I tried to assure Pollock we were not scorning his entertainment. 'I'm quite happy just to tipple the *raki* and watch.'

'That's OK,' he said, 'we'll move on to the hot spot shortly. You'll be surprised.'

It was there at the end of a street five blocks away, advertised by a large red neon sign strung out over the sidewalk. Pollock pulled up the car and watched our faces for a moment, waiting for us to take in the lettering.

The blazing letters spelled out: 'THE SOUTHERN CROSS CLUB.'

'My God,' said Bassington slowly.

'You guessed it already,' said Pollock, starting to giggle, 'Aussies. Once upon a time it was the Greeks who ran the whorehouses, then the Lebanese. Now it's the Australians. They got a taste for it in Manila, took over half of Bangkok until the Thais muscled back in, and now they got girlie bars everywhere, including here.'

'Are they selling Australian beer?'

'That they haven't yet managed in Istanbul,' said Pollock. 'They've fixed damn near everything else, though.'

Pollock got out of the car and led the way. Inside the Southern Cross Club was something almost straight out of Pat Pong Road in Bangkok, but cleaned up. The low-lit bar was long, faced by a maze of low-walled drinking booths, and heavily decorated along the walls with a mismatch of Australian football posters and Turkish peasant handicraft. It was populated with a sprinkling of men and a flotilla of girls in short silk-textured cocktail frocks. Heavy beat music played on the big juke box at the end of the room, and a couple of girls in bikinis writhed about on an elevated platform behind the bar as disco dancers.

'All that's missing is the sex exhibition,' I told Pollock.

'They put that on later,' he said, 'in the private bar.'

Bassington, baying joyfully above the crash of the music, called out 'I haven't seen anything like this in years,' and moved to the bar to buy us drinks.

'It's a novelty for Istanbul,' Pollock told him. 'Started up since you were last here. Must cost them a fortune in bribes.'

'Who runs it?' Bassington asked.

'A big Australian called Murray Tyler. I think he started in the Philippines, but his partner must have levered him out because he moved on, to most places in the east, I gather. Ended up here doing the thing he knows best. He's cashing in on the tourist traffic.'

'You interested in him?'

179

Pollock shook his head. 'He's too smart to be involved in anything you'd be concerned about, and this kind of tourist attraction isn't big enough to appeal to my travel trade investors. I bring some of the visiting Germans here from time to time, that's about it.'

Three of the watching girls moved quickly in to carry our glasses to a booth. Bassington, visibly happier than he had been all evening, bought them drinks as well. The girl who attached herself to my side was a slim brunette with a dress which suited her much better than some of the clothes her colleagues were wearing. She smiled, and pressed my leg. I discovered, as I might have guessed, that she came from one of the Greek families who remained marooned in Istanbul's poorer quarters after the Cyprus troubles. I imagined the Southern Cross Club might have problems attracting a reasonable kind of local girl in Muslim Turkey.

'One can make the usual arrangements later on in the evening, I suppose?' Bassington asked Pollock.

'Oh, can you ever.'

'I shall most certainly postpone sleep until the flight,' said Bassington.

When it came my turn to buy the drinks – we were sticking to *raki*, for safety's sake – the price demanded carved a deep trough in the store of lira I had exchanged on the ship. As I sat down, trying to calculate how much of this I could afford, I felt a new pressure on my left leg simultaneously with the return of my new Greek lady's amatory reminders on the right.

I looked at Pollock, surprised. He winked again, and nodded slightly downwards. 'I'll get it back from Basso in the morning,' he whispered.

I put my hand below the table and found his. His fingers pressed a wad of large notes into my grasp. They felt like 1,000-lira bills. I transferred them surreptitiously to my pants pocket, and began to look forward to the evening.

Bassington's girl was also Greek. He began talking about Athens: oh, how the two Greek girls wanted to go there, they told him wistfully, but their families were in Istanbul. They shrugged their shoulders, trapped in a Turkish whorehouse by the machinations of an uncomprehended nationalism. But the third girl seemed to come from some other, indeterminate minority group: she was talking softly to Pollock in Turkish.

The bar was filling up now with a mixture of well-walleted tourists and young Turkish businessmen. There was laughter coming over the beat of the music, but the only group who could be called noisy were a handful of Germans in the corner by the door. The place had the relaxing feeling of a bar that is well-run, and when Pollock in an aside pointed out the owner, I could understand why.

He stood well over six feet, and he was one of those Australians whose enthusiasm for the beer tankard has added bulk to a body already massively developed by youthful exercise, but without reducing the impression of physical power. His hair was brushed back in gentle grey waves that were curiously in contrast to the face below: with its large irregular bones and small eyes this gave the impression not of distinguished middle age, but smart moves on the waterfront. The bar owner was standing surveying the customers together with a younger man, broad-shouldered and sandy-haired, who was just as tall and looked almost as rugged.

'Handy pair if we ever need some muscle,' said Pollock. 'The older one is Murray Tyler. The other is his Aussie minder.'

Bassington by now was talking Greek to his new friend, but despite this absorption part of his mind was keeping track of the surroundings. He glanced up immediately and nodded.

Pollock looked back at me, but once again I could not quite read his meaning.

At the bar Murray Tyler signalled almost imperceptibly to his senior girl, and turned with his follower back into the interior of the establishment. The girl began passing between the booths, pausing here and there for a whispered word. When she came to our girls she merely nodded. Poppeia, the girl with me, considered briefly and nodded back.

'The back bar will be opening soon,' she told me. 'Would you like to go? There will be a show.'

'And the drinks are *really* expensive,' said Pollock. 'But we can't miss it.'

At the girls' signal we drifted discreetly to the rear, leaving the non-elect tourists carousing in happy innocence in the main bar. The room at the back was dark. Here the drinking booths were set around a dimly lit central stage which was almost the room's sole illumination. The booths' walls were higher than in the front and the booths themselves were smaller. Pollock and I and our girls sat at one table: Bassington and his Greek were at the next one, set two or three feet higher on a sort of platform.

After we ordered drinks, squinting in the dull light at the denominations of the bills in the change, a disco system began to play Turkish music with a heavy beat.

Poppeia took a cigarette out of a pack and removed the tobacco, mixing it with something out of her purse and skilfully replacing the result in the paper. She lit it and passed it round. 'It's OK,' said Pollock, 'just straight hash.'

Bassington, when the joint was passed up to him, took a breath his companion considered greedy. The girls shrieked softly at him, in jest more than anger, and Poppeia began to work on a replacement. Then the whole place hushed, and a girl came on the stage in the opening movements of a belly dance.

At the Southern Cross Club, we discovered, the belly dancers did take off their tops. They also took off their bottoms. And they finished the performance with a slow, languorous exhibition with a champagne bottle.

More was to come. Poppeia was very close to me now, pulling my hands to her breasts and rubbing hers over my groin, interrupted only for a second as a waiter appeared through the gloom to collect an exorbitant cover charge for the six of us. As soon as he had made his Stygian round, two new girls appeared on the dim stage. They stripped off their briefs, and as the music's tempo built up, with the crashing *zaz* and the heavy rhythm supporting the wild cadences of the Orient, one strapped to her loins, as she slowly danced, a monstrously shaped three-foot dildo.

The other girl sank rhythmically to her haunches, offering herself.

Poppeia unzipped my flies and got hold of me, firmly.

The girl with the dildo, in perfect slow time to the remote music, started to operate. No more than three or four inches was penetrating, perhaps; but the sight was astonishing.

183

A great groan came from Bassington, above.

'Christ,' whispered Pollock, 'you've haven't come *already*.'

'With a girl wanking me off like a threshing machine here, and a girl on stage in front of me fucking another girl with a three-foot dildo, what in God's name do you think I've done? Of *course* I've come, you fool.'

'I just hope you can stand up for the second round,' said Pollock, and ordered more *raki*.

Poppeia, softly at work herself, sensed I might be approaching a similar result, and slowed. 'Wait for later,' she said into my ear.

The show that continued was not quite up to the standard of Bangkok before the 80s clean-up, when well-trained Thai vaginal muscles seemed capable of almost anything, firing ping pong balls, smoking cigarettes, and 'drinking' a bottle of water before changing it through some labial legerdemain into what was claimed to be Coca Cola. But it had a slow erotic effect on minds drifting into soft fantasies with the *raki* and the wisps of hashish. When Poppeia suggested we go upstairs, I readily agreed.

Once up a narrow, wallpapered stair, the Southern Cross Club offered a floor or two of what passed, I suppose, for residential chambers – single bedrooms, with a tiny bathroom attached, their real purpose only suggested by the four walls of mirrors which surrounded the bath, and the large expanse of mirrored glass focused on the bed from the ceiling above and the wall on its near side. There was a kind of foyer on the first floor decorated as plushly as a hotel and equipped with a desk, over which a slim clerk entered bookings in a register and collected the house fee for the rooms. Pollock and Bassington followed me, and went off with their girls to their own destinations as Poppeia led me to our assignation.

Lust struggled with the effects of the *raki* within me, and was arbitrated by the calming hashish. *'Inshallah,'* I thought, with the Turkish phrase of submission to the will of God. But Allah had very little to do with what she was proposing.

This was to begin, I gathered, with a bath. 'And then a real Turkish massage,' she said. 'Afterwards, as you wish.'

She filled the bath and gently removed my shirt and slacks. As the bath was filling she added a scented mix which produced a mass of bubbles. Then she turned to to me and slowly took off her clothes.

Poppeia was lovelier by far than the girls who had performed in the sex theatre below. Although the only civilised thing you can do in these circumstances is to sit on the bed and make occasional light conversation, pretending the encounter is the most casual thing in the world – well, actually when you come to consider it that is strictly correct – I managed to observe that she was beautifully slender, with small breasts uptilted to the saucer-sized nipples that many Greek women possess, a combination that makes for unusual sensuality. Greek women at home put on comfortable flesh when they are past their twenties: Poppeia existed in the harder circumstances of the Istanbul slum, and had no such opportunity. She was thin, by Turkish standards. I understood despite the *raki* that she was lovely only to the foreigner's taste, and not according to the local preference for opulent flesh.

She watched my face while she stripped, and because I took the show as casually as I could, she seemed to

185

feel easier. The sense of slight tension with which we had entered the room had vanished. She motioned me into the bath and got in astride my thighs, wetting me, soaping me, and washing every inch with extreme care. Halfway through she turned a switch on the wall and an extension loudspeaker I had not noticed before began to play a radio station softly. Poppeia hummed to its cadences as she worked: she knew the oriental falls of the tunes perfectly.

'Turkish music,' she told me as she gently rubbed the soap into my thighs.

When I was rinsed, and sprayed once more clean of all soap with the hand shower attachment, she moved me out of the bath, carefully towelled me down, and lay me on the firm bed to be massaged not with oil but with talc, scrupulously administered from a vast jar on the side table.

Poppeia understood the art entirely. She began with the extremities, relaxing toes and fingers with pressure and then cracking all the joints to the ankles and wrists. Then she moved upwards, cracking each joint on the way and, it seemed, manipulating each separate muscle in turn. She ended with my back, and then shampooed my neck and the rear of the skull. It was a massage that somehow took the spirit away from the body, removed care, and destroyed concern for both past and future; I lay there totally in the present, as the Buddhists advise, incapable of anger or distress or any of the red passions.

'You want to make love?' she asked, very softly.

I don't think I wanted anything, except for the moment to continue. She must have seen this in my eyes. What she suggested now seemed to me a natural extension of the massage, but it was unusual to be offered it in the east Mediterranean. She gestured to her mouth. It passed my mind that in this place, cosmopolitan notions had percolated even to Turkey – probably via the USAF bases in Anatolia.

I don't believe I would have done anything else. It seems illogical, but part of me retained some sort of bruised intention for Nina. I wasn't even aware of this most of the time, but underneath there was a sense that I had been going to make love to Nina, and even though this hope had been thwarted by something that seemed very like betrayal, for the moment something in the back of my mind still intended her to be my next love.

Mind you, it was a curious kind of fidelity, this bordello morality of mine. I also wanted to do something with this lovely, tragic, soft-handed Greek. I let her know my interest: we bargained her massive price down by half, and she began letting more hot water into the bath, with a newly-sly smile.

At her indication I lay back in the re-warmed bath, with Poppeia crouching naked across me resting my buttocks on her thighs. She bent to work with her mouth. This was delightful; and yet because the bath was not made for someone my size I found that my feet were outside it, tensed in concentration and anticipation now against the wall at the end.

Now because of this – I did not intend the result, I swear – I was arched from my shoulder, up across her thighs, to my pushing feet at the wall, in perfect position for a monumental result.

But as a consequence of the *raki* I was very slow. Poppeia redoubled her efforts, and as she worked brought my left hand to her breast.

Without realising it, she was being enormously successful.

And just to compound this recipe for catastrophe, I had not only played a lot of locker room poker in my youth with the football squad, I had started my career as a lover before the easy days of the Pill.

Away in the Nirvana of *raki*, and hash, and loving lips, I made no sound in the approaching crescendo. Poppeia was at full bore, so to speak, when I unintentionally revived, out of those lost years, the perfect poker-faced example of the Silent Come.

The shrieking, the gagging, the retching over the edge of the bath and the garglings with Listerine that followed, as Poppeia choked in Greek and gestured down her throat, were a shocking marvel to behold.

I lay there, unable to say a word. Poppeia staggered against the door like a figure in an entirely new sort of Greek tragedy. We dried ourselves and dressed silently. I handed her the money with an apologetic face, but she barely softened.

I had taken so long with this act of desecration that Pollock and Bassington were already waiting in the foyer as Poppeia and I came down the hall. She was holding my hand, in the approved fashion, and Pollock called out a comment on my newly beatific expression. But Poppeia was not the loving partner she had been when we went in.

The massive Murray Tyler stood behind the foyer desk, counting the night's takings and giving a bland nod to departing patrons. Poppeia said something sharp and bitter to him in Greek and then left through a side door without another word.

Tyler swung his craggy gaze to me.

'I don't know what you did, you mongrel,' he said, 'but the lady didn't seem to like it.'

'No accounting for tastes,' said Pollock, with unfortunate and unintentional accuracy, taking me by the arm.

'Friend of yours, is he, Pollock?' said Tyler mildly. 'Well, I tell you what, mate, he wants to pick another girl the next time he comes.

'I like people to get along together here, know what I mean?'

'Sure,' said Pollock, 'no problem, Murray,' and led us away.

Tyler was smiling, but there was no joke in his small eyes. I certainly thought I knew what he meant, all right.

The three of us tumbled out through the now-empty front bar into the yellow-lit street. The city was empty. Pollock remembered finally where he had parked the Opel, and drove us back to his apartment, almost without stumbling over the gear shifts.

When I rose, unsteadily, the next morning, Pollock was sitting like a grey agonised ghost by the unopened venetian blinds at the balcony window. His greeting was no more than a soft moan. He gestured at the Turkish coffee pot for me to pour my own cup.

'*Raki* hangovers,' he said finally, 'are the worst.

'You wake up and you think you've got food poisoning, until you remember, Jesus Christ, *the raki*. I reckon there's ten per cent wood alcohol in that stuff.'

'I've felt better myself,' I told him.

He was silent for a while. I sipped the thick, sweet coffee and began to feel a little better.

'Bassington's gone to the airport,' said Pollock suddenly. 'He made a date for you with Ilderim before he left. You've got to be there at eleven, but I guess you'd better take a cab. I don't believe I could drive.'

Pollock subsided. For a few minutes I almost thought he was going to pass out. He was built on a smaller scale than Bassington and I, and the *raki* had taken a greater toll. But when I had finished my coffee he pulled himself together with an effort.

'Listen,' he said, 'Basso changed the plan this morning. He took my advice in the end. All he told Ilderim was that you are here to warn him of a possible terrorist drug run, that you had the guts of the girl's story of the murder, the kidnapping and the smuggling trip, and that we would provide hard evidence when the girl comes back here.

'So what you tell him will now be strictly limited.

'Last night wasn't entirely wasted. Bassington got the message in the end.'

'Ah,' I said, 'I realised you were doing something at the time. I just couldn't work out what it was.'

'I was trying to impress on him that there's a lot goes on in this town you won't get with London bobbies, or even straight Greek cops in Athens. He took the point eventually.'

'I guess he would.'

'So now you have to be careful with Ilderim. In the first place we got to book you in to the Park Hotel down the road, so you've got a legit address to give him without blowing my cover. While you're there you might as well get yourself some new clothes from the tailor's shop in the lobby, because right now you don't look too believable in that cheap Kraut seaman's gear from Piraeus.

'In the second, you go to Ilderim in your new disguise as a legit guy telling nothing but the truth,

190

but you don't let him realise that the boat's in Turkey or that the Apollo's Head is aboard it. All Bassington wants you to say is that you will able to provide him with an archaeological piece from the *caique* at the right time.'

Doubts rose immediately. I trusted Bassington, and Bassington trusted Ilderim. I did not understand Pollock's caution.

'What's the problem?' I said.

'I told you last night. If Bassington can't get the girl over to Istanbul, or some other kind of proof, this isn't a case for the anti-terrorist division,' said Pollock. 'And if the thing goes to another section, God knows what happens. Once they know about the boat, five minutes after the file leaves Ilderim's office and some other cop we don't know takes charge, you could find yourself without a yacht, and Basso could be minus one historic Greek statue. There's no telling.

'Just tell Ilderim you can lead him to the statue when the girl gets here.'

'He's going to be satisfied with that?'

'He's a Turk, he won't be in any hurry. And that way, if the whole investigation goes wrong, you've still got access to your boat. You could sail her down through Turkish waters one night and sneak her across the Aegean to Egypt, using the clearance papers you already have from Izmir. Dump the statue on the beach before you go and leave a message to tell Ilderim where to pick it up. From Egypt you'd be clear to sail along the North African coast to Italy, and you're out of trouble.'

'Jesus, Pollock, the Greeks could arrest the boat and have me extradited in any West European country.'

'The US Embassy can sort that out for you once Bassington gets the girl's story established. Shit, given time you can prove your voyage from Hong Kong. The Greek case against you will never stick outside Athens.

'But if you give the game away here before we know what's going to happen, you could lose the lot.'

I drank my coffee and considered this. Through the slats of the venetian blinds, the view of the Bosphorus seemed obscure this morning.

CHAPTER 9

Ilderim

Pollock worried me. After all, the only thing I really knew about him was that he had been a hospitable host for a few days.

Bassington told me to trust him, but when I considered Pollock now he seemed to have gone out of his way from the beginning to suggest doubts about Bassington – or at least, about Bassington's judgment. I did not even know who Pollock worked for, except that whatever shadowy organisation it was its interests were vaguely on our side. Could I believe this suddenly-mysterious New Yorker now, when he told me Bassington had changed part of the plan – without further discussion with me – in a last-minute aside on his way to the airport?

I felt naked in this situation. The big Englishman had been some kind of familiar reassurance in the sudden flood of unexpected shocks that had assailed me over the last seventy-two hours. I *knew* Bassington and from what I had seen of him in the past I believed he could cope; I'd understood that the underworld twilights into which I had so rapidly fallen were Bassington's familiar surroundings. At the same time, when you are exposed to unusual risks it's natural to approach the next step with caution: and part at least of what Pollock advised seemed to make sense. Knowledge you have to yourself is a kind of power. A sensible man keeps it in reserve when circumstances become doubtful.

So I did not immediately blurt out the whole story as I was ushered into Colonel Ilderim's bare-floored office. And as the interview progressed, this began to seem a wise insurance.

I did my best to come on like a public-spirited citizen, wearing an honest smile and a newly acquired good guys' uniform, in the shape of a Levantine businessman's white cotton suit, bought in the Park Hotel lobby that morning. But heavy-jowled Mustafa Ilderim was not exactly what they mean by your friendly neighbourhood policeman. He had been beautifully shaven a couple of hours before and his hair, not a strand longer than threequarters of an inch, had been meticulously razor-cut very recently. It lay precisely in place, like the lawn at Dachau. His uniform shirt was pressed into knife-edge box-pleats, and his shining face wafted a scent of Turkish lemon cologne across the desk towards me. He bent a clear plastic ruler between his fingers and gave me to understand he was less than excited by Bassington's telephone message.

'Mr Bassington did ring me, very early this morning,' said Ilderim, 'and informed me that you would be coming in to pass some interesting information.

'As I now understand it, what you are saying amounts in fact to the same message. You are saying that you will – eventually – be able to give me some interesting information.'

I thought of forcing things for a minute, and then I waited to see where this was designed to lead.

After half a minute or so Ilderim shrugged. When a Greek shrugs, he is saying to you, You and I, or at least our joint forefathers in the vast and all-encompassing heritage of our civilisation, have understood each other since the beginning of time, and therefore you appreciate, as I do, that at least on this issue, things are against us. When a Turk shrugs, he says simply, You are another fucking Infidel, and you are worth less than a pinch of shit from my dead donkey's asshole.

There was still enough alcohol going through my veins to inspire a slow-thinking man to play it sensibly. Years ago the big tennis players used to like to sleep with a woman the night before a major final for just the same reason. When the edge is off the mechanism of your nervous tension you play on the credit of acquired skill, on motor reaction, on instinct, or whatever you have, and sometimes – in the calm of mild fatigue – this makes you sharper. The tennis people used to talk about a player's 'eye': the big night, within limits, was supposed to be good for the 'eye' the next day. In something of the same effect, I had acquired enough balance from the night before to keep quiet for a moment.

Ilderim broke the silence. 'Bassington *bey* told me that a serious crime was committed, in the course of a smuggling attempt that probably involves drugs, and that you would provide evidence.' '*Bey*' is the strictly formal style of address for any male in modern Turkey – Ataturk made the change to stress the egalitarian style of his new regime – but no one ever uses it in another language. I felt Ilderim employed the term as a kind of tease. '*You* tell me that a serious crime was committed and that the girl will provide the evidence.

'Good: where is the girl? We must obviously now wait for her. I hope she does not suggest that still

195

another witness will furnish the proof. But even then, it will be just her story.'

'You *are* interested in drug-smuggling attempts by terrorist groups?'

'Of course,' he said. 'Once you show me where they occurred. Can you show me?'

'No. The girl said somewhere on the Aegean coast south of Canakkale. East of the Gulf of Syme.'

'Have you any idea how many kilometres of coast that covers?'

Ilderim looked down at his desk, suppressing a slow smile, and then glanced back at me in a friendly sort of way under his neatly trimmed eyebrows.

'There is really very little I can do.' He had given up the game of trying to see how far he could offend me. I think he really felt sorry for me at that point, as if he was talking to a simpleton who had bought shares in a South American gold-mine Bassington had invented.

It was probably that small flicker of sympathy that tempted me to tell him: 'Even without the girl, we do have certain evidence.'

'Indeed.'

'There is a large Hellenistic statue. It was part of the smuggling cargo.'

'Where is it?' said Ilderim. He seemed almost startled.

'I can't give you that information immediately. I know it is not in the possession of the Greek police, but I am unable to tell you where it is. It can be made available to you in due course. When you have spoken to the girl, perhaps.'

'If there really is evidence,' said Ilderim very seriously now, 'it may not be necessary to wait for her after all. What kind of statue?'

'It's a large bust of Apollo. An Apollo's Head.'

'Ah,' said Ilderim. He considered a while. He put the plastic ruler down and reached with one hand into his left desk drawer, without looking, for a set of yellow amber worry beads: he began to play with them while his eyes considered the far wall. 'Presumably the statue came from some archaeological site in Turkey.'

'That is one explanation, yes. Another is that it is a fake which contains some cargo to be smuggled.'

'Why do you think so?' said Ilderim, considering this carefully.

'It looked that way to me.'

'You took it off the *caique*, then. Where?'

'In Andros.'

'And you hid it there? Or on your boat?'

I gave him a few more feet in the fencing match. 'It's on my boat,' I said. 'Or it is, as far as I know. I don't have access to my boat right now. But when you have spoken to the girl, and you need the evidence to support her story, I should be able to provide it.'

'That is *quite* different,' said Colonel Ilderim.

'Of course, it still doesn't tell us where the murder happened, or who was responsible.'

'No,' said Ilderim. He got up from his desk, clicking the worry beads. 'Why did you decide it was a fake?'

'I don't know that it is. Bassington thought not, and he had more time to examine it than I did. But I chipped the head on a winch when I transferred it onto the ketch, and the exposed surface looked like epoxy resin with a stone finish. Bassington thought it was just a repair.'

'What do you think is inside it?'

'Drugs, probably.'

'Drugs,' said Ilderim, 'very likely.' He swung back to me. 'You must produce the statue.'

'I can't.'

'It would be better.'

'I don't have access to it now,' I insisted. Technically, I supposed, that was true. Ilderim looked at me for a long while, and then seemed to accept this suddenly. He went to the window and looked out for a time.

'The statue is your passport out of this trouble, Mr Lancaster.'

'And I'll use it, Colonel. As soon as I'm able to get hold of it, I'll hand it over, so long as you clear this whole mess up and I can straighten things out with the Greeks.'

'Ah, the Greeks. Are they important?'

'I've got a film I want to make there.'

'Of course. So when the girl gets back to Turkey and talks to us, you will produce the statue.'

'Something like that.'

Ilderim went back to studying the morning crowd on Taksim Square. 'Bassington may not persuade the girl to return,' he said after a while. 'Let us assume the statue is not a fake. Bassington believes it is real. We may be able to trace the story back from there, even without Miss Millen's evidence. But the archaeological area is not my province.

'What I would like you to do is to go to Ankara to tell your story to my colleagues there who specialise in archaeological crime. Describe the statue to them. Tell them every detail. They may be able to connect the statue to a gang operating from known sites – they are experts. Even if it is a fake, they would know who could produce such fakes in Turkey.

The epoxy repair, if that is what it is – they will under-stand that too.

'You have time to catch the day train. It is a delight-ful trip. I shall arrange you a ticket and a hotel, if you will go?'

'Of course,' I said. I had very little option, I thought.

Now that I had made contact with the police it seemed wise to be cautious about meeting Pollock. I rang him from the public phone in the Park Hotel lobby, rather than use the one in the room when I collected my spare shirt and pants and cheap suitcase.

He restrained his enthusiasm for the trip to Ankara without enormous difficulty. 'You might as well,' said Pollock. 'See Ankara at Turkish Government expense, I guess. And you never know, the archaeological service might just turn up a lead.'

'I haven't revealed the whereabouts of the large missing article,' I told him.

'Wise. Keep that one face down. We really need to take a good look at it ourselves before we turn it up.'

A black police car ferried me across to the Uskudar Station, and the escorting sergeant requisitioned a first class ticket for Ankara. He wished me a pleasant journey without going so far as to actually smile.

But not even that dark official face could hold back the dawning sense of vacation time. We had barely made the train, and almost the moment I'd settled into a corner seat of the old-fashioned carriage the diesel loco hooted for departure, and the dusty platform began to inch past. I was alone among the faded velvet cushions and ornate light-fittings of the compartment, feeling as if I'd strayed into an illustration in an early edition of Sherlock Holmes. The train crashed over junction points, and started to wind through the tattered suburbs of Uskudar: I began to feel like a tourist instead of a man on the run.

It was quite illogical, of course. In reality I was simply carrying a guilty secret between two police interrogations. But the fact that I was actually *moving*: that no one was on guard, minding the door, concealing my existence or forbidding my departure, made it seem I was simply there to see the sights.

The countryside changes rapidly once the train starts to climb out of the coastal bowl of Istanbul. After an hour or so the narrow-gauge single track begins to draw tight curves round a series of fertile valleys leading up into the inner Anatolian hills, and the dense, luxuriant greenery crowds so close it almost seems to push onto the permanent way.

I went to find the dining car, and settled back to a slow Turkish lunch, of salad, and aubergines, and roast beef, with a bottle of Marmara red. I watched the rich fields appear and vanish through the gaps in the trackside woods. Here in the hills the air was different. Every window in the long car was open, and the breeze of the train's slow ascent came in warm but clean, a wafting freshness drying any humidity left over from muggy Istanbul. As the train wound into new curves to follow the meandering valley, the labouring loco kept coming into view up ahead, making little bursts of noise whenever it left the sound-shadow of the intervening cars, and hooting occasionally on the bends.

There were half a dozen men scattered leisurely in the dining car, and three or four white-aproned waiters.

I took less notice of them than of the passing country-side. Occasionally there were women working in the steep fields, tending vines, or weeding vegetables, and covered always in their veiling head-scarves.

Back in the compartment the wine, and the long lunch, encouraged sleep. And then when I awoke, in late afternoon, the train had debouched out of the mountains onto the great Anatolian plain. Woods and crops were hours behind us in the lower hills: now there were just reddish buttes and flat-topped ranges, away in the distance across a khaki plain as flat as a huge sand-tray, and marked here and there by the single tracks of some long-hauling ox wagon. Here Timurlane's invading Mongols slaughtered the Turkish army and captured the Sultan Beyazit in 1402: the wagon tracks looked as ancient and forlorn as that distant disaster.

Some two hours after the sun died in long maroon shadows across the plain, the diesel express clattered into Ankara.

Timurlane had more immediate effect in Ankara than I did. The security authority had booked me into a high-rise modern hotel on the outskirts. It seemed about as much at home in Turkey as the capital's other square monoliths. The city's embassies and towers of bureaucracy sit baking listlessly on the Anatolian plateau like huge lizards, lazily inspecting each other's Mussolini facades across the empty boulevards, with eyes half-veiled by the blinds in every window drawn against the sun.

A Lieutenant Saklasun called at the hotel next morning from the archaeological section of the Central Police HQ. He left again after twenty minutes' desultory conversation, and I waited a day and half for the telephone to ring.

There are things to see in Ankara – the Hittite Museum, with its massive remains of a civilisation that rivalled Egypt and a Neolithic history the rest of the world is only starting to learn about – and Ataturk's tomb, another monstrous edifice in Mussolini-classical style. Thirty-six hours are about sufficient for a tourist to take all this in. Ankara has a few small restaurants where the food is poor Turkish, and cheap, and some grander places where the food is poor international, and expensive. Having discovered that the Turkish police were picking up the total hotel bill, I was eating in the hotel restaurant and drinking mainly in the bar. But of course I did not need to go the rounds of the tourist sights. I had the Hon Rosemary Bulltine's phone number.

CHAPTER 10

—◆—

Rosemary's News

Her voice was distinctly cool after her maid brought her to the telephone. 'Are you in Turkey, Harry?' she asked.

'Yes, I'm back. I'm sorry for ducking out on the Izmir date.'

'You weren't exactly my favourite person for a while.'

'I'm sorry,' I said. 'I had to go when I did. I was running out of time.'

'From what I hear, you've been running out of luck, too. Weren't you involved in some fracas with a stolen *caique*?'

'You know about that?' I was surprised: there had only been a paragraph or two in the Istanbul papers.

'A little. We heard you'd disappeared from Greece. I suppose that's why you're here. I don't know why you're ringing me, though.'

'I'm helping the Turkish police, Rosemary. That's if they *want* to be helped. Can't we have dinner or something? I'll tell you all about it.'

Her cold defence seemed to capitulate suddenly. 'All right,' she said. 'But don't come here. Where are you staying?'

I told her. 'I'll meet you in the bar at seven o'clock,'

said the efficient Miss Bulltine. 'I'll book the restaurant, if you like - there's a rather modern place up on the hill that's about the best going at the moment.'

Then she hung up. I congratulated myself, foolishly, on having smooothed that one over. I had liked the Hon Rosemary for a long time, and she knew it: I'd made that admiration obvious years before, in a sudden embrace at a stranger's London door. The lovely Bulltine had been the cool intellectual in a curious flotsam of young international agency journalists, second-string political writers from the heavy British papers, and budding career girls. We were all – apart from Rosemary – moving in a kaleidoscope of shifting joy between one another's beds, evenings in Soho Italian restaurants, and leafy summer beer gardens in old pubs on the west side of Hyde Park. Rosemary, fresh from a top-class languages degree at Cambridge and on the point of joining her country's diplomatic service, was the only one permanently unattached. Tall and blonde, long-legged, standing in a bar with a workmanlike pint of British bitter in her hand and the straight back they insist on at the better English girls' schools, Rosemary carried a kind of invisible armour against the vagaries of this minor Bohemia. She was protected by a mixture of her class, background, intelligence – and in a strange way, her own student naivety. No one would do anything so crude as make an obvious pass at Rosemary because they were either subsconsciously frightened, or thought it wasn't fair. Sitting in a Kensington pub with the *Sunday Times* at Sunday lunchtime, she would dissect political questions more perceptively than the professional com-mentators in the group, but you knew at the same time she was ruled by a logic so compelling it paid no regard to the realities of human reactions. In other words, I was in the group that was too frightened to make a real pass. I could not tell where her logic would take us if I did: if something made sense to Rosemary, she would do it, however extreme this appeared to anyone else.

I knew, for example, that the year before young Rosemary had fallen passionately in love with a handsome and wealthy Italian, who had some sort of aristocratic title like her own. That summer in Rome the Italian – idiotic tool of convention – had declined to sleep with the more-than-willing Bulltine because she was at the time a virgin. Rosemary did what to her was the obvious thing. She came straight back to London, screwed a young painter in the group who had admired her for some time (he was too dim to be nervous of her), went back to Rome and told the young nobleman 'Everything's all right, now, I fixed it.' She still could not understand why the Italian, hag-ridden by 2,000 years of patriarchal fixation, would never speak to her again.

It was partly because of this knowledge that the idea of having an affair with Rosemary seemed, then, to carry the same sort of hazards as getting into the saddle on an untrained racehorse. I felt you could never tell to what wild extremes of the landscape this unpredictable young thoroughbred's sudden whims might carry you.

Over the years, of course, I had come to regret that reservation. By the time I came to wait for her in Ankara I understood that what we had taken for neurosis in Rosemary's London days was really a kind of independent strength: but I was about to learn much more.

I took a shower before she arrived, and doused myself in whole handfuls of an Italian aftershave that I'd found in the hotel drugstore. It came in a bottle the shape of a pine cone, and as soon I splashed it round my face I was enveloped in a sort of overwhelming miasma of the Black Forest. Pino Silvestre reduced its wearer to a state of gentle intoxication coupled with vague guilt at the sacrifice of what evidently must have been entire pinewoods in the Italian Alps.

'Christ!' said Rosemary moving into the bar a few minutes later, 'I could smell you from round the corner. That stuff you're wearing would knock over the average Turk at ten paces. *And what in God's name have you done to your hair?*'

'I forgot to tell you I had to change my appearance.'

'You're in disguise as a faggot. Actually, the haircut is quite appealing: but the raving blond hair is a little hard to take on an empty stomach. What in the world have you got yourself into, Harry?'

'It was actually one of your people who suggested it,' I told her, and bought her a drink.

'What do you mean, one of our people?'

'British Intelligence,' I told her under my breath, turning away from the bar, 'in Athens.'

Rosemary moved off to a table on its own against the farther wall. I sat down after her and she said firmly, but without a change of expression: '*British* Intelligence?'

'Oh, nobody a respectable diplomat would know. But it was one of your people who helped me out.'

'This isn't the best place to discuss these things,' said Rosemary. 'Tell me later.'

She chatted about inconsequential matters for a minute or two and finished her drink. Then she said: 'I wonder if you'd mind showing me your room? I quite often have to book visiting firemen into hotels and we use this one a lot. But I've never actually seen the accommodation.'

Once we had taken the lift up to the eleventh floor, Rosemary looked briefly round the carpeted monastic cell, lifted up the telephone, inspected the picture on the wall, and declared the place quite satisfactory. 'Round about the level of the cheaper Hiltons,' she said, 'how's the shower?'

Then she went into the bathroom and turned on the faucets. 'Now,' said Rosemary, 'what's been going on?'

I told her most of the story, briefly, while the shower spewed water loudly behind the glass screens. Out of habit, now, I withheld the fact that the Apollo's Head was aboard *Andromeda*. I also left out most of the sexy bits.

Rosemary looked very thoughtful. 'I'll have to consider this,' she said. 'It's time we left for the restaurant.'

Once we climbed into Rosemary's little English car – 'very cheap here, with diplomatic privileges' – she drove at a leisurely pace onto the boulevard and began questioning me again. I gave her Bassington's name – after all, I knew Rosemary was safe – but did not mention Pollock's.

She was silent again for a while, still driving slowly. Then she said: 'Skipping out on the Greeks seems an awful risk for you to take, but I can see the logic of it.

'Your man in Athens was quite right. In the present political situation over Cyprus you would have been sitting in jail for a year, maybe more, before anything got sorted out. The Greeks aren't doing the Americans any favours just now, and certainly not the Turks. They don't like us that much, either.

'He's probably right about the terrorist link, too, though what you'll find aboard the *caique* is more likely arms than drugs.'

'We thought the opposite.'

'No. Oh, I think some of our European colleagues have suggested a terrorist drug link. The French *Deuxième Bureau* put out a paper on it and the people in Bonn are quite fixated with the notion. But we investigated the idea and we're in no doubt that what they're moving is arms.'

'I understood the British were convinced there was terrorist drug-running.'

'Quite the contrary,' said Rosemary. 'And don't forget we're pretty active in Northern Ireland where the IRA receives all the benefits.

'We've known for years the radical Muslim guerrillas in the Lebanon were providing guns to West European terrorists. They used to get the cargoes out from Tyre and other Lebanese ports, but the Israelis have gunboats patrolling that coast like traffic cops now, and the route is closed. So they've taken to bringing arms and explosives across the Turkish border and shipping them off north of the Israeli cordon. We knew, but the Turks have problems covering the whole Anatolian coastline.'

'Well, Bassington was quite sure the *caique*'s cargo was drugs.'

'That's a little odd, actually. But anyway, whether or not the Greeks find whatever was aboard the *caique*, your best chance of establishing the facts quickly is in Turkey – if you can get the Turks to help.

'The one thing that bothers me, my dear, is we don't have anyone called Bassington in Athens. And we've had no report to warn us we're involved.'

'Well,' I said, 'you wouldn't necessarily know the staff of British Intelligence, would you?'

'Believe me,' said Rosemary, 'I would. I don't have to spell all this out to you, do I?'

'What do you mean?'

'Really, Harry,' said Rosemary Bulltine, '*don't be so naive.*'

And of course I saw it, at last: it was just that I was slow to recognise the lovely Rosemary as the Turkish end of British MI6.

The restaurant sat on a terrace carved out on the top of a hill overlooking the distant capital. At night, the twinkling lights sprinkled all the way to the horizon far below made Ankara look almost like a real city. Once the waiter had brought us the large slabs of tough, pale meat that were passing for an Italian veal-and-asparagus dish, I said: 'If my Athens friend isn't one of yours, who do you think he is?'

'Be careful how you put things here,' said Rosemary mildly. 'You're all right so far, but this *is* a public restaurant in the most intelligence-conscious country in Europe.'

'Very well. But who is he?'

Rosemary chewed her veal for a while, off-handedly. 'Some kind of freelance, I'd imagine. I mean, he might even have done something for us, in the past. I'll check. But I doubt very much if he's one of the opposition, and as far as you're concerned the important thing is you feel certain he is not an ordinary crook.'

'For sure. But so what? I'd like to know who I'm dealing with.'

'Well then, give me the name at the Istanbul end. Don't say it, write it on this.' She reached in her bag and handed me her card and a ballpoint pen.

'Is it safe?'

'You can tear it up and put it in your pocket after-wards. Or eat it, if you insist. The tables aren't bugged, it's just the neighbours and the waiters you have to look out for.'

I considered. I had avoided mentioning Pollock, but things were starting to look black with this new doubt about Bassington. I gave her Pollock's name. After it I wrote: 'Mossad?'

My suave British Third Secretary snorted suddenly in a kind of schoolgirl's strangled laugh, projecting a small piece of the *ersatz* veal halfway across the table. I retrieved the card while she wiped it up.

'Oh Lord,' she said, 'sorry. It's just that we sort of *know* the regular people for that organisation in Istanbul and they're not very like your man sounds from what you said earlier. They're very respectable and very serious middle-aged Jews, not your kind of drinking mates at all, really.'

'Then who is he?'

'Another freelance, I imagine.' She regathered her composure and looked at me seriously. 'Listen,' said Rosemary, 'you say you've known your Athens friend for years and you trust him.' There was a pause while a waiter scurried from across the floor and refilled the wine glasses. When he had gone Rosemary went on:

'You know him. Certainly he seems to have done the right thing by you, up to now. What he did was probably the best course to take at the time. And I doubt if we could have handled it quite like that if the problem had happened here, you know.

'So far, so good, and you really don't have much choice but to stick with Plan A, Harry, do you?

'I mean, I can take an interest, because Her Majesty's Government maintains our usual magnificently superior position that it doesn't matter what new passports you've

210

acquired in the interim, you were born one of ours and you remain one of us. But I can't actually *do* anything except as an absolute last resort.

'In theory you should go to your own embassy right away, but I think they'd very much rather you didn't. They guaranteed you'd appear in a Greek court and then they had to say, "Whoops, sorry about that." If they're suddenly seen to be helping you in Ankara now, my dear, it all begins to look something less than accidental, doesn't it? I'm sure they'd prefer to hear the story after you've found the happy ending.

'So all in all, your best chance is to clear it up with the Turks. You'll find Ilderim is very energetic once he's convinced it's terrorists he's dealing with.'

'Perhaps I should have given him some harder evidence.'

'Do you have any?'

'Actually, yes. I shifted a piece of the antiques cargo onto my boat.'

'I don't think it makes a lot of difference,' said Rosemary. 'I'd imagine they were just smuggling antiquities as a profitable sideline. The real cargo would have been guns and explosives hidden in the bilges. You'll just have to hope the Greeks find it soon, and give Ilderim something to go on.'

She thought for a minute. 'Perhaps I may be able to push them along a little, if I get word to our people in Athens. The official people, that is, not your friend. Considering how important the discovery of this cargo may be to our side, London might even be willing to supply a naval salvage team from Malta to help.

'You'd better keep in touch. Don't phone me at the embassy, though. Better to talk to Jack Terragen at

211

the Istanbul consulate. But be careful what you say on the phone.'

We finished the meal with small talk of people we knew, watching the small twinkling lights of Ankara below. As we walked to her car afterwards, the air was pleasantly fresh, in comparison with the humid nights of Istanbul. Even the question of Bassington's real identity seemed a much smaller problem in the aftermath of dinner and the cool breeze: Ilderim would resolve everything, eventually.

'I'll drive you back to the hotel,' said Rosemary.

'We're not going home for a coffee?'

'Oh no, my dear,' said Bulltine firmly as she got behind the wheel. 'You've no idea how positively nine-teenth century diplomatic society is, particularly in a Muslim country. I can't possibly take you home after dark: it would be round the town in a flash.'

'Well, perhaps I can buy you a drink at the hotel.' I slid an arm gently behind her shoulder, and inclined a winning smile towards her cheek.

Rosemary kissed me, tenderly. She was wearing a French perfume that came to me like the promise of return to sanity from the underworld I had been occupying.

'I'm afraid there's going to be no nookie even there, Harry,' said Rosemary gently. 'If I visited your room at night it would certainly be observed – and reported.

'No,' she said, leaning back from me and starting the car, 'this afternoon was the time for fucking. That was rather the point of the heavy espionage stuff in your room, really. I was surprised you didn't suggest it.'

Lieutenant Saklasun telephoned next morning while I

still lay in my monastic bed, clutching thwarted desire and cursing my slow wits. He proposed to bring me into the office for a more detailed interview. I had something of a *raki* hangover, but I felt fit enough for interrogation after a shower. It did not materialise. Saklasun, translating for his superior, offered observations rather than questions. The section had traced Nina Millen to an American archaeological dig near Trebizond, on the eastern Black Sea coast: they had confirmed that she was missing, but her work in Trebizond could hardly give anyone a lead to what she might have been doing on vacation 700 miles away on the Aegean coast. They had identified the Turk she had been with as a student from Istanbul taking a sabbatical with the American expedition. He had not been heard of lately and could well be missing, but they could not begin to guess on what part of the Aegean coast the reported murder might have taken place.

There were many groups faking antiques, and others smuggling both fake and genuine artefacts out of Turkey. The investigation unit could not divine which group might be responsible for the offences I alleged without further evidence. An inspection of the actual antiquities being smuggled might assist.

If that was not possible, they shrugged their shoulders disinterestedly. I might perhaps return to Istanbul at my convenience. Colonel Ilderim would be in touch.

I took a cab from the police headquarters to the Hittite Museum, caught another once I was sure I had not been followed, and phoned Pollock from the general post office.

'You're not getting anywhere,' said Pollock over the crackling line from Istanbul, 'and there's no word from Bassington about the girl.'

'That's another thing. The Brits say Bassington isn't one of theirs.'

'The Brits wouldn't know their own *assholes*,' said Pollock. 'Listen, haven't you ever heard about left hands and right hands in this business?'

'The Brit I've been talking to seems pretty well-informed. Not only do they not know our friend, their official theory isn't his, at all. They say the cargo on the boat would have been the stuff that goes bang, bang, not the stuff that makes you giggle, you get me?'

'I understand,' said Pollock. 'Listen, so Basso's maybe not what you assumed, but you can still feel OK about him, understand? I can explain when you're back here. Or kind of, anyway. But I can't blame you if you feel this is all getting too complex.

'Maybe you should just leave the statue on the beach and piss off to Egypt, after all.'

'No,' I told Pollock. 'I've got too much invested in going back to Greece with a clear name. I'm going to hand over the statue to Ilderim as a gesture of good faith, and trust the Brits to push along the salvage of the missing goodies in the Aegean. I gather I've screwed up with our people.'

'Why the hell would the Brits do that?'

'They seem to think the things that go bang would have ended up getting aimed at them. Northern Ireland, you know.'

'That's a point,' Pollock said. 'I think you should come back to Istanbul as soon as you can. Let's have a good look at the statue before you hand it over. We should cut right into the middle of this and see what we've got.'

CHAPTER 11

The Striking Acquaintance

It was too late to get a place on the night train, and I went back to the hotel bar to buy a couple of *raki* on the police account. After the third, I was beginning to feel a little more philosophical. Bureaucracies are the same in most countries.

The only police force with a crime detection rate over fifty per cent is in West Germany, where, as they delicately put it, they have a certain tradition of detective work. There was not much chance that a normal cop elsewhere could make anything of the sketchy story I had to tell: perhaps, as he said, Pollock and I had to get hold of this thing ourselves, and wrestle it through to a conclusion. That was if I could depend on Pollock.

A slim man drinking a beer three stools down the bar remarked, in almost perfect English, on my air of content. We were the only guests in the place: evening had hardly fallen. I told him it was because I had just decided to accept fate.

'You are in Ankara for a business deal?' he asked. 'And it goes well?'

'No,' I told him, 'I was here to wrestle with the bureaucracy, and I've lost. Or rather, it was a no-decision bout.'

He lifted his chin in that patient, negative gesture,

and remarked: '*Inshallah*, as we say in Turkey. If God wills it.'

'God did not will it the way I wanted it,' I said. 'So I go back to Istanbul tomorrow, to square one.'

The man nodded, sympathetically. 'I, too,' he said. 'On the train?'

'Yes.'

'We may see each other. But you don't spend much time on trains, I think. Your face is very brown. Perhaps you were on a beach vacation?'

'No,' I told him. 'I've done a great deal of sailing in the last few months. Across the Indian Ocean, through the Red Sea and up to Turkey.'

This interested the thin Turk hugely. He himself was an engineer, he told me, but his father and his uncles had been captains of *caiques* in the coastal trade, and he liked to sail a small yacht on the Sea of Marmara. He moved to the next stool and bought me my next *raki*, his eyes lighting up the way they do when amateur yachties start speaking about the sea. Professional seamen never talk about it with our kind of intensity.

Whenever part-time yachtsmen get into a long conversation the discussion generally gets round to bad-weather sailing. People who have never experienced a really violent storm always have an intriguing doubt in the back of their minds about the way they would cope with it if they did. Selim Kasadar, as he introduced himself, had only been in minor blows around the Sea of Marmara and the northern Aegean coast: he wanted to know how a deep sea gale was best handled in a small boat.

I had to confess that the Indian Ocean had been extraordinarily kind, and that the worst weather I'd met on the whole trip had been in the Aegean.

'Ah,' he said, 'it can be bad there. The seas are so steep. Tell me about it.'

But I wasn't going to explain the details of Nina's rescue and that damned *caique*. I told him instead about the problems in the Straits of Malacca, and how yachtsmen in the East stowed a .30 cal machine gun in the cockpit whenever they could, for defence against the pirates of the Langkawi Islands and the Andamans. He raised his eyebrows. 'You got a machine gun?' he asked.

Despite the *raki* I shrugged, without committing myself. 'They're not easy to buy,' I said. 'But we did have protection.'

He nodded, seriously. 'The police would make great trouble if you had such a gun here.'

'I don't even have the boat here.'

'It's in Greece?' he said.

'Kind of,' I said.

'You have no troubles with our police then,' said Kasadar, assuringly.

'We've decided to leave one another alone,' I told him.

He put down his drink and declined my offer of another round. As he left he said: 'I may see you on the train tomorrow. It is rarely full.'

I thought little more about the conversation at the time. I bought a paperback from the hotel shop and went into dinner. Kasadar's questions seemed quite normal for one man interested in sailing to ask another who shared the same passion. It did strike me that he had been very quick to assume *Andromeda* was in Greece, although I had never told him that was my destination: but I supposed he had gathered this from my mention of the Aegean storm.

I was not surprised to see him on the platform for

217

the train to Istanbul next morning. Once again, there was only a handful of first-class passengers. We nodded at each other and boarded the train separately. I did not meet him again until it was time to thread down the corridors towards the dining car for lunch. Kasadar was sitting alone at the table against the furthest wall of the car. He waved at me, and I joined him.

'We have nothing to do for a long time,' he said, 'except eat and drink. Is not that wonderful? You shall be my guest.'

I protested, but Kasadar was too expansive to be denied. 'My company is very generous,' he said, 'hospitality is important to business in Turkey. They would wish you to be their guest, too. First we shall have some beer and Turkish *hors d'oeuvres*. Then they have steak, today, and some wine. The cooking is quite good on these trains.'

If you're going to be seduced, enjoy it. I settled into the dining car cushions, and began being appreciative as Kasadar called the waiter for a string of dishes and a flow of drinks. The food *was* good, as he said.

'What business are you in?' he asked, quite casually, as the entrées disappeared and the second bottle of Marmara arrived.

'I was in journalism,' I told him. 'Now I'm preparing to make some television programmes.'

'In Turkey?'

'No. Probably in Greece.'

'Ah,' he said, and began to pour the wine. 'Whereabouts in Greece?'

'Some of the islands.'

He nodded, as if I had just confirmed something I had already told him. Food came to the table in a leisurely succession of small dishes, and the long meal drifted on into the afternoon. We were under no pressure to vacate the table: there were not enough passengers on the day train to require a second luncheon sitting.

The rail line had left the high Anatolian plateau just after we started eating, and the train was following the Porsuk river valley down towards the coastal fringe. By the time we finished our coffee in late afternoon the loco was slowing down for the main stop at Eskisehir, a big provincial town halfway down the Porsuk. There were few people on the low platform as the train came to a halt. A handful of travellers got on and off, without haste. Then I saw a boy carrying a jagged square of cardboard with a hand-scrawled message, bawling unintelligibly into each carriage window as he passed.

The message on the card read: 'Lancaster: *telefon.*'

'Christ,' I told Kasadar, 'how can I take a phone call now?'

He leaned out of the window and barked an interrogation at the boy.

'There's a call from Istanbul for you. They say it's urgent. You can take it in the stationmaster's office – the train stops for half an hour here.'

'You sure?'

'Always.'

'Oh, shit,' I said. I hate dismounting from trains, despite all the confidence foreign travellers have in the immutable timetable which is always supposed to give you the opportunity to go buy a sandwich, feed the beggars, get a paper or whatever temptations are offered in the country you are travelling through. I knew a correspondent in Thailand who claimed to have fucked the waitress in the buffet at Phitsanulok during a stop on the Chiangmai express, but I could never show that kind of cool. My mind's eye always sees my travelling sanctuary disappearing into the distance with a farewell toot, leaving me stranded in the alien wilderness.

In addition, when I got to my feet I realised I needed to find a lavatory urgently, after the continuous flow of drink through the afternoon. There would be time, I kept assuring myself. As soon as I clambered down the car steps onto the platform I looked around for the toilets: happily there was one right across from the car door. I moved rapidly inside. As soon as I'd started to walk I'd become desperate for a pee, and the phone call would have to wait.

I stood against the wall there with relief assuaging even the usual stench of a Turkish shithouse.

Then, as I began to zip up with a satisfied languor, there was a rattle outside. I darted to the door, still trying to press the zip closed – the train was moving, lumbering up to go, just the way I always knew they would.

I sprinted for the car door I'd just left, got to the step, jumped aboard and heaved it open. Christ, I was going to have something to say to Kasadar. As the train gathered way I stood at the window, heaving with the exertion and the sudden panic: and then through the moving window I saw Kasadar, walking along the platform outside towards the stationmaster's office, with a purposeful expression on a face that no longer shone with expansive bonhomie.

The platform disappeared from view. The train picked up speed and began to wind again through the country-side. I called the dining car head waiter, who spoke better English than the others.

'Does this train normally stop for thirty minutes at Eskisehir?'

'No,' said the waiter. 'Never.'

There is nothing so immediately sobering as recognising a lethal set-up.

It was past dusk when the train slowed to crawl through the outer suburbs of Uskudar, and dark when we got to the main terminal. The rule in this kind of situation is never to be in the lead through the barriers, or hail the first cab. I let the main knot of passengers make their way off the platform ahead of me, while I pretended my suitcase was a weight I could only carry half a dozen paces before changing arms. There seemed to be no suspicious welcoming committee on the station concourse.

Once outside, I let the first three *dolmus* taxis fill with arriving passengers and drive away. It would safe enough to take the next – the forecourt was nearly empty now, and I did not want to be the last man left on a deserted cab rank.

Another *dolmus* turned the corner onto the carriageway and slowed besides me.

'Beyoglu,' I told the driver, 'Taksim Square,' and he nodded his head at the rear door. I did not propose to take the cab all the way to the Park, but from Taksim it was only a short walk downhill to the hotel area. I put the suitcase in the trunk and climbed in. There were two other passengers – half empty for a *dolmus*, which only runs at a profit if it is packed like a sardine can. One sat in the front with the driver, and the other on the offside of the rear bench seat.

The cab whisked quickly off the station forecourt and down the wide boulevard to the Bosphorus bridge. That wasn't standard practice either. It's cheaper in petrol for a *dolmus* cabbie to take the shorter route by car ferry.

As the driver found a lane on the bridge and began to drive quickly across the water, blasting the warm sea air through the open windows, it struck me suddenly that he had made no attempt to stop to solicit other passengers.

If he had taken the car ferry I could have got out, and slipped ashore at the Galata terminal. But there would be no point in trying to get him to drop me at the other end of the bridge: you come off the freeway there in an empty suburb, and if the Turks in the car had any malevolent plans for my future they would have the upper hand.

I sat tight and concealed my apprehension. As we came off the bridge the driver stayed in the central lane of the freeway, making the long left-hand curve towards Pera and Beyoglu. This was a slight reassurance, and I breathed easier. But as we came up to the modern city centre, he slowed and turned off right into the back streets.

'*Yok*, Taksim,' I said. At the same time the man on my right drew a short, heavy revolver from under his coat, and jerked his chin, signalling me to shut up. The man in the front passenger's seat turned for the first time, sneering, and slowly gestured with his left hand, palm downwards, for silence.

I sat back in the seat. I wasn't in any doubt that I had been targeted, now. A long breath of air escaped my lungs. My hands were on my knees.

I gestured at myself, and said 'Cigarette?' to the man with the gun. He hesitated for a moment and nodded, signing for me to do it slowly. I found a flat pack of Turkish cigarettes in my breast pocket and lit one. I'd been hoping the gas lighter might have enough fuel in it for me to tinker with the valve and thrust it flaming into his face – the man in the front seat did not appear to be armed. The notion failed. The lighter had only about half an inch of flame.

The car was heading briskly down an empty, slow-descending side street, but there was an intersection in the distance ahead. I had to do something quickly, I told myself. Obviously someone wanted the Apollo's Head and felt they needed it fairly badly, whatever it was. I foresaw a painful few minutes while they persuaded themselves I was telling them the truth about its whereabouts, and then a rapid end.

As the *dolmus* slowed towards the intersection I drew deeply on the cigarette until the end was white hot, and then threw it into the gunman's eyes with my right hand, while my left darted for the revolver. The man flinched from the sparks in his face momentarily. It was just enough for me to get hold of the gun and thrust it away from me. Then I gave him my left elbow an inch below his ear: as it landed, his hand tightened on the gun and blasted off a round. The driver in front screamed. The big slug had torn right through the seat into his back.

The car's ancient tyres screeched and the cab spun in a great skid to the other side of the street, crashing across the sidewalk into a building. The dying driver and his front passenger went into the windscreen like the devout Muslims they had no doubt been, butting their heads into an instantly-shattering crystal prayer mat.

I was cushioned from the impact by the front bench seat. The gunman wasn't so lucky. He'd been out cold even before the crash, from the moment I hit him, but his head had fallen forwards. When the cab cannoned into the wall it looked like he'd broken his neck against the seat. The man in front was halfway through the gap where the windscreen had been, bleeding a lot and groaning. I couldn't find the gun on the floor – the whole bench seat had shifted forward – but I decided to leave it with them anyway. The police were going to have one dead *dolmus* driver to think about, and they might as well find the evidence of the way he died.

As soon as that occurred to me, I had the presence of mind to get my case out of the trunk. From the look of the guy in what was left of the windscreen I didn't think anyone would be running after me for a while, but I sprinted down the first turn I found. Then I threaded through the alleyways in the general direction of Taksim.

I was headed, panting and sweating in the hot night, for Pollock's apartment rather than the Park Hotel. I had a fair idea, now, how the gang looking for the Apollo's Head – whoever they were – had gotten onto me.

Happily the elevator to the top floor of Pollock's apartment building was working. After a four-mile trot through the back streets to Taksim and down the boulevard to Pera, I was in no state to climb the stairs. Even more luckily, Pollock was at home: I had not worked out how to get into the place if he had been out.

His face showed clear amazement as he looked up at me in the doorway. I was still running with sweat and the white suit was ripped and grubby where I'd torn a shoulder in the cab crash.

'The neighbourhood cops are short on protection,' I told him. 'I just survived two snatch attempts on the trip back from Ankara.'

'Jesus Christ,' said Pollock, 'how did they get onto you?'

'That's an interesting question,' I said. 'I've been thinking about it half the afternoon. You're going to love the answer.'

'Sit down,' Pollock said. 'I'll get you a beer.'

My breath was coming back. I took the glass from his hand and drank deeply. Then I was ready for explanations.

'There is only reason anyone would want to snatch me,' I told him. 'The Apollo's Head. What else do I have anyone could want? It follows that whoever tried to kidnap me knows about it. They figure I have it — and it's equally clear they don't know where it is.

'How many people know about the Head? One, Bassington. OK, so he's not British MI6, at least officially. But he actually *had* the Head for two whole days while he was bringing the boat here. He didn't need me to get it.

'Two: *you* know, Pollock. I don't really know who you're with, either. But you've known where the Apollo's Head is ever since the night Bassington came here. Once I went to Ankara you could have taken it whenever you wanted.

'Three, my British contact knows I have the Head. But she could have talked me into handing it over without any trouble, believe me. Instead, she agreed I should give it to the Turks.

'The one special thing about the guys who tried to snatch me is that while they know I have the Head, they don't know where I have it.

'Neither does Colonel Ilderim.'

'Christ!' said Pollock in disbelief, 'Ilderim!'

225

'It's got to be either Ilderim or the police I saw in Ankara. Somebody tipped off the gang about me, where I was, and how I was travelling today.

'Somehow I don't think it's the sloppy cops in Ankara. I think the only logical answer is Ilderim.'

'It's logical,' said Pollock. 'Jesus, you were just going to give him the statue, too. So what now?'

'I don't know. But I have to work that out quickly. The mob who are involved with that statue know it's not on the *caique* any more.'

Pollock nodded, and started walking across the room to the balcony. 'Oh, they know that all right,' he said. 'They found that out a few days ago.

'Look who's here — and listen to what *she's* got to say.'

Out in the warm night, sitting in a flurry of white shirt-dress looking out dreamily onto the Bosphorus, I saw Nina.

When our eyes met she rose all at once, and came into my arms, and kissed me.

'Bassington must be more persuasive than I imagined,' I muttered into her hair, 'I never really thought you'd want to come back to Turkey.'

'I didn't, for a while,' she said. Then she pulled back to arms' length, still holding onto my shoulders, finding my eyes with hers.

'But then I realised I had to come to help. I've seen the real Englishman from the *caique*.'

CHAPTER 12

‒‒‒‒

Nina on Andros

Nina had seen the best doctors the American Embassy could recommend. She was pronounced, amazingly, to be in no danger from her ordeal, and she began to relax. By the time the call came from Theodoropoulos on Andros she had even been able to shop for some fresh clothes, on an Embassy-guaranteed advance from American Express.

When she got to the phone the police captain began with deprecatory remarks about island fishermen who thought that when a boat was half-full of water all they had to do was pump her out, to be ready for a tow across the roughest stretch of water in the Aegean. Then he asked for Nina's help.

'If they'd even bothered to look at the *caique*'s seams before they set out I would not have to disturb you,' he said. 'But now she's at the bottom of the Andros Strait. I need your advice about salvaging the cargo.'

'That's kinda deep out there, isn't it?' said Nina.

Theodoropoulos' voice was crackling down the submarine cable from the island. He said something about depth that got caught in the static, and then went on: 'I have one navy diver here. He says getting down is not easy, but experienced men can do it. I still need you to tell him what to bring up.'

The noise on the line cleared. 'Of course I would send the helicopter to collect you,' said Theodoropoulos, 'but it's here with me at Gavrion tonight and I have problems sending it back. We will buy you a first-class passage on tomorrow's ferry and pay all expenses, if you will come.'

Nina felt in no hurry to return to Turkey. She did not, at that point, even want to think about it much: after the nightmare on the *caique* she was not certain she wanted to see a Turk again. What Theodoropoulos was suggesting sounded like an all-expenses-paid diving holiday in the Aegean. She agreed almost immediately.

The ferry trip next day was rough, but Nina was a good sailor. She spent a little time drinking a slow Fix in the first-class bar, watching the tourists turn green. Then, once the old ship passed Sounion, Nina went out onto the top deck, just behind the wing of the bridge. The gale drove her skirt behind her as she leaned across the rail, filling her lungs with the blast from the sea. She was beginning to feel thoroughly clean again. The water was wild with white horses: she reflected idly that it would be some time before the weather was fit for diving. Then she went down to her cabin, and read a book. Working it all out later, she thought she never even saw anyone who might have been Bassington – she did not, of course, know him.

When the ferry pulled into the sudden calm of Gavrion bay late that afternoon, Nina went back on deck to see Theodoropoulos waiting on the quay with a car behind him. Life in this new position as consultant marine archaeologist had the compensation of a little luxury, she thought, descending the first-class gangway to meet him.

'I take you in the car to the helicopter straight away,' said Theodoropoulos. 'There is just enough light left to show you the wreck site, and tomorrow I must be back in Athens.'

Milo, the navy diver, was already in the back of the car.

Nina thought he showed a certain Greek irritation at the prospect of being asked to take orders from a woman. She settled herself beside him while Theodoropoulos climbed in beside the driver, and took a tactful approach. 'Do you think it's a difficult dive?' she asked him like a pupil diffidently approaching her master. 'How deep is the *caique*?'

Milo shrugged. Theodoropoulos turned round in his seat before the diver could go on with his answer. 'The fishing boat turned back to try to beach her when the *caique* started to sink,' said Theodoropoulos. 'They almost got into Aghios Nikolaos bay. She's in perhaps thirty metres of water.'

Say, 100 feet, thought Nina. Just about as far down as a scuba diver could work in comfort.

'That means staging,' she said to Milo, in doubt. Every time the divers came up they would need to pause for a period in the ascent to slowly ease the pressure build-up in the lungs. 'It isn't going to be easy for you.'

Milo shrugged again. '*Diskolos*,' he said, 'difficult.'

'Captain Theodoropoulos,' said Nina, 'if you've got a navy diver, you've got a salvage expert much more competent than I am. And you're going to need him, with a wreck at that depth. What exactly am I supposed to do?'

'I expect to find drugs,' said Theodoropoulos. 'They'll probably be in the boat's keel. That means we will have to get into the – what do you call them – bilges? Underneath that jumble of cargo in the cabin.

'I want it done quickly. We can't raise the *caique* anyway, and Milo says it will take time to bring up all the cargo. So I need you to go down to tell him what is valuable – what we *must* bring up – and what looks like it might contain hidden contents. Then he can dump the rest over the side and leave it at the bottom.'

'The Apollo's Head,' said Nina. 'That's what's valuable. But it's got to weigh at least 300 pounds – 150 kilos. Maybe more.'

Milo spoke a full sentence at last. 'We'll use underwater parachutes – lift bags,' he said.

Nina understood the system, of course. The diver took down waterproof sacks, attached them to the article he wished to bring to the surface, and then inflated them with air from his own system to give them buoyancy. But you couldn't do that efficiently on a big job with simple scuba equipment. She turned to Milo.

'You mean we've got a pump, and air hoses?'

'I have to get them from the mainland,' he said.

'Captain Theodoropoulos,' said Nina flatly, 'you better get used to patience. This is going to take quite a while.'

Milo looked at her sideways and his eyes began to twinkle, in spite of himself. He shot a glance at the back of his superior's head. Theodoropoulos was looking to the front while the car negotiated the narrow village streets. Milo winked rapidly at Nina, and recovered his calm.

'All you have to do is to mark any valuable historical pieces,' said Theodoropoulos. 'Your part will be finished in just a few days.'

230

The car pulled into a field on the edge of the village where the police helicopter stood, its navigation lights already flashing red in the approaching twilight. The three of them tumbled out and Theodoropoulos took Nina's arm to help her into the aircraft.

'We must hurry,' he said. 'I would like to show you the place where the wreck lies tonight. After that Milo will help. I have to go back to Athens first thing tomorrow.

'Not only is there no sign of Lancaster since he escaped the American Embassy official, my men now inform me they could not even keep track of Bassington – you know, the Englishman who let Lancaster walk out of that restaurant. He has disappeared too. No doubt there is a connection.'

The helicopter roared into life; and after thirty throbbing seconds lurched suddenly upwards and away across the village. Nina watched the long shadows behind the houses and the hills, and then as they crossed the coastline tried to study the water below. They had flown four miles to the beach south of the Aghios Nikolaos point, and the sun was low on the port side. In calm weather she would have seen the sea bottom as clear as a Kodak print through the crystal water. But the long, open bay ran with a savage chop, and reflections from the waves almost blinded her.

'There is the *caique*,' shouted Theodoropoulos, oblivious to the problem.

Milo's hand nudged Nina's inboard shoulder as she craned over the portside window. He held out his pair of Polaroids. Nina grinned at him and took them: the sea leapt into focus through the tinted lens, and she found the long shape of the *caique*, lying deep in the crystal water about 300 yards from the shelving beach. She nodded at Theodoropoulos, and automatically worked out the wreck's approximate bearing from the beach's southern headland. She could see from the jumbled movement of the water's surface that strong currents from the Andros Strait swirled around the wreck site. Theodoropoulos tapped the pilot's arm and gestured. The helicopter swung around again for the village.

'What do you think?' shouted Theodoropoulos. 'You can get down and take a look?'

Nina screamed back: 'Sure. Looks like there'll be enough light down there, even at that depth. But it's not going to be an easy dive. The work for him' – she gestured at Milo – 'that's going to be real hard, Captain.'

Theodoropoulos nodded, grimly, and turned back for'ards. At her side, Milo grimaced, hopelessly.

As Nina had anticipated, Theodoropoulos proved a pressing host at dinner. Once he had settled her into the main hotel – where she noted she received a larger, quieter room than the last time – he retired to his own to renew his shave, and picked her up half an hour later to escort her ceremonially along the quay to the restaurant. The table there had been chosen and prepared some time in advance, she thought. There was a white cloth and a cold bottle of Samos wine on the table. The restaurant owner and his waiter stood by deferentially. Once Nina was seated, the waiter brought out a plate of chilled, split sea urchin.

Nina had not eaten them before. Theodoropoulos showed her how to hold the shellfish in a napkin to keep her fingers away from the sharp exterior spines, while she spooned the yellow flesh from the interior.

It tasted curiously like a soft crayfish, she decided. The light hair on the back of Theodoropoulos' hand brushed hers casually as he handed her the next urchin. She was being wooed, she knew.

Over in the corner of the restaurant terrace Milo the diver sat at a less-favoured table. Nina looked up and caught his eye when a *bouzouki* player and a violinist filed into the central space, and prepared to play. Milo lifted his glass towards her, briefly, with a grave smile.

Knees pressed occasionally beneath Nina's table of honour. The captain, spick and span and expansive among this successfully ordered display, leaned back in his chair and inclined his head towards her, smiling widely, indicating the musicians. Simultaneously his right thigh touched hers. Nina expected his hand to follow it at any second. But the pressure faded. Captain Theodoropoulos was romancing her in the way of an attentive, but deliberately not over-familiar, Greek admirer. She was not sure where in this ritual of high-class mating the hard word was supposed to come. Perhaps not even tonight. But she was sure it would, eventually.

Nina understood all this, instantly, and yet as quiet withdrawals followed each soft approach, she relaxed. The *bouzouki* began to play. She did not, she was sure, particularly fancy the Captain. She wondered why for a moment: she was not normally against island romance, and he was good-looking enough, in a very intense, dark way. But as she had felt aboard *Andromeda*, it was too soon for her thoughts to turn to sex.

Theodoropoulos saw that she was suddenly quiet. She wondered if he actually knew what was in her mind. She had not expected him to be one of those singular men who can pick up nuances without words. But perhaps he could: he grinned suddenly, called across the restaurant to the diver, and got up with a handkerchief in his hand. Theodoropoulos was from Athens, and there is no consideration of rank in the slow formalities of Greek traditional dance. Milo came to his feet and silently joined the Captain, taking the other end of the handkerchief.

They dipped, and moved their feet in the set patterns: then one leaped, as the other fell away in choreographic counterpoint. Each in turn put on his show and then waited for the other, in a kind of competition in formal display, like mobile peacocks, while the *bouzouki* and the violin throbbed through the night air.

Theodoropoulos called for a tall glass of *ouzo* from the waiter, and handed it ceremonially to the diver, who bowed to the Captain, and across to Nina, and resumed his seat. Theodoropoulos was hardly even breathing hard as he returned to Nina.

'Later, I show you, perhaps,' he said, and began to attend to the red mullet the waiter now put before him.

Nina began to feel comfortably secure. And perhaps because of that, she started to sense something in the Captain's mood she had not recognised earlier. He was showing off, certainly, displaying the glamorous Athenian wooer's graces perhaps as much for the villagers of Gavrion as for her. But underneath his confidence was not entire. She felt it even before he mentioned his return to Athens again. Perhaps the case was not going as well as he maintained. Of course, with the boat and its evidence out of reach, and the suspects flown. . .

'You wouldn't think,' she said mildly, 'that Lancaster's still in Athens?'

Theodoropoulos' lower lip shrank into a hard, straight line. 'He's certainly still in Greece,' he said. 'Oh, very surely. All departure points have been watched constantly, and he hasn't had time to get up north to a land frontier.

'Maybe he's even still in Athens.

'What I don't understand is this Englishman Bassington. The one who let Lancaster escape. He has lived in Athens for years, his record is clean. He is very close to the British Embassy.' Theodoropoulos looked sideways at her. 'You understand, eh? Everyone has people in Intelligence in our capital. We think Bassington tells the British things.

'So, in the first place why is he friendly with an American drug smuggler? That's a little strange. Then, yesterday, he disappears.'

Nina suggested: 'Perhaps the British are involved somehow?'

Theodoropoulos shrugged his shoulders, and gave her a slightly helpless grimace under his lowered eyebrows.

Good God, thought Nina, he doesn't know. That's his problem – like the wreck, it's all too deep.

There was a movement at her left shoulder. Milo stood there erect, a clean white handkerchief in his right hand. He bowed correctly at the Captain, paused, and said hesitantly to Nina: 'I show you the dance, please?'

The musicians were playing something very slow, and it seemed to Nina they were looking expectantly over to the Captain's table. Theodoropoulos nodded, abstractedly.

'Of course,' she said, in a kind of relief, 'I might just manage a real slow waltz.'

Milo offered her the other end of the handkerchief. 'It's easy,' he said, 'I show.'

'Don't expect anything fancy.'

Nina watched his legs moving in the deliberate steps of the dance – which seemed to be more of a courtly island folk step than the flamboyant Piraeus exhibition the diver had danced with his Captain. She understood what this was, now: an acceptance ceremony. After a few seconds she was able to mimic the diver's steps. He smiled at her, leading her round the floor on the handkerchief until the music ended.

The musicians came to their final chord – and began clapping. 'Very good,' said Milo, grinning. He bowed. 'Everything works fine, now,' he said. Nina could not entirely follow what he meant. The diver saw her puzzlement and explained in a low voice as he led her back to the table: 'The Captain likes to hurry. But we know the best dance is slow, careful.'

Milo winked at her again and retreated. Theodoropolous refilled her glass and toasted her, but she felt the pressure was over. 'Success in Athens,' she wished him as she raised the glass towards him.

Perhaps the reference was not fair. At the end of the night, escape at her bedroom door was simple. The Captain remained deflated.

It was eight-thirty in the morning when somebody noticed *Andromeda* was missing.

Nina was breakfasting with Theodoropoulos in the hotel's little courtyard. There was a burst of voices, and the village police sergeant bustled up the steps with an expression of despair, breaking into a machine-gun volley of anguished Greek at ten yards' range. Milo, impassive, came behind him.

Theodoropoulos screeched back at the sergeant and ran to the courtyard archway and its view of the harbour, with the underling scrambling after him. Milo explained to Nina.

'The ketch is gone.'

'Christ,' said Nina.

Theodoropoulos ran back into the courtyard to snatch up his uniform jacket, still spitting rapid sentences in the direction of the sergeant.

'Lancaster must have come straight over to the island when he escaped,' he told Nina. 'Last night he took the ketch – he must be on the way back to Turkey.

'I'm going to start searching in the chopper, and radio the navy.'

Nina said: 'Maybe the Englishman is with him?'

'Impossible,' said Theodoropoulos, struggling into his jacket and waving the sergeant out ahead. 'Bassington was in Athens yesterday morning and every ferry arrival here has been inspected for days.

'It's Lancaster. Maybe we get him before he reaches Turkey.'

The policemen ran out of the courtyard again, and vanished. Milo sat quietly down opposite Nina, grinned, and ordered himself a coffee.

'If they've been watching every ferry, how did Lancaster get here?' said Nina.

Milo shrugged. 'Maybe before they told the island's police. Maybe on a fishing boat.' His slow, brown eyes were unconvinced. Nina pursed her lips, prompting him further.

237

'The police sergeant says they were only told to look for the American,' he told her suddenly. He raised his chin gently, telling her much more eloquently what he thought of his superiors, and watched to see if she understood.

'So the other man. . .?' she said, and left the question in the air.

'Who knows what he looks like?' said Milo. 'They had a *picture* of the American. They thought they were watching for one man, running, no money. Now there are two men. Maybe they hired a *caique* to bring them across, anything.'

'Will the police find them?'

Milo's chin went up again. 'Is the yacht a fast ship?'

'Pretty good.'

'She could have been taken any time last night. Gavrion was asleep, no? They will be somewhere off Ikaria, halfway to Izmir by now.

'If the police don't find them in three hours, they will reach Turkish waters.'

Milo drank his coffee, watching the morning wind beginning to shake the old hotel's shutters, and flatten the bougainvillea creepers on its walls.

'No diving today,' he said. 'Or tomorrow, I think. The sea is rough in the channel.

'I shall take the ferry to Athens to arrange for the pump-line and the parachutes. I will leave the scuba gear. If you want, use it just to have a look around – the police arranged a motor fishing boat for us. But don't dive on the *caique* till I get back, eh?'

'Of course not,' Nina assured him. 'Not at that depth.'

'OK,' said Milo.

As it happened, it was a full two days before the summer calms returned. Nina occupied the time very happily, looking around the locality. She caught a bus to the little village of Batsi, three miles away, went for a swim on a sheltered bathing beach and hired a ramshackle cab to the ruins of Palaeopolis. What was left of the island's ancient capital proved to be little more than the foundations of a few walls, a well-preserved arch, and two metres of harbourworks mouldering quietly in the clear water. Nina walked around, contemplated the mysteries of time in front of the archway, and went for another swim. Lying on her back in the flat water off the mole, she wondered why the Andriotes had chosen to move their main town from this comparatively sheltered south coast to the gale-swept north. The motivations of Cycladean history were never obvious: there was a period in the first millenium BC and another in the Dark Ages when certain islands shifted their major settlements inland, for fear of pirates, while others apparently in exactly the same situation ignored the risk. On Andros they merely moved from one artificial port on the south coast, good in summer but open to southerly winter gales, to another man-made harbour on the north which was equally defenceless against the violent northerly storms of summer. She could not imagine the reason.

Nina paddled idly in the still sea: her whole career as an archaeologist, it occurred to her, amounted to a forlorn contest between her wits and the logic of people thirty generations before her. That was no immense gap, in geological time, but it produced a mystifying barrier of miscomprehensions for an historian. How could she begin to understand the ancient past when she was so totally uncertain about questions even in her own time

– who, after all, had really taken *Andromeda* out of Andros? She was already beginning to feel even less sure of this puzzle than Theodoropoulos now appeared. And if she could not even answer that, she was in much more frustrating uncertainty about antiquity – though in historical terms it was no more than a couple of dozen lifetimes away.

Nina had grown used to doubts about history. She felt less accustomed to uncertainties about yesterday's fact. The thought made her impatient. She wished Milo would return from his Athens errand. The sea was so flat that afternoon she felt certain diving would have been possible, even across in the Andros Passage at Aghios Nikolaos.

The next morning dawned equally calm. But there had still been no sign of the navy diver on the evening ferry, and Theodoropoulos, after his failure to find *Andromeda* on the southern route to Turkey, had remained in Athens. Nina was anxious to be doing something constructive. She took an early coffee on the waterfront, and then piled Milo's scuba gear into the boat the police sergeant had provided. She had promised not to *dive* on the *caique*, she told herself: but there was no harm in going *snorkelling* in the water above it. Through a face mask she would get a much better view of the wreck's position, and anything which might have happened to it since.

The boat the police had provided was a little fishing *varca*, some sixteen feet long, designed to use a single lateen sail when the breeze was favourable and to be propelled when it blew the wrong way by an oarsman, standing up and facing forwards in the Mediterranean style. But since it was built, the corrupting influence of a son in America had financed the owner to the modern luxury of a neat little Evinrude outboard, which Nina considered was probably more than adequate for the boat's size.

She distrusted locally maintained outboards, but this one started without a qualm, coughing its busy racket into the silent morning, and Nina set out for the mouth of the mile-deep Gavrion Bay. The water was like a mirror, and she cursed Milo inwardly for not returning. In front of her she had her borrowed wet-suit, mask, and one of Milo's air tanks, in case her resolve to keep her promise failed. She knew the beach south of Aghios Nikolaos cape shelved steeply, and it might just be possible they were wrong about the wreck's depth. Perhaps she could drop the *varca*'s anchor close enough to the wreck to get down safely with the tank. But even if that didn't work out, Nina fancied a leisurely snorkel off one of the headlands: Nina knew that the north sides of most Cycladean islands are littered with amphorae and other relics, the debris of 3,000 years of summer storms and lost ships. There was always the chance of finding something interesting.

Once round the protecting headland, she had another two sea miles to motor past the second cape at Aghia Kakogremi. She was out into deep water here: the chart had indicated forty-five fathoms. But the sea was still flat and she had no doubt it was good diving weather at Aghios Nikolaos. Probably had been for most of the previous day, too. Nina was irritated at the delay, and gunned the motor.

To her right, now, was the two-and-a-half mile shallow bay which separates Aghia Kakogremi cape from the serrated beach below Nikolaos where the *caique* lay. It took the *varca* no more than twenty minutes. Then she rounded the small headland that masked the south Nikolaos beach.

She was not prepared for what was waiting there. Her eyes took in the whole scene in one instant of surprise. A large white trawler yacht lay anchored where the *caique* had gone down. No national flag flew from her jackmast. The boat's pilot house and flying bridge atop was well forward in the hull, leaving space at the stern for a large well. Four or five dark men in shirts and trousers stood there around the stumpy derrick mast. Every face was turned towards her.

And at the edge of the group a much taller European with yellow hair was peeling off a wetsuit. Mask and tanks lay on the deck beside him.

Nina's heart bounded. She did not doubt even for a split-second the trawler yacht's purpose. She waved her hand and smiled and shouted 'Good fishing?' and kept the *varca* headed straight past them, across the bay towards Aghios Nikolaos cape.

All at once, in almost the same moment she spoke, the men in the well began to cry, urgently, to the blond man. The words were Turkish. He looked across at her and called in English.

But she knew, even before she heard his voice, who he was. This was not Lancaster. It was the tall man she had glimpsed once before, in hazy outline through the blindfold aboard the *caique* that now lay below them.

With just the same flat English intonation she recognised so well, the exact voice that had told the two Turks to lose her at sea called now: 'Hey, come aboard – wait, we've got something to show you!'

The Turks, she knew, had recognised her. They were indistinguishable to her eyes, but some of them must have been in the party loading the *caique* the day of the kidnap. The Englishman was giving them orders, now. They ran to the bows to struggle with the anchor cable.

Nina turned the throttle handle of the Evinrude to maximum and ran for the Aghios Nikolaos headland. The yacht had been between her and Gavrion almost before that first flash of mutual recognition, and there was no turning back to safety now. But she had a chance: they probably had 150 feet of anchor cable out and by the time they could retrieve it and get under way she could be past the next cape.

Nina sat hunched in the stern of the *varca*, trying to get the bows up on a plane and willing the boat to go faster. Behind her she could see the Englishman urging the Turks on at a handwinch in the bows, and turning to stare in her direction. He was surely coming after her.

The *varca* seemed agonisingly slow, now. She guessed she had a mile and half to go for the cape. She had travelled about 700 yards past the yacht when she saw the anchor come bouncing across the fairleads at her bow, and the two puffs of diesel exhaust announcing that the blond man at the wheel was getting her under way.

The cape was still about a sea mile ahead of her. Almost as if answering the force of her will, the Evinrude seemed to cough slightly and then roar a little stronger from clearing its throat. Given that the trawler yacht astern was headed the wrong way, and now had to describe a tight circle to join her track, she thought she might make it. She began to fumble with her free hand at the air tank and wet suit.

When she turned her head again the trawler behind was headed straight for her. Inexorably it crept up on the little *varca*: the larger trawler, as she expected, slightly had the legs of the Evinrude.

As she got to Aghios Nikolaos cape, the trawler was no more than 500 yards behind.

Nina knew what she had to do. The cape stood at the tip of a high, rocky tongue of land, jutting threequarters of a mile out into the straits and no more than a couple of hundred yards across.

As soon as the *varca* rounded the headland she swung it two points to starboard on course across the next bay, jammed the Evinrude tiller in place with the air tank, and draped Milo's wetsuit over it to resemble a crouching helmsman. Then she pulled on her facemask and lowered herself rapidly – but carefully so as not to disturb the boat's course – over the side. For a moment she held on there. Then she plunged into the sea, as far from the side as she could to avoid the prop. In almost the same moment Nina dived, and headed back for the headland.

She surfaced quickly and struck out as fast as she could for about a minute, until she heard the trawler's diesel round the cape.

Then she dived deep, staying under with her lungs straining until she judged it had gone by.

Nina was gasping for breath when she re-surfaced. With relief she saw the trawler's stern, 600 yards away, on course across the bay away from her, in pursuit of the little *varca*.

Nina's breathing recovered a little. She hit out for the shore, swimming below the surface as much as she could to minimise the chance of being spotted.

A minute later she saw the welcome boulders of the shelving land come into view beneath her. Even better, she realised with a flash of fresh hope that the water on the north side of the point was shallow for a long way out. There was barely six feet of depth beneath her and she was still 100 yards from land: it would be difficult to bring the trawler close in.

She drove herself in towards shore. There was no surf, just the gentle lap of the last of the swell from the Andros Strait. Nina found her footing and splashed through into a small cove a few hundred yards inland from the point. Behind her the trawler was now a mile away, still heading across the bay after the *varca*.

She had a minute or two before they would catch up to the little boat and recognise her stratagem. Panting from the swim, and ducking as low as she could in case any eyes were looking after from the trawler, she scrambled up towards the ridge of the headland. Halfway up there were rocks to use as cover, and then a shallow gulley running off the ridgetop at an angle.

Thankfully, Nina rolled over into it, caught her breath for a few seconds, and then made for the ridge peak under cover of the outer bank. Near the top the bank fell to a height of no more than eighteen inches. She crawled behind it and looked out into the bay. The trawler was stopped now: the *varca* bobbed at its bow and the figures on the deck away in the distance there were stationary. She guessed they would be inspecting the shoreline. For a minute she wondered whether she should try to stay hidden. But the trawler began to edge towards the shore, heading at an angle back on its track, and she knew she could not remain where she was. They certainly could not find her quickly, but logic would bring their search back into this area. She crawled up to the ridge peak, and dropped quickly over to the other side, out of sight.

There was no problem here, for the moment, and she ran as rapidly as she could across the rough ground towards the mainland. The ridge began to descend, now. After a minute she found the reason. The long tongue of land which went out to the cape was split by a shallow channel, halfway to the mainland, which connected the north bay with the south. When she crossed it, she must necessarily be in view of watchers from the trawler still in the northern bay.

But there was no option. Nina collected her strength, left the cover of the descending ridge, and ran helter skelter through the shallows to the eastern side. At her left, she heard the sudden distant throb of the trawler's diesel in answer. They had spotted her.

She had barely 300 yards left to travel to get back onto the main island. By veering to her right as soon as she crossed the channel she returned to cover again under the lee of the ridge, which started to rise once more away from the water. As soon as she left the spit of land, and saw the shoreline bending off to her right, she paused to edge up to the ridge and place the trawler's movements.

Nina was lucky once again. As she had hoped, the trawler had come up against the shallows to the north of the spit as it headed to cut her off. It had moved off to her right, trying to land the Turks halfway up the northern beach, about a mile away.

Nina considered which way to run. There were no roads on this north-west tip of the island, only goat paths and dried gulleys. Neither was there any habitation nearer than the little village of Ano Gavrion, four miles off around the lower slopes of the main mountain, Oros Aghioi Saranda. To head there, or in any other inland direction, meant an uphill jog over rough country and the risk of being cut off on an angle by the Turks running across easier, flatter ground near the shore. But she had no choice: if she stayed on the shore the trawler could intercept her even more rapidly.

Nina, young and also fit after a summer's archaeological dig in Turkish heat, reckoned the inland route gave her the best chance. She sprinted up the first gradients of the mountain, slowed, found a convenient dry riverbed, and half jogged, half scrambled under its cover until she reached a point some 500 feet above the bay.

When her breath finally ran out, she threw herself to the ground and wriggled to a vantage point overlooking the beach. In the distance below, half of the Turks were uncertainly heading along the shoreline. The rest were struggling up the foothills vaguely in the direction of a point halfway between her present position and the inward end of the spit.

They had miscalculated her speed. This realisation gave Nina new energy. She started off again up the riverbed. After about a mile she found herself crossing a path running across to the north-east – to the left of her general direction – between the main bulk of Oros Aghioi Saranda mountain and a smaller peak about half its size, between the mountain and the straits. On an impulse, she headed up the path, putting the lower hill between herself and the trawler. She had now outflanked the searching Turks: they were moving south-east, along the shoreline and through the foothills, while she passed them going in the other direction inland, heading north-east in her hidden mountain valley.

There was no further pursuit. At about noon, north of the smaller peak, Nina fell exhausted into an empty shepherd's hut, and rested until the afternoon was half-way through. No one troubled her. But to be on the safe side, when she had recovered she took a route eastwards around the mountain, along a six mile detour round into Ano Gavrion.

It was dusk before the villagers returned her to Gavrion to break the news to the police sergeant.

Theodoropoulos returned with Milo in the Athens police chopper that night, as soon as he heard about the trawler yacht. His confidence in the Lancaster-Bassington theory was shaken, he admitted, by Nina's new identification of the Englishman from the *caique*. Next day, when Nina and Milo dived on the yacht under the Captain's armed protection, the lines around his mouth deepened further.

As Nina expected, they found the trash from the *caique*'s cargo scattered on the sea bed around her sagging bulwarks. In the cabin, floorboards had been ripped up to expose the bilges.

And the Apollo's Head was gone.

'Didn't Bassington tell you we had it?' I asked her.

'I've never spoken to Bassington,' she said. 'After I got back to Athens two guys in shiny CIA suits came down from the US Embassy and told me in a tactful kind of way they thought the whole investigation had miscued, and suggested I come back to Istanbul to help the Turks sort it out. They gave me a ticket, and told me I'd be met.'

Pollock said: 'I got a telex from Bassington in Belgrade to meet her at the airport. He'd arranged with the

US people to bring her over here, but it seems he didn't mention the Apollo. When he left, he didn't think it was all that important, remember.'

We'd broken out the *raki* while Nina was talking. She was sitting with her back to the window, wearing a slightly puzzled expression now. Pollock looked very serious. I felt that I was getting to grips with the mystery at last.

'The conclusion,' I said, 'is really pretty clear.' I was on my feet, walking around the apartment, thinking out the connection of one fact to another.

'Bassington was right the first time, and wrong the second. The only thing that really mattered aboard that damned *caique* was the Apollo's Head.'

I turned to Nina. 'How much is it really worth? On the boat you told me fifty grand.'

'I'm not an expert on the black market,' Nina said. 'Maybe I guessed high. Hellenistic statuary isn't that rare – most museums have that sort of thing. But I'd still say a collector would pay around that: thirty or forty thousand, anyway.'

'That's not enough to explain all this,' said Pollock.

This had been my conclusion, too. 'Still, the main value in the *caique*'s cargo was the Head. Perhaps there was some other stuff, but the statue was the big ticket item. So the Brits are wrong. It's not arms. Bassington was right – and wrong. It's drugs, but they're inside the fake Head. It wouldn't be difficult to hide a million bucks' worth of heroin inside that epoxy repair job.

'After the gang dived on the caique, they assumed Theodoropoulos and the Greek police had lifted it. Just as when Nina found it was gone, Theodoropoulos assumed the Turks had taken it back.

'No one knew any different until a few days ago. While the gang still thought the statue was on the *caique*, and later when they believed the Greek police had it, we had no trouble. But right after I saw Ilderim the trouble began.'

'If you hadn't been smart,' said Pollock, 'right now you'd be answering questions about the Apollo's Head with an electric flex taped to your balls. But can we be sure the leak isn't in Ankara?'

'Maybe there's a slim chance it is. But the Ankara police really didn't take much notice. The chances have to be 80 in 100 it was Ilderim. It all fits too well: he could hardly snatch me in police headquarters, and the Park Hotel is a fraction too public. But if he ships me off to Ankara to talk to the bureaucrats there, he's made the right official-type police move, it's off his doorstep, and when I'm snatched it can't come back to him. Plus Ankara doesn't care about the story anyway, so maybe the fuss will all go away.'

'Yeah,' Pollock said wearily. 'It doesn't gel with what we thought about Ilderim being a straight cop, but maybe he's only square as far as terrorism is concerned. And this is drugs, just as Bassington thought.'

'Sure. We're going to find that statue is stuffed full of heroin. Any idea how much 100 kilos of the stuff would be worth on the streets?'

'Millions,' said Pollock. 'But what do we do now?'

'I'm sure as hell not going back to the cops here,' I told him. He made a dissenting face. 'No way,' I said. 'You had your doubts about the drug section before, remember, and there's still a chance my problem is not just Ilderim, but other officers too.'

Pollock got to his feet, and walked away from where I

was standing. He thought for a while and said, 'Yeah, I suppose that makes some sense. I guess I couldn't guarantee your security in these circumstances. But what's the option?'

'Only one choice,' I said. 'I'm going to drive out to *Andromeda* tonight, and sail the Apollo's Head back to Theodoropoulos.'

'Shit!' Pollock said, laughing at the same time.

'Why not? It's four to one Ilderim's bent, but in view of the one chance in five it's someone else in the police force I can't take a risk on going to *anyone* in Istanbul. But Theodoropoulos already knows I wasn't one of the gang, from what Nina told him. If I take the really valuable evidence back to him I've cleared myself, in the country where it matters to me. Leave it to Bassington to settle Ilderim's hash.'

'You know,' Pollock said, 'it makes sense. You got to get out of here tonight, though, both of you. Do you reckon the boat's got enough fuel left to reach Greece?'

'Bassington said there was some. As long as there's enough left to get through the Dardanelles we'll be OK. There's a three-knot easterly current in the Straits to help us, and all we have to do then is sail down to Lesbos and get Theodoropoulos on the radio.

'I'd like to drive down and pick her up tonight.'

'Right,' said Pollock, 'I'll take you.'

'OK,' I said, 'but one thing first. I want to know, now, who Bassington and you are working for.'

Pollock's face was unmoved. 'Didn't anyone ever give you the bit about looking gift horses in the mouth? If your British friend didn't tell you Bassington's background, I'm not going to. The only thing that matters to you is that he and I are on your side, and Ilderim isn't.'

'I need to know.'

'You need a driver to take you down to *Andromeda*. You got one. That's all you get.

'But first the little lady and I need something to eat. You may be OK, you had a boozy lunch on the train by the sound of it, but we've been waiting for you all night.

'I'll ring down to the restaurant in back and get something sent up.'

I decided not to argue further. The real point, now, was to get to *Andromeda*. Pollock spent a little time on the phone, ringing through an order, and Nina started wondering aloud whether she wanted to return so rapidly to Greece. It seemed that what she really preferred was to go back to her digging site, collect her baggage, and try to forget about the whole thing. I suggested she might be safer coming with me, at least until the Apollo's Head was in safe hands. I thought this was true. But underneath I also wanted her around.

Pollock left the phone and told us the meal would be coming up a few minutes.

The main decisions taken, the three of us relaxed noticeably and Pollock produced a bottle of wine. I could see that Nina was moving over to the idea of coming with me.

The doorbell rang, and I went across to admit the waiter from the open-air eating house round the back of the building.

It wasn't the waiter.

On the doorstep were four large Turks, pointing revolvers unerringly at our stomachs.

CHAPTER 13

Night Ride

Nina and I lay bundled on the floor in the rear of a car, with some kind of tarpaulin over our heads and our hands manacled. They had Pollock in a second car behind. Every time I moved I felt a gun barrel pushed into my spine. The heat under the tarpaulin was stifling.

I tried to work out where we were being taken. The auto swung over long streets that created little traffic noise.

After twenty minutes or so I heard the swish of some kind of construction passing close by at short intervals: I guessed it was the Bosphorus Bridge again. At the end I felt the vehicle turn right. Then we rode, at a slower pace, for about three quarters of an hour.

The goon in the back with us finally pulled the tarpaulin away, inspecting us with a grunt. He made certain we saw his gun was still in his hand. I think he was more interested in being able to watch us than with giving us air, but the breeze from the open windows was a relief nonetheless.

I was on the right hand side of the car, and over my head I could see stars in a cloudless night sky. We were obviously out of the city and suburbs by now: the constellations seemed to belong in the southern sky, so I guessed we were travelling south-east along the Asian shore of the Sea of Marmara. I thought I could smell the sea occasionally in the blast from the window as the auto speeded up.

What I could not work out was how they had found us. I'd certainly not been followed from the crashed cab in Beyoglu. Bassington could not have told Ilderim that I'd taken cover with Pollock, yet the four hoods had done their walk-in as if they were totally confident of what they would find. I could only imagine that Ilderim had discovered more about Bassington's connection than the Englishman believed. When I began to mention this to Nina the hood with the gun barked urgently for us to be quiet.

He covered us with the tarpaulin again each time we came to a small town, letting us breathe freely once more only when it was gone. We had passed through three when the driver took a right turn. According to the stars we were now driving westwards: an hour and a half later this was confirmed when we came to the edges of a coastal town I thought I recognised just before the tarpaulin came down: Karamursel. This was proving an extraordinarily long trip. The car headed inland again and I lost myself for the next three hours. There were villages, towns – one of them large, and I thought it might be Bursa – tracts of dark wooded countryside, and endless driving, until at last we came out to the shore again.

We were off the main highway, now, bumping along a poorly maintained country road. There seemed to be sea on either hand for a while. Then the driver turned off onto a rough track, and after a few minutes we saw a large, ramshackle villa standing in darkness on a small promontory overlooking a little bay. The two sedans came to a halt; the men with revolvers motioned us out, produced flashlights, and led all three of us to the front door. Nina lurched suddenly against me, and as she caught my eye nodded briefly towards the sea. I followed her look and saw the distant object that had just emerged to view beyond the angle of the headland. It was an anchored trawler yacht, showing dim lights in the cabin. I had only a brief glimpse in the moonlight, but I judged she was painted white.

We were pushed into a large, musty-smelling downstairs room, and one of the Turks produced matches to light some large oil lamps on the single table in the centre. The two drivers sat down on the floor, evidently tired from the long drive, and stared at us blankly. The gunmen appeared more relaxed now they had reached the evident security of the villa. One of them left the room and the second, still holding his revolver on his lap, waved his free hand to a long divan standing along the inner wall of the room.

I thought we could talk, now. 'Where the hell are we, do you think?' I asked Pollock.

'On the Kapidagi pensinsula, I guess. Halfway down the Sea of Marmara.'

'A hell of a way from Istanbul.'

'Not by sea,' he said. 'Just about a hundred miles, straight across.'

I looked across at Nina. She seemed near the end of exhaustion, sick and pale after five hours on the bottom of the car.

Nobody spoke for a while. One of the drivers got up and went outside. I could hear him relieving himself against the exterior wall. There were other noises, too: cattle sounds in the distance, an occasional night-time murmer of cicadas. The villa was probably set in an old olive grove bordering the sea, I thought. There was the sound of an outboard motor, approaching.

Suddenly Pollock said 'Good place for a smuggler,' almost with admiration. 'Think about it. You'd expect smugglers to be based down in Anatolia on the open coast, instead of having to run through the Dardanelles every time they make a trip. These guys aren't stupid, they don't do the obvious thing.'

A bass voice from behind me said: 'That's a very percipient observation, sport.'

When I turned my head, I saw the mysteries unravel, all at once. Standing in the doorway was the huge frame of Murray Tyler. And behind the Australian bar owner was his sandy-haired muscle man. I knew now how the Turks had found me at Pollock's: Tyler, after all, had marked us together the night of the trouble at the Southern Cross Club. I understood something else, as well.

'Now I know why the Greek police took me for your big friend,' I said. 'Two witnesses, a Thai and an American. The Thais can't tell one European face from another. And no American can tell a British accent from an Australian.'

They came into the room, and the sandy-haired one laughed. 'I'm insulted to think anyone would confuse you with me, mate. I'm ten years younger and much better looking.'

256

Nina stared at him, her eyes tight, but with her shoulders betraying the tension.

'That's right, darling,' he said. 'We've met before, a couple of times.'

Murray Tyler sat down on the divan along the opposite wall. His four Turkish goons were in the room as well, now: Tyler nodded at one of them, who bustled away. I could hear a clink of glass at the end of the hall.

'I'm going to drink a beer while we have a nice friendly conversation,' said Tyler. 'At the end we might give you three a glass too, if you're in any condition to appreciate it.

'You've got something of mine.'

'Not any more,' I said, 'didn't Ilderim tell you?' I might buy time, I thought. But Tyler just laughed.

'No,' he said, 'he didn't. That's a nice try, sport, but you're trying to be too clever. You can't turn the heat onto my little friend Ilderim. In the first place that package is no good to him – not without me. Ilderim wouldn't know where to sell it, and he wouldn't be able to get something like that out of the country. He wants it, but he wants it with me. And that's where you're going to put it by the time tonight's over.'

The man he had sent for beer came back with a tray and two large bottles. The sandy-haired henchman poured two glasses. 'Thanks, Shane,' said Tyler without looking at him. To me he said: 'You've led us a right dance. You killed two of my best men yesterday, wrote off one of my autos, and stranded another couple of guys in the middle of Anatolia. If these four hadn't snatched you last night I'd be running out of hired help.

'Mind you, I suppose we owe you for saving the *caique* in the first place. But then you got everybody confused. When Shane couldn't find the cargo we thought the Greeks had taken it.

'We just couldn't understand why they didn't announce finding it. Seemed fishy, you know? But then the moment Shane comes back empty-handed from his dive on the *caique* we discover you've very kindly brought yourself over here. To tell the nice Colonel Ilderim that you've had it all the time.'

'It sure must be valuable,' said Pollock. 'For you to take a risk like this.'

'Oh, it is,' said Tyler. 'It certainly is. But I'm not taking a risk, Pollock. That wouldn't be like me at all.'

'Smuggling, kidnapping, and maybe in the end three murders,' said Pollock. 'I'd say that's plenty risk.'

I realised he was really saying this to me. I did not need the warning. I knew that the moment Tyler had the statue in his possession the three of us would be disposed of.

'Just remember, Pollock,' Tyler told him grimly, 'I don't need you at all. You could make quite a nice example to loosen people's tongues.'

'There's things you haven't thought of,' said Pollock. 'Who put us in touch with Ilderim in the first place? Somebody who's got a kind of official interest in proceedings, wouldn't you think? We disappear, that group'll start having a good look at your crooked colonel. How long do you suppose *he*'ll last when the Turks start sweating him?'

Tyler nodded suddenly at Shane. Indolently, the big man got his feet and backhanded Pollock across the mouth. Pollock fell backwards on the divan, and glared at him. 'It's still something to think about,' he said thickly.

'Cut the comedy,' said Tyler. 'This isn't Saigon, kiddo, and the CIA cuts no ice with me.' He looked back at me. 'Here's the way I read it. You must have switched the statue from one yacht to the other very early in the piece. Like a smart boy, you didn't tell the Greeks.

'The American Embassy gets you out of jail, and being an ungrateful bastard you get away from them, too. Then somehow you spirit your boat off Andros, hide it somewhere, and foot it up to Istanbul to get the reward. Very public spirited, for a guy who's just jumped bail in another country.

'So the statue has to be on your yacht, OK? Now, you just tell us where that is.'

'Then you kill us,' I said.

'Then maybe we come to an arrangement,' said Tyler. 'We let you have the boat back, perhaps, and you sail off and see if you can get past the Greek search party.'

Pollock said quickly: 'Don't believe this, you give him the statue and we're dead.'

Shane moved to him very rapidly and punched him twice in the head. Pollock crashed against the wall and was silent.

Tyler said: 'Maybe he wasn't too confident about Ilderim telling our life stories to the Turkish cops, after all. What do you say, Lancaster?'

'I didn't take the ketch off the island,' I said. 'It was a friend sailing her for me. I don't know for sure where she is now.'

'You told Ilderim, somewhere in Greece,' said Tyler, 'but I don't believe that. You're here, there's a thousand cops looking for you in Greece, why leave the boat there?

'The boat's somewhere in Turkey. And you know where.'

'I don't. I have to contact the guy who sailed her here. Bassington, the Englishman you saw us with at your club. He's in Belgrade.'

Shane spoke, at last: 'You know where she is all right, sport. That's about a hundred and twenty grands' worth of boat. I saw her on Andros. You'd have kept your tabs on her, all right.'

'I trusted Bassington to get her out for me.'

'That's tough,' said Tyler.

'You know, in my country we've got a beaut way of encouraging people to hand over what isn't theirs to keep. We take a pair of bolt-cutters and start snipping off their toes, one by one. By the time you get to the second foot, even an iron-tough bank robber is ready to cough up everything he has.

'Unfortunately, out here in the backblocks we don't have any bolt-cutters immediately to hand. Or should I say, to foot?'

Shane laughed, very readily. The Turks smiled, without understanding, but ready to join in the mood. Tyler lit a cigarette.

'I've got something nearly as good, though,' he said. He nodded at the two drivers, and gave them a short command. They moved to Nina and grabbed her arms.

Tyler got up and crossed the floor to her, quite slowly. With one jerk he ripped her dress apart at the front. She was wearing no bra, and her bare breasts were white and vulnerable.

Tyler took his cigarette from his mouth, examined the end, drew on it, and then in one sudden movement ground it into Nina's left breast, just above the nipple.

260

Nina screamed. The Turks gripped her. After what seemed a life sentence, Tyler withdrew the cigarette and looked across at me. I was already shouting at him.

'All right, all right,' I was yelling, 'the boat's at Izmir.'

'OK,' said Tyler, 'that's better. You don't want me to give her one more for luck?'

'For God's sake,' I said, 'I'll give you the boat.'

'Yes,' Tyler said, 'I guess the boat'd *have* to be at Izmir. Nearest port to the Cyclades. All right, we'll drive down tomorrow and you can show me.

'You three can spend the night in the cellar and think about it.'

He spoke briefly to the Turks. 'They'll look after you,' he said. Shane, who had watched Nina's branding with evident enjoyment, went over and gave her burned tit a heavy squeeze. Nina moaned again.

'I sure hope your ketch is going to be there, when we get to Izmir,' said Tyler.

'I got a lot more cigarettes.'

They shackled us to some kind of storage rack in the cellar, each with one end of our handcuffs fastened to an upright. Nina and I were at the far end of the room, lying on the dirt floor. Pollock was manacled to the wine rack or whatever it was on the other side, just to the left of the four steps leading down from the outside of the house. I asked for something to eat and drink, and Pollock translated. They bought us water in two of the brown earthenware pots, designed with a filling spout on the side and a smaller one at the top, which the peasants use to keep drink cool in the summer fields. Nina took ours up clumsily with her free hand. I showed her how to drink out of the smaller spout without spilling the rest. There was no food in the house, the main gaoler told Pollock.

The other Turks left him with us while he arranged an oil lamp to his satisfaction in the centre of the floor. Then he waited, expectantly, until Shane came down and tested our fastenings. The Australian nodded approval, and the two men left, barring the door behind them and from the sound of it securing the hasp with a padlock.

We were left in the dull light of the low-trimmed lamp, Pollock silent by the door, and Nina and I sharing the water pot between us.

'Are you OK?' I asked her.

'For now,' she whispered. 'But what happens in Izmir?'

'I don't know. We'll see.'

Outside the men's voices came to us from a distance. Then the outboard motor I had heard before started up again.

'The Australians are sleeping on the boat,' said Pollock. 'They're just going back, I think.'

The outboard noise was receding into the distance. After a while, it stopped.

'You were smart to tell them Izmir,' Pollock said. 'That should give us another day, at least, if we're going to drive down there.'

'Unless Tyler's got someone he can telephone first.'

'I hadn't thought of that,' Pollock admitted.

'Isn't the boat at Izmir?' Nina whispered suddenly.

'No.'

'Oh, *God*,' she said.

We could hear the four Turks talking from the central doorway of the house. It was some way from us, and Pollock could not catch the words clearly: the cellar was under the northern end of the villa and the main room where we had been interrogated was on the south. But three of the Turks seemed to go inside. Then we heard one of them return and sit heavily against the cellar door.

'Well, what are we going to do?' said Pollock. 'I don't see you escaping out of that car again. There'll be the two Aussies tomorrow, as well as the hoods.'

'Maybe attract attention in Izmir.'

In the shadows Pollock shook his head. 'They'll keep tight hold of us. Send someone to look for the boat and keep us under cover. What are your handcuffs like?'

'Solid army issue. I'm attached to this piece of timber for the night.'

'Me too,' said Pollock. He fell silent for a while. There was a little muffled noise from Nina. She was trying not to sob. I moved to get my free arm around her, and she fell onto my shoulder, crying freely now.

'Well, it's time for desperate measures,' Pollock said. 'Look at it this way, we got one Turk outside the door now, and the other three some way off relaxing after a long hard day.

'What do you say we give them time to get sound asleep and then try something? After this the odds will never be so good again.'

'You got me. But what?'

'I've got one idea,' he said. 'But I don't want you looking like you expect it. Just lie quiet for half an hour.'

The minutes on Nina's diving watch ticked endlessly by. I was so exhausted I was almost dropping off to sleep myself.

Then Pollock whispered: 'OK, we'll try it. Let Nina start kicking up a racket. I want the guard to come in to you. Make it sound like someone having a cardiac arrest, OK? Moans, gurgles, anything. But not so loud it wakes the other three.'

Nina began groaning, nervously, unaccustomed to the fake. I said, 'Not good enough, kid. Sorry about this,' and grabbed a handful of flesh around her midriff. She shrieked in earnest now as I twisted it. Simultaneously Pollock rose to his feet and reached up the little stairway to kick at the door behind the guard's head, calling urgently for help in Turkish.

We heard the man start, and rise. After a moment of incomprehension he rattled keys and began to take off the padlock. Then Pollock stepped back as the door opened and the guard came down the steps, squinting into the lamplight across to where I held Nina groaning in my arms.

'She's sick,' I said, 'she's having an attack or something.'

He understood the meaning at least, and came towards us.

Pollock rose in the shadows behind him. I tried to keep my eyes from glancing at him and warning the Turk. But from the corner of my eye I saw Pollock, yards away on the side of the room, slowly raise his heavy water jar to his ear with his free right hand. Then he pitched it, straight into the back of the Turk's head. The jar shattered, and the man crumpled on the spot. I think he was dead the moment the jar smashed his skull.

'Jesus,' said Pollock, 'that's the best beanball I ever threw.'

I let go of Nina and stretched across with my loose arm to grab the fallen guard by the shoulder. It was sticky with his blood, and his head was a dark wound in the lamplight. He was an enormous, inert weight and I could hardly shift him.

'Hush!' said Pollock. He was listening intently for the others. But there was no answering noise. After a moment he motioned me to continue.

'See if he's got the keys to the cuffs.'

I strained. Nina got her unmanacled hand onto the man's shirt collar and tried to assist. Finally we pulled him to the storage rack and I went through his pockets.

'Only the outside padlock key,' I said. 'He's one of the drivers. Hasn't even got a gun.'

'He's got to have a knife, then,' Pollock said. 'Or better, take off his belt and slide it across to me.'

'Belt?'

'Yes, quickly.'

It was a very broad, rough-fashioned leather belt, strapped outside the loops on the man's trousers. I threw it over to Pollock.

He took the big buckle in his spare hand and began to work at his handcuffs with its central spike.

'Learn a lot of things in the Army,' he said, 'including how to pick GI issue cuffs.'

In less than a minute Pollock was free, and working on my manacles. 'You first,' he said, 'because we may have to fight if the others wake.'

But all was silent at the far end of the house. Pollock freed Nina quickly while I watched cautiously from the door. Pollock, last out of the cellar, replaced the padlock in its hasp and led the way to the two sedans, parked one behind the other on the narrow track a little distance from the main entrance.

'Have to take the car behind,' he whispered, 'because I don't see where we can turn the other.'

Softly he slid behind the steering wheel and began to pull wires from under the dashboard.

'Don't know where the bastard kept his car keys,' said Pollock, 'but I'll get this started in a minute. Just see if you can pull the distributor head out of the other one.'

I left Nina with Pollock, and slipped back to the auto parked nearer the house. But the hood lock on the battered sedan had failed long ago, and the thing was secured with tightly wrapped bailing wire. There was no time to fool with this. I pulled the valves out of the front tyres and went back to Pollock.

From behind the wheel Pollock whispered 'OK, you ready?' I got in beside him. Nina crouched in the back. Pollock jammed two wires together and the engine coughed noisily into life. 'Here we go,' he shouted, revved the engine, and swung the car round, under an olive tree. We lurched and bumped – then Pollock came back onto the track heading away from the house.

'She's still got a little gas,' he said, 'we're going to make it,' and behind us lights flickered up in the villa as the three Turks came lurching out into the night. There were two shots, but Pollock was already seventy yards down the track and they came nowhere near us.

'You get the distributor head?' he asked.

'No, but the front tyres are useless.'

'We've got just a few minutes start then,' said Pollock. 'Till they get another car.'

He slowed a little, taking no risks on the uneven cart track. But when he got onto metalled road he let the car out. There was still no sign of pursuit. A few minutes later we were crossing the isthmus of land connecting the peninsula to the rest of Anatolia. I felt we might be free. I reached over into the back and hugged Nina to me. I think she kissed me: her face was wet with the tears of relief.

'Here's where you've got to make a choice,' said Pollock. Ahead, the road was rejoining the mainland. Pollock slowed to a fork in the road on the other side.

'If we go left we're heading for Istanbul. We steam in to the military command and get the heat on Ilderim and the gang. But Istanbul is a five hour drive and that's where Tyler will expect us to be heading. Those goons behind will get a vehicle from somewhere: Tyler could overtake us, or if he warns Ilderim there could be a welcome party. Even a roadblock, maybe.

'Alternatively, if we turn right, it's only ninety minutes to Karabuga and the boat.'

'Go back to Plan A,' I said. 'Head for the boat. She should have enough diesel left to get out the Dardanelles. Once we're in Greek waters we can radio for Theodoropoulos.'

'Yeah,' Pollock said with satisfaction, 'That's what I would do.' He accelerated again and turned the car to the right at the road junction. Then he dimmed the headlights and after a second or two slowed and switched them off altogether. The moon was still clear enough to drive by.

'Those guys will be after us sooner or later,' he explained. 'Keep an eye on the road over on the peninsula to your right. We may have only ten minutes or so in hand, if they got another set of wheels from somewhere.'

The right-hand fork paralleled the shore for several minutes. The tongue of sea between the mainland and the peninsula was less than a mile wide. Sure enough, after a minute or two I saw a pair of headlights travelling at high speed down the peninsula coastal road we had just travelled. As they raced towards the isthmus, we came into the outskirts of a small town. Pollock slowed and then stopped. 'We're pretty safe,' he said. 'Even if Tyler thinks we're off to Izmir he would have had to take the left hand turn to go after us. But just watch him.'

'Can't we go to the local police here?' said Nina.

'If we have to,' I told her, 'but not if we can help it. Ilderim is an officer in a powerful position and he can still screw us. The incriminating statue is on my boat, remember? Ilderim could make that a ticket to a Turkish jail.'

We strained our eyes through the dust-grimed rear window. With relief, we watched the speeding car cross the isthmus, come to the junction, and take the turn towards Istanbul. Pollock engaged his gears again, and started off for Karabuga.

Dawn was beginning to light up the surrounding hills as we bumped down the narrow road into the fishing port where Bassington had left my ketch at anchor. There were one or two people about, but no one near enough to notice when we abandoned the old sedan outside the mediaeval walls. We walked softly through the single storey streets to the waterfront, and commandeered a small fishing boat.

There was some way to row. Bassington, as he had told me, had left *Andromeda* out under the lee of the northern headland, several hundred yards away from the village itself on the seaward side of an exposed rock in the harbour's centre. There, she was not immediately obvious to passers-by on the waterfront. As we rounded the rock I turned my head to search for her. I felt almost an explosion of relief in the middle of my chest when she swung into view, her familiar lines and broad black hull promising safety and calm at last.

Pollock and Nina clambered aboard while I let the rowing boat go to her own tiny anchor, and then followed them.

'I don't think I ever want to leave this boat again,' Nina said. 'This is twice she's rescued me.'

I began to hunt in the side stern locker for the keys which Bassington had left there. Just as I found them, Pollock said: 'You needn't have bothered.'

He was looking at the main cabin hatchway. Someone had levered the padlock hasp away from its seating.

'Christ!' I said. Pollock opened the hatch, and we inspected below. There was really very little disarray. One or two bottles had gone from the liquor store. There was a smell of rotting food from the freezer, which doesn't work when the batteries are turned off. Apart from the drink, it seemed the local fishermen had come aboard for only one thing.

My double sideband marine radio had gone. There was nothing left but the empty bracket above the navigation table.

CHAPTER 14

To the Sea

The thieves had been in a hurry. They had little time to do much damage, apart from ripping the radio away from its mounting and rifling the booze that was immediately available. Other things which were equally useful but less accessible were still in place. They had not bothered with the charts, and the radar set was untouched: little point in taking it without the scanner, which would have required time and unwelcome exposure to curious eyes ashore to detach from its place at the top of the mizzen mast. Even the battery system was in place. Perhaps it was too high-powered for the requirements of the local fishing boats.

I found the keys where Bassington had left them in the cockpit locker and turned on the electric systems. According to the fuel gauge there was enough diesel left for six or seven hours running. The engine came to life without more than a couple of preliminary hic-cups: I left Nina on the wheel while Pollock helped me get up the anchor. Then I took over the helm and edged *Andromeda* out of the little bay. It was just after five a.m., and the dawn light was getting stronger.

Nina went down to the main cabin to open a can of Spam and fry up some breakfast: none of us had eaten since the previous day. Until we got to Greece we would have to depend on whatever she could find in the canned stores. There was nothing edible left in the freezer, and as the breakfast cooked in the galley she was already throwing some of it over the side. I headed *Andromeda* due north, towards the entrance to the Dardanelles. The sea was brisk, with a breeze springing up from the north-east and the light becoming more brilliant with every minute. Pollock brought us both sweaters from the cabin, and we settled back in the lee of the cockpit coaming, watching the land on our port for the sharp turn into the straits that led to escape.

Nina had found a can of milk to go with coffee, and eggs that were still in reasonable condition to fry with the Spam.

She brought the meal up to the cockpit and we all wolfed it, though there was no bread aboard to ballast the fat and fried meat. Nina had found me some cigarettes, too: I finished my mug of coffee and smoked two of them, beginning to think clearly for the first time since our escape.

'We've got a decision to make,' I said.

'We have just about enough diesel to take us through the Dardanelles. Now, two thirds of the way down the straits there's a port at Canakkale, where I could put in for more fuel. It's the last chance of getting any until we get to one of the islands. But Canakkale happens to be the Turkish control port for the straits, and if I put in for fuel the harbourmaster is going to want to see the ship's papers. And they're not in order.'

'How come?' asked Pollock.

'They show this boat as leaving Izmir for Greece nearly three weeks ago, and they don't record re-entry. That

271

didn't worry Bassington when he came back, because it was only a few days after I'd sailed from Izmir. He just said he'd changed his mind and returned to Turkey. The story was good enough for the harbourmaster at a little fishing port like Karabuga, and anyway Bassington was paying the guy a generous minding fee for the boat. But at Canakkale there could be a lot of questions, and a big delay.'

Nina said: 'Also I haven't got a passport with me. It's still in my bag in Istanbul.'

'There you go,' said Pollock, 'you're the only one of us with travel documents, Harry.'

'OK, so Canakkale's out. We motor down the Dardanelles and then sail. We'll have to hope there's enough wind to get us into Greek waters inside a couple of hours.'

Nina saw the implications here a split second before they dawned on Pollock.

'My God,' she said, 'you're expecting a chase.'

'I think it's quite likely.'

'How the hell would they know where to start looking?' said Pollock. 'They've never even seen this ketch, to know it from any other.'

'The lovely Shane was on Andros, remember. And it wouldn't be difficult to work out where to look for us, if you think about it. You've got to keep in mind that whatever Tyler is, he's not stupid.'

Up to port the sharp corner of the cape above Karabuga was coming into sight, lit in a light gold now by the early sun. I started to turn the wheel, bringing *Andromeda* on course for the straits. Asia lay close by on the left hand: the European shore was a smudge of brown on the other horizon.

'Just put yourselves in Tyler's place,' I said. 'He'd have to figure out sooner or later that he wasn't going to catch us on the road to Istanbul – or Izmir either if that was where we were going.

'I'd say that the moment he came to the fork where the road divides between the route to Istanbul and the turn-off for Izmir he started taking that idea on board. And very soon after that Ilderim's bedside phone would have started ringing in Istanbul.

'As soon as Ilderim could get into the office he would have had two or three policemen on the telephones ringing harbourmasters in every port they could think of. We were hardly likely to have just left the boat anchored off a quiet beach somewhere. Too much of a risk – logically you'd want to leave her in a harbour. Now, there's not more than twenty or thirty ports in Western Turkey where you would bring a large yacht.

'Somewhere along the line they'd get the harbour-master at Karabuga on the phone. "We're interested in a large European yacht, a ketch, named *Andromeda*, painted black with a stripe on the topsides." Shane mentioned last night he'd seen her at Gavrion, remember? So they have the description. "Oh, yes *effendi*, there was one like that here for ten days or so, but she left early this morning. ."

'So where do you go from Karabuga? Odds on we weren't heading for Istanbul. And there's nowhere else to sail from there but through the Dardanelles, to take the statue back to Greece.'

Nina said: 'If it's that easy to find the boat, why didn't Ilderim do it before?'

'Because he thought *Andromeda* was in Greece, as I told him. It was Tyler who worked out that she had to

273

be in Turkey, only yesterday. In addition Ilderim would have been trying to keep his hands clean. He wouldn't want the kind of questions he could possibly provoke by ordering a countrywide search.

'But once we escaped he was involved anyway. Tyler just had to say, look, they've got away and they know about your role in the affair, you've got to find them, Colonel.'

'In that case,' said Nina, 'why don't we just put into Canakkale and tell the whole rotten story to the authorities?'

'We can't,' said Pollock, 'the chances are we'd just hand the game to Ilderim.

'Look, we happen to be in possession of one hot Greek statue stuffed like a Thanksgiving turkey with God knows how many millions of dollars worth of drugs. Great, it's all a misunderstanding. And one of the top cops in Istanbul is the real culprit. I wouldn't want to find myself sitting in a Turkish jail telling that story, and answering the questions that Ilderim is going to dictate down the phoneline from Istanbul.'

'Can't risk it,' I said, 'too much could go wrong. We'd just give ourselves the same problem Theodoropoulos handed me in Athens, only worse: a long stay in jail, with no chance of proving the truth inside a year or two of argument.'

'And long before that time was up either Ilderim or Tyler would make sure we got shot attempting to escape,' said Pollock.

Nina sighed, and looked away at the passing coastline. After a moment she said: 'Well, OK: what are the chances of getting away?'

'Depends when Tyler actually works it out,' I told her.

'They can't catch us in the Dardanelles, anyway. *Andromeda* will do something over eight knots under power, and once we get into the straits we'll have a two-knot current behind us.

'I doubt if that trawler yacht of Tyler's will do more that twelve knots, and he has something like a thirty-mile passage to make before he even gets to the eastern end of the straits. Meanwhile we're heading out to sea nearly as fast as he can travel.

'It's when we run out of fuel at the other end that it's going to get sexy. He'll be bearing down on us and we'll still have two or three hours to go to Greek territorial waters.

'I think we've a good chance of making it. But it depends on the weather – and if he follows that far.'

'You're the sailor,' said Pollock. 'I believe you, running is the only thing to do. But you'd better be right.'

'We're already inside the entrance to the Dardanelles,' I said. The compass showed a course to the west-sou'west, now. At last we were heading for Greece.

Nina looked wistfully at the brown coastline of Anatolia and asked me, 'Do you really think we can get away?'

'I think so. The winds in the northern Aegean are flukey, but at this time of year once we get out from under the lee of the land at the mouth of the straits we ought to pick up a decent breeze. Remember the Byron voyage I was trying to retrace when I first picked you up? The British frigate Byron was aboard took a day to cross the Sea of Marmara and another to get out the Dardanelles and out into the Aegean.

'But once she hit the *meltemi* out there she crashed right down to Greece in a single day. Early that morning

275

she was between Limnos and Tenedos, just outside the Dardanelles – they landed at Piraeus the same night.

'When it blows in the Aegean, it doesn't matter whether you're sailing a British frigate or a Taiwan ketch, you've got the legs of a diesel trawler.'

This wasn't, I knew, quite the truth. But we were taking the best chance we had, and she needed a little moral support.

It was about seven-fifteen a.m. when I first began to notice the Dardanelles current. By that time we were three miles east of the Boz Cape, just as the straits show the first hint of narrowing. The European shore creeps in to a distance of ten miles, here, and I saw that the scrubby brown hillsides on the Asian side off the port beam seemed to be slipping by a little faster, although the patent log still showed a fraction under eight knots. The action of the current was bringing our real speed to a little under nine, I calculated.

I asked Pollock to bring the chart up from the navigation table. The current that flows through the Dardanelles starts in Russia, of course. The great Russian rivers which end in the Black Sea constantly replace evaporation in the Eastern Mediterranean, streaming through the Bosphorus first into the Sea of Marmara and then down the Dardanelles into the Aegean. For some reason the current flows fastest near the shore, but the straits are thick with navigation hazards here. At the eastern end there are long stretches of inshore reefs and submerged rocks. Further downstream lie the wrecks of the Allied battleships which attempted to force the Dardanelles in a major blunder of World War One. They remain, scattered along the southern shoreline where the Turkish batteries sank them, tangles of keel-ripping rusting steel threatening any small boat tempted to take incautious advantage of the current.

I had eighteen fathoms under our keel now, but when I looked at the chart I saw *Andromeda* would be entering a twelve-mile stretch of navigation hazards as soon as we rounded the Boz headland. To begin with we had to watch for an offshore reef less than a mile past the cape, and then a long stretch of underwater rocks pushing out into the channel from the Asian shore. Later we could save time and hold speed by changing course to take a short-cut: this would swing us through a narrow passage between the inshore rock hazards and a second offshore reef, which stands out a mile and a half into the waterway. There would be no rest for me in the next hour or so, until we passed the little town of Cardak on the southern shore. I sent Nina down to the cabin to sleep: she would need to relieve me at the helm later.

'You look completely beat,' said Pollock. 'I'll get you another coffee, and then you'd better teach me how to steer.'

He caught the trick quite easily. I might not have asked him to take the helm straight away with sail up and a good wind blowing, but he got the feel of the boat under power very quickly. I sat on the coachroof hugging my coffee mug, giving him the leading marks to steer to.

When we got to the second offshore reef I went back to the helm myself. The short-cut looked simple enough on the chart, but the current was much more obvious now, and I reckoned we were easily making the ten knots I'd hoped for. Our course through the narrow passage had to be carefully calculated: as we went out towards midstream, along the edge of the projecting onshore reef, the flow would be pushing us sideways towards the rocks. I brought *Andromeda* as close as I could to the reef to port, half a mile out from the southern shore now, and held the bow a couple of points to the right of the small town of Gallipoli on the opposite side of the straits. I was aiming off to allow for the current: the direct line would have been the town itself. The little lighthouse on the northern tip of the offshore reef was fine on my starboard bow. The reef itself extended half a mile south of the light: though the chart said there should be ten feet of water under our keel there, I preferred to stay within the channel, 300 yards wide, between the reef and the rocky shallows inshore.

In six minutes *Andromeda* slipped through the gap, and I swung the helm round to a full sou'west course towards the Narrows. Just before eight we passed the light outside Cardak, to port, and a mile or so later I sent Pollock below to wake Nina.

'Keep her about 1,000 yards offshore until the next headland,' I told her, 'and wake me when you come up to the Narrows.'

Down below on the portside berth, I fell into a sleep deeper than death the moment my head touched the pillows.

Nina woke me a little after ten. I felt as if my head was stuffed with cheap rabbit fur. 'It looks as if we're coming up to the Narrows,' she said. 'You asked me to give you a shake.'

I stopped in the galley to splash my face with water, and then followed her on deck. We were in the last third of the straits, now. The Asian and European shores were not much more than a couple of miles apart here, with the start of the Narrows barely three miles ahead. My helmsmen had steered an uneventful passage for the last ten miles from Lapseki onwards, Nina said: Pollock took the wheel for most of the way, insisting that what he called 'driving' did not tax him. To his left, the low mountains of the Asian shore stared at the hills of the Gallipoli peninsula across a calm waterway. They'd had the easy part of the passage, while I slept.

Pollock said he wanted to go on 'driving', and I let him. There were no great problems ahead, apart from a well-signposted offshore rock with one of the World War One wrecks just to its south, on the angle where the Narrows starts and the straits take a 90 degree turn to port.

And once we were around that, I felt almost safe. Canakkale was just ahead, and the Aegean only fifteen miles away. Surely Tyler would not follow us into Greek waters.

When you get to Canakkale the Dardanelles is little more than a mile wide. It was here, I told the others, that Xerxes built the famous bridge of boats between Asia and Europe to invade Greece with his Persian hordes, and Byron made his celebrated swim across the Hellespont – as the straits were called in classical times – in emulation of the mythic hero Leander. Byron and his Royal Navy companion were nearly dead when they were pulled ashore. The current had pulled them so far downstream they'd swum nearly four miles.

Now I had come awake again the sleep seemed to have injected me with glucose. I felt brilliantly aware of everything round me. I started to get involved in telling the story of Byron's swim. Then I noticed a helicopter, distant in the sky above the town, heading across the straits towards a big tanker plugging up against the current on the European side.

I watched the chopper while I talked. It was about 300 feet high, apparently taking a course towards the tanker, but actually taking a wide circle northwards across the channel. As I went on talking I realised that the centre of that circle was *Andromeda*. You would not have noticed unless you kept your eye on the machine for several minutes. Then it was possible to see that as the helicopter moved wide across the straits, her distance from our moving ketch remained constant.

Of course, I told myself, it would be easy for Ilderim to order a police lookout for a missing ketch without committing himself to reasons. A normal surveillance order, the Canakkale police pilot would assume. On its own that helicopter in the distant sky was hardly evidence. It moved away upstream after some ten minutes. By then we were almost opposite the town, at the very narrowest point of the channel. I told myself that I could easily be wrong. But I felt the chill conviction that Tyler was somewhere behind us.

'We ought to stick to the south shore,' I told Pollock. 'The rule in the Dardanelles is drive on the left. But I think you may as well cross over the channel here on the starboard turn. We'll save a lot of time cutting across the European shore, and we can easily avoid the big ships going eastwards.'

Pollock spun the wheel to make the crossing. As we crept under the lee of the low peninsula, I offered to take the wheel from him.

'I'm OK driving,' he said. 'You two should split the rest periods for the moment. When we run out of gas you'll be doing the sailing work between you.'

He made sense. I sent Nina down to take an hour on the bunk. Pollock, over on the European shore now under the deceptively peaceful hills which had proved so fatally impossible for the Allied landings in 1915, watched her drop down into the cabin from the corner of his eye. The sun was hot on our backs, as I stood at the break of the coachroof keeping an eye out for larger ships heading east for the Black Sea. A band of stray cicadas in some piece of scrub onshore found their voices in the heat, and for a moment the shrill chorus overcame the diesel throb.

Pollock waited until Nina had disappeared and said: 'That helicopter looked suspicious.'

'You noticed.'

'This'd be a good place to jump us,' said Pollock. 'OK, it's narrow, but from the look of that land there's no one about to be a witness later.'

'They can't catch us in the Dardanelles. And once we're in the open sea we should have three or four hours clear, sailing in pretty near any direction.'

'He'll have radar, you know. You do. He will. Is yours working?'

That wasn't a bad suggestion, now I thought about it. I believed it was, I told him, and slipped down to the main cabin to switch it on for a while. Nina was deeply asleep, up on the portside berth. She never stirred when I sat at the navigation table and clicked the switches of the set.

I had twenty-five miles range available on the radar, but the land was interfering with the image beyond the bend of the Narrows behind us. There were a few small boat blips in that area, but nothing that meant anything. I turned the set off again to save batteries and went on deck again.

'Nothing to worry about,' I told Pollock.

'But you reckon they're coming,' he said.

We kept close into the land all the way down the tip of the Gallipoli peninsula, with the Alci Tepe peak creeping slowly across the beam to starboard. I found some beer in the refrigerator, which was very slowly reviving now the batteries were charging, and hung it in a small net over the stern until it had cooled sufficiently to be drinkable. A cruise liner and a freighter passed us to port, the liner hooting her siren in irritation to find a small craft on the wrong side of the channel. About eleven-thirty we slipped by the village of Seddulbahir, just inside the mouth of the Straits. Just on noon the land on either hand began to disappear aft of the beam: we were clear of the Dardanelles.

I told Pollock to stick with his course of 240 degrees. We had no option. There was no wind under the land for a quick run south towards Lesbos, and we had to make as much of the direct line for Greek waters under diesel power as the remaining fuel allowed.

The diesel ran out about five miles outside the Gallipoli peninsula. It was just about ten minutes after noon, and the strong wind I'd hoped for by now was still not there. What breeze we had was due west. I roused Nina, and she took the wheel while Pollock and I hauled up the big genoa and then the main. Without the engine we were making about three knots on the wind. I gave Nina the best course for Lesbos, clipping the two small Turkish islands of Karaya Adalari and Bozca Ada – 215 degrees, almost sou'sou'west.

I must have betrayed my concern. Unless the wind got up we were not going to make Greek waters until almost dark.

'Do you still think they might be following?' said Nina.

'You saw Tyler last night. He'll follow as long as he thinks he has a chance of catching us,' I said.

'Has he?' Pollock asked.

'I don't know. That's a difficult calculation. I need to work on the charts.'

'Go ahead,' said Nina, 'I'm not tired, now. I can steer for as long as you want.'

I picked up the big Dardanelles and Approaches chart from the cockpit bench, where we had been using it to con the course, and went down to the navigation table. Luckily the Karabuga fishermen had left the nav. calculator in its drawer.

Now we had emerged from the Straits, we were near the bottom right-hand side of a sort of Isosceles triangle of islands: the side we were on went up north-west through the Turkish islands of Bozca Ada, at bottom right, and Imroz Adasi in the middle, to the triangle's peak at Samothrake, thirty-five miles away on the other side of Imroz. The left-hand side ran down thirty-five miles sou'sou'west to the other large Greek island of Limnos. The shortest route to Greek territorial waters lay due west: Greek waters began after about fifteen miles. From where *Andromeda* now sailed, towards the bottom right of the triangle, the coast of Lesbos lay some forty miles on a dogleg course south-west and then south-east – it would be foolhardy to attempt the hazardous inshore route directly south between Bozca Ada and the mainland under sail.

But it would be more sensible to aim for Lesbos rather than either north-west for Samothrake or sou'sou'west for Limnos. We could tack to either of the other two islands on the wind we had now, but in the summer

283

you get these westerlies only in the Turkish gulfs. Once we made a little way out to the open sea we could expect the wind to veer to the north, which put Samothrake out of the question, while a course to Lemnos meant tacking interminably for the next few hours. And, depending where Tyler was, this might be fatal.

I began to try to put myself in his position, twirling the dividers across the paper. Around me the boat rolled a little in the low swell, and Pollock's feet sounded lightly on the deck above as he moved around on the cabin top. It might have been a lazy summer cruise – the motion, the soft voices on deck, and the peaceful swish of the water past the hull – if I hadn't seen, almost immediately, the mistake I'd made in calculating the odds.

Tyler must not only *think* he had a chance of catching us. He had one.

The calculation depended, completely, on the time he got under way from the Kapidagi Peninsula. Now, when I thought about it – and I was thinking much better, after the sleep earlier in the morning – we must have cast off from Karabuga somewhere around five, after our ninety-minute drive from Edincik, the place where we had seen our pursuers chasing down the road on the peninsula across the water.

That meant Tyler must have realised we had not taken the road to Istanbul some time after four a.m., when he got to the Istanbul-Izmir crossroad. I had to assume he would have phoned Ilderim as soon as he could: it should not have taken the policeman more than a couple of hours to get an answer from Izmir about *Andromeda*'s absence from the harbour. If there had been some other European ketch there perhaps confusion could have dragged the time out for us, but I couldn't bank on it.

Tyler would have realised right then that *Andromeda* had to be somewhere on the coast west of him – we hadn't gone east for Istanbul, so we were presumably trying to get to her. He could safely calculate we would try to take her back to Greece, because the whole reason for my original call on Ilderim was to try to clear up the Greek charges against me: he'd reckon that in view of what I knew now, I'd be looking to make my peace in Athens.

If Tyler was thinking straight, he would have figured out fairly quickly that his best chance of finding us was to get out in his own boat and head down the Dardanelles. If we had left the ketch in a coastal port to the west, open to the Aegean, we would have at least a four hour drive to get there, and I saw now that he could be almost out the Dardanelles and into the open sea inside six. After that, chasing an auxiliary-engined ketch in a twelve-knot diesel trawler, he had a reasonable chance of catching us. If we were picking up the boat inside the Sea of Marmara – as in fact we did – he was even closer.

I marched the dividers across the chart, silently arguing the logic of the morning's timing. If Tyler had got under way before *Andromeda* reached the Dardanelles proper, seven-fifteen a.m., he must be right behind us. But if he had left after we got the benefit of the Dardanelles currents we had a fair lead.

I calculated that he would have just on three hours motoring at twelve knots to get to the eastern entrance of the Straits. If he left any time after seven, *Andromeda* with the current behind her would have been doing ten knots to his twelve and losing only some two sea miles in an hour until he got into the Straits.

Say Tyler had called Ilderim at about five. Ilderim gets an answer from Izmir back to him in two hours, so the earliest Tyler would leave is some time after seven. It might not even be that bad, I thought: he could have waited until Ilderim checked out the other ports, which could have meant our pursuers did not set out until nine or ten.

But if you took the worst case from my point of view, Tyler left at seven: he would be at our midday position about one-thirty in the afternoon.

Our chances all depended on the decision I made next. Somebody on Tyler's boat, I knew, would be making exactly the same calculations I puzzled over now, but in reverse. What would he do when he got to the mouth of the Dardanelles? Surely he'd assume he was chasing a ketch which would be motor-sailing, heading with her sails assisting her engine, on the best course to reach a Greek island as fast as possible. *Andromeda* wouldn't be trying to reach Limnos: that course took us into the teeth of what wind there was. Without the engine it was an impossibility anyway. He must work out, as I had, that Samothrake to the north would be equally unlikely. It must be as plain to Tyler as it had been to me that Lesbos was the best target. The island's north coast was forty miles distant, on an easy starboard reach, but the harbours on the north are scarce and small. He'd expect us to try to get round to the main town, Mytilene, another fifty miles round the corner. That would certainly have been my logical choice too, if I had not now realised he would be following.

The average speed for our size of craft when motor-sailing is about seven knots, although *Andromeda* in fact would have done a bit better if we'd actually had fuel.

Tyler would calculate that we could not make Mytilene before two a.m.: his faster trawler would catch us on the island's lonely south coast well before that.

He could not know that our fuel had already run out. If we made for Lesbos in this light air he would be on us even before we got to the north coast.

I shouted up the hatchway to Nina to change the course. We had to sail as high on the starboard tack as possible, now. I had seen that our only chance was to get out into the open Aegean, where the big *meltemis* blew from the north.

Up in the cockpit, Nina listened to the situation with a set face. She observed quietly that it might have been better to take a chance on Canakkale after all. Pollock asked how soon I thought Tyler could reach us.

'Late this afternoon, if he came straight for us, and if he left the peninsula at his first opportunity this morning. But by the time he gets to the mouth of the Straits we'll be over the horizon, and as soon as we are I'm going to go on the other tack for a while to confuse his radar picture.'

'What'll he do then?'

'Head south for Lesbos, if he's logical. There'll be plenty of small boat blips on the radar down there. They'll keep him busy investigating all evening.'

'What sort of range would he have on radar?'

'Depends on how high his scanner's mounted. For spotting small boats, perhaps six or seven miles. Unfortunately we've got a radar reflector up there on the top stay. If he knew where to look, he could pick this boat up at maybe twelve to fifteen miles.'

'Any chance of taking the reflector down?'

'None, outside a boatyard. It's a permanent fixture. But Tyler would have to know where to go looking.'

Pollock nodded. I took over the wheel from Nina and asked her to find us something to eat below. We were making nearly four knots now in the gentle westerly, and I got Pollock to grab the helm for a minute while I adjusted the genoa runners and the mainsheet traveller, slackening up the sails to make a little more of it. *Andromeda*'s long keel and stiff lines are not the best for light weather.

When I retrieved the helm I told Pollock to rummage down to the bottom of the longer starboard-side cockpit locker. He started taking out hanks of line, the grease-gun, and some creased club pennants. Next came the sea anchor: he looked up, doubtfully, when he got to the bagged spare mizzen and the storm trysail. I did not want to tell him what he was looking for.

'Just go on down,' I suggested.

He pulled out the sail bags and disappeared so far into the locker all I could see of him were his buttocks, heaving with the exertion. All at once they fell still, just for a frozen second. He had guessed what was under the stiff, heavy bundle he had now come to. He straightened up with it in his arms, breathing hard under the burden.

When he pulled the oilcloth off the .30 cal machine gun Pollock smiled for the first time that afternoon.

'That evens the odds,' I said.

Pollock grinned, and started wiping off the storage grease with a rag from the locker.

'Chances are they'll only have handguns and maybe a couple of sporting rifles,' he said. 'For some reason the Turkish authorities are dead against having machine guns around the place. We can stand 'em off with this as long as the ammo holds out.'

'That was the general idea of taking it into the Straits of Malacca.'

'Pity it's not a .50 cal. I could have sunk their whole fuckin' boat with one of those.'

'You need a special mounting for a .50 cal.'

'I know *that*,' Pollock said with irritation, 'When I was in Nam I was pulling triggers, not pounding typewriters like some people.'

I realised, with just a little surprise, that in all our talks at the Istanbul apartment he had never before admitted being there.

'On a ketch there's no place to mount one which gives you all round protection,' I told him. 'If you put it in the cockpit, you can't cover the bow: set the mounting in the for'ard hatchway, they can get at you from the stern. I thought about it.

'Anyway, I got the thing for Thai pirates. With them, one burst and you'd expect them to clear off.'

Nina came up the cabin hatch with plates of food.

'Jesus,' she said when she saw what Pollock was holding, 'we're in the damn Navy, now.'

Round about one o'clock, when we had eaten, I put *Andromeda* onto the port tack. The breeze had shifted to the south a little, and I had her heading almost west-nor'west. This course was carrying us off at ninety degrees from the line Tyler ought to take when he came to the head of the Straits, which were by now fifteen miles behind us and no more than a blue blur of mountains over the horizon. On Tyler's radar we would look as if we were a Greek island trader, calmly making our way round Imroz Adasi towards Samothrake to the north – not at all the direction someone making a tearaway escape from Turkish waters would be likely to follow.

Nina, thoughtfully sucking her teeth after the lunch, suddenly suggested: 'It looks like we're going to have calm sailing for the rest of the day.

'Why don't we take a look at the Apollo's Head and see what we've been lumbered with?'

'You better take the wheel again,' I said. 'It'll need two of us to get it out of the locker.'

Pollock bundled the other sail bags back into the starboard stowage to give us some room on the cockpit floor. I unfastened the padlock on the stern lazarette and pulled out the spinnaker and spare main. The Apollo's Head lay undisturbed where I had wedged it down with the figurine crate on Andros. The raw gash on its maimed ear showed through the carpet wrappings, like the reproachful memory of some childhood atrocity.

'It took a billy tackle to move it before,' I told Pollock, 'I'll get a couple of lines round while you rig it up.'

He passed me some spare lines from the locker he had just re-packed. I passed them round the narrowest part of the neck while Pollock found the billy tackle and hitched it to the mizzen boom above: the mizzen is fairly useless for a tight tack on the wind and I had not bothered to set it. We knotted the line to the tackle eye.

Pollock heaved on the tackle and I tried to wrestle the Head into position to come out of the lazarette. It was monstrously heavy.

'Christ,' I said, 'is this worth doing now?'

'Sure,' said Pollock. 'If we run out of ammo for the .30 cal we can start throwing heroin bags overboard and set up a Mexican stand-off.'

We caught our breath and pulled again. Pollock had the easy part, pulling on the tackle downhaul: my shoulders were wrenched with the effort of heaving the bulky stone past the obstructions at the locker opening. Slowly the Apollo's Head came free. A couple more minutes and we lay it heavily on the floor of the cockpit. Pollock rummaged in the toolbox and found the hammer and the chisel Bassington had blunted.

Nina was keeping one eye on this operation, but when she saw the fresh plastic revealed at the damaged ear she raised objections to Pollock's approach with the hammer.

'Let me have a good look first.'

I steadied the wheel with one hand behind my back, while Nina crouched and Pollock watched her, fingering the tools.

'I don't know,' she said, 'it could just be a repair. You can see where Bassington put the chisel in and came to old marble, an inch or two down.'

'That's another one of Bassington's mistakes,' said Pollock, 'like voting Ilderim as Square Cop of the Year. He put the chisel straight in, and hit something hard all right. But look here.'

Pollock scraped the chisel against the lower edge of the damage crater. Grey powder showered from the sides of the hole onto the Head's shoulder.

'That's fibreglass,' said Pollock. 'Fibreglass mixed with stone. Never mind what's in the middle of this for a moment. How much of the outside do you suppose is fake?'

He aimed the chisel against the edge of the hole, pointing downwards towards the shoulder, and whacked it with the hammer. Nina sucked in her breath sharply.

Then her shoulders loosened – the chisel had driven down almost four inches, and as Pollock levered it out the material was exactly the same.

'It's a fake shell,' said Pollock, and he began driving the chisel cut down the side of the Head.

Between blows he said: 'This is going to take a long time to get through. We'll have to take it in shifts, Harry.'

I watched him while Nina steered, and then took over. The fibreglass began coming away in great chunks. Pollock took a breather and I hacked through to the swell of the shoulder. When I got there the plastic cracked suddenly and the entire shoulder came away in one piece. That part at least was completely false.

'I can see a line of weakness in the mould,' said Pollock all at once. 'Give me the hammer again.'

He crouched down there at the stern of the cockpit and attacked the back of the Head. Finally – it seemed no more than a couple of minutes – a great section, perhaps three and a half feet high, came away all in one piece.

But the plastic was a strange shape, a kind of mould within a mould. On the outside it was formed to make up the back of the Head: we saw now that the inside followed a different shape, a sort of elongated oval with a long, pointed protrusion at the top.

'There's something inside to make that shape,' said Pollock, struggling to heave the statue round so that he could inspect the interior of the hole. 'Look, it's been wrapped in tar roofing paper or something.'

'No, it's just an outer covering of old paper and plastic wrapping. And inside – '

'Carpet again,' said Pollock, 'give me your knife.'

He started to rip through the worn material.

292

'And what's inside that?' said Nina.

'The old marble Bassington struck,' said Pollock. 'You know what? This is just another motherin' statue. Jesus, though. This one looks genuine.'

The last of the wadded carpet came away in his hand. Peering over his shoulder I saw what looked like the side of a female form, perhaps a little over four feet high. Its right arm was raised above its head – making the thin protrusion we had seen at the top of the oval bundle.

'My God,' said Nina, 'it's sure-enough genuine.'

'You sure?'

'I think so. I recognise it. It's the Praxiteles. The French took photos on the dig before it was stolen.'

'You mean that's all that this whole mess is about,' said Pollock. 'One lousy ancient statue?'

'That's what it's about,' said Nina. 'The biggest art theft in Turkey since the Crusaders sacked Byzantium. Never mind fifty thousand dollars. That's worth ten million. . .do I hear twenty?'

'Jeez,' Pollock said.

'I guess that makes it certain – Tyler is out there somewhere after all.'

CHAPTER 15

———— ❧ ————

Before the Wind

The light breeze held to the west, hardly raising a ripple on the low swell. It was one-thirty in the afternoon, and if my calculations were right Tyler was about ten miles east of us, turning south for Lesbos. There was nothing I could do about that, and with the steady wind blowing about ten knots, there was little risk leaving *Andromeda* to the self-steering gear. We were all below in the cabin, drinking the beer which we had left cooling over the stern for a couple of hours, and looking at the Praxiteles which now lay wedged amidships at the side of the saloon table. Pollock's face was drained after the effort of getting the thing below, but somehow he carried a look of relief as well.

He said: 'You know, in a crazy way this starts to make a kind of sense, now. I never saw Ilderim being into drugs, though you can't tell, and of course there's no way a good Turkish officer would have a piece of terrorist arms smuggling. But the idea of making a bit on the side spiriting away a statue that isn't even Turkish, that'd be almost respectable. I can almost understand it.'

'He'd make more than just a bit on the side,' said Nina. 'What's the Venus de Milo worth? Or the Mona Lisa? And this is the long-lost Aphrodite of Cnidos, which is right at the top of just that league.'

'Yeah. But stolen goods, though.'

'There's a market for stolen art,' Nina said. 'OK, no one's going to pay real values. But they'll pay a lot. In northern Italy thieves have cleaned out whole churches full of mediaeval art. The Italians have to keep them all locked these days. Dozens of the country's best Renaissance pictures have disappeared in the last twenty years. Rembrandt's *Portrait of Jacob van Gheyn* was stolen from a London gallery a couple of years back and never heard of again. Another Rembrandt, a Rubens and a lot of French Impressionists were stolen at gunpoint in Montreal, and just vanished onto the art black market. Twenty years ago someone stole the fabulous Queen Alexandra's emeralds from the Duchess of Windsor in Paris. That was supposed to be the British Secret Service, because the Royal Family wanted them back – but they've never been seen again, either.'

'Right, so somewhere there's a mad millionaire who would buy this. How much?'

'Who knows?' said Nina. 'Several million. It's impossible to put a top value on a genuine Praxiteles.'

I drank my beer. It was still too warm despite its hours in the water, but after the sweating effort of manhandling the statue down the companionway our thirst was desperate. I opened the last two bottles and handed them round. The drink started to revive me. When you are pressed, alcohol can bring you back to something like effectiveness. I got up to check the radar, and switched it on.

'How far are we from Greek territorial waters?' asked Pollock.

'With this light breeze, still another four hours.'

There were a mass of radar blips back towards the Dardanelles. One of them, I felt certain now, one of those innocent light flashes moving imperceptibly southwards, would be Tyler's diesel yacht.

'Surely they won't follow us into Greek waters?' said Nina. 'For all they know we've been hollering for the cops on the radio for hours.'

'I'm not so sure,' I said. 'That statue's not just a haul of heroin you could replace in a few months and recoup your losses. It's a few million dollars that once they lose they'll never see again. I think they'll keep coming. And they must know we haven't radioed for the cavalry so far.'

'How come?'

'To contact the Greek authorities we'd have to call them up first on the international communications frequency. That's the way ships' radio works. You call on 2182, the international channel, and then switch to whatever frequency you both have available on your sets – you can't press the first button you come to on the board and get through.

'Tyler will have had someone sitting on the 2182 channel listening out for our message. Naturally, we haven't sent one. So he's guessed by now that we either haven't got a radio working, or for some reason we don't want to call for help.

'And he's going to keep coming until the radio tells him different.'

Pollock pulled himself wearily to his feet and joined me at the radar screen.

'You guess he's over there with that jumble of traffic at the Dardanelles?'

'I reckon. We'll hold our present tack until we're under the shore of Imroz Adasi, and then head south-west for Greece. By that time he'll be set for Lesbos, because that's the first sensible place to look.'

'And later?'

'Hard to tell,' I said. 'If he doesn't find us on the north coast of Lesbos by nightfall, he ought to realise he's slipped up. But I'm calculating that he'll find enough small boats making radar blips down there to keep him busy checking up for hours, maybe halfway through the night.

'At that stage, he might reckon we've run out of fuel, and decide to take a last look out into the open sea. But by then we'll be off his radar screen, and it won't be easy to find us.'

Pollock stared blankly at the radar display. Nina joined us at the screen. She looked at it for a second, and then transferred her attention to the chart below. Nina was a sailor, where Pollock was not: she saw the alternative that was hidden from him.

She said: 'If you're right, and the wind will come round to the north once we're clear of the Turkish islands, we could make a fast beat westward to Limnos and be safe.'

'Too big an 'if'. Up at the top of the Aegean here you can't depend on the *meltemi* blowing from the north. It's just as likely to come from the nor'west or even the west. From here it's forty-five miles west-sou'west to the main harbour at Mudros. If we have to beat into a westerly that'll take us damn near a full twenty-four hours at the rate we're sailing – and if we're still tacking to and fro when Tyler comes out to look, we're sitting ducks.

'We have to head for the Cyclades. Where we know the wind blows for sure.'

Nina thought for a moment, and nodded. Then the strength seemed to drain out of her, and she moved up the cabin and fell on the starboard bunk.

'Just wake me when the shooting starts,' she said.

It was time Pollock got off his feet as well. I told him to bunk down in the stern cabin, and went back up to the cockpit to check the self-steering. The wind was lighter now that we were under the lee of the looming mountains and iron cliffs of Imroz. The island is barely six miles wide and its central ridge rises to over 2,000 feet. *Andromeda* was now about five miles due south, barely edging her way forward in the island's wind shadow. While I wasn't worried about our speed, because our radar trace up here would not arouse Tyler's suspicion, I was nervous of getting closer to land. I hadn't forgotten the hovering helicopter at Canakkale, and though there are few people on Imroz, there was always the chance that one of them might be a village cop with a pair of binoculars who had seen a message from Ilderim. By now the good Colonel was no doubt firing off alert requisitions in salvoes along the entire coast.

It was, regretfully, time to tack. I unhitched the self-steering and brought *Andromeda* easily round onto 220 degrees, almost due south-west. It meant sailing a bit high to get the best out of the breeze, and the course was not quite the direct line for the Cyclades: but on the other hand it kept us out from the Turkish coast and put Tyler's probable route to Lesbos over the horizon.

There was not much more I could do, so there was little point in worrying. The sun beat down from a clear sky, out here. Now that we were on the starboard tack there was no shade relief from the mains'l. I crept down into the cabin and found myself a white peaked cap. I had brown-tinted Zeiss Umbral sunglasses, the only ones that seem to be much use in the Mediterranean, and the light back on deck looked like molten copper.

A couple of dolphins broke the surface off the starboard beam, and gambolled about the side wake for a while before abandoning us. *Andromeda* was not travelling fast enough for their game. I watched the coast of Imroz slowly slip away to stern with the hours. The breeze was so steady I needed only to hold the wheel with a foot. It was quite a pleasant little sail that afternoon, as long as I made myself forget what might be over the horizon hunting for us. Round about four in the afternoon the colour of the shadows began to deepen as the sun fell away towards the western horizon. Now there seemed to be a suggestion of northerly cast in the gentle swell, which was otherwise so long and quiet you had to think about it a while to be sure it was there. That was a promise that the *meltemi* had been blowing somewhere. I was sure it would be with us tomorrow.

Just after five, by my reckoning, we crossed into Greek waters. We were about seventeen miles off the Turkish coast and the same distance away from Limnos. Tyler should be some forty miles south of us by now, down on the coast of Lesbos harassing fishing boats. I eased the sheets and dropped *Andromeda* back onto a course just a little west of south. She seemed to move more easily, almost with relief, and I thought we picked up a touch of boat-speed. It was worth putting up the mizzen, now. The sail adds little when *Andromeda* is sailing high on the wind, but with the breeze remaining slightly north of west we had come onto a broad reach, and the extra drawing power helped us. According to the log we were making well over three knots, which gave us a good four with the aid of the northerly current.

It was time to think about food again. I set up the helm and went below to find two cans of beef stew in the stores. With the aid of the spices in the rack they made a very reasonable curry. There was plenty of rice, but no beer, of course – and the water in the tap tasted as if it had been in the storage tanks since Noah's Flood.

But the sleepers, when they were aroused, were ravenous and almost light-hearted. Nina insisted on a second helping and gave her opinion that I was worrying over nothing.

'Now we're in Greek waters I'm sure we're out of trouble,' she said. 'When you've had a good sleep the whole picture looks brighter, Harry.'

'Tyler's out there somewhere,' I told them. 'But we've got a chance of slipping by. I've been checking the radar at intervals and there's been nothing to worry about – no small craft heading in our direction. Just normal coastal traffic and nothing at all as far out as we are.

'We can't leave the radar on all night or we'll drain the batteries. It'll be enough to check it every hour, because that's just about the time it would take Tyler's boat to get to us from the edge of our radar range.

'The closest we're going to come to Lesbos on this course is about thirty miles, between midnight and two a.m. At that distance we won't be visible on Tyler's radar screen, but he might just get lucky. If he does, the radar check will tell us. Any blip on the display that holds a steady bearing will be a boat on a collision course. It may be accidental – or it may be Tyler trying to intercept us. When you see a steady bearing on the screen, that's when I want you to wake me.'

I went up onto the for'ard bunk then, and left them to split the watches in the first part of the night. Tyler was not going to get to us that evening.

Nina touched me gently on the shoulder just after two a.m. I felt as if I had slept for twenty-four hours. I went into the shower up for'ard to try to come round. Nina came to the door to report our progress.

'We've been down every hour to check the radar,' she said. 'You were sleeping like a baby and there wasn't any reason to wake you.'

I grunted and started taking my clothes off, too dopey to worry much about Nina's reaction.

'I'm going to take a shower.'

'Go ahead. Anyway, according to the radar there's been nothing coming in our direction – there still isn't – so we let you slumber on until now.'

I dropped my clothes into a heap. Nina passed her eyes over me quickly, and winked. Just for a moment I felt a little like one of the girls in the Istanbul night club.

Then she said: 'The only thing is, honey, I think you made a small mistake plotting the course on the charts. I guess you must have been tired.

'We're off the edge of the Dardanelles and Approaches chart now, like you figured. The only thing is there's an overlap between that chart and the next one – you know, the Admiralty chart for the Greek Archipelago? The bottom edge of the Approaches sheet cuts in at 39° 20' North, but the top edge of the next one starts at 39° 35'. The way you've pencilled in the course it looks like you've taken the top chart position at the bottom edge and just transferred it to the first grid line on the second chart, thinking it was the same one.

'We're a lot further east than you anticipated.'

'Shit!'

The cold water of the shower hit me with a sudden shock at the same time, and brought me round in a second or two. Christ, if we were too close to Lesbos. . .

Nina continued: 'I don't think it matters too much, or I'd have changed the course when I spotted it.'

'So where are we?'

'Well, we're off the northern coast of Lesbos and miles from anywhere else. But instead of being thirty miles west of there, we're only about eighteen miles off the north-western tip.

'But think about it, it's two a.m. If Tyler got to Lesbos at all he's on the southern coast by now, snooping round the approaches to Mytilene harbour. That's an extra forty miles away from us, and there's nothing at all on our radar.

'So I stayed on the direct track for Andros. I hope I did the right thing.'

I was starting to enjoy the water, and thinking furiously. 'I guess you probably did. If the radar stays clear for the next few hours I might even start believing we've made it.'

'Well, we're on track for Andros, and that looks to me about as good a destination as any.'

I got hold of a towel and started back for the cabin, rubbing myself furiously to get some circulation back after the chilly water. I pointed out the clothes locker to Nina and she rummaged through to find some clean gear. She threw me a shirt and pants, and then went to turn the radar on.

'Pollock showed me, while you were asleep,' she said. 'Want to look?'

I zipped up the pants and joined her in front of the screen.

'See, there's Lesbos,' she said, as professional as a freighter's chief mate briefing the pilot, 'and there's nothing coming our way from there.

'By the time I realised what had happened with the charts it was too late to do too much about it. We only crossed over half an hour ago. I reckoned the best thing to do was to keep going straight for the southern Aegean, and let you sleep. I mean, we wouldn't make much distance away from Lesbos if we did turn off on a westwards reach. Not in this breeze.'

'You did the right thing. I got it wrong yesterday, obviously.'

'Well, doesn't look like there's too much harm done,' she said, with a reassuring tone. 'But Pollock could use some sleep now. I'll keep watch with you, if you like.'

Pollock was so weary by now that when I relieved him he stumbled down the companionway with hardly a farewell groan. Nina spread herself along the cockpit bench and studied the stars.

'They're brighter here than anywhere,' she said. 'You don't realise how many stars there are in the sky until you come to Greece.'

'Depends where you're coming from. You don't see such a full sky in Europe or America because our skies are cloudier – except sometimes on the Mid-West plains. But if you came from the desert countries to the east of here it'd be no surprise at all. That's why half the stars in the sky have Arabic names: they were the first astronomers.'

'Do you know which is which?'

'Not all of them. I know the Pole Star, The Big Dipper, Orion's Belt and the major constellations like that. But astral navigation's never been my thing.'

303

'You wouldn't need it out here. You're hardly out of sight of an island or two for long.'

'We will be tomorrow,' I said. 'We'll have Psara to port for a while, and you might see the mountains of Chios over the horizon to the east, but otherwise we won't see land until Andros comes up ahead.'

'I was wondering about that,' Nina said thoughtfully. 'Once we get past Lesbos, there are two other islands that are obviously closer – Chios, and Skyros to the west. I took a good look at the chart. You don't suppose we ought to aim for one or the other?'

'If we stay out here we're pretty certain of finding some wind tomorrow. If the Australians aren't chasing us, it doesn't matter how far it is to Andros. If they are, we'll need all the wind we can get.'

'I don't think we're going to see them again,' said Nina, sleepily. 'Not this far out.' Then she stirred herself, and reached over to a length of teak trim on the cockpit coaming to knock on wood.

Nina settled herself back again and looked at the sky for a while. After a while she asked: 'When all this is over, and you've made your peace with the Greeks, are you still going to make that Byron film?'

'I don't know, right now. It depends whether it'll be safe to go back to Turkey. What are you going to do?'

'I don't know, either. Archaeology has been my life since my second year at college. But all I've got out of this summer in Turkey has been a case of incipient skin cancer from the sun and a new scar on the left tit.'

'It'll look very erotic.'

'Every girl should have one. Just one. Any more would look plain careless. Make sure you remember that, Harry.'

Then she closed her eyes and fell silent. I put some cockpit cushions under her head, and let her sleep on.

The boat's head barely rose and fell in the low sea. Occasionally the big genoa flapped, with a slow subdued bark from the foredeck. The breeze was barely perceptible, blowing as it did from almost dead astern. But it was enough to keep the sails filled for the most part, and my boat continued to foot through the flat water, gently, with only an intermittent swish from time to time when the hull cleaved a slightly higher swell. Phosphorescence gleamed in the low bow wave streaming to either side. When I turned to look astern the wake glowed for fifty yards or so. I hardly needed to keep a hand on the helm.

The still Aegean was virtually an empty sea. Once a steamer's lights crossed our bows in the distance, right to left: an island ferry on its way to Lesbos, I imagined. A little later a prickle of lights near the western horizon announced the arrival of one of those nighttime acetylene fishing fleets which appear mysteriously miles away from any island, to put a match to the ancient gas lanterns at their bows and manoeuvre in silent unison netting the dazzled fish below. They were fishing the Mansell Bank, I supposed, forty miles out of Skyros and the same distance from any fishing port on Lesbos. There would not be a boat in the fleet longer than twenty-four feet. If they were prepared to venture so far out it was a plain indication the pattern of calm weather was general.

Paradoxically, that made it more likely it would blow in the morning. The Aegean's rare windless periods do not last long in the summer. The acetylene fleet would leave the bank while it was still dark, and enough time remained for them to reach home before the morning was more than two hours old. Then as the sun climbed we would expect a return to normal weather. In the meantime I could hardly find reason even to think, there in the night. I wondered vaguely whether to risk using the spinnaker when the wind got up the following day: it would give us extra boat speed, at the expense of a good deal more work controlling the sail. I put off the decision. Almost before I realised it, the hour hand moved to four a.m. in the glow on my diver's watch, and it was time to check the radar momentarily. The screen came to life in an underwater tint of green, still innocent of threat.

I went back to sit at the wheel, watching the coverlet of stars begin to fade. Time slipped by. Then the sky lightened slowly, and dawn broke lazily over the flat metallic sea. Nina came back to life with the first rays of the sun, and squinted blindly across the cockpit into the dazzling glare over the port side. I put a lashing across the wheel, and went down into the cabin to make coffee, and find a can of bacon for our breakfast.

Pollock woke to the smell of bacon, and came blearily across.

'How are we doing?'

'Fine,' I told him. 'Hungry?'

He grunted, and went for'ard to the head. Nina came to rummage in the galley storage cupboards over my shoulder, and found a packet of flapjack mix, some dried milk and Turkish honey.

'Just let me get at the frying pan when you've done,' she said. 'We're going to have a freedom feast. A kind of Aegean Passover: there's not a hostile ship in sight.'

By the time we had eaten we were well south of the fishing banks, roughly on a line between the north of

Skyros and the southern tip of Lesbos to the east. Just waiting for the wind to blow: the six a.m. radar check had been clear.

There was going to be no change for a while. I'd cleaned my teeth, washed, gone up on the foredeck to smoke several cigarettes in the lazy air, and even dozed a little by the time the genoa suddenly bellied out with a crack. The first puff of the day's *meltemi* had arrived.

I went back to the cockpit. Pollock was alone at the wheel, holding her on course while I strapped down the loose foresail a fraction to prepare for the rising breeze. It was eight-fifteen.

'Someone checked the radar?'

'Nina's just doing it,' he said.

'Hold her on 200 degrees,' I told him. 'The wind's going to be right aft, but she'll be easy enough to steer if we don't set the mizzen.' All the wind's effort would be concentrated in the sails at the head of the boat, so she would pull herself easily forward on track. He seemed to have the feel of the helm. After a second or two I went to the companionway to see what Nina was doing.

She was standing uncertainly in front of the screen.

'I just don't know about this,' said Nina.

'There's something a long way off, heading out of Lesbos.'

I clattered down the ladder to the navigation table. Lesbos was off our screen now, but Nina was right: there was a blip a little north of due east from us – the direction of the island's south coast. The range was something over twelve miles, exceptionally far to be picking up a small ship well over the horizon, but just possible if the boat was, say, a diesel trawler yacht with a lot of reflective clutter on its mast and high flying bridge.

'I've been watching it,' she said. 'It looks like what you said, a steady bearing. But it *can't* be deliberate: it's only just come up on the screen.'

'If it's Tyler, he'd have been able to see us long before we saw him. Because of our radar reflector.'

'Oh.'

I looked at the blip for a minute or two. Its direction was constant.

'Yes. That's a collision course all right.'

Nina said: 'It's probably just coincidence. After all this time, surely. They wouldn't follow us out here.'

'We're going to have to make certain. We'll switch courses. If he changes too, that's no coincidence.'

'Oh, Jesus,' said Nina. I left her to watch the screen while I went back on deck to haul *Andromeda* over onto a starboard reach. Pollock winched on the genoa and mainsail sheets while I steered round to a course 90 degrees off the track we'd been following, straight for the barren rocks of Skyros.

'The blip's moving,' Nina called up after three or four minutes.

'Now we need the mizzen up,' I told Pollock. 'Take the wheel while I get the lashings off.'

I had the mizzen hoisted in seconds, cranking the big Barlow winch, but it didn't seem to make much difference to the boat speed. Pollock felt easier, because of course it always *feels* as if you're going faster when you're reaching across the face of the wind or pointing into it, because of the extra apparent wind speed across the deck. But the log dial registered no improvement. We'd probably been footing better when we were running with the wind behind us, and in addition we'd now lost the advantage of the south-flowing current:

the boat's real speed was something like a whole knot slower than before.

I knew that if we were now in a chase we couldn't risk trying to make it to Skyros. Tyler would be on us before we were halfway there.

We made about a couple of miles westwards in the next twenty minutes.

Then Nina's voice came woefully up the companionway.

'Oh my God. The bearing's steady again.'

I went down. The other ship had altered course to match us. She was heading a touch south of west, to overtake and intercept our new course. She was also closer. Now, there were only ten miles or so between us.

'It's a chase,' I shouted to Pollock, and ran back up the companionway to get at the cockpit sail lockers. 'Get her back on the old course.' Nina, following, went to the portside heads'l winch. She was frowning at me doubtfully even while she went through the automatic motion of pulling the genoa sheet out of the cleat.

'The Australians are astern now and they *must* catch us,' Nina said, with the sheet in her hands. Pollock spun the wheel to port and she had to wind in the flapping headsail, gasping her doubts: 'Wouldn't we be better to keep heading away from them?'

Pollock paused, looking at me enquiringly.

'No. If we carry on west we may sail right out of the track of the *meltemi*. If we run before the wind we can't lose it, plus we'll have the current behind us as well.

'Not only that, I'm going to set the spinnaker, Nina. You take the wheel from Pollock when you've made the sheet fast. He'll have to haul in the spinnaker sheet as I hoist it.'

309

Andromeda came round to the southern track, now.

'What are the odds?' said Pollock, as Nina went to the helm and he joined me at the sail locker.

'If the wind gets up a bit and we fly the kite we can take 'em so far down the Aegean we'll all be too close to Greece for them to risk an attack. And if they do we can hold them off for a while with the machine gun.'

'Christ,' Nina said bitterly, 'they were prepared to go all the way down to Andros to dive on the fucking *caique*. Of course they're going to attack, you fool.'

Once we were settled back on the downwind run I slipped down into the cabin to have another look at the chart and watch the radar. The diversion had taken us slightly off track and I called up to Pollock to steer on 190 degrees to hold *Andromeda* on a course for Aghia Gria cape just above the main port on the north coast of Andros. The radar screen showed that the other boat across the horizon had quickly switched course too. The blip was steady again, bearing 076 degrees. She would be in sight within an hour, I thought.

Obviously the first thing to do was to pick up as much boat speed as we could. There were points for and against trying the spinnaker run. Normally, you use a kite in a race to get maximum speed downwind in a straight line to your destination – Euclid having shown that straight lines are the quickest, and so on. But you can only do that by having someone constantly man the spinnaker sheet on its winch in the cockpit: the big, fat-bellied triangular scoop of a sail up front needs to be kept at just the right angle to the wind to do its job. If a changing wind puff collapses its after edge – the one that's held outside the boat on the spinnaker pole – you not only lose boat-speed, you may tangle and split the sail, or see its lower tip disappear into the water, where it traps sea causing the whole damn thing to get run over by the speeding bow. Do that, and your yacht comes to a shuddering halt while everyone screams and runs to wrestle with the sodden canvas.

But with only three people on board *Andromeda*, all of them short of sleep and one of them an inexperienced sailor, we simply could not man the spinnaker winch all through a day-long run.

The other way of sailing with the kite is used by cruising yachts which don't much care about making the shortest distance between two points, as long as they're moving *somewhere*. You simply strap down the spinnaker sheet on a cleat, and leave it to the helmsman to alter the boat's heading to accommodate subtle changes in wind direction. The strapped-down sheet running to the outer end of the spinnaker pole holds the sail in a fixed position, and by steering carefully the helmsman keeps the spinnaker wind-full at the bow. That's fine and comfortable, but it means you may be making little track changes all the time as the wind shifts, and losing a bit of time against another boat which can steer a steady course – say, a diesel trawler yacht motoring down on you at twelve knots while everyone aboard it checks his automatic pistol.

Andromeda's only kite was a big, full-bellied running sail which could be something of a handful. Nina and I would have to share the steering, and I would not want to be caught with the kite up in a manoeuvring situation.

For the moment, though, this seemed the best option. It was more important to make speed rather than a straight wake. The wind was getting up, too.

Pollock stationed himself at the rear winch on the starboard side of the cockpit, with orders to haul like a maniac as soon as he was told. I dropped the genoa and wrestled the spinnaker bag up for'ard. There was not much motion on the sea yet, and once I had the pole attached to the mast I balanced myself easily in the pulpit to clip the sail attachments into place. The parrot's beak fitting on the outer end of the boom snapped onto the spinnaker sheet and we were ready. I jumped back to the mast and hauled the sail aloft on the halyard winch.

'Pull like buggery, Pollock! You've got to keep the bottom out of the water.'

The rear winch screamed and Pollock in a blaze of motion hauled in yard after yard of sheet line. The kite billowed out with a massive crack as she caught the freshening *meltemi*. You could feel the distinct surge as the power of the great spread of canvas jerked down into the hull.

'Hold on to her now,' I shouted, scrambling back into the cockpit. 'I'll just pull her in and strap her down. We're cooking with gas.'

We got the kite properly adjusted, nice and easy, with the boom out well back of the bow giving Nina a simple course to steer to keep her full. *Andromeda* had white water in her teeth now and spray dashing over her port side, with the noise of her rippling passage loud on the hull. I tied off the spinnaker sheet on its cleat. Nina's hair was blasting every way about her face and she stood at the wheel grinning, holding on with a manic grip as the boat lurched with a new violence across the shallow swells, and adjusting her course minutely with her eye fixed on the massive power sail out front.

312

'Great day for a spinnaker ride!' shouted Nina.

'Shit,' said Pollock, after a few minutes in a kind of awed silence under the cabin lee. He was looking at the speed log. 'We're hitting eight knots.'

'She'll go with the kite up, all right. The question is how long we're going to keep it flying, but we'll give them a run for their money.

'Still, come to think of it, do you want to try out the .30 cal?'

'That's an idea,' said Pollock, and he brought the gun out of the side locker.

At Nina's suggestion, I took down the mizzen while he was loading his first belt. We did not need the extra canvas at the stern now and it was only making steering more difficult by subtracting from the power at the for'ard mast. Once I'd lashed down the sail and the boom was taut in its fore-and-aft position, held by the mizzen sheet below and the topping lift to the mizzen peak above, I saw another advantage in furling the sail.

'You'd better practise shooting from a standing position,' I told Pollock. 'The sea's going to get up a lot higher by the time they come down on us. If the trawler is anything over fifty yards away and you're trying to fire out of the cockpit, you'll find the crests of the waves will keep getting in between you and the target.

'But if you stand up on the cabin top and hook one arm round the mizzen mast, you can fire across the boom.'

Pollock clasped the heavy gun in his left arm and climbed gingerly to the cabin roof. The deck was moving considerably now; Pollock, unused to the motion, had to catch hold of the mizzen boom to feel his way along. But once he steadied himself at the mast he had firm footing.

He nodded at me, aimed the gun to the weather side, and squeezed the trigger. The .30 cal barked with a reassuring crash, and the ammunition belt flailed against the brass winch handles on the mast. Pollock's teeth showed white on his face, burned a new red from the last day at sea.

'I guess Tyler's going to get a sudden shock,' he said. 'I sure hope they don't give up before I can smack 'em with a burst from this.'

He clambered back into the cockpit and busied himself arranging the machine gun and its belts where he could grab them readily out of the locker. The wind seemed to be getting stronger with each new gust now, as the morning heat increased: the needle on the log dial flickered over nine and almost to ten knots in the heavier blows.

'If the prizes in this race weren't so heavy I could kind of enjoy this,' said Nina from the wheel. She was in perfect control, keeping the heavy ketch at a perfect slant to the shifting blast of the rising *meltemi*. I went down to the navigator's table to try to work out lines on the chart.

The radar blip I was now sure was Tyler glinted steady on a bearing east-nor'east of *Andromeda*. He was still about the same distance off, but obviously on a converging track: in terms of where the wind was coming from he was only some five sea miles behind. Once we started hitting ten knots under the spinnaker his speed advantage would be down to barely two nautical miles an hour.

But I could see when I started to plot it that because of the angle he had much less distance to make up than the miles between us: it was not going to take him six hours to intersect our track, but perhaps three at the most.

314

Still, as I ruled the lines across the chart I thought that we would be within twenty miles of Andros port before then. Surely that would be too deep inside the Greek archipelago for Tyler to risk a piece of blatant piracy, hard by one of the busiest ferry tracks in the Aegean through the Kafireus Straits. I'd made the right choice this time, I believed, in sticking to the southern track instead of trying to make Skyros. Pollock might not get a chance to fire his machine gun after all.

The wind strength continued to build, blasting steadily from nearly due north, just on our starboard quarter. A steep short chop began to build on the summer swells, and Pollock's stomach started to feel it. He declined when he was offered the chance of a rest below, and I gave him a seasickness pill with a glass of water from the galley.

But just after ten I showed him something on the horizon that took his mind off the motion of the boat altogether. I'd been standing on the mizzen boom, clutching the mast, to get extra height for the lookout. And from there, away on our port stern quarter, out in the distance where the white-blue dazzle of the sky met the sea, you could detect a single notch in the skyline, steady in the east-nor'east among the moving lumps of water in between us. Pollock did not realise what it was for a moment.

'It's a ship,' I said. 'And it's the one that's been following us.'

The biggest binoculars we had were a pair of 12×50s – a touch too powerful for easy use on a moving sailboat but nowhere near the power of the massive World War Two U-boat glasses the raider-skippers were able to use to identify their distant prey. All I could make out of our pursuer, when I finally fixed the bobbing lenses on the target, was that she gleamed white in the morning sun. That established she was a yacht: small working boats in the Aegean, fishermen or the motorised *caiques* trading between the islands, are invariably painted black or dark brown.

Pollock took the glasses from me but did no better.

In a while he said: 'I think she's sideways on to us, though.'

'Naturally. It's an interception course. If she was bows-on in that quarter she would be passing way behind us in an hour or so.'

'When does she get to us?'

'They've got a long way still to go.'

Nina called me to the wheel then, and with only one squinting sideways glance at the horizon went below to catch some rest. Pollock sat at the weather cockpit coaming, silent, lifting the binoculars to his eyes from time to time to check on the shadowing yacht.

Andromeda crashed through the short chop, dashing plumes of spray as her bow cut down from each wave, and charging into the hollows under the huge press of her spinnaker bellying forward. Ahead the white caps became a solid glare of glittering reflection once midday came close, and the sun mounted into the southern quarter of the sky. The ketch was starting to roll a little now, as the sea rose, but nothing to worry about overmuch. I would come off the direct downwind run only if she began to arc her masts through the sky in the 'death roll', the lurch which can eventually make you broach-to across the wind all-standing, when the motion finally jabs the spinnaker deep into the sea and jerks the boat around. The spinnaker run is the most dangerous

316

point of sailing: but as long as the helmsman stays alert he can minimise the risk.

After a long while Pollock said: 'I reckon it's Tyler's trawler all right. How'd he come to find us again, after we gave him the slip at the Dardanelles?'

'Checked out all the possibilities off Lesbos, and came out to take a look around on the offchance, I guess. Just our bad luck we were the only small boat blip in the neighbourhood.'

'That's unusual?'

'I suppose not,' I conceded. 'Most of the little *caiques* tend to sail island to island – round the edges of the Aegean, rather than across. Once Tyler saw a boat making a track southwards right down the middle it'd have to be worth his while taking a closer look. Few other people would want to go direct for the mainland.'

'Next time you decide to make a getaway,' said Pollock lifting the binoculars again, 'try to make use of local cover.'

He was probably right, I considered. But while I thought about it, *Andromeda* slipped slightly off track, and when I over-corrected the bow slammed down askew off a wave, and a cascade of wild water crashed up over the portside, drenching him.

'Shit!' said Pollock, retreating under cover of the cabin break and trying to wipe the glasses clean.

He sat wedged into the angle of the cabin, working on the lenses with his shirt, scowling as if he thought I could do that kind of thing deliberately, like the skipper in *Captains Courageous*. I worked the wheel and tried to get some reason back into the boat's track. She was much harder to steer now, with the mastheads careering across the sky and the spinnaker overpowering her every minute or so. The needle on the log dial was approaching eleven knots. It was getting to be a wild ride – but the worse the ride, the better our chances of escape.

Pollock had got the binoculars clear again. 'Listen,' he said, shouting at me against the wind from behind the great jam-jars he was holding to his face, 'you know what you said about the intercepting boat being on a constant bearing?

'I don't know what's happening here, but the trawler's moving astern.'

'Christ!' I flashed an eye over my left shoulder. I saw nothing, and I could not spare longer from attending to the wheel, the way the ketch was starting to move around. 'Get Nina up from the cabin,' I told Pollock. 'I can't get time to look unless she takes the helm.'

In a second or two she followed him back to the cockpit, clutching at the companionway rail and the grab-handles at the hatch.

'Can you steer for a bit? It's getting difficult.'

'I'll be OK. My God, though, the wind's up.'

She caught hold of the wheel and moved behind the helm.

'Jesus,' she said, 'can we keep going like this?'

'As long as the sail stays in one piece.'

I took the binoculars from Pollock. He was right. The trawler was little more than six miles off, but she had slipped round to a point fine on the port quarter, almost astern.

Nina shouted 'What's happened? They turning back?'

'No, they're bows-on,' said Pollock.

I was equally puzzled for a moment. Then it came to me.

318

'You know what it is? They must have miscalculated the intercept course right at the beginning.

'When we turned back onto the southern track this morning, after we faked towards Limnos, they only had us on radar. They'd have calculated their intercept course off the screen plot. But the wind was lighter then, and we only had the genoa up.

'They never figured out the effect of the wind rising, and the difference the spinnaker makes to our speed. They've been steering the course they originally needed to come across our bows when we were still only doing seven–eight knots, and now we're hitting eleven. By the time they got close enough to realise the difference, they were falling astern.'

'We can outsail them?'

'Damn nearly. By the time they can overhaul *Andromeda* from that position we'll be at Andros, in this wind.'

CHAPTER 16

❧

Fire Fight

When the full implications of Tyler's mistake sank in, I hurtled down the companionway to the chart to check out our position. I managed to get a radar bearing on the little island of Psara, about nineteen miles due east of us, and calculated we were about forty-two miles off the Andros coast, and thirty-odd south-east of Skyros. At the rate we were scooting along, we had just over four hours' sailing to get to safety – and Tyler had only one knot an hour advantage on us.

'If the wind holds he won't get within two miles of us,' I shouted to the others.

'I wonder when he's going to realise it,' said Pollock. There was fair bit of spray flying across *Andromeda*'s decks now, and he was sitting huddled under the break of the cabin, wet and queasy. His face was set on the sea to stern, where the distant yacht came into view from minute to minute across the mounting wave peaks. Nina's fingers were white where she gripped the wheel.

'Better give me the helm back,' I told her. 'It's too much for you.'

'I'm OK,' she said. 'Take a break while you can, and I'll hand over when I can't control her.'

I took up a place on what passed for the lee side,

opposite Pollock, although with the wind almost aft it was little drier. *Andromeda* crashed and shuddered.

'The only doubt in my mind,' Nina shouted, 'is how long we can stick with the spinnaker. You ever done a kite run before in this kind of wind?'

'Not on this boat. I guess you wouldn't try it in the Atlantic, but the wave peaks don't rise so high here. There's not much chance of getting stalled in a trough and then swamped by the following wave. As long as we can keep her pointed in the right direction, she'll just keep going.'

'Like a steam train.'

'I never had a ride this rough on a railroad,' Pollock shouted, 'not even on Amtrak.'

'I'm going to find us something to eat,' I said. 'Anybody hungry?'

'Oh, Jesus,' Pollock groaned, 'no.'

I got Nina something out of the galley and brought up mugs of water, laced with Turkish *raki* to try to settle Pollock's stomach. There was no beer left and you can't cope with wine in a high sea. I felt pretty good, myself, despite the motion. I was sure now that we were going to make it, and my spirits were high. The plan had worked. When I finished eating I took over the wheel from Nina and aimed *Andromeda* southwards through the lower peaks in the raging sea. At the end of an hour we were holding our eleven knots and the pursuers were still five miles behind – with a safe port now only three hours or so ahead.

Then, about twenty minutes after midday, the disaster struck.

With a huge crack like a twenty-five-pounder cannon, the spinnaker block at the main masthead blew out. It was built to take a four and half ton strain, they'd assured me in Hong Kong, but the metal just exploded with the force of the bellying sail: the kite went straight for'ard and into the boiling sea, to be run over by *Andromeda*'s keel in the very next second. The whole boat jerked sideways as the sail caught a giant gutfull of water and grabbed at us from twenty yards astern like a giant obscene sea-anchor. You couldn't see much, just the line of white water where one edge broke the surface, but the ketch was beam sides on to the waves and tilting sickeningly towards them. Then a flash of time later the nylon spinnaker sheet parted and *Andromeda* surged free, with the sunken sail held only by the wire halyard.

I screamed at Nina to grab the wheel and ran for'ard to cast off the halyard from the winch. The end of it gouged my left forearm half an inch deep as the wire screeched off the drum and flashed over the rail to vanish in the sea. I hardly even noticed the blood as I felt my way back to the cockpit for the number two genoa. The boat was wallowing from side to side now like a drunken elephant, unbalanced without the force of the spinnaker on one side of the mast counterbalancing the main stayed out across the wind on the other. We had to get up another heads'l immediately before Nina lost control of her altogether.

Pollock threw open the sail locker and rummaged inside the moment I told him what to look for. The wind was too big to use the number one genoa we'd carried earlier in the day. I roared to Pollock to hurry while I tied a handkerchief round my arm, then gave up the attempt and grabbed the sailbag from him. He started to come for'ard with me: I made him stay by the winches. The genoa sheets were still in place at the foremast and I had only to hitch the sail onto the forestay and its halyard to haul it aloft.

The genoa screamed up the forestay, the force of the wind getting hold of it half-way up and almost raising the sail for me. Pollock wound in the starboard winch: the sail bellied out and we were on track again. Before I clambered back into the cockpit I disentangled the dangling spinnaker pole and pushed the parrot's beak end out into the genoa's leech eyelet, where the sheet was shackled. That way I poled out the small genoa like a miniature spinnaker. We might be able to keep up most of our speed.

At least the boat was handling better, now. Nina had her under control again and she was able to head more steadily through the leaping water. But without the spinnaker's power we had lost that exhilarating headlong rush to freedom. I watched the log dial as Pollock bound up my arm with the first aid kit. The needle was down to eight and half and nine knots.

'Pollock, you're going to get a chance to use the pop-gun, after all.'

'Look on the bright side,' he said. 'Now we've lost that sail, I might not be too sick to aim it.'

Tyler's diesel yacht was almost a mile closer already, after the minutes *Andromeda* had wallowed through the troughs while we rigged the genoa. He would be on us in an hour, I thought – unless by some fortunate chance we ran into the Greek navy on manoeuvres in the meantime.

The imperative now was to make the ketch as defensible as possible. I went below and locked the for'ard hatch, so that in the event we were boarded Tyler's men could not hold *Andromeda*'s crew down in the cockpit while taking us in a pincer through the accommodation.

Next, Pollock and I shifted sailbags and the heavier canned stores back into the cockpit, where we stuffed the side lockers as high and as thickly as possible. Rifle bullets might penetrate the fibreglass hull, but the locker contents should deaden their impact if they passed further.

The one thing that worried me was Pollock's intended firing position by the mizzen mast. The mizzen, with its winch gear at his chest level, was something like a foot wide, but there would still be plenty of Pollock visible as a target on each side.

It was not much cover, Pollock agreed. But other than lashing the storm trysail bag to the aft side of the mast — pretty tenuous kind of protection, but it was the toughest canvas we had — I could think of nothing.

Pollock was unconcerned. Given the state of the sea, he said, he would not bet much on anyone's chances of getting off an accurate shot at him with a handgun.

By the time we had finished, Tyler's boat stood a couple of miles astern. I could clearly identify it through the 12×50s, now. The figures on the flying bridge atop the wheelhouse were indistinct blots at that range, but the boat was the same one we had seen at Kapidagi.

Nina was exhausted at the wheel. I took over and sent her below to get us a drink.

'We've got about half an hour, Pollock. Try and give them a burst at about 600 yards. We're going to have to stand them off for at least a couple of hours.'

Pollock said: 'I don't have enough ammunition for that, kid. And I don't feel like wasting any into the sea.

'I'm never going to get in a hit at 600 rolling around like this. It'll be better to let 'em get in close and make it count. If you start blasting off a .30 cal, you want to feel it's doing some good.'

'If you let them get in close and don't stop 'em, they'll be all over us like a rash. We've got to string this thing out. Hold 'em off at long range.'

'Don't argue,' said Pollock, 'I'm the one with service time in on the shooter. I'm going to let 'em in easy range where I can subtract a few of the bastards. Remember they don't know we're armed – they'll be strung around the deck like clay pipes in a shooting alley.'

He wedged himself at the aft of the cockpit, keeping the binoculars trained astern.

'I was right,' he said after a while, 'they're all on deck without a care in the world.'

When I turned my head, the white trawler was shockingly close. Nina came up from the cabin again.

'Keep down, honey,' said Pollock. 'It's going to start any minute.'

'How close are they?'

'Less than half a mile now,' I told her.

'I found kitchen knives in the galley,' she said. 'They might be some use.'

'Maybe we won't need them,' Pollock said. 'I've a lot of faith in the dissuasive factor of a .30 cal. Particularly one you're not expecting.'

He handed the binoculars to Nina. 'I think it's time I got up behind the mast. Just watch the goons on the flying bridge and make sure they don't have their binoculars on us when I move. I don't want them to see the gun.'

Pollock lurched with the ammunition box up to the top of the cabin, and attached it to the foot of the mast. He pulled the lid open, tying it in the vertical position with a line as protection against the spray, which was dashing continually across the deck. Then he came back to the cockpit, staring sternwards.

'It looks safe,' said Nina. 'I can see Tyler and that other big loon up on the steering bridge. There's about four other men gathering up at the bows. Jesus, they're getting wet.'

Pollock gathered the machine gun in his arms. I looked aft again. The trawler was 300 yards away and closing fast.

'That's what I've been trying to avoid,' said Pollock. Holding the gun upright at his side, he clambered awkwardly back to the cabin top, and moved behind the lashed sailbag.

'Did they react to that at all?'

'No.'

'Good. Come on, kids, the meat market's waiting for you.'

Andromeda heaved and pounded through the piled-up, froth-lashed sea. I concentrated as hard as I could on the task of holding the boat on the angle to the near-gale which kept the poled-out genoa taut. But the minutes went by agonisingly. I had to look round. The white trawler was now 100 yards behind us, her bows crowded with the four or five Turks waiting crouched at her rail. I could recognise Tyler and Shane, standing confident behind the windscreen of the flying bridge steering position.

'For Christ's sake, Pollock, let them have it.'

'Just a little further.'

I transferred my attention back to the plunging bow.

'Any second now,' said Pollock. 'Keep down at the wheel, there.'

There were two loud cracks from astern, blasting down on the wind with almost unnatural force. Pollock laughed.

'You're not going to hit anything with a hunting rifle in this sea,' he shouted.

Then his head and shoulders came out from behind the sailbagged mast and the .30 cal broke into a stuttering, deafening roar.

I was on my knees by the wheel. I ducked my head, involuntarily, and then turned to the trawler behind. The first burst had missed but the men at the bows sixty yards away were a sudden heaving mass of motion, scrambling to flatten themselves on the pitching deck. Tyler and Shane had vanished behind the flying bridge rail and for a moment I thought Pollock must have hit them.

Then one head appeared above the solid bulwark and at the same moment Pollock fired his second burst into the mass of bodies on the foredeck.

The Turks were screaming in the sudden silence that followed: two of them writhed by the rail and the others scrambled rapidly aft for cover. Pollock blasted off for the third time, even as the trawler wheeled rapidly to port. One of the wounded Turks fell through the bow rail into the sea, spouting blood. The other was still and Pollock's hosing trail of fire cut through another who'd picked the starboard side of the main cabin for his attempted entry and then, as the boat turned, become exposed to the lead.

The trawler showed its stern as it wheeled, and that was Tyler's next error: the flying bridge was open to Pollock's aim now and he crashed off the rest of the ammunition belt at the men on top. One of them fell and lashed about suddenly as the last of the belt clicked through the machine gun and the explosions stopped.

'I think I got that fucker Shane,' Pollock said calmly in the unnatural silence that followed.

Andromeda was almost broaching in the trough after the seconds in which I'd left the wheel alone. The genoa cracked and slammed itself against the spinnaker pole's restraint, taking the gale at the wrong angle. I spun the wheel starboard to get her back on track, overcorrected and almost backed the genoa. I'd have lost it altogether, but at the last split-second I managed to get her to port again and the sail filled.

'Shee-yit,' said Nina, her head poked up over the port side, watching the retreating trawler.

Pollock came back into the cockpit, and cleared the last of the belt from the gun. 'What do you reckon they're doing? Heading back?'

I gave the wheel to Nina and took the glasses. Tyler had made rapid distance between us, but as I watched he turned again to match Andromeda's heading. He'd slowed his boat, too: she now parallelled our course, about 1,000 yards away. He was not bothering to try to pick up the man he'd lost. Somebody dragged the other one out from under the bow rail and back towards the cabin: there seemed to be a brief discussion with Tyler on the flying bridge. Then they pushed the second prone Turk off into the sea, as well.

I told Pollock: 'You scored two, anyway.'

'What the hell are they doing now?' Pollock asked.

There was a bustle of activity behind the cabin ports. I noticed that the for'ard windows of the lower wheelhouse position there had been shattered by one of Pollock's bursts. The Turks appeared to be packing the whole windscreen. I saw Shane's yellow head directing action, and Tyler descending from the flying bridge above.

'Shane's on his feet again.'

'Yeah, but are they trying to protect the wheelhouse windows or something?'

Pollock retrieved the glasses from me. 'They're going to try to do that with mattresses?

'Jesus, they are,' he said after a second or two. 'Maybe a cabin table, too.

'Looks like they're going to armour the boat with feather pillows and have a second go. Come along, baby: I know something about the power of a .30 cal you don't know.'

'They'd better be quick,' I said. 'We've got Andros up ahead, now.'

It hadn't registered in the excitement of the fire fight. In the few moments I'd had time to look at *Andromeda*'s course I'd been intent on the sea immediately ahead and not the horizon. But the mountains of Andros were clear in the distance now.

'Jesus,' said Pollock, 'how far have we got to go?'

'I don't know, maybe twelve miles.'

'An hour and a half. We're going to make it.'

Nina said: 'They're trying to get ahead of us.'

Tyler, steering from down in the trawler wheelhouse now, had gunned his engine and was starting to overtake us, on a course about 800 yards off.

'I can see what he's trying to do,' said Pollock. 'If he can get to abreast or a little way ahead of us he can turn and get across into close range quicker than he would just by overtaking from astern.'

'Then he tries to blast us.'

'He's got to get there first,' said Pollock. He moved back to his position at the mizzen mast.

'They're only safe until they show themselves to get a shot off,' I told Nina.

Laboriously the trawler gained the position Tyler was aiming for, up a couple of points on our port beam. Then he wheeled his craft quickly, and the trawler came bearing down towards us, leaping in the white sea and dashing spray higher than her flying bridge.

As the two boats converged, the trawler now at a range of 100 yards, Tyler turned a little to port to bring his starboard side to bear on us.

Right at that moment Pollock opened fire again. This time he was not trying to sweep the decks of the other boat. He just held the gun steady on one area of the hull low down on the waterline just abaft of the bows.

From behind the barricaded side windows of the wheelhouse Tyler's men blasted a fusillade of rifle fire at Pollock's position. The metal stays on *Andromeda*'s mizzen twanged to occasional bullets, Most of them didn't even come that close: the trawler was rolling in the troughs like a sick man and *Andromeda* leaped and surged in the short following seas, and single shots could not be aimed. Pollock, though, had a steadier firing platform because under sail the ketch only pitched and hardly rolled. He was able to hold his machine gun more or less on its target, like a hosepipe.

All of a sudden I saw what he was doing. A three-foot square of the trawler's hull just behind the bow was riddling and jumping with the force of the .30 cal bursts. At the same time the hull was pounding into the driving sea, leading with just this section. Within a few seconds the shattered fibreglass started to give way. Then there was nothing there but a growing black gap, filling with rushing green water every time the sea crashed and rose along the boat's side.

The trawler shuddered, and seemed to lean more to starboard. Then she slowed, and turned her other side to us, falling rapidly off to stern.

'That's kept 'em busy,' said Pollock.

'She's going have a focs'le full of water in a minute or two,' I told him.

'My God,' said Nina, 'have we sunk them?'

'I doubt it's that bad. It's just that when he started taking in water it suddenly slowed down his rush.'

'I don't think they'll try again, though,' said Pollock triumphantly, coming down from the cabin top.

Nina watched the trawler astern.

After a while she said: 'If that's right, they're taking a long time about turning back to Turkey.'

That did not worry me much for the moment, because if you have to plug a hole in your bow you naturally do not turn the boat's head to the weather. Of course they would not turn back yet. Tyler could find something to stuff in the gaping hull easily enough – a bunk mattress would do it – and get rid of the flood up for'ard with his bilge pump. But only when that was done would he risk turning round.

But in the next thirty minutes it became clear that he was not going to turn his boat yet. There was heavy activity on the trawler for a while, Nina reported with the binoculars. Then, when they seemed to have patched the bow, the boat once more began overtaking us on a course which took her past *Andromeda* at a range of 900 yards.

'What the hell happens now?' asked Pollock.

'He's going to try to hit us from dead ahead this time,' I said. 'The idea will be that you won't have a clear field of fire from the bow, with the genoa and the main between you and the target.'

'Jesus,' said Pollock, 'I don't fancy my chances trying to get off a burst from the bow pulpit. Not in this sea, and without any cover at all.'

'That's OK. Let him burn his fuel off trying to get up ahead of us. All I've got to do is take the pole off the genoa so we can manoeuvre again – then when he turns and runs for us, I just twitch the boat round to give you a clear field of fire from the mizzen mast.'

'The timing'll have to be good.'

'It will be. Don't forget, a sailboat is much more manoeuvrable than a power boat at speed.'

It took Tyler almost half an hour to get into position. We had plenty of opportunity in that time to unrig the spinnaker pole from the genoa and arrange ourselves so that I could turn the ketch as fast as an ocean yacht juggling for position at the start line, whenever they came within range.

Then they started their run, from almost half a mile ahead just fine on the port bow.

I had Pollock back to his gunner's position at the mizzen as soon as they turned. I had learned from his earlier tactics the advantage of waiting for a close range situation, and now I hung onto our southerly course until they were barely 100 yards away, converging on us at a combined speed that must have been near twenty knots, before flicking *Andromeda* out from under the trawler's charge with a quick turn to starboard. Because they were on our port I did not even have to gybe the main – swing the boom across the boat with the dangerous force of the gale effecting the switch from one side of the boat to the other. All I had to do was turn the boat's head starboard, while Nina threw off the sheet which held the genoa out on that side of the boat, and then jumped to the portside to winch the sheet in on the opposite side.

Andromeda flew over on a new course 90 degrees to the trawler, and Pollock, suddenly given a clear field of fire as the mains'l which had obscured him from Tyler's boat swung clear, blasted the flimsy protection of the trawler's wheelhouse windows with a continuous stream of fire from the .30 cal.

In the face of that stream of lead not a single head showed its face out of the blocked windows. The trawler kept on course straight past us, from the sheer inertia of its rush and its helmsman's Pavlov's-dog reaction under fire to keep behind cover, hands rigid on the wheel.

They were 400 yards further on by the time they got themselves together and began to turn the boat. And by that time I had *Andromeda* back on course.

And with every lunge by Tyler's boat the coast of Andros was coming closer.

'So much for that idea,' said Pollock. 'You seem to know how this game works, Harry. What would you do now, if you were them?'

'Fuck off back to Turkey,' said Nina.

'That's not a bad idea,' I said. 'But they seem pretty unwilling to fold their hand on this one. If it was me, I'd keep making approaches from astern until we've exhausted our ammunition.'

'Gloomy bastard,' Pollock said. 'We very nearly have.'

And Tyler, once again, was doing the logical thing. We watched from three-quarters of a mile away as his crew dragged up everything they could find from below decks to bolster the defences of the wheelhouse. They struggled up with floor gratings from the engine room and chopped-off cabin furniture, lashing them into position as extra layers on the mattress and table-top protection on the starboard side of the wheelhouse. Then they brought up their big liferaft canister as the final armouring.

'They must reckon the front of the wheelhouse is strong enough,' Pollock said.

'Probably is. Where the helmsman stands he's got a mass of equipment plus the whole bulk of the for'ard cabin in front of his body. The only thing that's exposed is the top of his head. What they're trying to protect is their gunmen's position, firing out of the side of the boat when it comes alongside.'

Tyler made the first of these attempts a few minutes later.

Once the wheelhouse protection was in place, his crew took their positions, rifles and pistols at the ready on top of the starboard-side wheelhouse barricade. Tyler increased revolutions to come up from astern.

Pollock blasted economical bursts from the .30 cal. The trawler was coming up bows on, and the machine gun bullets would only bounce off the angled planes of the oncoming hull: we could not puncture it again from this position.

The trawler fell back a little, and then came on again.

'I got one more belt left,' said Pollock.

'Don't let 'em guess,' I told him. 'Just half a mile further, and I've got another trick to play.'

We were just 1200 yards now from the steepling rocky coast of northern Andros. The great granite cliffs to the west of Aghia Gria were two points off my starboard bow: the grey-green mountains of the interior loomed over us all. My logical course, as Tyler must have known, would involve a slight deflection to port under the shadow of the lighthouse on Aghia Gria point, and a straight fast sail down the coast to the protection of Andros port.

But I knew something I now took a bet he didn't know. I'd had to set *Andromeda*'s course for Andros and I'd looked at the chart. Tyler could not have done so — at the beginning he did not know where we were heading. I'd noticed what lay just 350 yards to the west of my landfall at Aghia Gria. It was not much of a mark on the chart and you could be forgiven for missing it. But such things automatically strike any skipper of a sailing boat with six-and-a-half foot draft.

Tyler made his third run from astern as we came up under the island's shadow. In his desperation he totally ignored the certainty that anyone ashore tending the lonely light on Aghia Gria must inevitably notice what was happening out to sea just below the cape. He brought the trawler up on our port side this time, ready to cut off my turn towards Port Andros.

Pollock's machine gun barked, and then stuttered to an empty silence. I don't know whether we sensed, or saw, the triumph on the faces behind the trawler's barricades.

Then I spun the ketch's wheel starboard. Nina was ready at the genoa winch. She threw off the sheet and dived to the other side of the cockpit to take it on port: we were on the starboard tack in a second and heading west up the coast instead of down to Port Andros.

Tyler brought his trawler smartly around, but he had lost a hundred yards or so in the process. I'd banked on that.

As the white power boat drew up astern the men in the wheelhouse began cracking off their rifles and even a pistol. Occasional bullets sang around *Andromeda*'s cockpit but the sea was even wilder here in the coastal shallows than out in the centre of the Aegean. I crouched on the weather side of the wheel. I'd seen what what I was looking for. It was a patch of water, just a little whiter than the rest, that was now 300 yards ahead. It was coming closer every second. I prayed that Tyler might not notice that the white water showed suddenly dark whenever the troughs of the wave swell passed across the point directly ahead of my bows. I hadn't got the time now to notice the risk from the gunfire.

Tyler's boat was thirty-five yards off, then twenty. They were shooting so hard it sounded like Pollock's machine gun. Or my machine gun, whatever. I was not able to think clearly about anything except the target ahead of me.

Then, when it was ten yards from my bow, I told Nina to unhitch the genoa sheet.

And immediately what was represented on the charts by two small dots and the figure '3' disappeared from view under *Andromeda*'s bow, I jerked the steering wheel savagely to starboard and spun the boat through a vicious tack, gybing the main boom as we came about and turning round in her tracks past the advancing trawler.

Tyler ploughed straight on.

He must have run the whole length of his boat over what the Australians call a 'bombora' – two large rock ledges, three feet below sea level at low tide, just a couple of hundred yards out from the Andros cliffs and breaking the surface of the water whenever the trough of a wave passed over them.

Tyler's boat was hitting all of twelve knots. He would have ripped the whole bottom out on the first rock he hit.

The rest of the boat crashed through onto the second rock ledge, hung there for a second as the storm-packed seas burst into mountains on its obstruction, and then separated like a silent explosion, nothing left of it but huge shards of shattered fibreglass being thrown across 180 degrees of boiling sea.

My crew were silent.

Then Pollock said quietly: 'How come they didn't see it?'

'You had to know it was there.'

Nina said: 'And you knew.'

'I knew.'

'I'm glad,' said Nina. 'Are you going to try to pick anyone up?'

'Pick what up?' Pollock said. 'There's nothing left.'

And there wasn't. There'd been broken pieces of boat for perhaps thirty seconds. There'd been here and there a dark wet shape like a man struggling for a hold on a piece of wreckage. Shane's yellow head, just momentarily.

But now there was nothing but white water between the bombora and the shore.

You don't go too close to the north shore of an Aegean island in a sailboat during a full *meltemi*. The undersea litter of shattered amphorae on the north coasts of places like Andros and Naxos record 3,000 years of wrecked sailing ships which ignored that caution. The seas mount higher than fifteen feet as they crash in to the rockbound shore, and always the wind blasts inexorably in on the scene of destruction.

'I couldn't take *Andromeda* inshore there even if I wanted to,' I told them.

'No one's asking,' said Pollock.

'Let's just go to Andros,' said Nina, wearily, 'and tell them to pick up the pieces. It's over.'

CHAPTER 17

The Prizes

When the storm eased next day and the surf at Aghia Gria had subsided to its normal nine foot wave-height, Theodoropoulos' men found two bodies. One, clearly, was a Turk. From its size, the other had been Tyler. There was no certain way of knowing: the boiling maelstrom under the cape had left no recognisable feature. Shane and the rest of Tyler's crew were never found.

The morning after we made Andros I woke looking forward to enjoying triumphant irony at Theodoropoulos' expense. Vindicated innocence expected at least the satisfaction of watching his embarrassment. It proved quite impossible. He arrived beaming fresh from his helicopter and warmly shook my hand, even before I had time to rise from the table on the hotel terrace where the three of us were having breakfast with the Andros police captain. I'd forgotten Greek philosophy: there never was a mistake, yesterday was simply a sad misunderstanding which we won't discuss, a totally unnatural event which is now forgotten because we are as always excellent friends. Embarrassing facts have simply ceased to exist: no one therefore feels in the least awkward.

Theodoropoulos gave us to understand that our

survival gave him the most exquisite personal joy. He was particularly delighted that, as he put it, everything was clear for me now. He'd known, of course, ever since Nina recognised her mistake on encountering the real villains on Andros, that I had been wrongly identified and falsely accused. He took my hand again, this time in both of his, piercing me with his dark lustrous eyes and smiling with gleaming, generous exuberation. 'I'm very glad now that we are friends again,' he said.

The thing was, I knew he meant every word. It is one of the great strengths of Greek life that with each new dawn the whole world begins afresh.

With careful circumspection, Theodoropoulos inquired how we'd got the boat back to Turkey from Andros. With a conspiratorial glance he suggested, 'Friends, I presume. . .'

'That's right.' I said nothing else. We had all agreed to keep Bassington's name out of the story.

Theodoropoulos nodded. 'Well, of course, your boat was not under official detention. Perhaps technically she should not have been sailed out of Greek waters without proper notification, but we'll let that pass.'

When the congratulations were over – and as much of the story told as we could – Theodoropoulos diffidently suggested we might go back to Athens, as soon as it was convenient. We were offered a lift in the helicopter, but I told him I preferred not to leave *Andromeda* on the island again. There were a few bullet holes along the topsides I needed to get re-glassed in Piraeus, for one thing, not to speak of work on the rigging. The others said they would sail with me.

It would be an advantage to do that fairly soon, said Theodoropoulos with a deep, meaningful glance in my direction. There was the question of salvage money on the *caique*: it might be possible to arrange something, there.

Not even Pollock could work that one out for a while. We discussed it later on the long, leisurely sail round the south coast of Andros and across to Piraeus, when the *meltemi* died down.

There was properly chilled beer in the fridge, now, together with fresh food in the galley, and Pollock said he enjoyed sailing this way. He lay up on the lee-side cockpit cushions with a Fix in one hand, a handful of bread and *feta* in the other, and debated Theodoropoulos' hint.

'I can't see the salvage making your fortune,' said Pollock. 'After all, the fucking boat was so rickety they sank it in the first rough sea they met, didn't they?'

I didn't get the explanation until the next day. Our new friends and admirers at police headquarters had booked us into one of the modern hotels near Omonia Square. The night we arrived we'd fallen into our separate beds after luxuriating in what felt like the first hot showers in months, and left orders to block all phone calls. The story of the recovered Praxiteles was already all over the Athens papers, of course, and next morning the foreign reporters were besieging the hotel lobby. I left Nina to handle interviews – Pollock refused to be seen – and strolled out into Omonia Square's distinctive olfactory cocktail of *doner* kebab restaurant cooking smells and traffic fumes to join Theodoropoulos for lunch, at his request.

Over the *mezzes* all was made subtly clear. The authorities were naturally delighted with the return of what was, after all, a masterpiece of Greek art and a treasure of the national heritage. Since it was undeniably Greek, there would be no question of returning it to Turkey. Certainly not. The more particularly since the Turkish police had been so inimical to the noble soul responsible for its restoration. I forbore to observe that the Greek police had been something less than the model of friendly assistance, either.

It might be expected that there would be an international argument on the matter, Theodoropoulos conceded. He shrugged at this unconcernedly. Now, to the matter of the *caique*'s salvage. She had of course sunk, since then, and the owners were not in Greece. But in order to expedite matters the Greek authorities would be prepared to value her, as found on the day I took her in tow, at $US40,000, and hand over half to me forthwith as an *ex gratia* payment. There would be a further *ex gratia* payment of, say, $10,000 each to Pollock, Nina and myself for the return of the Praxiteles. It remained only to get our signatures to a document declaring, as a pure formality of course, that we relinquished any possible claims or rights to the statue.

'It might be more acceptable if we made it $20,000 for the salvage, and $20,000 each,' I said. Theodoropoulos drew a deep intake of breath. Then he nodded slowly. That could well be arranged, if we would sign.

'Of course,' said Pollock, when I discovered his hiding place in the hotel bar and broke the news. 'Why not, we haven't any rights that'd stand up in court anyway. The thing is, the Greeks don't have any legal right either – not to a statue they haven't seen for two and a half thousand years that got itself dug up by Frenchmen working in another country.

'So they're in a slightly tricky situation trying to

hold on to it. Of course they *will*, but if they get our agreements nicely parcelled up it'll make it so much the easier for Athens to outbluster Ankara. And on to the International Court.'

We signed that afternoon, and banked the cheques with American Express.

Pollock excused himself from the celebrations I planned for that night. He was catching the night plane back to Istanbul.

'There's a lot of clearing up to do,' he said.

'Ilderim?'

'Bassington's taking care of him. No, I'm going to pack up the flat. My time in Turkey's about over, I guess. There's not a lot more bread to be made selling strips of prime coast land to German developers – not until they've finished building on the lots I already sold them. And I don't fancy a two-year stint in the provinces handing over bribes to the local honchos on behalf of the boys in Munich.

'And let's face it, my. . .' – he paused over the word for a moment – '*usefulness* in Istanbul is now a bit compromised.'

'Cover blown? I'm sorry.'

'Something like that. Don't apologise. I'd had enough of the place anyways. I don't know where I'll be moving to, but wherever it is, it'll be a welcome change.'

'Tel Aviv?' I suggested, mischievously. I supposed they might take him back to headquarters, to debrief.

Pollock laughed suddenly. 'That's the last place *we*'d operate,' he said.

I was still wondering about this after Pollock left, when I was paged in the hotel bar to take a call. Amazingly, it was a message from the Hon Rosemary. I was to meet her on a café terrace in a quiet square off the main street between Omonia and Constitution. I could hardly imagine what the Third Secretary from Ankara was doing in Athens. But I arranged to rendezvous with Nina later, and walked down to find her.

Rosemary sat in the shadows under the sidewalk trees, away from the waiter standing at the café door. She was wearing an olive-green cotton suit, and smoking Egyptian cigarettes. I joined her, opening my arms to express a kind of overjoyed amazement and she smiled up in a composed kind of fashion.

'I'm delighted to see you, too,' said Rosemary. 'It's really in the cause of duty, though.'

'So Bassington *was* one of yours.'

'No, certainly not.'

The waiter came scurrying up and I ordered us drinks. When he went, Rosemary said:

'Your recovery of the Aphrodite was a wonderful thing for culture, Harry, but it gives the world of diplomacy a certain problem. One more reason for a row between the Greeks and Turks.'

'Still, if Bassington really isn't MI6 you're not really involved.'

Rosemary gave me a level gaze while the drinks and *mezzes* were set down between us.

'They're both NATO allies, you see.'

'Yes.' There was more to it than that, I knew, so I just returned her look.

'You'll recall,' she said suddenly, 'that when you came to see me in Ankara I advised you to return the statue to the proper authorities.'

'You didn't. You told me to stick to Plan A – which at the time was to give it to the Turks.'

344

'Ah,' said Rosemary, 'now do you happen to have mentioned that to anyone?'

I considered. 'Well, Pollock knew. And agreed, incidentally, at the time.'

'Pollock doesn't matter.'

'You mean Theodoropoulos?'

'Just so.'

'No, I haven't discussed it with him. You weren't mentioned.'

'Yes,' said Rosemary. 'Well, it would suit HM Government very well if that detail were to remain obscured.'

I saw it all, suddenly. 'Of course,' I said, 'and naturally, HMG is going to support the Greeks in the argument on the statue.'

'We will be even-handed,' she said, defensively.

'While privately encouraging the Greeks,' I told her, 'because supporting the Greeks on the Aphrodite will very nicely take the heat out of the argument between London and Athens over the Elgin Marbles.'

Rosemary laughed. 'You put it with the brutal cynicism of a percipient journalist,' she said, 'but that is the nutshell of the thing, just about.

'The point is that the fact you saw me in Ankara may very well be known to both sides, even though I made sure that what we actually said was secure. My people obviously don't want the Turks assuming that we masterminded the return of the Aphrodite to Greece, but at the same time we don't want the Greeks to think we opposed it. Ideally we'd rather that I was left out of the story, so I don't want you to mention me if you can avoid it.

'But if you're pressed, try to put it that my official view was that the statue should be returned to the proper authorities wherever it came back into your possession. Do you see?'

'Not entirely.'

'When you found it on the *caique* it was in Greek territory, so it should have been handed over to the Greeks. It was removed from Greece by someone else. When you recovered it, it was in Turkey and should – *if you had been free to do so* – have been handed to Turkish authorities. But by the time you were out of danger you were back in Greece, so you passed it over here.'

'And so,' I said, '*perfide Albion* can continue to play its historical game of both sides against the middle. OK, I'll stick to London's line. But one condition. Come clean about Bassington and Pollock.'

'What do you mean?'

'You say Bassington isn't British MI6 but he's certainly part of some kind of intelligence group. Who is he? Who's Pollock? Pollock said at the beginning he wasn't CIA, and I knew he wasn't yours. Putting together the fact that he was from New York, and handy with a machine gun, I assumed he was Mossad.'

Rosemary's laugh filled the warm blue night.

'You really are a little naive, Harry, even if you got my motives right just now. How do you think you got your West German passport? I gave you a clue, as well, when I told you Bonn had a *bête noire* about the terrorist networks. Your friends are with the German *Bundesnachrichtendienst*, dear boy. I really thought you would have guessed.'

'But Bassington's British. Pollock's New York Jewish, I thought.'

'A security service is never limited to using its own nationals. I don't know much about Pollock, but

Bassington had a Bonn connection even before he was in the Far East.'

'Well, Bonn is going to have a vacancy in Istanbul, apparently.'

'I'm not surprised Pollock's thinking of moving,' said Rosemary. 'And Bassington is under something of a cloud in Athens as a result of your little escapade. You're sweeter than a rose around here, of course, having brought back a national monument. But Theodoropoulos is damn certain Bassington lifted *Andromeda* off Andros for you, and he's not a little huffed.'

'I don't suppose the US Embassy is too pleased, either.'

'Not the bit that matters. Oh, the diplomatic side was a bit peeved with you, of course, but the intelligence people thoroughly approved. They couldn't get directly involved themselves, because of the delicate situation between Washington and the Greek Government, but they realised what the Germans did was the only quick way to hit something that looked at the time like an undercover terrorist route. It was the US people who persuaded Nina Millen to go back to Turkey, in the end. Unhappily what you uncovered turned out to be a stolen work of art and not an arms shipment. But at least Ilderim is out of the way, and he was a potential danger we didn't even know about.'

'More than just potential as far as I was concerned.'

'Yes. Well, don't worry about Ilderim. The Germans tipped off the Turks very quickly, once your story came through from Pollock. Don't forget Ilderim was Turkish Army on secondment, not regular police. Their army doesn't approve at all of senior officers going bent. You won't read of a court charge, but you

347

won't hear of him again, either. If he's lucky he might end up as second in command of some army district out on the Iraki border. More likely he'll meet with a quiet accident.'

'Couldn't happen to a more deserving guy,' I said.

'Come to that, my dear, I'm prepared to say the same about your reward money.' She stood up, and bent to kiss me lightly.

'Good luck, Harry,' said Rosemary. 'Good luck to both you *and* your fascinating archaeologist.' She moved smoothly away into the night.

When I had watched her go, I finished my *ouzo* and went through the back streets to find Nina in Constitution Square.

I'd vaguely thought of celebrating at the taverna in Diogenes Street where it all began. But Nina had her heart set on somewhere with music. We launched out on a taverna crawl in the steep, narrow streets underneath the Acropolis. We ate snacks of octopus in red wine in a place where the street climbed in steps up the hill and each table perched on a different level. We stopped for eggs and *dolmades* in another round the corner, and then followed the sounds of *bouzouki* music to a roof-top taverna where crowded tables jostled each other around a handkerchief-sized cabaret floor, and agile waiters swooped like conjurors on tightropes whisking fingertip-poised trays of food through the narrow maze.

Overhead the Mediterranean stars prevailed even against the electric lanterns wired across the roof garden. The music wailed, and the waiters raced, and the table disappeared under piled plates and twinkling glasses. It all made a considerable hole in my wallet, but we were in no mood for temperance or caution. We told ourselves that we had days of privation to make up for, and an amazing deliverance to celebrate.

When the meal was over I think we both knew where we going. We chose my bedroom, almost without debate. There wasn't an urgency about going to bed, so much as a triumphal determination: we went to each other with a kind of slow, joyous intensity, like two finalists in some sort of voluptuous Olympic festival.

'This is long overdue,' said Nina's lips close to my face. 'We've owed ourselves this for a long, long time.'

A little while later we were idly examining the scar on Nina's left breast when she said: 'With the money from the salvage and the reward, will you be able to make the Byron film?'

'It'd pay for the film stock and a cameraman, I guess. And outfitting for the trip. I don't know about processing and editing.'

'Supposing I put my twenty grand in, too?'

I looked at her for a while, and kissed her.

'I think I've had just about enough of cruising the Aegean for a while. I'm kind of cool on Byron's lost months in Greece, at the moment.

'What do you say we go and look for some of the islands Ulysses visited, round the west coast of Italy and the Balearics? The wine's good, there, maybe there's a film in it – and there's plenty of new skin diving for you.'

'I'll get the people in Turkey to pack up my things, and send them on,' said Nina. 'I don't think I'm going back.'

'Poste Restante, Naples. We can be there in a week, if the weather's good.'

'Just one thing,' Nina said. 'Let's be sure to buy a new radio before we go.

'And Harry, always remember. For a well brought-up girl like me, one scar on the tits is enough.'

Fontana Paperbacks: Fiction

Fontana is a leading paperback publisher of fiction. Below are some recent titles.

- [ ] CABAL Clive Barker £2.95
- [ ] DALLAS DOWN Richard Moran £2.95
- [ ] SHARPE'S RIFLES Bernard Cornwell £3.50
- [ ] A MAN RIDES THROUGH Stephen Donaldson £4.95
- [ ] HOLD MY HAND I'M DYING John Gordon Davis £3.95
- [ ] ROYAL FLASH George MacDonald Fraser £3.50
- [ ] FLASH FOR FREEDOM! George MacDonald Fraser £3.50
- [ ] THE HONEY ANT Duncan Kyle £2.95
- [ ] FAREWELL TO THE KING Pierre Schoendoerffer £2.95
- [ ] MONKEY SHINES Michael Stewart £2.95

You can buy Fontana paperbacks at your local bookshop or newsagent. Or you can order them from Fontana Paperbacks, Cash Sales Department, Box 29, Douglas, Isle of Man. Please send a cheque, postal or money order (not currency) worth the purchase price plus 22p per book for postage (maximum postage required is £3.00 for orders within the UK).

NAME (Block letters) _____

ADDRESS _____

_____